Wolf Tales 10

Also by Kate Douglas:

Wolf Tales 10

KATE DOUGLAS

APHRODISIA
KENSINGTON PUBLISHING CORP.
http://www.kensingtonbooks.com

APHRODISIA BOOKS are published by

Kensington Publishing Corp.
119 West 40th Street
New York, NY 10018

All Kensington Titles, Imprints, and Distributed Lines are available at special quantity discounts for bulk purchases for sales promotions, premiums, fund-raising, and educational or institutional use.

Special book excerpts or customized printings can also be created to fit specific needs. For details, write or phone the office of the Kensington special sales manager: Kensington Publishing Corp., 119 West 40th Street, New York, NY 10018, attn: Special Sales Department, Phone: 1-800-221-2647.

Aphrodisia and the A logo Reg. U.S. Pat & TM Off.

ISBN-13: 978-0-7582-4266-2
ISBN-10: 0-7582-4266-2

First Kensington Trade Paperback Printing: July 2010

10   9   8   7   6   5   4   3   2   1

Printed in the United States of America

Acknowledgments

My sincere thanks to my fantastic group of beta readers who do their best to keep me honest and try really, REALLY hard to make me look like I know what I'm doing—Ann Jacobs, Sheri Fogarty, Karen Woods, Rose Toubbeh aka Mo, and Jan Takane. Even though I'd rather blame any or all of you for whatever mistakes make it into print, they are, unfortunately, all mine. And ladies, as much as I love writing this series, you make it even more fun. I couldn't— and wouldn't want to—do it without you.

Many thanks, as well, to my agent Jessica Faust of Book-Ends, LLC and my editor, Audrey LaFehr, both of whom manage to keep me on track with this series that has taken off in directions none of us imagined. Thanks also go to editorial assistant Martin Biro, who goes out of his way to make my life easier. I don't think he has any idea how much I appreciate him!

Last but not least, my very sincere thanks to Kensington Publishing. What a fantastic company—when offered a series that fit absolutely nowhere, they merely started an entirely new imprint. Boggles my mind and still makes me smile!

From an author's point of view, it just doesn't get any better.

This one, as always, is for my readers—I love hearing from you and hope you'll find me on Facebook at www. facebook.com/katedouglas.author or join my newsletter. There's a link on my Web site at www.katedouglas.com for the newsletter, or you can write to me directly at kate@katedouglas.com. I answer all my mail.

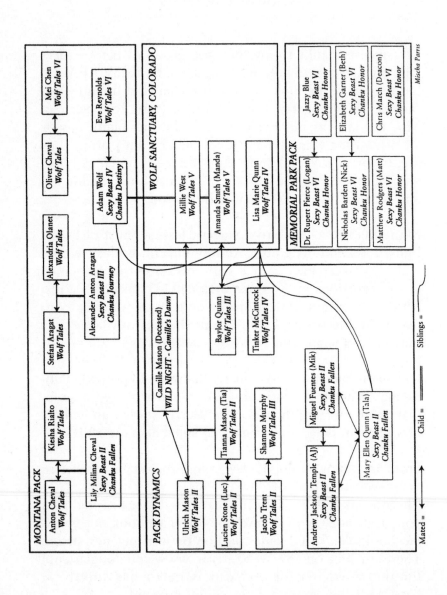

MONTANA PACK

Anton Cheval — *Wolf Tales*
Kiesha Rialto — *Wolf Tales*
Stefan Aragat — *Wolf Tales*
Alexandria Olanet — *Wolf Tales*
Oliver Cheval — *Wolf Tales*
Mei Chen — *Wolf Tales VI*

Lily Milina Cheval — *Sexy Beast II Chanku Fallen*

Alexander Anton Aragat — *Sexy Beast III Chanku Journey*

Adam Wolf — *Sexy Beast IV Chanku Destiny*

Eve Reynolds — *Wolf Tales VI*

WOLF SANCTUARY, COLORADO

Millie West — *Wolf Tales V*
Amanda Smith (Manda) — *Wolf Tales V*
Lisa Marie Quinn — *Wolf Tales IV*

PACK DYNAMICS

Camille Mason (Deceased) — *WILD NIGHT - Camille's Dawn*

Ulrich Mason — *Wolf Tales II*
Tianna Mason (Tia) — *Wolf Tales II*
Baylor Quinn — *Wolf Tales III*
Tinker McCintock — *Wolf Tales IV*

Lucien Stone (Luc) — *Wolf Tales II*
Shannon Murphy — *Wolf Tales III*

Jacob Trent — *Wolf Tales II*

Andrew Jackson Temple (AJ) — *Sexy Beast II Chanku Fallen*
Miguel Fuentes (Mik) — *Sexy Beast II Chanku Fallen*

Mary Ellen Quinn (Tala) — *Sexy Beast II Chanku Fallen*

MEMORIAL PARK PACK

Dr. Rupert Pierce (Logan) — *Sexy Beast VI Chanku Honor*
Jazzy Blue — *Sexy Beast VI Chanku Honor*

Nicholas Barden (Nick) — *Sexy Beast VI Chanku Honor*
Elizabeth Garner (Beth) — *Sexy Beast VI Chanku Honor*

Matthew Rodgers (Matt) — *Sexy Beast VI Chanku Honor*
Chris March (Deacon) — *Sexy Beast VI Chanku Honor*

Mischa Parris

Mated =
Child =
Siblings =

Chapter 1

Eve Reynolds raised her hands above her head and grasped the iron railings of the headboard. Who needed handcuffs when there was hard iron to wrap her fingers around?

And a gorgeous guy ready and willing to have his evil way with her?

She had to bite back the giggles, but damn this was great.

It was so rarely just the two of them. She'd almost forgotten what it was like to be the entire focus of Adam's attention, but Mei was working in the garden with Keisha, and she'd last seen Oliver heading across the driveway to the main house to talk to Anton.

But why was she wasting her time, thinking of them?

Not now. Not when she was naked and quivering with need and Adam was still partially dressed, wearing nothing but faded jeans and a sexy grin. She licked her lips, admiring him. Letting him know exactly what it did to her to see him this way.

Powerful muscles rippled over his chest and arms. His belly was flat and hard, the sharply defined six-pack accented by a trail of dark blond hair that grew darker, as it followed a line from between his copper-colored nipples, down the center of that gorgeous belly to disappear beneath the half-opened placket of his worn Levis.

He knelt between her thighs and ran his strong, callused hands from her knees to her hipbones. She whimpered with the pleasure of his touch, loving the way his work-roughened hands glided over her sensitive skin, the strength in his long fingers, the energy that always seemed to arc between the two of them when they touched.

Adam might be a powerful healer, one who fixed what was broken, but damn, he was an even more powerful lover. Especially now, in the bright morning light while the rest of the pack went about their normal morning routines.

There was something decidedly decadent about lying here naked on the bed with sunlight streaming through the windows and such a gorgeous man between her legs. Soft denim over his hard muscles rubbed against her inner thighs and sent shivers through her body. Dark blond hair curling out above the unfastened steel buttons of his fly teased her with the hint of what lay beyond.

Adam tugged at the blond curls between her legs. Eve twisted her hips, silently begging for more.

He flashed her a knowing smile as he slipped his warm palms beneath her butt and raised her up until her legs dangled over his forearms. Raised her closer to that smile, those lips, that amazing tongue.

He nuzzled the blond curls covering her mons, inhaled deeply and mentally shared the rich scent of her arousal. The connection was always there, that amazing mind link they'd forged when they finally mated as wolves. As sensual, as familiar as their shared arousal had become, she wondered if she would ever grow used to such a powerful union, to the sense that she was in him, a part of him even as he was part of her.

His tongue touched her clitoris, a quick little lick that

still managed to send a strike of lighting straight to her womb.

She could have been growing a baby there, but it hadn't happened. Not the one time they'd tried to conceive—that magical night late in the spring when Tia's babies were born—but she refused to let her disappointment ruin this glorious fall morning. She focused on Adam, on his magical touch and the deep sense of his love.

Arousal blossomed. Desire primed the quick rush of her fluids. Adam groaned when he licked her, taking long, slow strokes with the flat of his tongue that quickly had her quivering in his grasp. His lips circled her clit, swollen now and slick with cream.

Close. Dear Goddess, she was so close, but he stopped and lowered her butt to the bed, leaned over and kissed her mouth. She ran her tongue over his lower lip, then the upper, tasting Adam. Tasting herself. Her fingers tightened on the iron bars.

He backed away, grinning like the amber-eyed devil he was. Eve returned his knowing look with one of her own. She might have been a doormat for most of her life, but not anymore. Not now. Now she was a Chanku bitch, more powerful than she'd ever imagined. Self-assured, confident, complete.

If she wanted to open the rest of that button fly on his jeans, she could. If she wanted to turn the tables and mount him, it was her call, but she loved this game, this playful lovemaking that took her higher than she'd ever imagined. So instead of calling the shots and taking what she wanted, Eve clutched the iron bars in almost desperate need, arched her back and whimpered.

He laughed. The deep joy in his voice, the sparkle in his eyes forged an even stronger bond between them. He used both hands to shove his tangled, dark blond hair out of his eyes. "Eve, my beautiful Eve. What would I ever do without you?"

He stared at her a moment as if he didn't dare even contemplate such a thought. Why should he? She was his. She would always be his. Teasing, she bucked her hips against him. He shucked his jeans in a heartbeat, grabbed the thick length of his erection in his hand and pressed between her legs.

The slick mushroom head forced her swollen lips apart. She arched her hips just so, taking him deep. Thick and long and hot—so amazingly hot—he filled her. Pressing closer, deeper, until the dark blond hairs at the base of his cock meshed with her lighter thatch.

She groaned and tightened her fingers around the iron bars until her hands ached, but it was good. So damned good. So much better than she'd ever imagined. Than she'd ever dreamed.

"I love you, Eve." His lips moved along her jaw, over the curve of her ear, kissing her gently while he drove into her with almost painful force. Claiming her.

Owning her.

"You're mine," he whispered. "Forever."

A chill raced along her spine, cold and unwelcome. She shrugged it off, arched her hips and hung on to love for all she was worth.

Eve wiped steam off the bathroom mirror, shoved her wet hair over her shoulders and frowned at her image. The face of a contented, well-loved, *pregnant* woman should be staring right back at her.

Definitely well-loved. Just thinking of how she and Adam had spent the morning made all her feminine muscles clench in response, but as far as being pregnant?

Maybe tonight. Her heat was due.

Maybe this time I'll get it right . . .

Lisa Quinn had gotten it right. She'd popped out an egg right on time and now she and Tinker were expecting their very first baby in just four more months. Even Tala had figured it out, though how that tiny little thing was going to bear twins to two big bruisers like Mik and AJ boggled the mind.

But Eve? Nope, not her. She shrugged and grinned at her reflection. Typical. If anyone was going to blow it, she was the one, though she still wasn't quite sure where she'd gone wrong. Everything had felt right. The sex as wolves that night in the forest, her body ripe with her heat and Adam so emotionally high after helping Tia deliver, had been amazing. Her hormones were certainly pumping and her heart had felt so full after Tia's babies were born, things couldn't have been more perfect. And, as always, Adam had left her smiling.

She just wished he'd left her pregnant. Thank the goddess Adam wasn't upset. In fact, if anything, he'd acted more relieved than disappointed when she'd told him they hadn't conceived, but with both Tala and Lisa expecting their babies around the same time, he probably figured he'd have enough on his hands helping Logan with deliveries.

The last thing he'd want was his own mate pregnant and needy at the same time as Tala and Lisa, especially now that Anton had built the clinic here in Montana. Both women had already said they'd be coming here to deliver, the same as Tia had last April.

Which was why Eve hadn't brought it up again through the long, busy summer. Logan and Adam had certainly had their hands full delivering Tia's twins. Adam could be so damned focused at times, so busy taking care of everyone else Eve sometimes wondered if he even remembered he had a mate. Not that he didn't love her. He did. She knew she was in his head and his heart most of the time, especially when they made love. When they linked, his love was strong and true, and she never had cause to doubt him.

But she'd learned to accept the man as he was, and Adam was, first and foremost, a healer.

It hadn't taken Eve long to realize that if she wanted his attention, she'd just have to reach out and take it. If she wanted his baby, she figured she'd have to take control there, too. After a lifetime of abuse, it was an empowering thing, to know she could take control without losing her man's love.

All her adult life she'd been attracted to the bad boys. Whether it was her conviction that they somehow needed her to love them, that she could find their warmer, nurturing side, or what, she'd ended up as a doormat and punching bag for every single one of them.

Until Adam. He was a bad boy, all right, and sometimes rough around the edges, but good where it counted. She never had to fear him, never had to wonder if he was going to hurt her. That alone was empowering.

Eve checked her lipstick, grabbed her purse off the big bed and headed down the hallway to the front door.

A scream stopped her. Primal. Agonizing.

Male.

Eve jerked to a stop with her hand on the door. *Adam?*

Her heart pounded. She spun around and raced through the living room to the media room beyond. Terrified of what she'd find, she burst through the door into the darkened room.

Adam lay flat on his back on the floor, arms spread wide, a video game controller clutched in his fingers.

Oliver stood beside him, doubled over with his hands on his knees, laughing hysterically.

Adam moaned.

"No!" Oliver barely got the word out. "You can't moan. You're dead."

"Good Goddess!" Eve leaned against the door jamb with her hand pressed to her thundering heart. "You scared me half to death! I heard you scream and thought something terrible had happened."

Adam raised his head and grinned at her. "Something terrible did happen. That's the third time in a row the bastard's killed me. I'm getting tired of always being the one who dies."

"And does dishes," Oliver added. "That's three nights you owe me." He held out a hand. Adam grabbed hold and Oliver tugged the larger man to his feet. "It works for me."

"You up for another game?" Adam palmed the controller and aimed it at Oliver.

"Always. I love a good loser."

Eve took a deep, controlling breath and slung her purse over her shoulder. "Don't ever do that to me again! You scared me half to death. Look, I promised Xandi I'd make a run to town. She's low on diapers for Alex, plus she needs a few things for dinner. Adam, you want to go with me?"

He shook his head. "Are you kidding? With my honor on the line?" He strolled across the room, his tall, lanky frame taking her breath as only Adam could. Leaning down, he kissed her. His fingers traced the line of her jaw as his lips melded perfectly to hers.

Eve felt the kiss all the way to her toes, though as always, it settled in that ever-needy spot between her legs.

After an entire morning of sex, she still wanted more.

"You sure you have to go to town?" His question was nothing more than a breathy whisper against her mouth.

"Yes." She smiled against his lips and ended the kiss, even though her body cried out to stay and see just what else Adam had in mind. Oliver, too, for that matter. She shook her head in mock dismay. "Far be it from me to interfere with the reclamation of your honor." She turned to leave, but glanced over her shoulder at Oliver. "Oliver, be gentle with him. His ego can't take much more."

"You're kidding, right?" Oliver jabbed Adam with his elbow.

Both men were laughing when she closed the door behind her. With Xandi's grocery list tucked in her pocket, Eve crossed the driveway to the little red convertible Volkswagen bug she shared with Mei. A soft breeze lifted her hair and the hazy late September sun made her squint. She plucked her dark glasses out of her purse and put them on as she slipped into the driver's seat.

The morning had been cool, but now the leather upholstery felt warm against her legs and back. Cicadas hummed in the trees along the drive. She sat there for a moment in the driveway, just listening to the familiar sounds that always gave her such pleasure: Keisha's laughter and Lily's giggles, Xandi's soft voice as she sang the Barney song to Alex. A phone rang in the big house. Eve's sensitive Chanku hearing caught Anton's deep voice as he answered. A raven flew overhead, its long, black wings sounding almost mechanical in flight.

She heard a rustle in the grass to her right, and looked up just in time to see a fox carefully picking its way through the dry weeds along the forest edge. A large doe with two speckled fawns at her side grazed in the strip of greenery between the houses and the deep woods.

The sense of peace that settled over Eve brought tears to her eyes. After so many years with abusive men, so many lost years when she'd barely managed to survive— this life, this beautiful home and this amazing group, this pack of Chanku shapeshifters that welcomed her as one of them, who loved her unconditionally—was more than she'd ever hoped for.

More than she'd even known to want, yet now all of it was hers. Life was good. So good, in fact, that sometimes it made her nervous for things to feel so perfect.

Which was downright stupid. She needed to be more

like Tala and learn to live in the moment, because this moment, right now, was great. Smiling with the conviction that life just couldn't get any better, Eve started the car and followed the curve of the long driveway. She loved driving into town, especially when it was warm enough to drive with the top down on the bug.

It was especially nice being able to go by herself.

Not that she didn't love the pack. No, she loved them all. Adam, of course, but Anton and Keisha, Stefan and Xandi, Jazzy and Logan, and Mei and Oliver as well. They were the family she'd dreamed of having one day, friends and lovers who accepted her for who and what she was.

Even so, loving and being loved, she still needed time by herself. Time when she could count her blessings and think of all that she had as much as all she'd escaped.

Sometimes she ran alone as the wolf, but that always made Adam nervous, especially since she'd once been so badly injured by a grizzly that still roamed the area. Adam had saved her life then. Saved her and loved her and made her love him back.

At least when she went into town on errands, Adam didn't worry. Didn't feel as if he needed to be with her every moment. Now that the attacks against the Chanku had ended, these shopping runs saved her sanity.

Togetherness was good, but a girl needed her space.

She sped down the highway toward town. The breeze was cool and fresh, the sun warm on her head and shoulders. It was late enough in the year that the tourists had mostly gone home, so the traffic was light. The day couldn't be more perfect.

Smiling as her hair whipped around her shoulders, Eve reached for the radio and flipped it on. Loud heavy metal blared out of the speakers.

Laughing, she fiddled with the channel. Obviously Mei had been the last one to drive the bug. She was the only one in the pack who really liked the stuff. Eve glanced at the radio to check the station. A horn blared. She looked up.

Directly into the grillwork of a huge truck.

She'd drifted into oncoming traffic.

Eve jerked the wheel to the right, but the Freightliner barreling down on her clipped the left front panel of the bug, spinning it out of control. She slammed her foot down on the brake. Tires squealed. The little car skidded, hit the berm at the right side of the road and flipped, end over end.

Light and color spun. Sound and time compressed into a kaleidoscope of sensation. For Eve, time ceased to exist.

She was going to die. She knew it with a deep, soulful regret. She'd never been so happy. Had never known such peace.

If only she could have held on to it just a little longer.

Time resurfaced. The ground rushed up to meet her. She screamed a single word, her final word before death reached out to claim her. A word powered with love.

His name.

"Adam!"

"Eve!" Adam fell to his knees with his hands over his ears. "Eve!" He cried out again. Burning, his mind was burning but it was cold as ice and barren. He searched frantically for the connection, the sense of his mate. She was always there, always in his head, the soft sense of her love, her nurturing warmth.

Nothing. He'd felt the blast of his name, the power of her scream, the pain of sorrow and fear and regret.

Then nothing.

Oliver knelt beside him. Wrapped his arms around his shoulders and held him. Vaguely, Adam heard the front door slam open, the pounding of boots against wood floors. Anton and Stefan raced into the room.

Still he searched.

Logan, Jazzy, and Mei crowded in behind, but he ignored their questions. Ignored them in his frantic hunt for Eve's thoughts. For her love.

He was still looking, still huddled on the floor surrounded by his pack, all of them trying to find her when the call came from the highway patrol.

Still numb and unresponsive hours later, unwilling to believe when Anton Cheval returned from the morgue, from the horrible task of identifying Eve's broken body.

If he'd only gone shopping with her. If he hadn't been so damned self-centered and selfish, he could have saved her. She would be here with him now, alive and whole, not lying on a slab in the fucking morgue. She wouldn't be broken. Not anymore.

Slowly, he lifted his head. Stared at his hands. At the scars and calluses, the stains at the edges of his fingernails. He fixed things with these hands. Broken bones. Torn muscles. Damaged brains. He could have healed her, if only he'd been with her.

He raised his head and looked into Anton's sorrowful eyes. "That's what I do," he said. His voice cracked on the words. The useless words. "I fix things, Anton. Anything that's broken. No matter how badly. If there was a spark of life, any life, I could have saved her." He let out a long breath of air. "But I wasn't there."

"No." Anton shook his head. "You couldn't have. Not this time. Eve died instantly, my friend. Her injuries were fatal, too much even for you."

Adam raised his head and gazed into Anton's amber eyes and refused to believe. He slowly folded the fingers of his right hand into a tight fist and stared at it a moment, hating his hands. Hating himself.

He slammed his fist into the floor, through the oak boards, into the concrete below. And again. Splintering wood. Breaking bones. Crushing flesh.

Anton was the one who stopped him, the only one who had the strength to grab Adam and hold him back. The one who wrapped his arms around Adam and held him as he wept.

Held him, linked minds with him, mesmerized him. Made him forget. At least for this one night.

Eve.

Darkness descended like a soft blanket covering him. Protecting him. Insulating him from pain.

Anton's gentle hands supported his mangled fist. His voice seemed to echo in Adam's numb mind. "Logan. We need your healing skills. His hand's a mess."

Someone helped him to his room. Pulled back the covers and made him lie down. Logan was there and then he was gone, leaving Adam alone. Alone and locked in the darkness in the same bed where he'd made love to his mate just a few hours ago. He lay there with nothing more than his memories. Memories, and Eve's subtle scent still clinging to the bedding.

He had no idea how many days had passed. Couldn't remember eating or sleeping. He'd not shifted. Hadn't spoken, though Adam didn't think he'd been left alone. It seemed someone was always beside him, a silent presence.

Not Eve, though. Never Eve.

Stefan finally came to his room and dragged him out of the big bed that no longer carried Eve's scent. He helped Adam undress and made him shower, stepping under the spray with him, bathing him like a child.

Adam hadn't shaved and his beard had grown enough to give him a ragged, unkempt look, even after he'd washed the sour stench from too many days of mourning off his body.

He refused to shift, so they walked him up the mountain, all of them silent and filled with grief. They'd come from all over the country, all of them grieving. Somehow,

Adam understood that their distress was as much for him as for Eve, which made no sense at all.

Eve was gone. He was still here, still drawing breath. It wasn't right. Not right at all.

Anton spoke. Adam tried to pay attention, but it was so hard. Impossible to focus, to make sense of what the fuck Anton was trying to say. Lies. All his compassionate words about life and death and rebirth. All lies.

There would be no rebirth.

Eve was gone and Adam was hollow and his life might as well be over. His heart might be beating, but there was no soul to keep alive. His lungs might draw air, but there was no reason to breathe.

They scattered her ashes across the small meadow, one Eve had loved because of the wild pink primroses that flowered in late summer, but it was almost October and they should be long gone. The primroses bloomed now, which was wrong. So terribly wrong, that her favorite flowers should bloom when she could no longer see them.

The others left and walked down the hill. Adam stayed behind, aware of Anton watching quietly from the shadows beneath the dark branches of an ancient cedar. Adam waited, standing in the center of the meadow, hoping for some sign, something that would tell him Eve hadn't suffered, that she was okay, that she had found peace.

There was nothing of Eve here. The dust of her bones, but no sense of the woman he loved. Not yet. Later, maybe?

Just in case, he stayed. Night fell, and still he waited.

Anton stayed on in silence, waiting with him.

The eastern sky glowed with the silver gleam of the rising moon. A wolf howled, and then another. He heard a rustling in the brush, sensed the hearts and minds of the pack. Felt their sorrow and was comforted by their pain.

Pain was something he understood. Something that made sense.

Within minutes they surrounded him. He recognized Stefan, Xandi, and Keisha. Mei and Oliver. Then Tinker and Lisa, her belly already round with their coming child. Luc was there, though he didn't see Tia. She must have stayed behind with the babies—hers, Keisha's, and Xandi's.

Eve had wanted a baby. He hadn't been so sure, hadn't shared her disappointment when she'd not conceived. Hadn't broached the subject again when she'd come into season.

Damn it, be honest! He'd been relieved. Glad she'd not gotten pregnant the one time they'd tried.

Selfish bastard. Had he been the reason it hadn't worked? Maybe she wouldn't have gone out, if she'd been with child. If only . . .

Regrets. He had time enough for regrets.

More wolves entered the meadow, arriving in twos and threes. Ulrich and Millie came together. His mother looked his way with so much love in her heart. So much sadness. He couldn't meet her eyes. She didn't need the burden of his pain added to her own.

Matt, Daci, and Deacon stepped into the moonlight. Beth and Nick and the pack from Maine—Baylor, Manda, Shannon, and Jake. He shared a quick glance with his twin. Manda understood pain. She'd known loss for most of her life, but now she had Bay.

Someone to share her burdens. Someone to love. It hurt too much, and Adam looked away. Manda had Baylor. He was alone. Just as he'd been most of his life, but he hadn't minded before. Before Eve, he'd not understood what love could do. How it changed a man. Made him need the other half to his soul.

Mik and AJ trotted into the meadow with Tala between them, moving slowly, her belly already big with their twins. More babies. Another reminder how he'd failed Eve.

Jazzy and Logan slipped into the meadow. The entire pack had arrived.

All here to honor Eve. He glanced toward Anton. The alpha waited patiently, still standing alone beneath the dark cedar. Anton's eyes sparkled with tears, his grief an almost tangible entity. Once again, Adam sensed Anton's sorrow was as much for himself as for Eve. And once again, it made no sense.

None at all.

Slowly Adam began to disrobe, removing his heavy boots, his shirt and jeans, folding the items neatly and setting them to one side. The upper crescent of the moon broke over the mountain, spilling more silver light across the meadow as Adam shifted and found his place within the pack.

All of them mated, in pairs or in groups of three, each wolf here with the ones who loved them.

He'd never felt so alone, never loved his packmates so much. They'd come for him. For Eve. Together in their grief, they'd come across the country, left their homes, their work, to celebrate Eve's short life, to mourn her death.

Adam gazed across the small meadow and once again caught Anton's eye. The pack alpha had shifted and the big wolf stood alone, as if waiting.

Waiting for Adam? Not for Eve. There was no reason to wait for her. Not anymore. She was gone.

Adam lowered his muzzle almost to his paws. *Gone forever.*

The full moon finally crested the mountain. Need rose up in Adam and he raised his muzzle to the sky and howled, spilling his grief across the landscape even as silver tears of moonlight spread across the earth.

The others joined him. Their voices echoed over the mountains, growing in power and strength, a powerful, heartfelt tribute to one of their own.

Then, long minutes later, almost as one, their song ended. A harsh scream, the cry of the panther Igmutaka, rose and died in a haunting, final crescendo. Silence followed, a long pause of sound before the crickets once again took up their song and the deep hoot of an owl ended the spell.

One by one or in pairs, the wolves blended back into the forest. To hunt, to run, to make love in the dark woods.

Keisha stood beside her mate just this side of the forest. Anton pressed his muzzle to hers. Then he left her and trotted across the meadow. He rested his muzzle on Adam's shoulder.

Will you be okay?

Adam thought about that a moment. Would he? He honestly didn't know. This was the first time since Eve's death that he'd even left the house. That he'd been aware of anything beyond the emptiness of their bed, the silence in their room, of his own heavy burden of grief. He gazed across the moonlit meadow.

Once again he searched in vain for her presence.

There was no sense of Eve. She was not here. As far as Adam could tell, she was merely gone. Dead and gone, her ashes scattered among the primroses. He sighed. *Go, my friend. I need to stay here awhile.*

Anton raised his head and stared at Adam with eyes that were much too perceptive. Then, without a word, he turned and followed his mate into the forest.

Adam lay down amidst the drying grasses and wildflowers and rested his muzzle on his paws. He opened his heart, his mind, his entire existence, to his mate.

Alone, he waited in vain for her voice as the moon crossed the nighttime sky and disappeared below the horizon in the west.

* * *

Eve awoke in the meadow she'd always loved, lying in the cool grass beneath a perfect blue sky. Bright pink primroses blanketed the ground.

She frowned and slowly sat up. It was the same, but not. The sky seemed too blue, the trees too tall, the colors brighter than she'd noticed before. She looked down at the white gown she wore and slowly shook her head.

Memories filtered into her mind, confused and disconnected. Thoughts of Adam, of the little red car, the shiny grill of an oncoming truck.

There was no memory of pain. No sense of death, though she knew she'd died. Knew there must be a reason she'd awakened here in this place without her mate.

Adam seemed but a distant memory, a love she'd known and treasured, yet she felt no sense of loss. Shouldn't she miss him? Grieve for her own death? Wonder more at her circumstances?

All in good time.

Eve sensed another and looked over her shoulder. A woman of average height stood directly behind her. She held her fingers to her lips. Her eyes were wide and she had a look of utter shock on her face.

"What are you doing here?"

"Don't you know?" Eve stood up and took a good look at the woman. She had an ethereal beauty about her, a pale face framed in shimmering blond hair that draped over her full breasts and flowed over rounded hips. Her eyes seemed to change color, from green, to gray, to brilliant amber. Back to green.

"You shouldn't be here," the woman said. She stepped closer. Her white gown flowed around her bare feet as she stopped directly in front of Eve. "How did you come here?"

Eve thought about the woman's question for a moment. "I died," she said. "Isn't this heaven?" She smiled and held her hands out to her sides. "I was hoping this was heaven."

"No." The woman shook her head. "This is my *where*. My *when*. My world. It is where I exist. Where I rule."

"Ah." Eve smiled. It was all beginning to make sense in a wonderfully convoluted fashion. "You're our goddess," she said. Knowledge flowed into her. "I wasn't supposed to die, was I, Goddess? Where were you when my life ended?"

"I was . . ." The goddess snapped her head from one side to the other, almost as if she were afraid. "I was here. I was busy, and . . ."

"And once again you were not watching over your charges." Eve shook her head, unsure where her knowledge came from, yet very certain of the words she spoke. "Because of you, I'm trapped here, on this plane. I can't go back. I can't move forward. Looks like maybe you're stuck with me."

The goddess narrowed her eyes and looked down her perfect nose at Eve, not easy to do with Eve towering over her. In another life, Eve might have felt intimidated. She wasn't. She'd never felt so powerful, never been so sure of herself, even trapped here in an unfamiliar place with a woman who obviously had allowed her to die before her time.

Power flowed through Eve's veins. Unexpected power, thrilling beyond belief. She raised her chin and smiled. Spoke gently, as if explaining an unhappy truth to a small child. Again, she spoke from the heart, but without any idea how she knew what she knew.

"From what I understand, my Lady, there's only room here for one of us. I hate to be the one to say it, but I believe your days in paradise are numbered."

Chapter 2

Adam awoke beneath a sunny sky. He took a moment to regain his bearings before he realized he was in Eve's meadow, lying naked among the drying primroses. Somehow he'd returned to his human form as he slept. He sat up, surprised to find himself back here, in the same spot where he'd said good-bye to his mate so many days ago.

Or had it been weeks? He wasn't sure, but frost edged the leaves around him and the air still carried the chill of night. Time had lost all meaning to him. Just as life had lost meaning.

He'd been a wolf so long he'd almost forgotten what it felt like to be human. He rubbed his hand over his chin, shocked to find the thick growth of beard covering his face. His hair hung almost to his shoulders. He passed his fingers over his face and felt tears on his cheeks.

Memories slammed him in the gut and he doubled over with a harsh cry. Eve was gone. The pain sliced through him, cutting a jagged rip through his heart.

It was too much. Too much for his human mind, his human heart. With another cry, he shifted.

His world, his perception of grief, shifted as well.

It was easier this way. Almost bearable. Life and death

and time meant little to the wolf. Blinking, he stood up and shook himself.

This perfect meadow had once shimmered with the brilliant dark pink of wild primroses. Now, though, only a few dry flowers remained on the withered leaves. The bright blooms had dried and turned to seed. How much time had passed?

Time. He'd lost track of time since she'd left him. He knew he'd not been back here since they'd scattered her ashes among the flowers. He couldn't recall coming here the night before, but then he rarely paid any attention now to the places he wandered, the paths he traveled.

His first thought was to turn toward home, to the cottage he shared with Mei and Oliver and . . . no. Not with Eve. No longer with Eve.

What was the point? He turned in the opposite direction and trotted into the woods. It was easier as a wolf. Less complicated. He felt his grief, but it was a distant thing. Not as consuming as when he took his human form.

This morning's shift had been an aberration. He preferred it this way, on four legs with his human memories shoved aside, buried while his feral nature took control. Now, instead of mourning the loss of his mate, he noted the sounds of life in the forest, the scent of game.

He'd grown adept at hunting alone. Before, he'd always run with the pack or hunted with Eve at his side. Now, he slipped naturally into the silent posture of a lone wolf on the prowl, moving through the dark woods as quiet as a wraith.

The cares of his human self faded once again and slipped away. The overwhelming grief subsided, the feeling that a part of him was missing. When he ran as the wolf he felt whole, and if not entirely alive, at least capable of hunting, of feeding himself.

He scented the rabbit as he slipped through thick grass

along the bank of a small stream. Moving carefully, he concentrated on the cottontail, coming in downwind of the tiny creature.

By the time he finally pounced, leaping over a patch of bracken fern and grabbing the rabbit in his powerful jaws, he'd left his human self entirely behind.

And with it, his grief.

He ate the rabbit, wiped his bloodied muzzle off in the dry weeds and paused at the creek to drink. Then, stomach filled, he found a sunny patch and stretched out in a bed of soft grass.

For the very first time since her death, Eve came to him as he slept.

His beloved Eve, dressed all in white, her blond hair flowing about her shoulders, her beautiful gray eyes filled with compassion. She was his mate, yet not. He didn't understand what was different, but she had changed.

He reached for her, human now in his dream state, but she stepped back and shook her head. *No, my love. No more.*

I don't understand.

Our time is over. It was too short, but I've been called for another purpose.

He shook his head in angry denial. *What purpose? What's more important than our love? Than the child we hoped to make?*

Her sigh was audible and obviously frustrated. So typically Eve, even in his dream. *I don't know. Only that I have been called and you have a life to live. Much to do in the years left to you. Don't waste them grieving for what cannot be. Look forward, as I am. I'm not asking you to forget me, but you must move on.*

No, damn it!

He blinked, aware he was awake, that the sun had moved to the west and the air had grown cool with the coming of night. And he was human again. Why had he shifted now without intending to, twice in such a short span of hours?

How could he have lost the entire day, here beside the creek?

And what of Eve? She'd come to him in his dream, or was she merely his own wishful thinking?

No. If he'd wished for her, imagined her, she would never have told him to move on without her. He ran his fingers through the hair covering his chin. Then once again he shifted, stood up and shook himself. He gazed once in the direction of home. Then he turned and trotted in the opposite direction, into the woods.

Anton stood on the back deck, staring at the forest. He sensed his mate before he heard her, knew she worried, just as he did. Her hands slipped around his waist from behind and he covered her fingers with his.

"Did he come home?"

There was no need to say his name. They both worried about Adam. "No. I'm thinking of going after him."

"Do you sense him? Is he okay?"

Anton nodded. "I've been with him most of the day."

He'd left Adam alone for weeks now, checking in throughout each day to make sure he was okay, that he remained on familiar ground. Adam's thoughts had been easy to find amid the myriad mental signatures of his packmates. Feral and dark, the mind of the grieving wolf was a dark morass of anger and frustration.

But each hour saw him turning more toward the wolf, hiding his human grief in the complex mind of a predator. Avoiding those who loved him, who worried about him. This was the first day Anton had stayed with him. The first day in weeks he'd truly run with the wolf in Adam's mind.

He turned and wrapped his arms around Keisha. He'd

tried to put himself in Adam's place, tried to picture going on without his beloved mate.

He couldn't do it. Even to imagine such a loss was more than he could bear. It was impossible to criticize Adam's withdrawal from the pack when Anton feared he wouldn't find the strength to even draw his next breath, should he lose his beloved Keisha.

"He's not okay," he said, nuzzling her hair, inhaling her scent. "He's dreamed of her and she's told him to move on. He can't. Not yet."

Keisha leaned back from his embrace and looked into his eyes. Her perceptive gaze was so intimate, so powerful, he almost looked away. "Was it a dream, or did she come to him?"

He took a deep breath. "I believe it was a visitation. She was Eve, but not. I sensed something more in her. Something powerful. She reminded me of the goddess."

"The goddess? I thought you no longer held her in such high regard?"

He chuckled. The first time he'd seen humor in anything beyond his daughter's sweet hugs since Eve's death. "I'll rephrase that. She reminded me of the goddess, but in a good way. There was a sense of something more than Eve about her. I just couldn't place it."

"Come to bed. Sleep. Give Adam his time alone. He'll come back to us when he's ready."

Anton turned and gazed out over the forest. He sensed Adam moving farther up the mountain, near the tree line where forest gave way to rugged cliffs and snow-covered rock. "I hope so," he said, but he wasn't all that certain.

Adam's grief was still too powerful, and his loss too great.

Keisha tugged on Anton's hand. He gazed into her beautiful eyes and sighed. He could stand out here on the deck and worry about his friend, or he could make love to his mate.

The worry would wait. He followed Keisha into the house.

Adam awoke at dawn beneath the twisted branches of a dying spruce. Once again he was human, but as before, he couldn't recall shifting. He clearly remembered coming here, though, to this rocky promontory perched above Eve's meadow.

It would always be her meadow, now that her ashes nourished the primroses.

He sat up, shivering in the chilly morning air, remembering his silent run down the hill last night, sneaking into his workshop while everyone slept.

Racing back to the meadow with the coil of rope clenched in his jaws. It lay on the rock beside him now, a tight coil that promised a final answer to his grief.

There was one thing left to do.

He'd sensed Anton in his mind yesterday. He'd blocked him during his run down the hill, his silent return up the mountain.

Now Adam dropped his shields. *Anton?*

I'm here, Adam. You've been blocking me. Why?

I needed to be alone. But now . . . will you meet me?

Of course. Where?

The rock above Eve's meadow. Come alone. Please, Anton. For me?

I will do anything for you, Adam. Half an hour. Be safe.

Anton's compassion would be his undoing. He didn't deserve this, but it was the only option, the only way. Adam didn't want any of the others to find him. Only Anton. At least the alpha might understand.

Eve was dead. Adam gazed at the thick branch high overhead. It was the only way he knew to be with his mate again. He looped the coil of rope over his shoulder and climbed up the tree. Bark flaked away beneath his bare feet and broken branches scratched his hands and legs.

He smiled, thankful for the awareness of rough bark, sharp branches, the cool air blowing across his bare skin. Thankful to have these last sensations before they were gone forever.

He reached the branch and lifted himself up until he straddled its thick length. He tied one end of the rope off and figured how much he'd need to keep his feet from touching the ground.

He took one last glance at the sunlight dancing off the meadow below and another long, steady look at the glorious snow-capped spine of the Rocky Mountains.

He thought of Eve. Of how much he loved her, how she'd always loved the sight of snow shimmering on the high peaks.

Then he tied the rope around his neck and quietly slipped off the branch.

"You jackass. I can't believe you would actually do something this stupid."

Adam blinked. Slowly he sat up. His throat hurt like hell. He swallowed carefully and rubbed his fingers over the bloody, abraded skin under his jaw.

He blinked again. Joy blossomed in him, suffusing his entire body with a warm glow. He'd done it! Dear Goddess, he'd found Eve! He was looking into her gray eyes, her beautiful . . . No. They were different, somehow. She was different, but her eyes . . . They shimmered in the morning light, going from gray to green and then gold . . . and back to gray.

"Eve?" He reached out and touched the line of her jaw.

She slapped his hand away. Her southern drawl was thicker than ever. "Don't you 'Eve' me. What in the hell did you think you were doing?"

"Am I dead? Is this heaven?" His voice sounded horrible, all scratchy and raw. He swallowed again, but damn, it hurt. Heaven shouldn't hurt, should it?

"No, it's not heaven, and no, thanks to Liana and me and Anton, you're not dead. If Anton hadn't suspected what you were up to and called on the goddess, we wouldn't have known you were planning such an idiotic stunt. We wouldn't have gotten here in time and then you *would* be dead."

She stood up, slammed her hands down on her hips and glared at him. "And if that had happened, trust me, heaven wouldn't even be on your radar."

He tried to stand up, but his legs wouldn't work. Why didn't any of this make sense? "But you're dead and I can see and hear and touch you . . ." He reached for her hand.

She whipped back, out of his reach. "Only so I can make a point. Look, what you did was wrong. I came to you yesterday for a reason. I told you it's time for you to move on and it's definitely time for me to get to work. I have a lot to do, and so do you. Killing yourself is not an option."

Adam shook his head. She looked like Eve, but she sure didn't sound like Eve. This woman was coming across as the original alpha bitch. He looked up, and realized for the first time they weren't alone. "Who are you?"

The blond woman standing silently behind Eve shrugged and shook her head. Eve turned to glare at her. "That's Liana. The *Goddess* Liana, the one who screwed up and let me die before I should have, which is the only reason we were able to save your life."

The blonde stepped forward. Her hands were clasped in front of her, her fingers twisting nervously. "Because of my inattention, Eve died too soon. When you tried to take your own life, you compounded the problem." She took a deep breath, shot Eve a guilty glance and turned back to Adam. "You can't die now. You have too large a role to play. I'm sorry, Adam. So very, very sorry."

"You? It was your fault?" This time he managed to stand up, and he towered over the smaller woman, standing over her on very shaky legs. Eve stepped aside and folded her arms across her chest. The white robe billowed around her thighs, and her eyes flashed in shades of gray, green, and gold.

Liana didn't back down. Adam focused on the goddess. "Because of you, my mate is dead? Because of your *inattention*? What the fuck kind of goddess are you, anyway?"

Not a very good one, in my opinion.

Adam spun around. A huge, black wolf stood behind him. "Anton!"

The wolf shifted. Became man. "Adam. Are you okay?" Anton stepped closer, tall and naked, and absolutely beautiful. He touched the torn flesh beneath Adam's jaw and focused intently on his eyes. Then, possibly satisfied with what he saw, he folded his arms across his chest and gazed at Liana with obvious displeasure.

"Again, Goddess? Is it your job always to fail us? To fail an entire people?"

Liana hung her head.

Eve raised hers. Eyes flashing, she glowed with an inner light. "It's the last time, Anton. Liana is Goddess no more."

Liana gasped. She jerked around and stared at Eve.

Eve went very still. She opened her mouth, but the voice was not hers. Deep and sonorous, it carried the weight of ages.

"For eons, Liana, you have put yourself first. You've placed your people, those who depended upon you, behind your own desires. No more. Eve has known pain, she has survived evil. She knows loss and she understands true love. She cares for the welfare of others beyond her own, and thus is a more fitting guardian to my beloved Chanku. I cast you away, Liana. Be gone."

Liana cried out. Her legs collapsed. She dropped to the

ground and lay there. Adam ignored her as Anton rushed to the fallen woman's side.

Eve turned to Adam, and she was Eve once again . . . and not. Tears filled her eyes. She glanced toward the fallen goddess and shook her head. "You have to take her, Adam. You have to teach Liana to live as a mortal or she won't make it on this plane. She'll die."

"No. Absolutely not." He stared at Eve. How could she ask him to help the bitch? "She let you die. She deserves death. She's not my responsibility."

"Adam." Eve sighed. She reached for his hands and wrapped her fingers around his. Her loving touch, so familiar and yet so distant, made him want to howl his pain to the skies.

"You fix things, Adam. That's not just what you do, it's who you are. You heal the sick, repair broken bodies. Fix broken souls. You can help Liana. You're the only one who can."

He glanced at the woman lying on the ground and his muscles tensed in anger. He clung to Eve, but his gaze was trapped by Liana, by the disbelief in her eyes, the fear. Anton knelt beside her and supported her shoulders. Both of them watched him. Waited for his answer. Desperately he looked toward Eve. How could she ask this of him? The last person he wanted anything to do with was Liana.

Urgency and despair powered his words. "Babies, Eve. You wanted babies. What about . . . ?"

Eve shook her head, but she was smiling. "Don't you see? Every baby born to every Chanku will be mine. I'll thrill at their birth, watch their first steps, hear their first words, and I'll know that my protection helped give them life. Every new Chanku brought into the pack will be mine. Every single one of you . . . mine. When you make love, I'll share your arousal. When any one of you finds completion, I'll know the utter joy of your climax. I will be all of you, and I will know myself as I never have before.

"Please, Adam. Grant me this one request. Give Liana her chance to understand what life can be. She really has no idea."

The bitch had ruined everything. She'd taken Eve from him. "Eve, I . . ."

Her eye color shifted and swirled, mesmerizing him. Gray, green . . . gold. Gray again. "For me, Adam. If you truly love me, you'll do this for me. Care for Liana. Know that it's the last thing, the only thing, I ask of you."

"That's damned unfair, Eve." He took a deep breath and it hurt. His heart ached and Eve looked at him with so much hope. "I'm not a good man. You know that. You're asking me to be better than I am, better than I know how to be." He gazed at her through tears he couldn't shed and felt as if his life were ending. But wasn't that what he'd wanted?

"Adam, you're so much more than you know. So very much." Eve blinked back tears that clung to her long lashes. She shook her head and smiled so sadly at him. "I would gladly have spent my life with you, my beloved. Carried your babies, grown old with you. It's too late for that. Remember me, but grieve no more. Do this for me. Teach Liana. She needs to understand."

He didn't want to. Damn it all, the last thing he wanted was responsibility for that bitch. Adam glanced her way. Liana stared at him, unblinking, but her face was streaked with tears.

Probably worrying what would happen to her if he refused. Well, it served her right. She should be worried. She should be dead, damn it.

Eve turned his hands free. His fingers felt chilled, empty without her touch. She placed one hand on his chest, over his heart. Adam felt the warmth of her palm, but his heart thundered loudly in his ears and he fought an overwhelming need to reach for her, to hold her and never let her go.

Instead, he clenched his hands into tight fists and pressed them against his thighs. "Eve . . . ?"

"For me, Adam? Promise you'll do it for me?"

"Shit." He turned away, took a deep breath. Damn, but he'd never been able to deny her anything . . . except, he'd denied her the baby she'd wanted. The baby she'd never have. He looked back at his beautiful Eve and gave a short, sharp jerk of his chin.

"Thank you." She smiled at him and shook her head. "Oh, Adam." She sighed, and the sound of loss was almost more than he could take. "I will be here forever. Right here in your heart, as you'll be in mine. I'll not forget what we shared, but that time is over. Live your life, Adam. Find love again. It's out there, waiting for you."

He shook his head, hard, so that the long strands of his unkempt hair slapped the sides of his face. "Never. Only you, Eve. Only you."

She raised her head and smiled. Lifted up on her toes and pressed a light kiss to his lips. Then her eyes went wide and her smile grew brighter. "Oh! Oh, Adam. It's wonderful. Absolutely wonderful, the life you'll lead. Embrace it. Embrace love." She touched fingertips to his cheek, the very lightest caress. "Good-bye, my love. Remember me."

He choked back a cry and reached for her. Swept his fingers through her long, blond hair as it turned to stardust in his hands and Eve faded from sight, as her glow grew brighter and her corporeal form disappeared behind the shimmering light.

Within seconds, the meadow was empty. Empty except for Anton Cheval and the woman who had cost Adam his one true mate. He turned toward her and snarled.

He felt uncommonly gratified when Liana flinched.

Numb. That was the only way to describe how she felt. Absolutely numb. Liana looked into those amber eyes of

Adam Wolf's and knew she'd screwed up for good this time. Really fucked things up royally.

She couldn't remember not being a goddess. Could hardly recall the details of her childhood, that faraway time in a primitive world. How in the name of the Mother was she ever going to survive? Already she felt the difference. Her body was heavy now, her muscles ached with the strain of unfamiliar activity.

She felt the beginnings of a headache, and her hands actually hurt where she'd scratched them when she fell. She raised her right hand and stared at her palm, at the blood welling up from a small cut below her thumb. She'd never cut herself before. Never known pain. Ever.

And she had to pee. Really, really bad. Bodily functions hadn't been a consideration when she was a goddess. Now she was overwhelmed with so many unfamiliar signals, things her mortal body expected her to understand. Her stomach rumbled and she recognized hunger. What would she eat? She had no idea how to prepare food. She'd never really hunted in her wolf form. What if she starved? Would these ungrateful Chanku let her die?

What do they have to be grateful for?

Her heart stuttered in her chest. She'd failed them. Every single one of them. Maybe she didn't deserve to live . . . but she didn't want to die. She really didn't—not now. Not when she finally had a chance to experience real life.

The trick, though, was to figure out how to survive it.

It wasn't like she could count on Anton for help, either. Their history wasn't all that great, not since she'd held him in her world for some of the best sex she'd ever had in her life. Unfortunately, Anton still hadn't forgiven her. He hated her for taking away his choice, for sending him off on a quest he'd always thought was his own.

Finding out he'd merely followed orders from the goddess when he made his pilgrimage to Tibet to learn about the Chanku hadn't set well with him. Not at all, which meant she'd have to count on Adam, a man who'd just as soon see her dead.

She'd never dreamed her mistakes would actually get her kicked out of her world. The Mother had always seemed a bit more forgiving than that.

She glanced at the blue, blue sky overhead. A single black cloud drifted across the sun, paused, and moved on. *Obviously not.*

Anton stood, but his attention was on Adam, not Liana. She stayed on the ground and wrapped her arms around her knees.

"Adam? You going to be okay?" Anton went to Adam and wrapped an arm around Eve's mate's shoulders. Adam was a big man, so strong looking. Powerful, in a rugged, work-roughened way. Not conventionally handsome, not like Anton, or that beautiful young man, Matt.

She really hadn't been very nice to Matt, either, now that she thought about it. Keeping him as her consort without his permission, forcing him to want her even when he only wanted to go home to the two he loved. She wondered if she'd see him again, if he would forgive her.

She had a lot of forgiveness to seek.

Liana swallowed back the uncomfortable sense of choking on her own sins. Somehow, she had to learn to move forward. To move beyond all her mistakes.

She hoped Adam could move forward, but the pain in his eyes made her ache. It didn't bode well for her. Anton hugged Adam close. His soft words barely carried to Liana.

"Eve's made the only choice she could, Adam. The only choice."

Adam didn't say a word, but his shoulders trembled. He drew in a breath. Liana caught the sound of a keening whimper that suddenly exploded into a harsh cry. She hugged herself as Adam set his grief free.

She felt like a voyeur, watching him like this, but where

could she go? What should she do? This was her fault. All her fault. Liana turned away. The least she could do was give the man his privacy.

The harsh sound of his cries, the almost animalistic keening as he gave in to the enormous weight of emotions he'd buried over the past few weeks couldn't be ignored. Anton's soft words of comfort, words Liana wished she knew how to share, made her feel even more worthless, if that was even possible.

Adam's agony was her fault. All because she'd been playing with one of the many young human men she loved to bring to her bed. Too busy gratifying her own needs to pay attention to those she should have been guarding.

Too busy indulging herself when others depended on her. Choking back her own tears, she raised her eyes to the now cloudless sky. *Don't make my mistakes, Eve. It hurts too much.*

Silence descended on the meadow. Liana glanced toward the men, only now they were wolves. Both Adam and Anton had shifted. One of the wolves, a deep brown with shades of russet in his dark fur, was already trudging slowly down the hill. Leaving her behind.

Liana struggled to her feet. She recognized the other wolf, a big, black animal with brilliant amber eyes. He stared at her with such complete disinterest, there was no doubt it was Anton.

Adam hated her. Anton was merely disgusted by her.

She wasn't certain which was the most painful.

She slipped out of her tattered and stained white gown and left it on the ground. Then she shifted.

And sighed. She'd always loved her wolven colors, the molten silver sheen that looked metallic in the sunlight and seemed to flow and ripple over her frame. Now she was merely gray, and not even a very pretty gray at that, at least from what she could tell from her wolf perspective.

First things first. She trotted to the tree line, away from

Anton, and squatted in the weeds. It felt so good to empty her bladder she practically sighed in relief. Then she turned and kicked dirt over the wet spot on the ground with her hind legs.

Adam had moved out of sight on his way down the hill. Anton waited a moment longer. Then, obviously impatient, he turned away and trotted in the same direction Adam had just taken.

Liana shook herself and felt her thick coat settle into place. Then with a last look at the rumpled gown, the only reminder of her life as a goddess now lying in a soiled heap in the meadow, she followed Anton into the forest.

Chapter 3

Liana paused in the shadows at the edge of the dark woods and gazed out across the meadow. Anton's palatial home rose up out of the rocky ground, almost as if the cedar logs and stone supports had grown in place like some living, breathing creature. For all its massive size and rambling shape, it crouched there, an alert guardian fitting the surroundings perfectly, blending in rather than standing out.

Welcoming her, not holding her back. Making her feel cherished, accepted. She felt it in the warm cedar, the solid stone, and yet she waited here in the shadows, unsure how to continue on, now that she'd come so close. Anton proceeded across the meadow, heading directly for a children's play area near the broad back deck. Laughter and childish squeals drifting on the soft breeze called Liana.

Adam's unforgiving stare held her in place. He stood on the deck above the play area, wearing only a pair of soft, gray pants, glaring at her. Daring her to come into his space.

Daring Liana to invade the home where he'd lived and loved with Eve.

Her first instinct was to flatten herself to the ground, to display submission. To beg his forgiveness once again.

Then Anton shifted and looked her way. He glanced over his shoulder toward Adam, turned back to Liana and called to her. "C'mon, Liana. You're going to have to meet everyone at some point."

Was he laughing? She wondered if she'd ever understand how Anton's brilliant yet convoluted mind worked. Unable to resist the command in his voice, she trotted slowly across the meadow, focusing on Anton Cheval, not Adam. It was so bizarre, to think that Anton would be the one welcoming her, after the way she'd treated him.

She thought of the challenge she'd issued Anton when she'd still been the goddess, when she'd last brought him, against his will, to her *where*, her *when*. He'd come to her with Matt, but she'd sent Anton away—again, against his will—with nothing more than that stupid riddle she'd told him he needed to solve. Had he truly forgiven her for that arrogant request?

No. But constantly reminding you of my anger does none of us any good, especially Adam. He's the one we need to worry about, Liana. Not a selfish, self-centered ex-goddess.

She cringed against the slap of his deceptively soft mental words. Paused a moment, shook herself. Held her head up and looked Anton directly in the eyes.

If she ever hoped to be treated with respect, she was going to have to earn it. Cringing in the shadows had never been her way. If she was going to survive, she would have to act strong, even if that wasn't exactly how she felt.

It wasn't easy. Anton stared down at her wolven form from his impressive human height with only the barest of interest. She took a deep breath and moved forward.

What choice did she have?

None at all. Get over it.

She blocked him and felt a flash of anger—hers, not Anton's—and it was a surprisingly empowering feeling.

She took the last few steps toward the alpha and shifted, standing tall with her head held high.

He held his daughter in his arms. The baby giggled and squirmed. Then she reached out her chubby little arms. Reached for Liana.

At the same time, Anton's mate joined him. Liana knew it was Keisha. Remembered the first time she'd empowered the woman to shift, long before Keisha should have been able to make the dramatic change from woman to wolf—from victim to predator.

It had been the only thing that allowed Keisha Rialto to survive. At least, that time, Liana knew she'd gotten it right.

Keisha smiled at her, held out her arms in welcome. The first true and personal sense of welcome Liana had felt. She slipped into Keisha's warm embrace and felt tears she hadn't expected. For some reason they wouldn't stop, but Keisha merely hugged her harder.

"It was you, wasn't it? That night, in that filthy apartment with those men?" Keisha backed away and stared at her, but she didn't turn her loose. Her fingers squeezed Liana's arms so hard she was certain she'd have bruises.

She sniffed and nodded. "I wasn't supposed to, but I couldn't let them kill you. I had to let you shift, but then there was nothing else I could do. It had to come from you. Your strength, the predator inside you, your need to survive."

Keisha nodded. "I did survive, obviously. Thank you." She released her hold on Liana and grabbed a piece of bright blue fabric off the low fence surrounding the play area. "Here. It's an extra, in case you want to cover yourself."

Liana realized Anton had already slipped into a pair of soft pants, similar to the ones Adam wore. She was the only one unclothed. It wasn't modesty that had her wrapping herself in the silky sarong. No, it was a powerful desire to be like everyone else. Not to stand apart.

She'd been apart for eons. That needed to change now.

"Thank you." She glanced up at Anton and caught his quizzical gaze on her. "What?"

"You were the reason Keisha was able to shift and defend herself? You gave her that ability?"

For some reason her mouth felt dry. Too dry to form the words. She licked her lips and nodded. "There are very few times when even a goddess can interfere. That was not supposed to be one of those times, but I couldn't let them kill her. That was their intent. I had a feeling that Keisha was meant for so much more, though I didn't know what."

She smiled and reached for Lily. The toddler wrapped her fingers around Liana's thumb and giggled. "I imagine this beautiful little girl is why Keisha had to live."

Anton merely studied her. His silence was unnerving. She turned again to Keisha. "Did your mate tell you why I'm . . ."

Keisha nodded. "You're welcome here, Liana. I owe you my life. I imagine Tala does as well." She raised one eyebrow in question.

"To some extent." Liana smiled. She hoped to meet Tala one day. Once known as Mary Ellen Quinn, a tiny woman who had proved to have a heart big enough to ensnare two powerful men. She'd love to be more like Tala. She wanted to be more like all of the women she'd come to know through their dreams, their lives.

"Where's she going to stay?" Adam glared at her from the deck. "She's not staying with me."

Anton still had a bemused expression on his face, but he frowned when he looked at Adam. "Why would you think we'd expect her to stay with you, Adam? Liana is welcome here, no matter the circumstances of her arrival. The house is large enough for everyone."

Adam turned away and stalked into the house. A smaller, dark skinned man stood up. He'd been sitting in the shadows so Liana hadn't noticed him. *Oliver.* It had to be Oliver.

"I'll stay with Adam," he said, nodding toward the closed door. "I don't think he's ready to be alone. Welcome, Liana. Mei's over at our cottage, but I know she's going to want to meet you."

Liana nodded. "She has questions. I sense them in you."

Oliver nodded and went into the house.

Keisha glanced at Anton and then reached out and took Liana's hand. "Come with me. You're about Xandi's size. She's taller than you, but no bigger around. Let's get you settled in a room and then see what's in her closet."

"She won't mind?" For some reason, Liana glanced at Anton. He was smiling at his mate, still holding his beautiful daughter.

Laughing, Keisha tugged her toward the house. "She wouldn't dare," she said. "Anton, you hang on to Lily for a while. Liana and I have a closet to raid."

Adam stalked through the house, out the front door and across the drive. He'd not been back to their room in the cottage since Eve's memorial service. Now he stormed into the house, radiating anger and frustration, not sure why he'd come back here, what he wanted, how he was going to find his way without his mate.

He grabbed the bedroom door and jerked it open. Mei stood in front of the big walk-in closet, staring at the rack filled with Eve's clothing.

"What the fuck are you doing in here?"

His snarl scared the crap out of her. Mei spun around and stared at him, wide-eyed. Afraid? Damn it to hell, he hoped so. She had no business . . .

"I was looking for this." She straightened up and stared

at him, obviously shocked by his appearance but not at all cowed. She reached into the closet and pulled out a jacket. "Eve borrowed it from me ages ago. I couldn't find it, but I hadn't even thought to look in her closet." She held the multicolored fabric against her breasts. "It's mine, Adam. I was merely taking it back."

"Get the fuck out of my room." He stepped aside.

Mei glared at him. "This is Oliver's cottage, Adam, and I am his mate. Therefore, while you sleep here, this room is not exactly yours. You might think of that before ordering me out of my own home."

She slung the jacket over her arm and approached him. He wasn't sure what came over him—anger, loss, his inability to change what was, but as she passed by him on her way out the door, he grabbed her wrist and viciously jerked her around. She cried out in pain and tried to pull free, but he ground his hips against hers, snarling in a blatant display of . . . what? He had no time to consider, no time to try to understand his own bizarre behavior.

Something slammed into him from behind. Oliver, barreling into him in leopard form, his strike so fast, so silent, Adam didn't have a chance to defend himself.

Raking claws, sharp teeth, the weight of the big cat's body flinging Adam to the floor in a ruthless, slashing attack. His hard head met the even harder oak floor. He felt a flash of pain, and nothing more.

Consciousness returned slowly—small flashes of light over darkness, a fierce pounding behind his eyes, pain in his skull. The sharp sting of claw marks down his left arm explained the rich, coppery scent of his own blood. His right shoulder hurt like hell and he recognized that agonizing burn for what it was—leopard bites. Oliver must have sunk his fangs deep into the muscle for the pain to be this intense, but discomfort was the least of his problems.

Adam tried to move, just to be sure, but he was shackled securely to the bed, spread out, facedown with a collar fastened tightly around his neck to prevent his escape by shifting.

Oliver sat on a chair beside the bed, glaring at him. Mei was nowhere to be seen, though he recognized the room as Mei and Oliver's, not the one he'd shared with Eve.

Adam tugged on the restraints, but handcuffs were Mei's specialty. Handcuffs, toys, implements of erotic torture that Mei'd learned to use with an expert's finesse. From past experience, he knew there'd be no escape until she or Oliver let him go.

In the past, he'd relished Mei's inventive mind when he'd shared the experience with Eve. Not now. He tugged at the shackles. "Release me, Oliver. Now. I'm not into your games."

Oliver stared at him for a long time. Finally, he stood up and walked away, out of Adam's range of vision. "This is no game, Adam. You're not going anywhere, and don't think to call on Anton for help. He knows I've got you here and he approves. You hurt Mei. Badly. She's with Logan right now so he can repair the broken bones in her wrist."

Adam shuddered. He'd broken her wrist? No . . . he fixed things. He would never have hurt Mei. Never.

But the image of her face when he'd grabbed her, the sound of her cry, the sharp crack of bone beneath his fingers . . . shit. His head fell forward onto the bed.

"I wanted to kill you."

Oliver's voice had an edge to it Adam had never heard before. It sent shivers along his spine.

"Even though I owe you more than I can ever repay, I wanted you dead. Mei stopped me. That's the only reason you're still alive, Adam. The only reason. Think about that. When Mei comes back, you're all hers."

* * *

42 / *Kate Douglas*

"C'mon. We need to get you settled."

Smiling broadly, Keisha took her hand and led Liana into the house. This all felt surrealistic, coming here to Eve's home, taking the place of the woman who now held Liana's position as goddess.

She wasn't certain how she felt about that.

She'd loved the power of being a goddess, the sense she was above all the petty issues that bedeviled the Chanku. She'd called lovers to her whenever she wanted, could alter her surroundings with the wave of her hand, change *what was* into a totally new *what will be*.

Being an immortal with so many different powers certainly had its good points, but she couldn't get over the sense of freedom she had now, the awareness that she was the only one depending on her choices and her actions . . . or lack of action.

Keisha closed the door behind them, shutting out the soft sounds of Anton's laughter, the childish squeals as he pushed his daughter in the swing. Liana glanced out the window and felt one more layer of fear melt away.

Anton was smiling, holding Lily's swing in both hands, rubbing his nose against his beautiful little girl's as he teased her with kisses. Even though it had been many years ago, Liana had felt those same lips kissing her intimately, had slept with his strong arms around her.

Had felt his anger, his arousal, his frustration.

Most of all, she'd felt the goodness within the man when he'd called on her, a supplicant to the goddess.

He hadn't called on her since their last meeting, when she'd pulled Anton and Matt into her world without their permission. She hadn't known, then, that free will meant so much to her Chanku. Had always assumed the power of their amazing libidos superseded their need for freedom of choice.

Hadn't she seen men cleave to men, women to women, going against what she considered their natural choice of partner to satisfy their physical need for sexual release? She'd always thought that sex was more important to them than freedom.

Maybe she'd been wrong. Maybe she'd misinterpreted more than she'd realized.

"Liana?"

She jerked her chin up and caught Keisha's worried look. How long had she been standing here, staring at the floor? "I'm sorry." She shrugged, embarrassed to be caught woolgathering. "There's so much I'm trying to understand. So many things I thought I knew."

"Whatever you want to know, you only have to ask. Come with me. I'll show you to your room and then we'll find some appropriate clothing for you."

Liana followed Keisha down a long hallway. It came to her slowly as they walked, that she was mesmerized by the sensual swing and sway of the woman's full hips, the curve of her spine, the thick fall of dark hair cascading over her shoulders.

She'd spent so little time with women in the past. The last few weeks with Eve had been stressful, not sensual, but now she recognized a familiar clenching in her womb, the sense of moisture between her legs. She was becoming aroused, but by a woman? She knew her Chanku often chose partners of the same sex, but she'd always preferred men.

Only preferred men.

Keisha paused before a door that looked just like others they'd passed. As she reached for the handle, Liana touched her shoulder. "Keisha, explain something to me, please? Why do I feel aroused by you? I've always been with men, always chosen men as my partners, yet I'm watching you and desire is building inside me. Is this normal for mortals, to desire one another no matter the gender?"

Keisha reached out and stroked the backs of her fingers along Liana's cheek. "Ah, Liana. Anton is right. There is so much you have to learn. It's normal for Chanku. You've just shifted from your wolven form to your human form. Your body recognizes the change and needs the sexual release a shift always brings on. Gender doesn't matter. It's the emotional and sexual connection with another of our kind we crave."

The connection. Liana blinked as a trickle of moisture left a cooling trail down her inner thigh. She fought the need growing inside her, the overwhelming desire to trace her fingers over Keisha's beautiful, dark skin. To savor her full lips with tongue and teeth, to suckle at her plump breasts, to explore all those feminine places she'd not gone before.

Keisha smiled at her with a look that carried more questions than answers. Before Liana had a chance to figure out what she was thinking, Keisha pushed the door open and stepped into the room. It was smaller than she was used to, though it had a large bed, a comfortable sitting area and a sliding glass door that led to the back deck. There was a partially open door to another room, one Liana recognized as a bathroom.

She was going to miss her beautiful pool with its constant flow of bubbles, but she told herself this was more, so much more than she should have expected.

She had, after all, been cast out of her home by her own failure. She must learn to be thankful for each kindness. Must learn to appreciate simple things.

"Will this be all right?"

"It's lovely." Liana glanced around, taking in the soft colors, the natural light, and she realized that was true. It was a beautiful room, exquisite in its very simplicity.

And it was hers—her very own space. She'd been given a room of her own, even though they all knew it was her fault one of theirs had died.

Confused, shaken more than she'd first realized, Liana turned to Keisha. "I don't understand. You're accepting me into your home, even though I've failed you. All of you."

Keisha shook her head. "You're right. You failed Eve, and in so doing, you failed Adam as well as the entire pack, but what happened is over. It's time to move on. We have all made mistakes, each one of us. Me. Anton . . . even Adam. And remember, when I needed you, you didn't fail me, Liana. You didn't fail Tala. You gave both of us the tools we needed to survive at the time when we needed them most. I like to think that balances out at least some of your mistakes."

She stepped closer and grabbed both of Liana's hands in hers. "Eve's not truly gone, not if she's taken your place as the goddess who watches over us. She has always been a most wonderful caretaker. When someone was down, Eve was the one to make them laugh. When someone needed help, Eve was there. She's the one who took over much of the nursing care when Daciana Lupei was so badly injured. You know of Daci, don't you? From your position as goddess?"

Liana nodded. "I do. I sent her here, hoping she would find her way. I also learned what a powerful force she's become when she challenged me for her lover." Liana glanced down at their clasped hands, Keisha's so dark against her own fair skin.

All thoughts of Daciana Lupei floated away. She imagined those hands on her body, touching her in places only males had touched. Imagined Keisha's lips moving across her own, and wondered if her imagination even came close.

"Anton is watching the baby."

"What?" Liana stared into Keisha's dark amber eyes.

"You're broadcasting. I feel your desire, your need. Your curiosity. It's just the two of us. You're free to explore all you want."

"You wouldn't mind?" Liana swallowed as arousal shot

through her, a charge of lightning sparking from head to heart to womb that left her shivering with desire.

"I would welcome it." Keisha reached for the knotted fabric holding her saffron-yellow sarong over her full breasts. Her body was full, ripe and womanly, her curves more generous than Eve's, but Keisha had borne a child. Was that the difference?

She let the fabric slide to the floor and Liana's mouth went dry. Full, rounded breasts with nipples so dark they were almost black against her bittersweet-chocolate skin. Her waist nipped in, but her belly was rounded, her hips full and lush.

The pink lips of Keisha's sex glistened, moist and inviting. Already the smooth little head of her clitoris protruded from its protective cover. Liana wondered if she would look as ready, as lush with desire as Keisha.

She'd never felt desire for a woman before, never known the sweet rush of arousal for any other than a man.

A man she'd forced to come to her side.

This was unique, to be approached by someone of their own free will. To be the object of desire, not because she'd insisted, but because the other person truly wanted her. Liana reached for the tie on her own sarong, and shivered when the silky fabric slithered to the floor.

Keisha's smile welcomed her. Her arms drew Liana close in a warm, comforting hug that ignited an entirely new level of need. Their breasts touched, nipple to nipple, but as they hugged tighter, the soft pillows of flesh seemed to meld and become one body, connecting on a level beyond physical.

Shivering now with growing arousal and her sex clenching in wave after wave of frustration, Liana had no idea what to do next. Then the slight pressure of Keisha's hand on her arm directed her to the bed. She crawled across the patterned spread and stretched out on her side. Keisha lay beside her, and stroked her warm palm from Liana's thigh to her breast.

Her trembling increased with each silken glide, with every beat of her heart. Keisha leaned close and wrapped her full lips around one distended nipple, and Liana's world imploded.

Lightning and fire spread through her veins. Liana whimpered and the muscles between her legs tightened. Empty. She felt so empty, clenching around nothing. She wanted the fullness of a man's cock, his thick length penetrating her, but she sighed as the suction of Keisha's mouth drew fire from her toes to her breast.

Using tongue and lips to work her magic, moving from one breast to the other, licking and sucking, Keisha teased and nipped until Liana's back bowed in a spasming arc atop the bed.

But it wasn't enough. Not nearly enough.

Clutching frantically at the bedspread, Liana gasped when Keisha slipped three fingers through the thatch of blond curls covering her mons, teased her protruding clit and slipped deep inside her sex. The suddenness of the intrusion, the unexpected sensation of soft fingers forcing entry and curling against her taut inner walls shocked her into orgasm.

Screaming, Liana clutched at Keisha's hand. It was too much, too unfamiliar, this deeply personal touch, this woman's touch, but Keisha merely smiled around Liana's nipple, slipped her mouth away and latched on to her other nipple.

Keisha's fingers continued pumping in and out of Liana's tight sheath, the pressure perfect from one intimately familiar with a woman's needs. Her thumb rode directly over Liana's clit. Her soft, full lips suckled and nursed at Liana's breast. Tongue flicking over the tip, lips clasping, teeth nipping, she added layer upon layer of sensation to a body that was already hovering on the edge of yet another orgasm.

Liana tried to move away, but Keisha refused to be deterred. Slowly thrusting her fingers in and out of Liana's tight channel, rubbing the soft pad of her thumb over her sensitive clit, Keisha took her once again over the edge.

Liana'd never imagined what it would be like, to be touched so intimately by another woman, by someone who knew where and how, what and how hard, to touch, to lick, to rub. Her arms and legs shivered in reaction, but Keisha kept on. Liana's orgasms rolled one into the other. She couldn't take anymore. No more. Her body had reached its limit.

And then Keisha shifted. The dark brown wolf ran her tongue over Liana's belly and then settled between her thighs. This was more familiar, exactly what Matt had done for her as lover to her goddess. She reveled in the heat of a warm, furry body holding her legs apart, the cold brush of a wet nose, the long, sensuous lick of a mobile tongue.

Liana arched her hips as Keisha's wolven tongue stroked the inner walls of her vagina, soothing and inflaming at the same time. Her heart thundered in her chest and she realized she was plucking at her own nipples, teasing the points higher, tighter.

The wolf lapped between her legs, dragging her long tongue the full length of Liana's cleft, licking between her cheeks and running the tip all the way to her navel. Whimpering now, her body continuing to spasm and clench with each lick, Liana drifted in a sensual fog of warm touches and long, leisurely licks.

Lips encircled her nipples, and somehow both breasts were encased in warm mouths with busy tongues licking, sucking, teasing. The wolven tongue was gone, but in its place were mobile lips and the same sensual suction over her clit that she still felt on her breasts.

Fingers slipped inside her vagina and then teased at the tight pucker of her anus. Penetration was smooth and simple, a single finger that breached that taut muscle and slipped inside.

Still her body rolled with each new sensation, each new touch, welcoming lips and tongues, fingers and breasts. A nipple brushed her lips and she suckled, drawing the turgid tip into her mouth, aware on some level that this was a stranger to her in some ways, a familiar friend in others.

She was, after all, their goddess. She'd been with all her Chanku, at one time or another, as they made love to their packmates. She opened her eyes, curious now, to see whose breast she tasted, and looked into Mei Chen's beautiful amber eyes, her lips parted in her own sensual haze of pleasure.

Alexandria Olanet lay beside her, running her hands over Liana's belly, softly palming her breast and bringing it to her mouth. Liana raised her head and recognized Jazzy Blue as the one who teased her anus, knew she was one of the younger women who had recently joined the pack.

These were the women of the Montana pack. All of them here, welcoming her. Loving her. She felt their warmth, their arousal, the sense of family. Their thoughts were open to her, their desire that she know she was one of them such a powerful force, Liana did the only thing left to her.

Her body shuddered with yet another orgasm, and then she burst into tears.

Oliver sat on the corner of the deck, waiting for Mei while Anton played in the sandbox with Lily, and Stefan strapped Alex into the swing. Finally, Anton raised his head and winked at him.

"What was that for?" Oliver frowned.

"You going to tell me what you plan to do with Adam

now that you've got him trussed up like a sacrificial lamb?"

Oliver shrugged. "It was either that or kill him."

"If it helps any, he feels absolutely terrible about hurting Mei."

"He fucking broke her wrist, Anton. There's no excuse for . . ."

Anton nodded. "I agree, but have you wondered at all what's going on in the man's head? Why he's hidden himself away from us since Eve died? Why he tried to kill himself this morning?"

Oliver's breath caught in his throat. "He what?"

Anton nodded. "He hung himself. It was only through Liana and Eve's intervention that he's still alive, and he's pretty pissed off about that. Adam blames himself for Eve's death. Liana has already acknowledged that the fault was hers, but Adam figures if he'd gone with Eve instead of staying to play video games with you, she'd still be alive." Anton shrugged. "Perhaps he's right, but that's not what happened and Eve is dead—at least, dead to Adam. She's actually achieved immortality, but that's another discussion for another time."

"So what's that have to do with hurting Mei?"

Anton shook his head, but the sad smile on his face spoke volumes. "Even Adam doesn't know how that happened. He's a healer. He snapped when he walked into the room and saw Mei going through Eve's closet. You've taken the right action though, as long as you follow through in a satisfactory manner."

Oliver stared at Anton, but Lily had claimed her father's attention once again. Finally, frustration won out. "Okay, give. What do we do to help him?"

Anton tickled his daughter's tummy and watched her giggle for a moment before turning his attention to Oliver. "I would suggest you have Mei punish him. For hurting her, of course." Anton lifted Lily up and tossed her in the air. She squealed when he quickly caught her and hugged her close to his chest.

"I've already told Adam I'm leaving him to Mei. I wanted him to think about it for a while."

Anton nodded. "I know, but Adam needs to hurt right now. He needs to feel pain, and then he needs to come through it. Mei is a natural dominant, but can she inflict real pain on a man she truly loves? Can she force him to submit to her?"

Oliver shook his head. "Adam's not a submissive. He won't like it."

Anton shrugged. "Do you want him to? You just told me you feel like killing him. He hurt Mei. She's the one who should have control, though there's no reason you can't take part in his punishment. Think about it, Oliver. How do you really feel about Adam Wolf?"

Oliver shook his head and his eyes filled with tears. "I don't have to think about it, Anton. I love him. I owe him everything, but even if he hadn't been the one to give me back my life, I would still love him. He's a good man."

"That he is. A good man who needs to get past a horrible agony that's tearing him to pieces. His mate is gone. Her killer, for all intents and purposes, has been accepted by his pack. He's feeling betrayed, but more than that, he's feeling guilty on so many levels. You and Mei can help him, Oliver."

"Help who do what?" Mei stood on the deck behind Oliver. She had a band wrapped around her wrist, but she was smiling.

"How's your wrist?" Oliver stood up and wrapped his arm around her waist.

"Logan healed it, but Liana took away the rest of the pain. She's a healer, just like Adam. The tape's just to support the repairs for a day or two, but everything is fine."

Mei leaned close and kissed him. He tasted an unfamiliar flavor on her lips. "Who . . . ?"

She giggled. "Uh . . . Liana. I stopped off to meet her. She and Keisha were getting to know each other." She turned and winked at Anton. "Real well. Xandi and Jazzy were already there. I think Liana feels more like one of the pack, now."

Anton raised one expressive eyebrow.

"Well, I don't think she really understood the way shifting affects your libido. Keisha offered to help and she's never been with a woman before, and Xandi and Jazzy and I sort of picked up on the mental screams and . . ." She shrugged and grinned at Oliver. "You know how that goes."

Laughing, he kissed her. "That I do, but we've still got a problem."

She frowned and watched him.

"Adam. I left him tied up so you could have your evil way with him."

"He didn't mean to hurt me, sweetie. He lost it. He . . ."

Oliver shook his head. "No. Don't make excuses for him. He hurt you. Broke your wrist, Mei. That's not a small thing." He nodded at Anton. "Anton says Adam wants to be punished. You're very good at that."

Her eyes went wide and she glanced at Anton and back at Oliver. "Well, if you really think this is what he wants . . ."

"He may not recognize it, but I know it's what he needs." Anton stepped out of the play area with Lily perched on his hip. "Not necessarily arousal, not sex. Punishment. He wants to feel pain. Enough pain to let him begin to heal. Can you do that?"

Mei winked at Anton. "Well, he did break my wrist . . ."

Anton smiled as he bounced Lily on his hip. "I knew you'd understand."

Chapter 4

Adam wasn't sure how long he'd been left here on Oliver and Mei's bed, trussed up like a damned pig. He'd actually fallen asleep, which meant time now had no meaning whatsoever.

Oliver had blindfolded him before he left, so he couldn't tell if it was day or night. He figured he couldn't have been here for too long, though he'd awakened with his shoulders screaming in agony, as much from the scratches and bites as the way he'd been restrained with his arms tightly stretched up and apart. But he wasn't thirsty, didn't have to take a leak . . . so he'd only been here an hour or two at the most.

He did, however, have the world's hardest boner. Must be the result of so many weeks in his wolven form. He hadn't jacked off, hadn't had sex since Eve's death.

Eve. Would he ever be able to think of her without wanting to weep like a lost child? Without needing her arms around him, her lips on his, the warm, wet clasp of her pussy on his swollen cock?

She wasn't just dead, though. He couldn't think of her that way, not when the truth was so much better—at least for Eve. As weird as it seemed, it was easy for him to think of her as their goddess. She'd always had that quality about her, that sense of otherworldliness that kept him in awe of her even as he loved her.

He would always think of her as he'd last seen her, gowned in white, her eyes swirling in that mesmerizing shift of colors. She'd actually looked happier than he could ever recall, as if she'd finally found her true purpose in life . . . or death, as the case might be.

He heard a door open, the sound of footsteps, whispered words he couldn't quite discern. Oliver and Mei were back. Damn. He owed Mei an apology. He hadn't meant to hurt her.

No. The only one he wanted to hurt was himself. What a bastard he was. He hadn't deserved Eve. Didn't deserve Oliver and Mei.

Didn't deserve to live, but he hadn't even been able to kill himself. He'd failed everyone he'd ever loved. His twin sister, Manda, during all those years when he'd not tried to find her, hadn't saved her from a life of torture and pain. His mother, the woman who'd given him birth. He could have searched for her, but instead he'd taken the easy route. He'd believed the lies he'd been told and he'd cursed her instead.

Cursed Millie West, one of the sweetest, most loving women he'd even known. His own mother . . . and he'd failed Eve most of all. Taken her for granted. Accepted her love as if it were his due. Had left her to make that last trip to town alone even after she'd asked him to go with her.

If he'd been along, she'd still be alive. The wreck wouldn't have happened or, at the very worst, he could have saved her. He fixed things, didn't he? He fucking fixed everything.

But he'd be damned if he'd fix Liana. This was the goddess's fault as much as it was his. The bitch was on her own. If she couldn't figure out life as a mortal, it was just too fucking bad.

"You're right, Oliver. He's still here."

Mei's voice carried a note of disgust. Well, did he deserve anything else?

"I saved him for you. I think you need to show Adam how badly he hurt you."

He heard Mei's derisive laughter. "Oh? You think I should break a bone or two?"

He sensed Oliver moving closer to the bed. An involuntary shiver raced over Adam's flesh. He felt the anger pouring off his friend. He'd never known Oliver to be this angry. Never imagined his anger directed so personally.

"You don't have to break bones to make a point." Fingers—Oliver's fingers—trailed across his flank. Adam's shivering increased until his entire body trembled.

He sensed the change in air pressure a second before the flat of Oliver's hand connected with his left cheek. His buttocks clenched. It wasn't a love tap. Not meant to arouse. No, it was meant to hurt, and it did.

"I have something better than the flat of your hand," Mei said. "Something that will remind him long after I'm finished."

He heard the soft slide of a drawer and knew that Mei was looking in the top drawer of the bedside table, the one where she kept her toys. Most of the items she kept there were designed for pleasure.

Some she'd never used, but he'd seen them. Knew they were specifically designed to cause pain. The kind of pain guaranteed to take the recipient to a different place, another reality.

Would she use those on him? Dear Goddess . . .

What was he thinking? Could he really pray to Eve? To a woman he'd made love to? One he'd taken in every way possible, both as a man and as a wolf?

There was no warning. The sharp hiss of leather straps whistling through air, the agonizing pain of the metal tips of the flogger cutting into his lower back, just at the base of his spine.

Shock. Unbelievable shock that anything could hurt so bad.

"Fuck!" He shouted, surprise as much as pain empowering his voice. Cursed again as air touched what had to be open wounds.

"Perfect." Mei's soft voice held an angry note of satisfaction. "Oliver? Leave me alone with him. An hour, please. He deserves at least an hour."

"Look, Mei. I'm sorry." Adam tried to raise his upper body but the restraints were too tight.

"Too late for that, Adam. I don't want to hear you."

He heard the brush of fabric as she moved away, then a blast of discordant sound, shrieking voices . . . fuck. Mei and her damned Finnish heavy metal. He hated that shit, hated what it told him about Mei right now.

She loved heavy metal, but she only played the Finns when she was pissed. Really, really pissed. She turned it up loud, so loud he couldn't hear the whistle of leather through air, had no time to prepare for the next stinging barrage of metal beads cutting into his buttocks.

He hoped she couldn't hear him curse. He bowed his head forward just before she hit him again, and then once again. The music reverberated off the bedroom walls, seemed to beat within his blood as fire touched his thighs, clipped the curve of his buttocks, slashed across his lower spine. After a moment he realized she danced behind him, swinging the flogger in time with the powerful beat of guitar and drums, cutting him in a bloody rhythm, his right shoulder, then his left, one strike following the other leaving tracks of flame behind.

The first song ended. Four minutes? Wasn't that about the length of each piece on that damned CD? He heard Mei breathing—deep, rasping breaths that whistled in and out of her straining lungs.

Or was that his own breath he heard? The next track

began, a clash of guitar and male screams, the powerful yet primitive beat of the drums and the fiery slash of beads across his left cheek and then his right, the snap of leather and the blazing pain fitting perfectly with the raucous heavy metal.

There was a sensual beauty in the rhythm, an erotic depth to his agony. He floated on the beat, on the slash and sharp impact of tiny metal beads and thin straps of leather against vulnerable flesh. Mei swung again and again, and he moved beyond the pain, into a place he'd not discovered before, floating on a sea of blinding agony that was somehow good and pure.

His heart beat with the rhythm of the drums, each breath tied to the guitar and the powerful riff that sang in his veins and fired his soul. He felt at peace for the first time in weeks. At peace with the pain, with the anger, with the memories. His thoughts wandered beyond the pain and he wondered if she used her right arm, if the wrist was strong enough for swinging the flogger with so much force.

The second track ended. Eight minutes, give or take a second or more. His body was on fire, his dick so hard it practically lifted him off the bed. When Oliver'd tied him to the bed, he'd somehow positioned Adam's cock so that it pointed down between his legs with his balls pressed against the underside of his shaft.

So far Mei had missed his cock and testicles, but he didn't expect his luck to hold out forever. He didn't want to think of the pain should she connect one of those metal beads with the swell of his balls. For now, the pain had become a companion, just as the rich, coppery scent of his blood had become familiar, an almost welcome perfume.

How long, he wondered, would it take Logan to heal him when Mei was done?

Would she ever be done? He waited for the next track

to begin. Waited for the slash of the flogger, the slight rattle of the beads as she lifted it over her head, the whistle that announced the downward stroke.

Instead he felt the soft touch of fingers caressing his skin. Heard the quiet catch in her breath.

"Oh, Adam. What the hell have I done to you? I'm sorry." Mei knelt beside him on the bed. He felt her lips against his shoulder, his back, his buttock. Why the fuck was she apologizing? She couldn't stop. Not now. He felt cheated. She'd cheated him out of . . . what? Shit, he had no idea, but he knew they weren't finished. Not yet.

"Don't stop," he said, well aware he was begging. "You're not done yet."

"You're bleeding, Adam. You could end up with scars. I didn't intend to hurt you like this. I need to get Logan in here."

"An hour, Mei." He tried to see her, but he couldn't turn enough to find her, and even if he had, the blindfold wouldn't let him see. "You told Oliver you needed an hour."

"Well, I don't. Okay?" She sounded angry. He wanted her angry. Wanted her so pissed off at him she'd hit him again, take him back to that place where he'd actually felt a sense of peace.

"Why, Mei? Can't handle it? A little blood and you chicken out?" He tugged at his restraints, pulling until the bed creaked beneath the strain.

"Oliver?" He sensed her backing away from the bed. "Are you out there?"

No! He wasn't ready. Not yet. She needed to go back, needed to do exactly what she'd *been* doing. His heart thundered in his chest and he realized he was panting, a regular "fight or flight" response because she'd quit beating on him.

Was he a sick fuck or what? "You two are a pair, aren't

you, Mei? A couple of rejects. Oliver sold like a damned dog, castrated like the mongrel he is. I heard your mother threw you away, wrapped you up in a newspaper like day-old garbage and left you in a park. A couple of real winners, aren't you?"

"You bastard!"

Oliver's soft curse made him smile. Maybe Adam hadn't been able to kill himself, but with any luck, Oliver'd do it for him.

"Oliver, no. He's just trying to get at us. Ignore him. I'm going to get Logan. Some of those cuts are deep."

"Logan's gone. Tala's having some trouble with her pregnancy and he and Jazzy just left for the airport. No one talks to you like that, Mei. No one."

The straps whistled through the air with twice the force behind Mei's strikes. There was no music this time. No drums forcing a steady rhythm. Nothing but blinding pain, anger like he'd never felt before as Oliver slashed at his back and legs, crisscrossed his buttocks with brands of fire.

A metal bead caught one of his nuts and he screamed. Another hit the underside of his shaft. Excruciating pain flashed the length of his spine. Oliver must have realized what he'd done because he focused his strikes, hitting his buttocks and balls, his cock, the cleft of his ass, spread wide by his restrained legs. Flicking the metal beads over his anus until each cut was a knife thrust, each slash causing unimaginable agony.

He thought he heard Mei screaming, or maybe he was the one. He didn't know. Not anymore, but at least he was back in that same place, floating beyond the pain. Beyond anger or loss.

Beyond everything.

It had happened before, during orgasm, though he didn't think he'd actually come from the beating, but Adam found himself floating above his body, looking down on Oliver as he swung the metal-tipped flogger with his own dark and rhythmic grace.

Suddenly Oliver stopped, stared at the whip in his hand and tossed it on the floor. He crawled up on the bed between Adam's legs and removed the shackles from his ankles. Still Adam watched, separate yet very much a part of the scene taking place beneath him.

Oliver slowly unbuckled his belt, shoved his jeans down over his thighs. He lifted Adam's hips, his hands slipping in the blood that covered his flanks. Though separate from his body, Adam somehow drew his legs forward and raised his ass for Oliver.

His mind floated, mere spirit overhead, and watched, mesmerized, as Oliver wrapped his fingers around his thick, black cock, stroking his full length while staring at Adam's bloodied ass. His anger pulsed, almost a separate entity in the bedroom as his hand moved faster and faster, up and down his thick shaft.

White fluid leaked from the tip, but just before he came, Oliver shifted his knees, let go of his cock and parted Adam's buttocks. Then he grabbed his cock once more and drove forward, shoving the thick, dark glans against the tight, unprepared opening to Adam's ass.

Excruciating pain sucked Adam back into his body. Still suspended by his shackled arms, he cried out as Oliver grasped his hips in both hands and forced entry, tearing his path through Adam's tightly clenched sphincter. Adam twisted his body in an attempt to throw Oliver off. He tightened his muscles against penetration, but Oliver was stronger, his anger a driving force.

He hadn't used any lube, but there was so much blood he didn't need it. His cock finally slipped through the taut ring of muscle, burning through Adam's defenses—but what was one more injury in a world of pain?

Adam groaned. He flexed his shoulders and wrapped

his fists around the restraints. He thought of fighting Oliver anyway, of cursing him, but there was nothing left. No anger, no strength.

He gave up the fight and took it, the thick slide of Oliver's cock tearing into him. The dark pleasure in spite of the agony of forced entry, the sense of connection he always felt when he coupled with a man.

But with Oliver, before, it had always happened with love.

Never with hate, never in anger.

Never like this.

He'd lost something important today. Something he'd never truly appreciated. The love of a good man. Oliver's love. He'd fucked himself this time. What they'd had was broken.

Irreparable. One love dead and gone, another destroyed, only he'd done this one all on his own.

Adam pressed his face into the bedding and wept. Oliver plowed into his ass, cursing Adam with every driving thrust, tearing his flesh, destroying whatever was left of his heart.

Adam heard a door slam, sensed others coming into the room. Heard Anton's soft voice in his head and knew he spoke to Oliver as well.

It's okay, Oliver. Come and be done with it. Finish in him. Both of you needed this, but no more. Not anymore.

Oliver grunted and cursed. Adam felt the thick spasm of muscle as Oliver shot his seed deep inside. Groaned with his own release. Unexpected. Unwanted.

Adam kept his face buried in the tangled bedding. He didn't know if he had it in him to move, even if he'd wanted to. Anton removed his blindfold and gently unfastened the shackles binding his wrists. He unbuckled the leather collar around Adam's neck and set it aside. Then Anton sat beside him on the bed, gently rubbing the circulation back into his hands.

The tears wouldn't stop flowing. Embarrassed, aware now of the pain of a hundred cuts, of bites and bruises and bloody tears to his body, he tried to find that place once again, the peaceful spot in his mind where he'd gone during the beating.

He heard a man crying, loud, desperate cries. Oliver, and then Mei's soft, measured tones. But why? It made no sense. He was the one bleeding. The one who'd just had his ass violently fucked. The sound of unrestrained grief ended, but only because Mei must have taken Oliver from the room.

Anton remained. He sat on the bed beside Adam and ran his fingers through Adam's tangled hair. It was unusual for Anton to remain silent. The fact he'd not said anything frightened Adam more than anything.

Now that he'd finally returned to the compound, would Anton kick him out? Was he no longer welcome here? He had only himself to blame, if that was the case.

He heard a soft gasp, a choked cry.

"Thank you for coming, Liana."

That bitch! Adam tried to push himself up, to tell her to get the hell away from him, but he couldn't move. After being stretched so tightly in the restraints, his arms refused to lift his weight.

The bed dipped on the other side. He turned his head away, refusing to acknowledge her presence. Pain rippled and rolled across his shoulders, along his spine, across his buttocks. He had a pretty good idea how badly he'd been injured, but why was Liana here?

Anton's thoughts slipped into his mind, a subtle intrusion not entirely welcome, but then Anton Cheval went wherever he pleased, welcome or not. Adam sensed his soft, sad laughter, and then he saw what Anton saw.

Liana sat across from Anton and held her hands out over Adam's bloodied back. Shit. He was worse than he'd imagined. His shoulders and back were crisscrossed with bloody stripes. Some of the slashes on his right shoulder went deep into muscle. He figured Oliver had done those.

His buttocks looked like hamburger. His testicles were covered in blood as was the length of his cock visible between his spread legs. So much semen and blood—it had to be a combination of both his release and Oliver's, but Goddess, he was an ugly mess.

But the pain was gone. *You?*

Liana. I don't have that ability.

Damn. Why did Anton sound as if he was laughing? The last thing Adam wanted was to feel grateful to the bitch, but now that the rush of the original pain was past, he welcomed its absence.

Adam wasn't sure how long he lay there with Liana working her healing magic and Anton lending his mental strength. He knew he slept, and it must have been awhile, because the first thing he thought of when he awoke was that he really had to take a leak.

The second, that Liana was gone.

Anton remained. Adam shook his head to clear the cobwebs, slowly rolled over and sat up. Before he could speak, Anton said, "You stink. Go take a shower. I'll be here when you come out."

Like that was an incentive to hurry? He really didn't want to face Anton, but the shower felt wonderful and he was amazed to see his injuries were entirely healed. Liana was good. He'd give her that much. He dried himself and looked at the face in the mirror, not exactly certain what to expect.

The man who returned his gaze was different than he'd been a few short weeks ago. Bearded. Older. Sadder. As if the lights had gone out.

They had. Eve was gone, and everything had changed. Wrapping a towel around his hips, Adam walked out to face Anton.

* * *

A cloud of steam preceded Adam as he stepped out of the bathroom. Anton got hard just looking at the man. When he'd walked in earlier and witnessed Oliver slamming into Adam's ass, Anton had almost come in his pants. The violence of the act, the innate sensuality of one man dominating another had been unbelievably erotic in spite of how wrong it had been.

Not a very proud moment for a man who wanted his people to respect his ability to control not only himself but those around him. He'd never expected Oliver to go so far over the top.

He stood up and glanced at the bloodied bedding. "Help me clean this mess up," he said, reaching for the twisted blankets.

Adam nodded and grabbed the sheets, peeling the fitted one off the mattress and tugging them all back. With Anton's help, they had the filthy sheets and blankets off and the bed remade within a few minutes. Neither man said a word. Adam carried the bedding out of the room when they were done.

He returned a few minutes later. "Sorry to be gone so long. I wanted to get the bloody stuff in the washer so the stains wouldn't set." He gazed around the room as if he wasn't quite sure what they were doing there.

Anton stood up. "Let's go out on the back deck. It's private and quiet, and I could use some fresh air."

Adam nodded, a short, sharp jerk of his head. He followed Anton, took a detour into the kitchen and came out with two cold bottles of beer. "It's not cognac, but thought you might like one."

Anton flashed him a grin and took the bottle Adam held out to him. This was beginning to sound more like the man he knew, but then he recalled what he'd walked in on and realized that man, that Adam Wolf, was gone forever.

They each took a seat, looking across a small stretch of

the meadow and into the dark woods beyond. Adam sipped his beer, but his thoughts were blocked, just as they'd been since Anton first walked into Oliver and Mei's cottage.

"I owe you an apology," Anton said. He stared at the dark bottle in his hand and realized he was overly fascinated by the drops of condensation running down the long glass neck.

"You? What for?"

Anton turned and forced himself to look into Adam's direct gaze. "I'm the one who told Mei and Oliver I thought you were looking for pain. They never would have hurt you like they did if I . . ."

"No." Adam turned away and stared at the forest for a long, uncomfortable minute. He took a deep breath and gazed at Anton. "Mei took me exactly where I needed to go, but then she stopped. She hated what she was doing. Mei's into playing the dominant, but she would never hurt anyone on purpose. She was hurting me. It was what I wanted, but she stopped before I was ready."

He swallowed and bit down on his lips. Took a deep breath. "I goaded her. Goaded Oliver. I said some inexcusable things to make them lose control." The corner of his lips quirked up in a self-deprecating smile. "It worked better than I intended. Oliver and Mei helped me exorcise my demons. Unfortunately, my poor choice of words brought in an entirely new set."

Anton nodded. He felt as if he was finally beginning to understand the man who had always been such an enigma. "You can't continue to stay with them."

Adam smiled as he agreed. "I know. There's a room over the garage. It's close to the clinic. I planned to ask you if I could move there, fix it up as an apartment."

Frowning, Anton stared at Adam. "Why? We have plenty of rooms in the main house."

"Liana's there." The smile was gone. Adam turned back to his study of the forest.

"Ah. She's actually very sweet. She's trying hard to learn, to lose the spoiled goddess persona."

"She should have tried that before Eve died." Adam lurched to his feet and paced the length of the deck. Came back and stopped in front of Anton. "She was fucking one of her borrowed boy toys while my mate was skidding off the highway. Probably didn't hear Eve scream because she was too busy enjoying her orgasm."

Anton nodded. "Quite possible. She's failed us in many ways. She realizes that. She knows she can't fix what she screwed up, but she's trying to be a better person."

"Like I said, it's a little late."

"The room above the garage is yours. I'll have it remodeled as soon as I can get a crew out here to do the work."

"It's not necessary." Adam tightened the towel around his waist. "I'm a good carpenter. I'll do it myself."

"Will you at least take meals with us?"

Adam stared at him for a long, silent moment. "Is that an order?"

"An invitation, Adam. Nothing more than an invitation from one friend to another."

There was no point in staying. Adam's mind was locked down. Anton knew he could break through the barriers if he wished. Adam would never know the difference.

But Anton would.

He stood up and finished the last of his beer. He might have left without another word if he hadn't caught the look of utter loss on Adam's face. Instead of leaving, Anton stepped close to Adam and drew him into his arms.

He felt Adam's shoulders shake, felt the powerful shudder that passed through his body, and still he held him, a man his equal in height, whose shoulders were broader, whose powers, though different, might equal his own. Held him close like a child, gently stroking his back while he cried.

* * *

Adam sat on the deck until well after dark. Neither Mei nor Oliver had returned. It bothered him, to think his presence made them unwilling to return to their own home, but he waited anyway.

He'd showered again. Shaved off his beard, changed into jeans and a light sweater as the temperature dropped with the setting sun. His clothes and belongings were gathered in a pair of duffel bags that sat beside him on the deck. It was well after ten before he heard the front door open, heard the sound of voices inside the cottage.

A few moments later, Oliver stepped out on the deck. He was alone. Adam wondered vaguely where Mei was as Oliver walked across the deck and sat in the chair Anton had vacated just a few hours earlier.

"You okay, buddy?"

Adam smiled, but he watched the forest and hoped his face was hidden from Oliver. "I'm good. You?"

"I've been better."

"Haven't we all? Oliver, I'm so goddamned sorry." Suddenly it all came crashing down on him. The careful speech he'd planned went out the window. Adam spun around and forced Oliver to return his gaze. "I never should have said those things about you and Mei. Damn, I'd take it back in a heartbeat if I could. I was so afraid you'd stop, that Mei would stop and . . ."

"No. You listen to me, Adam. I know you were hurting and I know you said those things specifically to piss me off. It worked, all too well. I raped you. Rape, Adam. There's no excuse. You were tied up, captive. I beat you with a metal-tipped flogger with the intent to draw blood. And I raped you."

Adam shook his head. "It's not rape when the person's willing. I was no victim, Oliver. I knew Logan could heal whatever you hurt, and I needed to hurt. Hell, I still do."

Disgusted with himself, Adam turned away. "I'm moving out, taking the room over the garage. I wanted to apologize to you and Mei first. I used you. Both of you. It was damned unfair."

Oliver chuckled, but there was little humor behind the sound. "Well, for what it's worth, you know I don't want you to leave, though I think I understand. As far as what happened . . ." He sighed. "Anton thought that's what you wanted. The pain. Punishment."

"He was right."

This time Oliver's laughter was freer. "Isn't he always?"

Adam grinned and shook his head. "Yeah. He is." He took a deep breath. "I am sorry, Oliver. I said things that I don't believe, that were just cruel. I wanted you to hate me."

Oliver's eyes seared him. "That's because it's easier if we hate you. Makes it easier for you to hate yourself. Sorry, bud. It won't fly. Mei and I were pissed. I think she still is, but we could never hate you. Never. We love you too much."

"Thank you." He sighed and stood up. Walked over to the door. Tugged it open. "Mei? You in there?"

The silence sounded loud as a shout. He sighed and stepped into the house. Locked on to her scent, the unbelievably attractive aroma of a Chanku bitch, and followed his nose to the kitchen.

Mei sat alone at the small kitchen table. She held a wineglass wrapped in both hands and stared out the window that looked toward the main house. Adam waited a minute to see if she would acknowledge his presence. He wasn't about to force her.

She ignored him. He realized he was worrying the inside of his cheek with his teeth, something he hadn't done since he was a little kid worried about what some adult was going to say.

"Mei?"

Her shoulders stiffened and then visibly relaxed. She took a sip of wine, but she didn't answer. "Mei, you don't have to like me anymore, and I don't blame you for hating me, but I want you to know I'm truly sorry for what I said. You're a beautiful, loving, classy lady, and I'm proud to know you. I'm not very proud of my behavior, though. I just wanted you to know that I'm sorry for what I made you do, for what I said. My words and actions were inexcusable."

Her shoulders relaxed just a bit, but she didn't look his way, didn't acknowledge his presence. Adam cleared his throat. It was so damned hard to talk. "I already told Oliver, but I wanted to tell you, too. I'm moving out. I'll be in the room above the garage. Thank you for opening your home to me and Eve. Those were the best times of my life, living here with you and Oliver. The best."

He turned before she had a chance to answer him, which he figured was another sign of his cowardice. He didn't want to stand there and find out she had nothing to say. He went back out on the deck and nodded to Oliver. Feeling like a damned fool, he lifted the first duffel and threw it over his shoulder. Wrapped his hand around the strap on the second one and held it. He wanted both his hands full so he couldn't hug Oliver.

He didn't want to risk another meltdown like he'd had in Anton's embrace this afternoon. Damn. He hadn't felt this washed out in ages. Not since . . .

No. He couldn't go there. He couldn't think about Eve. Not now. Not after a day so overfilled with emotion. He'd been sucked dry. As painful as it had all been, in some ways it was a good feeling. Peaceful, almost. Better than he deserved.

"You need any help with your stuff?" Oliver gestured at the heavy bags.

"No. I'm good." He turned away, feeling awkward

with Oliver. He'd never felt awkward around this guy. Not once. He glanced over his shoulder. "Anton said I have to come down for meals."

Oliver nodded. Took a deep breath and looked away. Obviously he was just as uncomfortable with this as Adam. What they'd had was lost. The most important friendship he'd ever known in his life, lost. Feeling as if he'd just killed his best friend, Adam practically ran down the back steps off the deck and headed toward the garage.

As he climbed the stairs to the empty room, he thought about what he was doing, why he was doing it. He wasn't leaving Oliver and Mei. He was leaving the home he'd shared with Eve. The one place in his entire life where he'd felt as if he belonged. Where he'd known unconditional love. Where he'd actually been free.

He stepped inside the room. It was empty except for a few boxes stacked in one corner and a small bathroom with a toilet, sink, and shower in the other. He'd have to get some furniture, maybe hook up a computer or a television. He stared around at the four plain walls and tried to picture it fixed up as a place to actually live.

All he could see was a prison. No bars on the walls, but a prison nonetheless.

He dumped his bags on the floor, slipped out of his clothes, and shifted. Shaking himself, he raised his head and sniffed the air, familiarizing himself with the myriad scents of a room long unused. Then he curled up on a small rug near the door and drifted off to sleep.

Chapter 5

Liana sat alone on the deck just outside her bedroom, well aware she needed a quiet evening on her own. She'd showered and wrapped a warm, faded blue chenille robe around herself. Now, relaxed and comfortable after a pleasant dinner with the rest of the pack, she wanted to take some time to think about her new, unexpected situation as a mortal.

A terribly flawed mortal.

Adam hadn't joined them at dinner, but she was actually relieved he'd not come. Of course, he was probably exhausted after his day. Physically and emotionally exhausted. She sent a prayer to the goddess on his behalf, and hoped Eve was a better listener than she'd been.

She heard a high-pitched whine in her ear and slapped the bug away. Then she lit a candle to repel the mosquitoes she'd never had to deal with as a goddess. She bit back a smile with the thought that the little bastards wouldn't dare feast on the blood of an immortal. Mortals were obviously fair game.

The flickering light barely eased the darkness that enveloped her. At dusk, she'd watched Anton and Keisha shift and race into the forest, their long legs stretching out as they ran across the dark meadow into the woods, but now even the meadow was lost in shadows.

Anton and Keisha had run alone. She knew Xandi and Stefan watched the babies, taking turns with their pack-mates as they often did so that all of them could have a chance to run as wolves at least a few times each week.

Liana had been invited, but the day had been long and she was still exhausted from healing Adam. She'd drawn on Anton's mental strength, but it had taken all of her own powers as well as what the über-alpha had shared in order to heal the grievous wounds covering Adam's back and legs.

The violence of the damage Oliver and Mei had inflicted on a man they loved still had her feeling shaken. Almost as shaken as she'd been by Adam's stoic acceptance of his injuries. He'd resented her healing him, had wanted the pain to last at least a little longer.

Her fault. All Adam's pain, the sundered friendship with Oliver and Mei, Eve's death. Maybe she was the one who should have been beaten. Would pain help her accept her horrible mistakes?

No. Not mistakes. *Outright failures.* She'd not done her job and others had paid. She glanced toward the small room over the garage, barely visible from her corner on the deck. Adam had moved up there, essentially isolating himself from the rest of his pack. It felt wrong, for her to be here, in the middle of things, while he hid away in a barren room.

"Liana?"

She whipped around at the soft question. "Mei? Hi. I didn't hear you."

Looking like a gangly teenager in her cropped linen pants and ragged sweatshirt, Mei flopped down in a comfortable Adirondack chair next to Liana's and looped one long leg over the arm. "I just wanted to make sure you were okay. Oliver decided to run with Anton and Keisha

tonight and . . ." She shrugged. "It's been a long day. I figured I'd stay and see what you were up to."

"Just thinking about everything that happened today."
Liana exhaled and wished she could make all her problems go away as easily as she emptied the breath from her
lungs. "It feels like it must have been weeks ago that Eve
and I found Adam. It's only been hours."

"He really tried to kill himself? That's so hard to believe of Adam. He's a healer." Mei's dark eyes reflected the
light from the house. She rested her chin on one hand and
gazed directly at Liana as if searching for answers.

"He did." Liana stared into the flickering candle, and
tried to see the morning's emotional beginning from an
observer's point of view. She couldn't. Not yet. She was
still too close, her emotions too tightly involved. "Anton
warned us, or we might not have gotten to Adam in time.
He'd jumped with the rope around his neck. Eve caught
him before the rope went taut. I was able to cut it just in
time. A fraction of a second longer and we couldn't have
saved him, not if he'd broken his neck. It's frightening to
think how close he came."

"But you did save him. That's what counts."

Liana nodded, remembering the terror of the moment.
The fear they might have been too late. She looked at Mei,
and then paused. There was something else going on in the
girl's mind. Some horrible question. "Mei, are you okay?"

"I . . ." Her lips trembled. She shook her head, and the
thick cascade of her long, black hair swept across her
shoulders. "Today Adam said some ugly things. He wanted
to make me mad, and it worked. I can't believe how badly
I beat him." She stared at the ground. "I had no idea I had
that kind of anger festering in me. I thought I'd dealt with
my hang-ups a long time ago, but obviously I haven't.
Today got me to thinking that maybe you, because you
were our goddess, that maybe you know things."

Liana reached for Mei's hands and squeezed her icy fingers. "What kinds of things?"

Mei blinked, and the words spilled out. "Why my mother abandoned me. How she could leave a newborn wrapped in newspaper like so much garbage and then just walk away. Do you know why?" She sniffed and wiped her nose on the sleeve of her sweatshirt. "I'm sorry. I try to make myself not think of it, but Adam brought it all back and now I can't let go."

"Adam hurts. It made him act with cruelty. I imagine he feels terrible about the things he said, but that doesn't help you, does it?" Liana let go of Mei's hand. She leaned forward and linked her fingers around her knees. "Right now, at this moment, I don't know the answers. Give me tonight to see what I can learn. Your mother was not Chanku—obviously she carried the genes, but she didn't have the nutrients that made her a shapeshifter, so I would not have been watching her. Sometimes, though, the Mother of us all allows me to see things, to understand what I didn't know before. That's all I can promise you, Mei. I'll do my best."

"Thank you." Mei covered Liana's clasped fingers with her own. Then she stood up. "I need to go back. Oliver should be home soon and I don't want him to be alone tonight."

Liana nodded. "It's been a rather difficult day, hasn't it?"

"No shit." Mei laughed and shook her head. "I like you, Liana. I didn't want to when I found out what happened. I miss Eve something fierce. She was like my mom and my big sister and my very best friend and my lover, all rolled into one beautiful, giving soul. No one will ever take her place, but I can see her as a goddess. She was made for the job. Maybe more than you, eh?" She winked.

Liana couldn't resent her honesty.

"I think you're going to do just fine, here, Liana. I really hope so."

Liana stood up and wrapped her arms around Mei. "Thank you. Your words mean more than you can possibly imagine. I'll do my best to learn what I can about your beginnings. I promise."

She watched Mei as she walked the length of the deck and slipped into the house through the doorway at the far end. Then she found herself thinking of Tala and her pregnancy, and the fact Logan and Jazzy had flown to San Francisco to help her.

If she were still the goddess, she would know exactly what was going on. Now, though, she had to wait, just like everyone else. Wait and pray, and hope Eve was on top of things.

Liana sat back in her chair and smiled into the darkness. Mei was right. Eve was the perfect goddess, a definite upgrade from the one the Chanku had been blessed—or cursed—with when Liana held the position.

She'd failed, but at least she'd done a few good things during her tenure. Keisha and Tala were excellent examples. Maybe she needed to do as Keisha suggested—concentrate on the positives, not the negatives. Think of the good things she'd accomplished and the good she could do now, as a mortal. She was a healer. She'd healed Adam today.

At least she'd healed his visible wounds, but what about the wounds none of them could see? Did she have the power to heal those as well?

She'd never know unless she tried, but she'd have to figure out how to help Adam without him realizing she was the one. He'd resented her interference today.

Tough shit. She laughed. Already she felt freer. Hanging out with Mei was good for her mortal development. She needed to find out what she could about the girl. Mei deserved to know the truth.

"You're still up. Is everything okay?"

Liana didn't recognize the voice at first, coming out of the darkness. Then Stefan stepped into the flickering light from the tiny candle. He was dressed in worn blue jeans and a soft knit shirt, but his feet were bare. He carried two fat, round crystal glasses filled with an amber liquid in his hands.

"I hardly had a chance to meet you today. Xandi sent me with a glass of cognac to welcome you." He offered one of the glasses to her.

Liana took it, held it to her nose and sniffed. "I've never tasted this before. What is it?"

Stefan sat in the chair Mei had just vacated. "Anton calls it the nectar of the gods. It seemed apropos for a retired goddess. Here's to your life as a mortal."

He held the glass out and Liana realized she should tap his with hers. She did, and the crystal rang like a bell. Stefan took a sip. She sipped hers.

It burned her throat, but it tasted good, too. She blinked her eyes and looked at the glass. "I've never had spirits of any kind, but I like this. I think." She smiled at Stefan. "As far as referring to me as a retired goddess, you're glossing over the truth of it. I was fired, Stefan. The Mother kicked me out and put Eve in my place. Not a very glorious ending to a long and less than illustrious career now, is it?"

Stefan tilted his head and studied her for a moment. "Is it so bad, being mortal?"

She shook her head. "No. Not at all. It's not something I ever dreamed could happen, so I can't say it's anything I actually wanted, but now that I'm here, I find I'm anxious to learn more, anxious to fit into this world. I've observed it for so many eons . . ." She stared at the amber liquid in the glass, caught in the reflection of candlelight across the crystal bowl. "Observed, but never participated."

"And what do you think of the participation so far?"

He smiled at her, his entire face lighting up with humor. "Xandi told me she was part of your welcoming party."

Liana blushed. She didn't think she'd ever blushed before, but she recognized the hot flush across her face, throat, and chest for what it was, and wondered if Stefan could tell he'd caught her by surprise. "Xandi is beautiful. Beautiful and very sensual." She shook her head and stared at the deck beneath her feet. "I'd never been with a woman before. Today I was with four, all of them intent on my pleasure. It was an amazing experience."

She raised her head, caught instantly in Stefan's deep amber eyes. She was learning to read expressions, catch small nuances of mood. After so many years of viewing her Chanku through the lens of her immortality, it was a totally different experience, trying to understand what these amazing individuals were actually thinking, what they really wanted in spite of their words.

There was much boiling beneath Stefan's surface. Anger, frustration. Regret?

She reached out and touched his knee, aware of the tension vibrating beneath the worn denim. "Ask me, Stefan. I can sense your questions, even a certain amount of anger, though I can no longer read what you don't wish to share."

He covered her hand with his larger one. Breathed deeply, as if centering himself. "Why, Liana? Why did you leave me in hell for five long years? What had I done that I deserved such treatment?"

She shook her head. She should have expected this question. Should have prepared a fitting answer. Unfortunately, all she had was the truth. "There was no reason, Stefan. None beyond the fact that I did not truly know you were Chanku, not until Anton gave you the nutrients and your dual nature became apparent. Remember, other than Keisha's line, which was the only family among all of you that had maintained the ancient connection to their Chanku birthright, all of you were lost to me."

"But once you knew? I spent five years in hell, Liana. Five fucking long years trapped in a body that was neither man nor beast." Abruptly he stood up and turned away from her. "You couldn't help me then?"

"No." Liana rose to her feet, unsure of herself, but she had to make Stefan understand. "You hadn't had enough of the nutrients. Your change had come upon you out of anger, a rush of adrenaline that forced the shift before your body was ready."

"Keisha was able to shift without any nutrients. Tala, too. Why not me?"

"The moment you made your partial shift, I knew you were Chanku, but I couldn't force you to complete the shift one way or the other. Tala and Keisha's lives were at stake and their inability to accept death gave them the strength to complete their shifts without the nutrients. You were angry, but never at risk of dying." She shrugged. "I'm sorry. There was nothing I could do. Nothing."

He turned and stared at her. "Not much of a goddess then, were you?"

Ashamed, she refused to look away. He was right. She'd been a horrible goddess. "I was still learning my way, just as I'm learning to be mortal now. It's never easy, learning new ways."

"Five years, Liana. Five fucking long years." He was the one to look away. He turned and paced, long, angry steps before he turned again. Paced like a wolf in a cage.

She clasped her hands over her belly as Stefan's remembered pain washed over her. "In my defense, such as it is, time has little meaning on the astral plain. Five years for you was . . ." She snapped her fingers and sighed. "Different. It was not the same for me. I didn't understand, then, what you suffered. To be honest, I did not truly understand mortals. I'm sorry."

He planted himself in front of her. "Five years. It's a damned long time for a man to want to die."

His anguish rolled over her, a flood of such deep, unrelenting pain that she blinked back tears she'd not expected. "I am so terribly sorry, Stefan. Once I knew what you were, I didn't forget you, but there was little I could do. You hadn't had enough of the nutrients to complete the shift, and you weren't frightened enough or angry enough to force the shift."

She held up her hand to stop him before he said something they'd both regret. "No. I'm not blaming you. Far from it. You were mentally, emotionally, too strong for the shift to take over. Subconsciously, you must have been fighting it. Tala and Keisha had reached a point of total desperation, knowing death was imminent. Their shifts happened because of that desperation."

Stefan snarled and spun away. Anger boiled off of him in waves—anger and arousal. What was it about these Chanku? She almost smiled as her own awareness of him as a powerful, sensual male blossomed.

"I searched for answers, Stefan. Believe me. It wasn't until I found Alexandria that I was able to put a solution in motion. When she caught her fiancé cheating on her, the spike in her pain enabled, if only for a moment, her Chanku spirit. I sensed her, locked on to her as one of my own. When her vehicle went off the road, I helped you find her. I'm sorry. It was all I knew how to do."

He stopped his angry pacing and stared at her, frowning. "It was you? That night when I chose to run through the storm?"

She swallowed and wrapped her arms around herself, suddenly chilled as she recalled the horrible storm, the sense of Alexandria's life force fading as she lay in the snow. "I couldn't let her die, but she was a long way from your home. I carried her scent to you that night and hoped you would be able to find her."

"I remember looking out into the storm, watching the snow blow sideways and suddenly realizing I had to go out. Oliver tried to stop me, but I raced out into the blizzard with the sense of something waiting."

"Alexandria. You barely got to her in time."

He nodded, and Liana's mind filled with the images in Stefan's memory. An unconscious woman lying barely visible beneath the falling snow, Stefan reaching for her, brushing the ice crystals away from her tangled russet hair, lifting her in arms that were thankfully more human than wolf.

The long walk through howling winds as he carried her back to his home, removed her sodden, partially frozen clothing and wrapped her in his arms beneath the heavy down comforter on his bed. Wrapped her in the warmth of his fur-covered body.

A night of lovemaking unlike anything he'd ever imagined, her body so perfectly attuned to his he'd wept as he held her. And then he'd set her free, only to realize he couldn't go on without her. His life had been forever changed that night.

He'd been reborn, because of Xandi.

Because of Liana? "How did you know?" he asked. "How did you know she would be the perfect one?"

She shook her head. "I didn't. I was no more than a tool of the Mother." She sighed. "We all are. The Mother, or fate."

Stefan threw back his head and laughed. "You would say that. Please, don't tell Anton." He ran the backs of his fingers along the side of her face. "I've cursed you for years, Liana. Hated you, if you want the truth. I'm sorry. I had no idea you'd been the one to lead me to Xandi. You saved more than her life that night. You saved mine as well."

He cupped her face in his hands, leaned close and kissed her. She hadn't expected it, hadn't prepared for the amazing sense of warmth when his lips moved gently over her mouth, the heat of his body as he pulled her close.

"Stefan?" She backed away and gazed up at him. He was so much taller than she was, his dark silver-streaked hair flowing loose around his shoulders, the sharp cut of his jaw and the fullness of his mouth were a sensual invitation she didn't want to deny.

But he was Alexandria's mate.

"Xandi knows I'm here," he said, answering her unspoken question. "She suggested I welcome you—and yes, she meant in exactly the manner you're probably imagining—but I didn't want to. I was too angry to offer love to a goddess I believed had sentenced me to hell for no reason."

A shiver raced along her spine and she felt the pull of her womb, the tight clench of muscles between her legs. "And now?" she asked, sensing exactly what was to come. Wanting him now, with a need that seemed to grow with every breath she took.

"Now?" He stepped closer and placed his big hands on her shoulders. She had to look up to see his face, all shadows and sharp angles in the candlelight. He had a feral intensity she hadn't noticed before. She'd always thought of Stefan as the jokester, the one who teased and laughed his way through most situations.

Now, though, he was anything but funny. The searing intensity in his dark gaze, the tight clasp of his fingers over her shoulders, the tension that was so obvious in the way he stood, studying her as if he'd never actually looked at her before.

"Now," he repeated, "I find that I'm drawn to you on an entirely different level. You are Chanku. I can sense the need in your body in spite of your exhaustion. I hear your heart pounding in your chest and know your body is fighting a very strong pull between us. Now I realize I want to know what it's like to make love with a goddess. One I could be friends with, not one I want to hate."

She laughed as the tension flowed out of her. "I'm no longer a goddess, though I must admit, I'm glad you've decided not to hate me. That would be a bad thing, especially since I love your mate so much. Things could get awkward."

Stefan smiled. He traced the line of her jaw with his fingertips, pressed the pad of his thumb against her lips. She slipped her tongue between her lips and licked his thumb, tasting salt. "Awkward would be a waste of time," he said. Then he leaned close and kissed her.

The smooth glide of his full lips over hers was a revelation. Sensual, almost sweet as he nibbled and sucked at her mouth, slipped the very tip of his tongue along the seam between her lips and then slowly gained entry.

She felt as if it must be someone else in this deliberately sexual embrace. As if Stefan urged another woman close, until her body melded with his from knees to groin to chest, but there was no denying that her nipples hardened against his muscular chest, her mouth opened to his.

All of her men, every one over the years, had been someone she'd chosen as a sexual partner, someone she'd spirited away to her own private world. Though she knew Stefan loved his mate with all his heart, he'd chosen Liana tonight. He'd come to her of his own free will, had not even been certain he even liked her when he at least took the time to make her feel welcome.

Now, though . . . now she whimpered and pressed her pubic mound against his thigh, desperate to ease the sudden rise of need. Now she knew his desire wasn't a sham, his growing need for her was every bit as real as the powerful desire she felt for him.

He ended the kiss and, breathing hard, his heart thundering against her breasts, pressed his forehead against hers. "Here?" he asked, and there was no question in Liana's mind what he wanted. "Or inside?"

She swallowed, struggled to slow her pounding heart.

"Inside," she whispered. "Naked, on the bed. Just you and me."

She felt his chest bounce with his soft chuckling laugh. "Xandi wanted to come, but she's got Alex and Lily to watch over. I promised she could join our thoughts, but I promise to keep her presence in my head alone, if that's what you prefer."

She thought about that a moment, about sharing a man with his mate, even if the sharing was merely through their thoughts. She'd already made love with Alexandria, had climaxed with Xandi's lips suckling her breast and again, when she'd licked and suckled between Liana's legs.

Remembering all they'd done this afternoon made her hot, made her vaginal muscles clench in a needy rhythm. Made her smile when she answered Stefan. "That would be selfish, don't you think? To keep her all to yourself?"

Stefan's eyes sparkled and he burst into laughter. He grabbed Liana's hand and tugged her toward the door to her room, but it wasn't only Stefan's laughter that made her race him to the door. It was Xandi's chuckle, the seductive sound of her laughter in Liana's mind that spurred her forward.

Stefan closed the door behind him, locking out the world, enclosing the beautiful blonde inside the four walls of her room where the big bed had suddenly become the dominant piece of furniture.

He'd come here with such conflicted thoughts tonight, following Xandi's bidding that he make Liana feel welcome. She didn't want her to be lonely tonight, didn't want Liana to have time to consider all she'd lost with her privileged life as a goddess coming to such an abrupt ending.

He no longer felt conflict. No, right now he felt nothing but gratitude and an unusually healthy dose of lust. If not for this woman, Xandi might have frozen to death that night. Instead, she'd not only lived, Xandi had given Stefan back a life he'd believed he no longer wanted. She'd shown him what true love could be—the love between a man and a woman, the love between packmates.

She'd given him a son. Alex. The most perfect creature on earth. And, every bit as important, if not for Liana, if not for Xandi, he might never have faced his desire for Anton, might never have known what being a shapeshifting Chanku really meant. This woman had been the catalyst to all that was good in his life—his mate, his packmates, his son.

Liana walked around the room with a box of matches, lighting candles. One on the dresser, another on the table beside the bed. She turned off the overhead light, leaving the room bathed in candlelight. Then she went into the bathroom. He heard the striking match and smelled the small burst of sulfur. A soft glow followed Liana.

She paused just outside the bathroom door and studied the candle burning atop her dresser. Then she sighed and her shoulders drooped. "I once could wave my fingers around a room and every candle would burst into flame. Now, this." She looked down at the matchbox in her palm before setting it on top of the dresser. Then she turned toward Stefan.

He stepped into her path and slipped his fingers beneath her thick bathrobe. It was a simple thing, to shove the fabric over her shoulders and down her arms, so that she stood before him with her perfect breasts exposed, her pale skin glowing.

He opened his thoughts and found Xandi waiting. Her presence in his mind added an extra caress, and he was glad both babies slept soundly, glad she could take this time to join him, even if it was only in his thoughts.

Liana gazed up at him. Her eyes were wide, the pupils so large they almost hid the soft gray-green of her irises. He cupped her face in his palms, tilted her just so, and kissed her once again. She was so sweet, her lips soft and strangely untutored, as if she'd not been kissed very often.

I haven't, she said, answering his thought. *No man has ever truly courted me. I brought men to me for my pleasure. They did as they were directed. Even Anton, when he took my body with all his amazing skill as a lover, avoided the intimacy of kissing.*

Then he missed the best part. Smiling against her lips, Stefan made love to her mouth, kissing and sucking at her lips, stroking the sharp edge of her teeth, running the tip of his tongue across the roof of her mouth.

His cock strained against his jeans until the pressure was more pain than pleasure. Before he could unzip the fly, Liana broke their kiss and slipped to her knees in front of him. The robe fell entirely from her shoulders and puddled on the floor in a soft cloud of pale blue chenille.

Her small hands caressed the front of his jeans. The slight pressure almost made his knees buckle. She fumbled with the metal button, but he didn't help her. He was too busy watching the way she worried her bottom lip with her teeth as she struggled to unbutton his pants.

When the button was finally free, she glanced up at him and smiled with a look of pure innocence. His heart almost seized in his chest as he watched her return her attention to his fly. He'd worn jeans with a zipper, never realizing how long it could take one determined woman to unzip a pair of jeans.

She raised the tab and lowered the damned zipper one set of teeth at a time. He'd dressed carelessly this evening and his cock lay against his groin to the left instead of down the leg of his pants where he'd at least have room to expand. Now it throbbed in time with his pounding heart, swollen hot and hard beneath the unforgiving denim.

Liana paused opening the zipper just over the thick base of his cock. Instead of opening the fly all the way and giving him some relief, she leaned close and put her mouth over the root of his shaft. Her hot breath tickled and more blood rushed the full length so that he swelled even larger. She licked the small patch of exposed flesh with the tip of her tongue, teasing him unmercifully.

A damp circle appeared on his pants, marking the spot where he'd begun leaking pre-cum. Liana stared at the spreading dampness. Then she placed her open mouth over the spot, clasping his crown through the denim in her teeth.

Goddess! Help me! Groaning, he clenched his hands into tight fists and prayed for his legs to hold him. He heard Xandi's soft chuckle in the back of his mind.

You realize, my love, you're calling on Eve? A woman we both made love with just a few short weeks ago?

He burst out laughing. Liana raised her head, frowning, though the dreamy expression in her eyes made him want to laugh even harder.

"Was I doing something wrong?" She licked her lips.

He ran his hands through her silky blond hair. "No. Good Lord, you're doing everything right. Don't stop. Please?" He knew he'd beg if he had to, but she slipped her hands inside his jeans and eased them down over his hips until his cock was finally, blissfully free.

She ignored it though, laying her cheek against his groin while she carefully massaged his buttocks with supple fingers, slipping along the crease between his cheeks, running her fingertip over the sensitive ring of muscle guarding his ass. His balls pulled up so tight and hard between his legs that they ached and a steady stream leaked from the slit in the end of his cock. He shivered, concentrating on remaining upright, trying to figure out when Liana had totally taken control of his planned seduction.

His jeans had fallen to just below his knees, where they held him imprisoned while Liana had her way with him. He couldn't help but compare. She was so much tinier than Xandi, so much quieter, but right now she had complete control.

She turned her head and licked the tip of his cock. Watching her tiny pink tongue bathe the end while her fingers stroked his ass just about took him over the top.

"You're killing me here."

"You'll live," she said. Then she wrapped her lips around the entire crown and swallowed him. There was no hesitation, no pause to fit his thick shaft through the stricture of her throat. She just opened her mouth and took him all the way, until her lips were planted against the base of his shaft and her chin pressed into his sac.

"Oh. Shit. Don't move. I really don't want to come right now."

Her eyes twinkled. Then she pressed her finger against his tight sphincter and slipped inside. Overly sensitized to anything she did, he felt first one knuckle and then the next one stretching him. When she added a second finger he whimpered.

Xandi's laughter exploded in his mind, but it was too much. Too damned much. The intense shock of impending climax raced from the small of his back and coiled through his balls, but just before he exploded into orgasm, Liana's fingers clamped firmly down on the base of his cock between her lips and his belly and squeezed him tight.

His entire body jerked with the pleasure and pain of orgasm denied. Groaning, he rocked his hips within her grasp, but she offered him no stimulation at all, merely the grasp of an iron fist around the base of his swollen cock and the tight clasp of her mouth holding firmly to his entire length.

Slowly, she slipped her fingers out of his ass and his thick erection out of her mouth, licked the tip of his cock and planted a soft kiss on the smooth curve. His entire body quivered with frustration and arousal such as he'd not experienced in far too long.

She raised her chin and grinned at him. Then she planted her hand against his belly and shoved.

"What?" Flailing his arms, Stefan went over backwards and landed on the bed. He'd totally forgotten it was behind him. With his jeans tangled around his ankles he had no control over his fall.

Liana tugged his jeans off over his bare feet. Then she crawled up his body, tugged off his knit shirt and straddled his chest. "Is Xandi enjoying herself?"

He growled. "Yes, damn it. She's having way too much fun."

"Good. This is for Xandi, too. She gave me a wonderful welcome this afternoon." With that, Liana scooted closer and stuck a pillow under Stefan's head. Then she parted her thighs, tilted her hips, and presented him with her sex.

She was lush and ready, her pink petals glistening with moisture, her little clitoris pulsing out of its protective hood. He knew he teased her with his long study, could tell by the way her muscles tightened and relaxed, by the sound of her breath catching in her throat.

He slipped his palms beneath her butt and lifted her just enough so that he could reach her clitoris with the tip of his tongue. With precise licks and soft swirls, he concentrated on that tiny bud of nerves, stroking and licking until her breathing came in short bursts and gasps and he felt the muscles in her legs begin to quiver.

Then he stopped.

She glared at him, caught right at the very edge of orgasm. Laughing, Stefan lifted her off his chest and slipped her the length of his torso until she straddled his hips. When she raised up on her knees and came down over his straining erection, he felt her link blossoming inside his head.

Xandi, thank you for sharing your mate with me to-night. Are you with us?

I am. The babies are sleeping and I'm in a warm bath, enjoying every move the two of you make.

Laughing out loud, Stefan interrupted. *Hey, girls. What about me? Am I invited?*

Oh, yeah, Liana said, raising herself and then coming down on his cock. *You're the main attraction.*

He left his thoughts open, invited Xandi and Liana both inside his deepest feelings, shared the sense of impending orgasm, the tight clasp of Liana's vaginal walls around his cock.

She rode him hard, her perfect heart-shaped ass slapping down on his thighs with each rise and fall of her lithe body. Her fingers clutched the thick hair on his chest and her vaginal muscles rippled and clenched around his shaft. Her breasts jiggled and bounced on each downward thrust, her long blond hair swept over his thighs and belly, and still she had the look of an innocent about her, even as she took him to the top.

They peaked together, bodies tensing, muscles clenching, hearts stuttering in synchronized thunder. Stefan cried out and wrapped his hands around her tiny waist, raising his hips and slamming deep inside her warm channel. Liana's voice joined his. Xandi's cry of completion took them both even higher.

Wrung out, his body barely capable of responding, Stefan caught Liana as she toppled forward against his chest. He'd felt her thoughts at the moment of climax, sensed her fear, her utter humiliation at her failure as their goddess and her powerful desire to finally make right some of the wrongs she'd done.

In spite of her natural mental barriers, he'd found Adam as she'd seen him today, his back and thighs bloodied and torn, his heart closed to everything but his need for pain.

He had no idea what had happened to leave Adam in such a mess, but one thing was obvious—they could be a damned confused and troubled pack at times. Even so, he refused to worry. They had each other. They had hope, and most of all they had love. He'd learned on the day he met Xandi that love had the power to heal just about everything.

He kissed Liana, shared with her his powerful belief in love, in family. Then he pulled a blanket over her shoulders and left her sleeping soundly and alone in her big bed.

Chapter 6

Stefan's kiss was but a warm memory, though her thighs were still slick, a mingling of her own fluids and his ejaculate. A pleasant postcoital euphoria held her in thrall. Liana drifted, half asleep, half awake in that quiet darkness before dawn, her thoughts a slowly flickering kaleidoscope of the myriad events of the day before, her long, long life as a goddess, her search for answers to Mei's beginnings.

She'd planned to ask the Mother directly in her prayers, but that was no longer her path. Eve was the one who must intercede, and so she sent her request to the one who was now, after all, the goddess of the Chanku.

And maybe Eve would have more luck reaching the Mother than Liana had. She'd always been intimidated by the awesome power of the One who had created everything . . . Eve, on the other hand, didn't seem like the kind of woman to be afraid of much at all.

Liana sent her prayer to the goddess. As she drifted in sleep, a vision took shape even as her subconscious mind regarded Eve with a newly found sense of awe and adoration. So often Liana had asked the Mother for help and been denied. Already it appeared that the Mother had heard Eve's request—and answered Liana's plea.

There were no words, no warning that this was vision, not dream as she slipped into a dark and distant scene that grew closer, more distinct, as if a camera slowly rolled into focus. Though her body slumbered in a big, comfortable bed in Montana, Liana's consciousness was in Florida again, not far from the magical place she'd chosen as her home on an astral plane just beyond the world she lived in now. In her dream state, she hovered over a park, one that slowly filled with shadows and life and the sounds of night creatures.

Out of the darkness came the cries of someone in pain. Liana floated closer until she discovered the source of the distress—a young woman, hardly more than a child still in her early teens, lying on a filthy blanket in what must have been a homeless camp hidden among the trees. A flickering lantern cast shadows over the girl. Naked, her belly distended, knees raised against her skinny chest, with a deep, animalistic groan, she pushed a bloody mass out from between her stick-thin legs.

The mass moved. A tiny arm reached out, a leg stretched. A small mouth opened and a thin, mewling cry cut the night. The woman reached for her newborn, touched dark hair slick with blood and birth fluids.

Liana wanted to weep as she watched the poor girl, all alone, giving birth in the worst possible conditions. Then a movement caught her eye and she realized there was someone in the shadows beside the young mother, someone who reached out, lifted the newborn and laid her across her mother's chest. The young woman looked up, her eyes filled with gratitude as she stroked her baby with gentle, loving hands.

The umbilical cord still connected them. Tears rolled across the young mother's cheeks, but still she managed a soft smile at the new life she'd just brought into the world.

Then she convulsed. Her body jerked as first the placenta and then a huge rush of blood poured out from between her legs. She cried out, holding tightly to her baby as blood continued to flow. Whoever was beside her pressed the blanket between her thighs, but it couldn't stop the hemorrhaging.

In a few brief minutes, the woman's hand dropped limply to the dirty blanket and her final breath rattled in her lungs. Liana sensed the girl's death with a horrible ache in her heart. All she could do was watch, helpless to interfere with what had happened so many years ago.

The woman's companion moved out of the shadows. A tall man of indeterminate age, he knelt beside her in the darkness, gently touched her brow and slowly closed her eyes. He knelt there for a moment. His shoulders shook as he wept and his tears fell on the baby lying quietly on her dead mother's chest.

After a few minutes, Liana heard his sigh and watched as he carefully gathered up the baby with the umbilical cord and placenta still attached, wrapped her in a newspaper and carried her away. A few minutes later he returned. He knelt beside the young woman as if in prayer. Then he wrapped her body in the filthy, bloody blanket and carried her toward a sluggish river that pulsed and ebbed its way through the park.

At the water's edge, he paused a moment. Finally he unrolled the blanket and carefully placed the woman's body in the dark water. He stood on the bank, watching bubbles rise to the surface as she disappeared.

Long moments after she was gone, Liana wondered why the vision remained. Wasn't this all the answer she needed for Mei? But even as she questioned the vision, the man suddenly took a step back from the water's edge. An alligator slid off the opposite bank and slowly wound its way across the river to the place where the body had disappeared.

There was a dark and silent swirl of muddy water as the creature rolled and dove. Once again the surface stilled.

The man stood for a moment longer, shoulders slumping in an attitude of utter despair. Then he wadded up the bloody blanket and carried it back to the camp. He stuffed it into a metal garbage can, struck a match and lit it on fire.

Thick, black smoke poured into the night sky. The man stood beside the barrel and watched while the flames turned to glowing ash. Then Liana followed him as he threaded his way through the thick brush and squatted down behind a tree, as if he waited for something.

The sun rose, moving quickly through the sky like a movie on fast forward. A baby cried. A child's voice called out, "A baby! Mom, there's a baby here!" Liana continued watching, but the images were blurred now, as she observed through the man's tear-filled eyes. He and she watched as adults came, found the tiny newborn wrapped in newspapers and carried her away.

Liana blinked. She felt the man's tears on her face, recognized his grief and knew his heartrending loss, knew he'd loved the mother as he loved the child she carried. Then all sense of him faded and Liana's consciousness slowly returned to the silent bedroom in Anton's Montana home.

Her face was damp with tears. She knew without any doubt she'd witnessed Mei Chen's birth, and the death of her mother. Mei hadn't been abandoned by her mother at all. No, in that one, soft touch, that single connection, Liana had witnessed a mother's love.

And possibly a father's? It was impossible to tell the age of the man who'd been there during the birth. Impossible to know his connection to either the mother or child, but she knew he'd loved them both. Knew he'd wept when the mother died. He'd watched and waited until Mei was found, but Liana wondered if she'd ever know why he'd destroyed all evidence of her mother's existence.

No matter. The mother was the one who counted. Homeless, alone and dying, she'd passed her love on to her daughter. Her love, and her Chanku heritage. Whoever the man had been, whether Mei's father or merely another faceless, nameless, homeless denizen of the park, he'd done the best he could. He'd wrapped Mei warmly and left her where he knew she would be found.

And then he'd waited, hiding close by until she was safe.

"Thank you." Awake now, Liana felt the Mother's blessing. Her prayer had been answered. In thanks, she sent another prayer to Eve. A simple one to thank her for her intercession and to wish her well in her new life.

Liana had taken her time in the shower and was late to breakfast, but she hadn't really felt up to carrying on a conversation with anyone this morning. The dining room appeared empty when she stopped by and grabbed a bagel off the only tray left on the buffet.

Anton's voice startled her. She hadn't seen him sitting in his chair near the window. He finished his phone call, hung up and nodded to her.

"Good morning, Liana. You're just in time for some good news," he said, folding his newspaper and standing up. "That was Logan. Tala is fine, she's not in labor, and both babies appear to be healthy. He and Jazzy are going to stay over for a couple days' visit with Beth and Nick, and then they'll be heading back up here. I need to let Xandi and Keisha know. They've been worried."

"That is good news. Thank you." Liana smiled at Anton as he left the dining room, thinking of how great a difference in circumstances between Mei's birth and what Tala's babies would experience. An entire world of difference.

Liana heard the sound of laughter and followed it into the kitchen. She found Mei wiping down the last of the counters. Oliver stepped out with a wave of one hand and a bag of trash in the other.

Mei paused with the damp sponge in her hands, slowly wadding it into a tight knot. Her tension enveloped Liana like a tight band around her chest. "Did you find out any—"

Liana touched Mei's hand. "Are you finished here? Run with me. It's easier to share what I learned when we're both wolves."

Mei nodded. She raised her head and gazed out the door. Then she smiled at Liana. "I've told Oliver I'm going. He wanted to come, but I'd rather it just be the two of us."

"Good. Now?"

Mei nodded and set the sponge beside the sink. She led Liana back through the dining room and out to the back deck. Within seconds both of them had disrobed and shifted. As Liana leapt over the porch railing, she realized this was her first time to actually run as a mortal wolf, beyond that horrible trip off the mountain the day before.

What a difference it made, to shift and run beside Mei now, compared to that nightmare journey following Anton, not knowing what her reception would be.

It had been beyond her wildest dreams. Knowing the Chanku were ruled by a powerful libido hadn't remotely prepared her for the welcome they'd given her, the intimacy she'd shared with so many members of the pack— first the women and then last night with Stefan.

If only she wasn't so worried about Adam!

When she was a goddess, she merely had to think of the different Chanku and their thoughts would often appear in her mind. Now though, when she thought of Adam Wolf, it was as if he no longer existed. Had his grief closed him off to everyone, or was she the only one he blocked?

Liana glanced toward the room above the garage. Was Adam inside, so late in the morning, or was he working on one of the vehicles, or helping someone with a project? Was his pain from the beating gone? Had she healed him well enough? What was he thinking right now, at this very moment?

Would he ever accept her as a member of the pack?

Liana returned her attention to the trail they followed into the woods. Who did she think she was kidding? She didn't care if he accepted her as a member of the pack. Didn't need his acceptance.

No. She wanted his forgiveness.

Such a simple thing, and yet, from Adam Wolf, something she feared she might never have. Somehow, she'd just have to figure out how to find peace without it.

Mei ran with a single-minded determination, almost as if she wanted to run away from whatever information Liana had to share. Still, it felt good to race through the forest. The grasses were dry and brittle now in late October. She'd heard Anton and Stefan discussing the lack of rainfall, the danger of forest fires even at this elevation.

She had no idea what was normal or dry, what weather to expect here in the Rocky Mountains. It was certainly different than she was used to, after the semitropical existence she'd chosen for so many eons.

Leaves and grass crackled beneath her feet, and the morning sun beat down on her back whenever Liana's run took her out from under the shade of the huge pines and firs and cedar trees along their route. The air was heavy with the pungent smell of resin from sun-warmed sap. Bees and other bugs zipped and buzzed out of their way, except for the tiny black gnats that hovered around Liana's eyes and nose whenever her pace slowed.

The trail seemed familiar to her, and when they finally burst out of the forest into a small meadow, she realized where Mei had led. Eve's meadow, the one where her ashes were scattered.

The place where Adam had tried to kill himself.

Mei went straight to the sluggish creek and drank. Liana followed her to the water and quenched her thirst as well. Then she looked up into Mei's glowing eyes. *Why here, Mei? Why did you choose the place where Adam tried to end his life?*

Mei blinked and slowly shook her head. *I didn't think of Adam when I came here. I chose the place where I feel closest to Eve.* She turned away and walked out into the center of the meadow and shifted. Tall and slim with her straight dark hair falling almost to her waist, she clasped her hands in front of her and bowed her head.

Liana waited in her wolf form, giving Mei this moment of communion with her friend. After a couple of minutes, Mei raised her head and smiled at Liana. "I sense her presence. I've felt her close by when I've come here before. I guess I wanted Eve with me when I found out whatever you have to share with me."

She shoved her hair back from her eyes and frowned. "Does that bother you, Liana? That I wanted Eve? I'm sorry. I guess I didn't think that through."

I think it's wonderful. I needed Eve last night when I called on the Mother for help. She interceded for me. Shift. It's easier to share my thoughts when you're in your wolven form.

Mei shifted, going from woman to wolf in a heartbeat. Someday soon, Liana hoped to see Mei's leopard form, but today it would have to be the wolf if they were going to share the dream Liana carried in her mind.

Mei's light gray coat with the darker markings rippled in the sunlight as she crossed the few steps separating her from Liana. Were the colors in her coat, the white and gray and black, the same she wore as a leopard? Liana had followed Mei's life as Chanku, had watched her first shift when she'd shocked everyone—including Liana—by turning into a snow leopard instead of a wolf, but seeing things through the variations of the astral plane could be deceptive.

She would have to ask Mei to shift for her. Some other

time. Now, they touched noses. Then Mei sat back on her haunches and studied Liana through dark amber eyes.

Liana lay down, crossed her paws and opened her thoughts. She sensed Mei's mind linking with hers, felt her tension as the dream began to gain form, as the visual of the young woman lying on a dirty blanket in the park grew in strength and clarity.

She stayed out of Mei's reaction, kept herself closed off from the other woman's feelings about the images she shared. It would be too much of an intrusion to go so deep into Mei's personal feelings, though she thought of ending the connection before the man placed Mei's mother's body in the river.

Thought of it, but didn't carry through. That would be unfair. The Mother had given the images to Liana to share with Mei, not to edit or censor them. That was not her place, but even as she tried to stay apart from Mei's reaction, Liana felt the young woman's pain deep in her heart when the dark water swirled and the alligator disappeared into the murky depths.

She felt Mei's stunned disbelief as they gazed at the spot where her mother's body had slipped beneath the surface, sensed her confusion as the man took the bloody blanket away to burn. More unspoken questions as he hid in the brush and waited beside the tiny newborn, but Liana sensed Mei's relief when the little boy found the baby and called for grown-ups to come and see.

She hoped that Mei felt the man's tears on her cheeks as he watched strangers carry the baby to safety, but there was no denying what they had just observed. It was horrible. Such a tragic and terrible way for Mei's life to have begun.

There was a brief moment of stunned disbelief. Liana opened herself completely and felt Mei's unimaginable pain. She shifted immediately, just in time to catch the sobbing girl as she tumbled into Liana's embrace.

Now when Liana tried to see into her thoughts, Mei's blocks were tightly in place. All Liana could think to do was hold her, rub her hands over Mei's back and let her cry until she couldn't cry anymore.

Finally, Mei pulled away from Liana, got up and walked over to the creek. She knelt beside the water and splashed her face. Then she shifted quickly to her wolven form and back to human, drying her tears with the shift. Obviously exhausted, she sat on a flat rock beside the water and sighed.

"You okay?" Liana walked over and flopped down next to her.

Mei nodded. "She was so young." She raised her head and gazed at Liana. "What? Thirteen, maybe fourteen? Not old enough to have a baby."

"That's what I thought. No older than that." She took Mei's right hand in both of hers and looked at her fingers. "These fingers were so small. You were so tiny. So was she, but she didn't abandon you, Mei. Did you see the look on her face when he placed you on her chest? She loved you already. I'm so sorry you never got to know her."

Mei sniffed. "I wonder if that was my father? It would explain my height, but whoever the man was, he cared for her, I guess. At least as much as he could in a homeless encampment. Why didn't she go to a hospital?" Mei looked at Liana and her eyes glowed with a terrible ferocity. "Why would she give birth out in the dirt like that?"

Liana shrugged. "Fear. Poverty. We don't know who she was or why she was there. She might not have known any better. Maybe she was an illegal, or maybe the man didn't want her to go to a hospital because of her age. She looked so young. If the father of her baby was an adult, he could have been jailed for sexual abuse. So many reasons, but one thing we know for sure, Mei. Your mother didn't throw you away as you've always believed. She gave birth to you and she loved you. Even the man, whether he was your father or not, left you where you would be found quickly, and he waited close by, protecting you until you were rescued. They could have done so much worse. As tragic as the circumstances of your birth were, your mother and her companion acted out of love for you. Because of their actions, you're alive now. You're healthy and you have a man who loves you. A pack who claims you as their own, who will always stand beside you and protect you."

Mei stared out over the meadow, still and silent for so long that Liana began to worry. Had she done the right thing? Said the right things? She wished Eve were here. Eve always knew what to say, what to do. *Which is why she's the goddess now and I'm sitting on this damned rock.*

Mei turned and smiled at her. "You're broadcasting, you know. I heard that."

"Oh, crap." Liana felt the warmth of her blush spread over her chest and up her face. She'd had no idea how easily a blonde could blush, but she was beginning to think she'd better get used to it giving her away.

"It's true, though," she said. "Eve always had the right thing to say, knew how to act. She's a perfect goddess."

Mei took Liana's hand in hers and squeezed. "Yeah, she probably is. But ya know, Liana, I think you're gonna be a perfect friend."

She stood up and held out her hand. Bemused, Liana reached up and grabbed hold. Mei tugged her to her feet.

"Do you really think so, Mei? I want to be, but I am so unsure of myself. I know Adam hates me. Anton isn't all that fond of me, either."

Mei laughed. "Anton cares about you much more than you realize, and Adam will come around. He's already accepted the fact Eve is gone. He misses her, but I think he's also a little angry—and jealous, maybe—that she seems so happy in her new role. That anger is good—it'll help him move past all this. He's got to realize at some point that what has happened has been, in many ways, for the best."

Liana wasn't so sure. "For everyone but Adam," she said. "While things are working out great for Eve, Adam is the one who's suffering a loss that can't be fixed. When Anton called me to help Adam last night, he was in horrible pain, but he didn't want me to heal him."

Mei dipped her head and sighed. "Blame Oliver and me for that. We went too far."

"No." Liana hugged Mei and kissed her cheek. "According to Adam, you didn't go far enough." She took a step back. "C'mon. Let's go back, but this time I want to see you as a snow leopard. Do you mind?"

Mei laughed. "Mind? I'm so much happier as a leopard. Thank you, Liana, for giving me so much today. You have no idea what a wonderful gift your vision was." She bit her lower lip as if she might say more, but instead gave a short, sharp jerk of her chin, bent at the waist a woman, and touched the ground with broad leopard's paws. Mei gazed up at Liana with her long whiskers framing an astoundingly beautiful snow leopard face.

Liana was speechless. She'd underestimated the power, the absolute beauty of Mei's feline form. Just as she'd underestimated so much about the world her Chanku inhabited.

Liana raised her eyes to the heavens and gave a word of thanks—to Eve—for taking on the role of goddess, to the Mother of them all for giving her a second chance at life. For allowing her the opportunity to experience the amazing beauty that was all around her.

This world was nothing like the plane she had inhabited for time out of memory—it was more. So much more than she'd ever realized. Liana shifted. She took a deep breath of the hot, dry mountain air and her feral instincts immediately catalogued and identified the scents of dirt and pine, flowers and prey.

She glanced over her shoulder at the great plume of a tail raised behind her and gloried in her simple gray wolven coat, in the instantaneous change from woman to wolf.

She was one with her world, awash in the scents and sounds that surrounded her, in the friendship of the woman, now leopard, waiting patiently beside her.

Liana glanced once more at the cobalt-blue sky overhead. Then with a swish of her tail, she led Mei back down the trail to their home.

"Hey, Adam. How's it look?"

"Shit!" Adam's greasy hand slipped off the wrench and he slammed his knuckles against the engine block. Cursing, he grabbed a dirty rag out of his back pocket and wrapped it around the shredded skin. As much as he loved working on Stefan's vintage '51 Ford pickup, the thing was a damned knuckle-buster.

"Like it always looks," he said, nursing his sore knuckles. "Absolutely gorgeous. Now, if you were to ask me how it's running, I'd give you a different answer."

Stefan leaned over and looked under the hood. Then he cocked an eyebrow at Adam and grinned. "Do I look like I know what I'm doing? There's something really manly about staring under the hood of an old Ford truck."

Adam leaned against the front fender and peeled the bloody rag off his hand. "Yeah. You look manly." He reached out and swiped his greasy fingers over Stefan's cheek, leaving a dark stain. "Now you look manlier. A little grease adds realism."

Stefan stood up, grabbed a clean handkerchief out of his pocket, and carefully wiped the grease away. "I was perfectly content being clean and manly, thank you."

"Look." Adam pointed to the forest's edge. A snow leopard and a gray wolf trotted out of the shadows and headed toward the house. "Can't tell from here. Is that Mei or Oliver? Who's with the cat?"

Stefan turned and leaned against the fender. "Mei, I think. And that's Liana with her. They must have gone for an early run. I'm surprised to see Liana out so early. I thought I wore her out last night. I know I slept like the dead after I left her bed."

Stefan? With Liana? "What were you doing with Liana? Was Xandi there, too?"

Stefan laughed, but he didn't look away from the wolf and the leopard crossing the meadow. "In a way. Xandi was in my head. She sent me down to welcome Liana. I didn't want to, to be honest. I've been pissed at the goddess for years, blaming her for leaving me caught mid-shift." He shook his head and glanced at Adam. "She explained that there was nothing she could do to help me, until she sent me to Xandi."

"Liana sent you? I don't get it." Adam sucked the blood off his scraped knuckle. "I thought Xandi drove off the road in a blizzard and you rescued her."

"She did. Miles from my home. I always figured it was pure luck that I stumbled over her that night, but it was Liana. She sent me to Xandi. I got there just in time to save her life. I'd forgotten how close I was. She was hypothermic, hardly breathing, almost entirely buried in snow and ice."

"So, you did what? Heard Liana's version of what happened and stayed for a pity fuck with the ex-goddess?"

"It was hardly that, Adam." Obviously irritated, Stefan shoved himself away from the truck and stepped back, putting even more distance between the two of them. "If I hadn't found Xandi, I doubt I'd still be alive. I know she wouldn't be, because she was very close to death when I got to her."

He shook his head and glared at Adam. "She is the key to everything good in my life. Xandi loved me in spite of my impossible appearance, she forced me to face Anton, to face the convoluted love and hate I felt for him. Through Xandi, Liana gave me back my life, so no, it was not a pity fuck. It wasn't even a thank you fuck. It was good, hot sex between consenting adults, a way to welcome Liana to the pack and to share that welcome with my mate."

Adam stared at the ground between them and wished he could crawl under a rock somewhere. "I'm sorry, Stef. That was uncalled for."

"You're right, it was uncalled for. Look, bud . . . we all miss Eve and it's got to be eating you up, knowing she's still out there, existing on another plane, actually living a new life apart from you, but you can't keep blaming Liana."

"Why not?" Adam threw the bloody rag on the ground and glared at Stefan. "She admitted Eve died because she screwed up, and you expect me just to forgive and forget? Sorry, Stef, it doesn't work that way. My mate is gone. For all intents and purposes, Eve is dead. Calling on the goddess in fucking prayer is not the same as sharing what happened during the day with the woman you love. It's not the same as curling up with your mate and burying your nose in her hair just to inhale her scent. And it is most definitely not the same as making love, or coming together as wolves and hoping to make a baby."

Adam's voice cracked and the anger flowed out of him, leaving him empty and shaking. He sighed and shook his head. Took a deep breath to keep from breaking down altogether, and stared at the oil stains on the driveway. "It's fucking not the same," he said, wondering why he even tried to explain.

"Hi, Liana."

Adam snapped his head up when Stefan greeted the bitch. He jerked around. She stood directly behind him and he wondered how much she'd heard. He certainly hadn't been trying to keep his voice down, not that it mattered. "What do you want?"

"Adam."

He ignored Stefan's soft rebuke and glared at Liana. She didn't back down or act at all put off by his rudeness. He had to give her credit for guts.

"I wanted to see how you were feeling. I don't want to bother you, but I felt I should check on you."

"You've checked and I'm fine. Now go, okay?"

She stared at him without any noticeable expression, and it was unnerving, to say the least. He didn't have a clue what was going on behind those gray-green eyes of hers.

"Your hand is bleeding. Let me take care of it."

He glanced at his knuckles. The cuts must be deeper than he'd realized. Blood dripped down his fingers into a small puddle on the concrete. "I'll be fine. I don't need you."

"Adam, don't be an ass." Stefan grabbed his arm. Adam tried to tug free of his grasp, but Stef was surprisingly strong. Adam really didn't want to stand here having a childish tug of war with another man.

"Besides," Stefan said, "I don't want blood stains on my truck. It doesn't go with my choice of décor."

Liana flashed a smile at Stefan, but she didn't come any closer. "Adam? May I look?"

He glared at Stefan and practically growled at Liana, but he was feeling decidedly outnumbered and just a little foolish. For some reason, something Eve had said to him on more than one occasion flicked into his mind—*pick your battles.*

This was not one worth fighting. He nodded his head, a single quick jerk. Tugged his arm free just as Stefan released him, and held his hand out for Liana.

She supported his hand in hers, cradling his long fingers

in her much smaller ones. He expected her to cover the injuries with her free hand, but instead, she raised his hand, leaned close and put her lips against his bloodied knuckles.

He felt warmth from her kiss, and a sense of calm he'd not expected. Pain disappeared immediately and he was actually disappointed when she lifted her lips from his hand and set his fingers free.

He opened and closed his hand. The bleeding had stopped and the scrapes no longer hurt. He couldn't tell how well they'd healed, because his knuckles were still covered in drying blood, but he had to assume Liana had repaired the damage. He raised his eyes and glanced at her.

She was wiping his blood from her mouth with a tissue. "Is that better?"

He nodded. "Thank you."

She stared at him a moment. The corner of her mouth lifted in a slight smile, and without another word she turned and walked back to the main house.

He and Stefan stared after her. Finally, Stefan let out a deep breath. "Give her a chance, Adam. She's good people. Sweet. Caring. In many ways, I think she's a lot like Eve."

Adam spun around and snarled at Stefan. "She's nothing like Eve. She's a self-centered bitch and not a damned thing like Eve, so don't even go there."

Stefan's eyes narrowed and he returned Adam's glare with a narrowed stare of his own. "Fine, Adam. She's a bitch. Is that what you want me to say? That she came down here to check on you because she's so nasty and self-centered? Right. Face it, Wolf. You're the last one who should accuse her of being self-centered. Eve is gone, and I miss her. We all do, but Liana's here and she's trying her best."

He turned and walked away from Adam, but after just

a couple of steps, Stefan spun around and looked him up and down. Adam felt as if he'd been measured, and found woefully inadequate.

"It's not all about you, Adam. It's about the pack. About forgiving and moving on with life. Eve has already made her choice and moved forward. Liana's doing her best to adjust to life as a mortal. Maybe it's time you tried adjusting to your new circumstances as well." He spun away and walked back to the house without a backward glance.

Adam watched him go. Stefan's words weighed heavily on his mind, but no matter how hard he tried, he couldn't get past the anger. He was pissed at Liana for screwing up his life, but as much as he hated to admit it, he was every bit as mad at Eve. She'd accepted her new role in the afterlife way too easily. Hell, he got the feeling she hardly even missed him, like she'd just written off what they had.

Like their love wasn't important. It was eating him up inside and he had no idea how to make the anger go away.

No idea at all.

Chapter 7

"This corner goes to this corner"—Liana stuck a clothes-pin in her mouth and quietly continued her litany of instructions, stretching up on her toes to reach the clothes-line and carefully folding the cotton sheet as she unpinned along its length—"and this corner here."

So many of the simple things she had yet to learn in this mortal life. Doing laundry and hanging sheets on the line was actually one she loved. She hadn't mastered cooking, yet, but Oliver had promised lessons whenever she was ready.

She wasn't. Not yet, at least not for something as in-volved as preparing meals. She stretched to remove an-other clothespin, carefully grabbed the crisp sheet. *Fold it here, smooth the crease, and fold it here . . .*

"Hey, Liana. I've got some more wet ones. Keisha ran a couple of extra loads." Jazzy set the basket down, straightened up and stretched. She watched Liana for a few moments and then chuckled. "It'd be easier if you weren't so short."

Liana spit the clothespins out into her hand and laughed. "Well, if the rest of you guys weren't so blasted tall, I wouldn't be considered short."

Jazzy stepped up to the line beyond Liana's and started

folding the dry sheets hanging along it. At a full six feet tall, she towered over Liana. Laughing, she peered over the top of the sheets, emphasizing her height. Then she quickly folded the sheet and set it on top of the others in Liana's basket and brushed her sweaty hair back from her forehead. "Xandi said it's unusual to be able to line dry them in October, much less in the middle of November. I think it's usually raining and snowing by now. Instead, I heard we've got a forest fire burning up north of us. It's a long way away, but still . . ."

"It's cold at night, but the days do seem awfully warm and dry. What's normal? You should know—you've been here for a year, now, haven't you?" Liana pulled the sheet she was folding aside and smiled at Jazzy. "Doesn't seem that long, I bet."

Jazzy laughed and shook her head. "Ya know, sometimes it seems even longer, like a whole 'nother life, but it is, after living on the streets in San Francisco. Like that life happened to someone else. Hard to believe it's been a year this month since I moved up here to Montana."

Liana thought of all she'd experienced in just the past couple of weeks since finding herself among mortals. "It is another life. You're another person. You went from being human to Chanku."

"Like you went from being a goddess to a mortal?" There was so much compassion in Jazzy's dark-eyed expression that Liana felt almost guilty admitting the truth.

"It's not like that for me, Jazzy. I don't miss my role as goddess. I love it here. I hope Eve's happy with the job, because I wouldn't trade what I have now for anything. I've never been this content, never felt as if I belonged anywhere before. You've all been wonderful to me."

Jazzy's snort brought her up short.

"What?"

"Adam's been a little less than wonderful. He avoids you like the plague."

"Adam has a different set of issues than I have to work through. Grief, for one. He lost his mate barely seven weeks ago." Liana reached for another sheet and noticed the faint, rust colored stains. Blood stains. She wondered if it was Adam's blood, from that horrible night when she'd first arrived.

"Well, I hope he works through them soon. Logan's worried about him."

Liana dipped her head and sighed. "Me, too, Jazzy. I'm worried about him as well." She raised her head and gazed at the small room over the garage. He was up there, now. She sensed him. Realized she'd become more attuned to him as the days passed until she knew when he shifted, knew when he worked on some project or other around the estate.

Knew when he sat alone in the dark, his mind entirely empty of thought in that lonely room. She glanced at Jazzy and sighed. "I haven't told anyone, not even Anton, but I called Manda. Adam and his twin have a link that goes back for years, even before they actually met each other."

"Manda's wonderful. Did she have any ideas?" Jazzy finished folding the dry sheets and began to hang the wet ones. Liana pulled them out of the basket, one by one and handed them to the taller girl. Jazzy easily reached the line and carefully clipped the sheets in nice, neat rows.

Liana shook her head. "She's been worried. She can sense his misery clear across the country, but she said he's blocked her out. He doesn't want her help."

Jazzy stopped hanging sheets and stared at Liana over the top of one she'd been pinning. "Just because he doesn't want it doesn't mean he doesn't need it."

"I know." Liana gazed once more at the small room. He was there now. Alone and grieving, caught in a hell of her making.

* * *

They gathered on the deck at dusk—Anton and Keisha, Stefan and Xandi, Logan, Oliver, and Liana. As usual, there was no sign of Adam. He'd not run with the pack at all since his return. She knew he occasionally shifted, but he stayed in his room, often sleeping in his wolf form but avoiding the rest of them.

Worried it was due to her presence, Liana had remained at home rather than running for a few nights. It hadn't made a difference—Adam had stayed in his room over the garage.

The nights she'd remained behind, Liana had taken care of the two babies, but she'd missed the chance to run as a wolf, to learn the ways of the pack. Tonight Jazzy and Mei had offered to stay with Lily and Alex, so Stefan and Anton could run together with their mates.

Liana loved their reasoning. Jazzy called it birth control and Mei quietly agreed. As the two youngest female members, they figured watching over the toddlers on a regular basis would remind them why they chose to remain childless for at least a few more years.

As Keisha and Xandi often admitted, babies were a lot of work. As a goddess, Liana hadn't even thought of motherhood for herself. Each baby born to the Chanku had been like one of her own. Now, as an unmated female, motherhood was still the furthest thing from her mind. Secretly, she agreed with Mei and Jazzy. Learning how to be part of a pack as large and dynamic as this one took all her energy and then some.

Stefan and Anton and their mates shifted and took off across the dark meadow. Oliver and Logan were still stripping out of their clothes. Liana shifted, but she waited for the guys before heading out into the night. She'd never gone by herself before. The forest was a dark and scary place and she lacked the confidence to run on her own. It was better, knowing there were others running beside her familiar with any danger they might come across.

Oliver shifted. Logan was still folding up his clothes. A shiver ran along Liana's spine. She turned toward the far end of the deck and her ears flattened to her broad skull. A beautiful dark wolf stalked slowly toward her. Not black—his coat was a deep russet streaked with gold beneath the soft glow of the overhead lighting. A dark mask outlined his eyes and spread over his back.

Adam. He watched Liana, but walked directly toward Oliver. His ears flattened, his tail slapped down between his legs and he turned his head to one side, exposing his throat in a blatant gesture of submission.

Oliver growled, but his ears tilted forward and his tail stayed up. His entire stance remained relaxed. Whatever he and Adam said to each other was exclusive and private.

Let's go.

Oliver's sharp command spurred all of them to action. Logan leapt first, then Adam and Oliver, followed by Liana. She loved this feeling, the rush of air through her fur, the blast of scent that flooded her sensitive nostrils as her big front paws hit the springy grass just beyond the deck.

An explosion of night sounds as she fully embraced her wolven senses pulled her forward at a full run toward the forest. An owl hooted, crickets chirped and dry grass rustled beneath her feet. Tiny things—creatures of the night—scurried away through the grass, and bats that should have migrated south weeks ago still zipped and squeaked overhead.

She'd not lived in a real world for so long that the concerns of the pack were still foreign to her. Worry about the drought, about the change in seasonal temperatures, the dryness of the forest and the thick grasses underfoot. She'd heard them talk of the risk of forest fires, knew the ground was dry and the creeks running unnaturally low, but now, racing through the cool night air with the wonderful amalgam of scent and sound and touch buffeting her senses, Liana could only feel joy.

Not worry for Adam, not shame for her failings—no. Her feral self knew only the joy of the night, the freedom of stretching out her powerful legs and running as the alpha bitch among these beautiful males.

She accepted their instinctive deference to her as the lone female among them, an homage that meant more than any obeisance she'd ever received as goddess.

This was something else, something freely given, not because she held a rank of power and could crush them with a single thought. No, this was more, this went to the very heart of her, to the sense of her femininity, her existence as a female in a matriarchal society.

They were male, physically more powerful, yet they deferred to her by virtue of her gender, her position within the pack. Even Adam, though she knew he fought his nature, fought the instinctive deference his wolven self gave to the bitch.

He wanted so much to hate her. He did hate her, but he respected her position as a dominant female even when he wanted to despise everything about her.

Liana accepted his dislike, just as she accepted his respect. She might be mortal, no longer a goddess, but she was Chanku, she was female, and she deserved his respect, no matter how much he wanted to deny Liana her place in the pack.

So now they ran, with Liana occasionally taking the lead, with Logan or Oliver running ahead, but never Adam. Not Adam. He had relinquished his place at the head. Given it up in shame over the words he'd said to Oliver. To Mei.

Liana knew the story. Had talked of it with Mei in that woman's talk she was still learning to appreciate. Had heard how Adam had cursed Mei and Oliver in his search for pain. They all knew it had been a ploy and nothing more. Foul words to elicit anger from those who loved him too much to truly hurt him.

What complex minds Chanku had, and Adam's more convoluted, more fascinating, than most. Liana realized she couldn't not worry about Adam.

She'd failed him when he needed her most, long before Eve. Long before he'd realized his true heritage as Chanku. Her failure went back generations, before his mother, before his mother's ancestors, back to the earliest times when Liana had allowed her people to disperse without their goddess's knowledge. Had lost them all when she allowed them to leave their birthplace on the Himalayan steppes.

Their huge diaspora had taken them out into the world, but it had also taken them away from the grasses they'd needed to ensure their birthright. Once they'd lost their ability to shift, Liana had lost her ability to find them.

They had stumbled in the darkness, just as Liana had stumbled. Only she'd been so damned self-centered, she hadn't worried about them. She'd taken her lovers among humankind, filled her own needs and neglected those she had been charged to protect.

If she hadn't found Anton, hadn't recognized his Chanku heritage, she might never have found her people. Never have known the utter bliss of watching over those she was meant to guard from harm.

And yet, she'd failed them again. Failed them so terribly that Adam still suffered and Eve had lost her mortal life. But even with her failure, Liana had been given a second chance. Why?

She paused in her headlong rush through the woods. The males slowed up ahead and returned to her side. They milled about, confused by her stopping here, long before they'd hunted.

Stopping for no reason they could understand, but

Liana had to do this. She raised her muzzle to the heavens and howled long and loud, her voice rising and falling in a crescendo of homage.

Not to the goddess. Not to Eve, who, she knew, watched over their kind with a much more prudent eye than Liana had ever done.

No, she raised her voice to the Mother over all of them, the one who had shown her more mercy than any failed goddess ever deserved. And the males, not realizing the reason for her song, but somehow understanding the power in her voice, joined her. Gave their strength to Liana as they howled to the heavens.

When she finally stopped, the others quieted as well.

A moment later, an answering howl from the western flank of the mountain broke the silence. Others joined in—Anton and Keisha, Stefan and Xandi, pausing in their run to add their voices. Their song echoed off the dark mountains and drifted on the silent breezes.

When silence reigned once more, Adam was the one who turned to Liana with a question in his amber eyes.

Why?

If only she knew for sure. Liana bowed her head and tried to explain. *To show my appreciation. I owe the Mother my thanks for her mercy. She could have ended me for all my mistakes. For my terrible failures. Instead she gave me another chance, and for that I owe her not only my life and respect, but my deepest appreciation.*

I'm still waiting for my second chance. Your failure took my first. He stared at her for a long, uncomfortable moment. Liana refused to look away. Instead she met his amber eyes with a steady gaze of her own.

Time stretched between them.

Adam was the first to turn away. Without another word, he trotted slowly along the trail, heading deeper into the forest. Silently, Logan followed him.

Oliver paused beside Liana. *Don't expect too much of him. He's trying to understand.*

I know. I wish there were some way I could help, but he has to do this on his own.

Oliver yipped, a sharp sound of agreement. Then he trotted after the others, with Liana on his heels.

Adam tried to blot out Liana's scent but the ripe, sensual aroma of the bitch seemed to envelop his senses like a shroud. He chose to run ahead. He'd tried following, but he'd been constantly immersed in her perfume. At least when he foraged out in front it wasn't as powerful, as compelling.

He tried to think of Eve, but her scent was lost in his memories, overwhelmed by Liana. He didn't want to think of the bitch. Didn't want anything to do with her, but it was growing harder and harder to find reasons to hate her.

She obviously felt horrible for her failure. She'd lost her immortality because of her mistake, yet she was adjusting to life as a mortal with good humor and determination. He'd never once heard her bemoan her fate, never heard her complain that any job they gave her might be beneath her, no matter how difficult or menial it was.

The women had accepted her immediately. The men had come around. He knew she shared their beds, that she'd joined sexually with everyone in the pack at one time or another, even Logan, who rarely strayed from Jazzy.

Everyone but him. He couldn't. He wasn't emotionally ready to open himself to anyone besides Eve. He'd avoided the other men, though he hoped that his apology to Oliver might help repair that broken friendship.

Anton and Stefan had approached him, tried to get him to join them with their mates or alone, but he hadn't been interested. Of course, he'd not been running as a wolf. If he'd learned anything over the past long weeks, it was that his libido wasn't as affected by the shift as it was by the run.

He'd definitely been aroused after his return from his own self-imposed exile after Eve's death, but Oliver and Mei had beaten and screwed that out of him. He hadn't climaxed since, even by his own hand.

He'd never gone this long without sex, not since he'd had his first erection as a kid. Now, running beside, ahead, or behind that damned Liana, he fought desire such as he'd not felt in weeks.

Not since Eve's death.

Liana caught up to him. Passed him. Her scent seduced him. Snarling silently, he steeled himself against her powerful allure.

The sharp scent of an elk saved him. *Prey.* The others paused and circled back to him. He gazed silently to the left, in the direction of a small meadow with a spring at the far end, one of the few spots in the vicinity where water still ran fresh after so many months of drought.

They separated and reached the meadow from different points downwind of the spring. The elk drinking there was an old one, its body scarred from past battles, eyes dimmed with age. Liana took the lead, practically quivering with excitement. She'd taken part in hunts, but Adam didn't know if she'd actually been in on a kill before or not. He had no idea what she knew, how strong she was.

It was obvious she followed instructions. Adam glanced toward Oliver and realized from the wolf's rigid stance that he directed Liana, told her where to hide, how to approach, when to strike.

She crept through the tall grass at the edge of the meadow, coming up on the bull from the direction downwind. At the last moment she struck, exploding out of the thick grass in a flurry of streaking gray fur, sharp teeth and sparkling amber eyes. The elk pivoted on its back legs and she caught him beneath the jaw, a bit too high for a quick kill, but her weight and the velocity of her strike took the big animal to his knees.

He swung his head to fight back, but Logan leapt up on the elk's broad back and sunk his fangs into the animal's neck. Between the two of them, Logan and Liana brought the animal down for the kill.

It struggled for a bare few seconds, and then the body went still in death. Liana continued to hold on, using the crushing strength in her jaws to choke the life out of the animal. Logan had managed to sever its spine with his powerful jaws and heavier weight. He backed away now, standing over the body with his sides heaving and saliva dripping from his open mouth.

Liana finally turned it loose as well. She walked around the elk, stiff legged, establishing her dominance and claiming the kill in spite of Logan's much-needed assistance.

Adam snarled. Typical. The bitch didn't even acknowledge the help she'd gotten after her crappy attack.

Then Liana stalked over to Logan and touched his nose with hers. Adam had no idea what she said, but Logan's tail wagged slowly behind him. Then he moved close and tore into the elk's soft belly, feeding first.

Before Liana. Adam felt the anger flow out of him. She'd not only acknowledged Logan's help, she'd ceded the kill to him.

C'mon. What're you guys waiting for? She wiped her muzzle in the grass, cleaning the blood off. Oliver and Adam both approached the elk, but she'd not fed yet. Usually the women insisted on eating first.

Go ahead. I'm calling the others. There's no way we can finish this off, and no need to kill more tonight.

She finally approached the dead elk and found a spot beside Logan. *They're coming. The pond in the meadow where they went to hunt is dry. Anton said there isn't any game.*

Adam tore into the elk's haunch, gulping huge pieces of

the warm, bloody flesh. He'd not fed like this in weeks and his body craved meat from a fresh kill, the thick, coppery scent of blood and the sense of the hunt, the adrenaline flowing furiously through his bloodstream in spite of his issues with the bitch.

Logan stood up and trotted over to the spring to drink. His ears perked up and he stared at the edge of the dark forest. *I think I hear them,* he said, trotting forward to meet Anton and the others.

A bear rushed out from between the trees, a massive grizzly headed straight for Logan. He didn't even try to run. Instead he leapt at the animal's throat, going directly for the kill.

The bear reared up as Logan jumped, catching the big wolf in his paws and deflecting his attack. He caught Logan's shoulder in his big jaws and shook him like a rag toy before casting him aside.

Logan yipped, rolled through the grass and lay still.

Liana was the first to react. Before Adam had time to consider a course of attack, she'd leapt on the grizzly, scrabbling for hold on the beast's huge back and clamping her jaws down on the side of his throat. Oliver rushed him from the back, grabbed a hind leg and tumbled the bear to the ground.

Adam dove beneath the bear's snapping jaws and grabbed hold of its throat on the other side, but unlike the elk, the bear's neck was padded with layers of fat stored up for winter and all the wolves seemed able to do was make it even angrier.

Anton raced into the meadow and the bear reared up on its hind legs. It shook its head and both Liana and Adam were flung from the huge body. It turned, saw the four fresh wolves running into the meadow and took off with Oliver hanging on to its leg.

Oliver released it when it was obvious the bear was trying to escape. Adam stood up and shook himself. Liana knelt beside Logan's body. She'd already shifted, and now she ran her hands over him as she checked his injuries.

What happened? Breathing hard from their run, Anton glanced at Logan but kept his attention on Adam.

Bear attacked without warning. Logan got to it first. I need to see how badly he's hurt.

Go.

Adam shifted and knelt beside Liana. "How is he?"

She shook her head. "Unconscious, but I don't sense a serious head injury. His shoulder is broken, some internal injuries. I think a lung may be punctured." She turned and looked at him, so close he could see the speckles of gray and green in her eyes. Smell her human perfume, which was every bit as seductive to him as her wolven scent.

"I'm new at this healing business, Adam. What do we do?"

He shook his head. "We can't move him. Not like this. Let's see what we can fix now, before we take him back."

She nodded. "I'll follow your lead. Just let me know what you need from me."

He nodded and placed his hands over Logan's shoulder, felt the shattered bone and the blood pooling in his lung. He was reminded of Anton's injuries when he'd been shot and then had tumbled off a cliff. They'd been much worse than Logan's, and he'd been alone.

With Liana here, Adam had help. He glanced at her. Naked and so beautiful she'd take the breath of any man with breath to lose, she knelt beside him with her hands folded in front of her. Waiting.

"Do you know how to go inside, to repair injuries from the inside out?"

She nodded.

"Okay then. I want you to concentrate on his lung. He's got a couple of broken ribs and one of them's pierced the side of his left lung. That's why you see the blood around his nostrils. I want you to move the bone back in place, but repair the tear in his lung before you actually try to heal the bone. I'm going to work on his shoulder."

She nodded and gently placed her hands over the area where she needed to work. Adam sensed the others around them and drew from their strength. He felt Liana's presence, her powerful concentration as she mentally slipped inside Logan's body, but then he focused on the badly damaged shoulder, on the splinters of bone and the massive bleeding from torn veins and arteries. Liana's nearness faded from his conscious thoughts, though she never entirely disappeared.

Time lost meaning as he worked on Logan with Liana's presence a subtle yet powerful shadow beside him. Carefully, as if he put together a fragile puzzle, Adam repaired the shattered bone and rebuilt Logan's shoulder.

He felt Anton's hands on his back and strength surged into him, enough that when the shoulder was back the way it should be, he had the energy to check the rest of Logan's body, to ensure that there was no other damage.

Liana was completing her repair of his broken ribs. He sensed her as a warm, compelling light, a being of pure energy moving within Logan's cells. Was that how he appeared to her? He'd have to ask her. Sometime.

Once again he realized he was admiring the one he hated, and it came to him that it was difficult to hate one he admired so much. That line of thought didn't belong here, not now while he wandered through Logan's physical body, checking for damage.

There were bruises and contusions, things a healthy body could heal on its own. A couple of bites went deep into Logan's shoulder. Adam cleaned away the filthy bacteria that had coated the grizzly's sharp teeth and repaired the deep punctures.

When he finally returned to his body, the night was half gone and Mei waited patiently beside Oliver with Jazzy holding tightly to her hand. Keisha and Xandi must have gone home to their babies so that Mei and Jazzy could be here with their mates.

Adam sat back on his heels and rested his palms on his thighs. A moment later, Liana did the same. She shook her head as if coming awake from a long sleep. Then she glanced his way, realized he was looking at her and smiled so brightly she lit up the night.

Adam caught himself before he smiled in return. Instead, he nodded and rose stiffly to his feet. Logan slept on, but it was a healing sleep that held him now, not unconsciousness from his injuries.

"How is he?" Anton addressed Adam as he held out his hand to Liana and tugged her to her feet.

Without stopping to even wonder why he did so, Adam glanced at Liana. She smiled and nodded. Deferred to him.

"I think he'll be fine," he said. "Liana repaired his broken ribs and punctured lung. I took care of his shoulder. Hopefully everything went back where it should."

"You did a wonderful job, Adam. I looked." Liana offered him a tentative smile. He couldn't blame her for her caution. He'd been a real bastard to her. He still felt anger toward her, but it wasn't as focused as it had been. Not as strong.

Liana was still speaking. Praising him. Making him feel like even more of a bastard. "It was completely shattered, Anton. I wasn't sure it could be repaired, but after looking at the repair job Adam did, I imagine Logan will regain full movement once the swelling goes down."

"Good." Anton sighed as if he were relieved the long night would be ending well. "Stefan's brought a stretcher. Let's get Logan on it and back to the house."

Jazzy stepped forward and slipped her hands under the unconscious wolf. *Her mate.* Tears marked her cheeks and Adam felt the fear rolling off of her in waves. He understood, better than most. He knew what it was like to lose the one you loved.

Anton and Oliver carefully lifted Logan's shoulders. Adam helped Jazzy support his hind legs. After they got him settled, Stefan and Oliver grabbed the stretcher and started back along the trail. The others followed.

Adam was left alone in the meadow with Liana, yet neither one of them seemed ready to leave. Liana gestured toward the stripped carcass of the elk. "Looks as if they decided to eat while we were working on Logan."

Adam nodded. "Thank you," he said, surprised at how easy it was to say the words. "I don't know that I could have done that on my own."

"I think you could have. You have amazing powers. Powers you've hardly begun to use." She turned and gazed at him for a long, silent moment. It was obvious she had more to say. Just as obvious she didn't have a clue how to say it. She sighed. "I'm going back. Logan might need more help before the night's over."

She turned away and shifted. Without a backward glance, she trotted out of the meadow and followed the others back to the house.

Adam watched her leave, aware of a strange yearning, a powerful desire to follow her. Instead, he waited until the forest fell silent around him. Then he shifted and made his way back to the house, following another route to ensure that he traveled alone.

Liana caught up to the pack and walked alongside the stretcher. Logan slept the entire way, though he didn't appear to be in any pain. Still, they walked slowly so as not to jostle him more than necessary, and it took them over an hour to get back to the house. Jazzy made him comfortable in their room near the clinic while Oliver and Mei went home to their cottage to get some sleep.

Liana was so keyed up she felt as if she'd never settle down. She'd thrown a voluminous caftan over her head, and now it billowed out and about her legs as she paced the length of the great room and back again. It was Anton who stopped her agitated pacing with a gentle touch to her shoulder. "Go get a shower. It will help relax you. Then join Stefan and me in my study. We're going to clean up and have a glass of cognac."

"Cognac?" Her laughter sounded brittle, even in her own ears. "I'm not sure that's a good idea." She glanced at Stefan. He'd entered the room with Anton, but he was still naked after shifting. He leaned casually, unselfconsciously, against the frame of the open door with his arms folded across his chest. He was so utterly gorgeous he made her mouth go dry. Liana licked her dry lips. "I remember what happened last time I had a glass of cognac."

Anton briefly glanced toward Stefan. Then he leaned close and kissed her, shocking Liana all the way to her toes. "With any luck, that's the same thing Stefan and I are hoping will happen if you share a drink with us tonight. Now hurry. Please?"

She blinked. Was that an invitation for sex? She stared at Anton's lush smile, sensed the power of his heightened arousal and blinked again. *Definitely an invitation.* Her agitation went up another notch. Without another word, Liana turned and headed to her room for a shower.

Chapter 8

Adam stood beneath the spray and prayed for the shower to wash away the adrenaline high that had his hands shaking and his cock hard as a post. He hadn't run in weeks, hadn't thought about the boost his libido would get from the combination of running with his packmates, a successful hunt, and the amazing rush that swept over him when he called on his healing skills.

In the past, he would have been buried deep inside his mate by now, their bodies so perfectly connected that the energy would have burned away in one searing climax after another. He thought of Eve, of her warm and welcoming body, of the way she fit him so perfectly when they came together, and the memories made him ache. Steam billowed around him and the pain grew, the need for release, the need to somehow tame the beast he'd always welcomed in the past.

He wrapped his fist around his shaft and his body shuddered with the contact of callused palm to erect penis. The water beat against his shoulders and over his buttocks as he stroked himself, sliding his right fist up and down his thick shaft, cupping his balls in his left hand and rolling the orbs within his sac.

He pulled Eve's image into his mind, and it was her hand that held him, her fingers wrapped around his sac, taking him closer, deeper into the well of arousal that billowed up from his spine to his groin, from his balls along the full, fat length of his dick.

Harder, faster, squeezing and pulling until he writhed against his own hand in pain as much as pleasure, until he felt the coil of heat that meant he'd almost reached the crest.

His eyes closed, his lips parted and he drew quick, harsh gasps of air in through his mouth as his hands flew. Almost there, just a few short, sharp strokes along his length and he felt it—his seed bursting up out of his balls, the seed that should have gone to Eve, that should have made that baby she wanted so badly . . . seed that should have been for the one he loved.

"Eve! Damn it, Eve. Damn you!"

His voice cracked and broke on the curse. Anger, not at Liana but at Eve, boiled up as hot and thick as his damned ejaculate. She'd told him to move on. She'd embraced her new world, the one that didn't include him. But she was dead to him now and it was over.

Adam slid down against the warm tile until he sat on the floor in the corner of the shower stall while the water beat about his head and shoulders, while his sperm swirled down the drain along with his utter loneliness, his unbearable pain.

He sat there and the water cooled and he cried. Shoulders shaking, nose running, eyes streaming, he cried until the hot water ran out and his body shivered beneath the icy spray.

He opened his eyes and saw himself as others might, sitting on the floor of the small shower, shivering like a man half frozen, which he was. Frozen and getting colder by the second.

Damn, what a fucked up ass.

Enough. Eve was right when she called him a jackass. She wasn't coming back. Liana wasn't going away. He needed to accept the inevitable and move on. Eve used to tell him to pick his battles. He'd picked this one and lost, and he knew he'd fought it long enough. Tonight he'd run with the pack, he'd healed Logan, he'd managed not to be too terribly rude to Liana. He felt as if he'd taken his first step back into the world of the living.

Maybe tomorrow he'd take another.

He didn't have to like it, but if he took one step at a time, he figured he'd eventually get used to walking among his packmates once again.

He stood up and finished rinsing, cursing the cold water and his own stupidity. Half frozen, he turned off the shower and toweled dry. His dick was so cold it was barely a fraction of its normal size, all shriveled up and practically blue, but the only trembling in his legs now was from being so damned cold.

His balls were sucked up between his legs in search of a warm spot. He would have laughed at the picture he made, except that for the first time in weeks, he actually felt alive.

It was late. He wondered how Logan was doing and thought about checking on him. Changed his mind. Logan and Jazzy knew where to find him if there was a problem, or they could call Liana. The main thing was that Logan was alive. Adam didn't think he could stand another loss at this point in his life.

His mind drifted and he thought of the times he and Logan had gone into the woods and fucked each other until they could hardly crawl back home. Logan still couldn't bring himself to ask Adam for sex, but he'd never once turned him down.

Remembering Logan beneath him, his cock buried in

the guy's ass, his hands wrapped around Logan's thick shaft, helped warm Adam up and he finally stopped shivering. He wrapped the towel around his hips and finger-combed his hair back from his face.

It was almost like looking at a stranger in the mirror. He'd aged over the past few weeks. There was more gray in his hair. The lines bracketing his mouth were more pronounced, his face thinner, his eyes set deeper.

So be it. At least he felt as if something holding him prisoner had cracked open, had freed him, at least a bit. He opened the window a little to let the steam out. Then he opened the door to the bedroom.

Oliver sat on the edge of his bed.

"Oliver? What are you doing here? Is something wrong?"

Oliver shrugged and stared at his hands hanging loosely between his knees. His sigh was audible clear across the room. "I couldn't sleep. Tried to, but all I could think of was you. Of me . . . I miss you, Adam." He raised his head. Adam sucked in a quick breath, reminded once again how deceptively beautiful Oliver was. Skin like dark chocolate, piercing amber eyes, the soft British accent that gave his voice a sensual power Adam had never been able to escape.

"I've missed you, too," he said. "Shit, man . . . what I said, what I did to Mei. Unforgivable. I am so sorry." He wanted to walk closer, but Adam felt as if his feet were glued to the floor. He stood there, staring into Oliver's gorgeous eyes, wishing he could take back every vicious word he'd said, every crappy thing he'd done.

He'd hurt Mei. *Entirely unforgivable.*

Oliver sighed and stood up. He wore nothing more than soft mustard-yellow sweats hanging low on his hips. The color emphasized the rich chocolate of his skin, the perfect condition of his lean hips and taut belly. He wasn't a big man, barely as tall as his mate, but his shoulders were broad and his smooth chest curved in all the right places. His flat stomach rippled with taut muscles. A thin line of coal-black hair led from his naval down the center of his belly to disappear beneath the flat waistband on his pants. Adam curled his fingers into fists to keep from reaching out and stroking his fingertip along that dark line.

Oliver's voice rose barely above a whisper. "What you said and did came from your pain. What I did was purely from anger gone out of control. I am so sorry, Adam. I'll never get that out of my head, the way your back looked when Anton finally stopped me. I went too far. I will never forgive myself for hurting you the way I did."

"It was what I wanted." Adam took a step forward.

Oliver shook his head and glared at him. "It doesn't matter. It was wrong. It's not what friends—what lovers do to each other. They find other answers to problems. They don't set out to cause pain."

He closed the distance between them by another step.

"Is that what we are, Oliver? Are we still lovers?" Emotion surged through Adam, harsh and painful and so utterly perfect he was trembling again, though it wasn't from arousal or the cold shower this time. It was so much more, the amazing power that filled him as he stood almost close enough to touch the man he'd loved from the first time they met.

Memories battered his mind, that first time when Oliver's truck died along the road where Adam was walking. The way Oliver invited him to share the cab while rain drenched the area. Somehow, Oliver had known. Somehow, he'd realized Adam was linked to this amazing group of shapeshifters, and he'd taken Adam in and brought him home.

But the most powerful memory of that amazing night was the secret he'd shared with Adam—a secret that only

Anton Cheval had known—that Oliver had been castrated as a child. Denied not only the chance to become a whole man, but denied his Chanku heritage as well.

And Adam, the one who fixed things, had fixed Oliver. Even more important than returning Oliver's sexuality, he'd given him full passage into the pack as a shapeshifting Chanku.

Only Adam understood, though, that as much as he had saved Oliver, Oliver had saved him. He stared at Adam now with tears tracking across his cheeks and a soft, sad smile on his lips. "We're more than lovers, Adam. So much more. You are my brother, my best friend, the one I will always need in my life. The way I look at it, you hurt me. I hurt you. People who love as much as we two sometimes do cruel things to one another. I think we're even now, don't you agree?"

His accent had become more pronounced. His need seemed to fill the space between them. Adam didn't re-member taking the final steps that brought them together. Wasn't sure if he had been the one to move or if Oliver had bridged the gap, but they clung to one another now, both of them holding on for dear life.

For the second time tonight Adam wept. He'd never been a man to cry, had seen it as a weakness when he was a whole lot younger and way more stupid. Now he knew it for what it was, a cleansing, a catharsis as important to healing as any step he might take.

His chest was damp and he smiled against Oliver's dark hair, knowing how much his friend hated any weakness in himself. He leaned close and kissed Oliver full on the mouth, tasting the salt on his full lips, parting his own when he felt the first timid thrust of Oliver's tongue.

They so rarely kissed. It was a revelation to discover how much he'd missed this connection. As his lips and tongue explored Oliver's, Adam realized the grief that had consumed him was as much over losing Oliver and Mei's love as it had been over the loss of his mate, of Eve's death.

They made it to the bed, a clumsy segue of tongues and lips, teeth and searching hands until they lay together on the rumpled spread, their bodies straining together. Adam's skin was still chilled from his icy shower, but Oliver's was hot. Adam felt branded wherever they connected. His towel ended up on the floor with Oliver's sweats in a crumpled heap on top.

They grappled like wrestlers, desperate to connect. Adam needed to feel again. His body was cold, his heart too goddess-be-damned empty, but Oliver's hands were everywhere, stroking, brushing, pinching. Touching.

Connecting. Adam kissed Oliver's chest, his belly, the inside of his thigh, the side of his shaft. He suckled the wrinkled sac and tongued first one ball and then the other, sucking each solid orb into his mouth, frantic now to taste and touch, to feel. Oliver thrust his hips forward. Adam took him in his mouth, tonguing the tiny slit, slipping the tip of his tongue beneath the edge of foreskin bracketing the broad glans and then wrapping his lips around Oliver's thick length and swallowing him deep.

He teased him for just a moment, taking Oliver right to the edge before releasing him and sitting back on his heels. Oliver lay on the bed, his cock standing tall, slick with Adam's saliva. He reached down and stroked himself, slowly rolling the foreskin over the broad tip and back down again. A tiny drop of white cream pooled in the dark slit.

Adam stared at that perfect drop, breathing deep, imagining the taste, the texture of it on his tongue, but he wanted more. So damned much more. He shook his head and broke away from the seduction of that one white bead of cream against the dark, smooth tip of Oliver's glans. Another deep breath and he closed his eyes, searching in the darkness behind his lids for strength.

Finally, fully under control now, he reached for the small dresser beside the bed. The drawer caught when he tried to open it. He jerked the handle. The damned thing fell out on the floor and shattered.

Any other time, such a stupid move would have had both of them cracking up. Not now. The tension in the room seethed with expectation and arousal, heightened by the sound of their labored breathing, the pounding cadence of hearts powered by need and desire. Adam reached down and grabbed a tube of lubricant out of the splintered drawer. He tossed it on the bed. "You or me, bud? It's your call."

Oliver's steady gaze hadn't flinched. Now he grinned, raised his legs and grabbed his knees and held them close against his chest. Adam released a deep breath he hadn't realized he'd been holding.

He backed away and slipped off the bed, grabbed Oliver and turned him until his butt rested on the edge of the mattress. Kneeling beside the bed, Adam leaned close and planted a kiss on the underside of Oliver's erect cock.

Then he sat back on his heels on the floor beside the bed and ran his fingers over Oliver's perfect ass, stroking his dark flanks, marveling at the smooth, sleek skin, trailing a fingertip along the warm, damp crease between his cheeks. He picked up the lube, removed the cap and pressed the tip against Oliver's anus, covering the taut, sensitive ring of muscle with a thick layer of clear gel.

Oliver's eyes closed. He sighed, and his head fell back against the bedding.

Adam squeezed some of the gel into his palm and slowly, carefully stroked his own cock, covering the thick shaft from tip to base. Normally they used condoms for anal sex, not to prevent disease which wasn't an issue between Chanku, but because the women insisted.

Tonight, though, it was just the two of them.

Aesthetics be damned. He needed the intimacy of fucking raw, the feel of heat and moisture and taut, clasping muscles tightening around his bare shaft, the skin-on-skin connection only full, naked sex could give him.

Images flashed through his mind, frame after frame of visuals—the way Oliver's tight ring of muscle would stretch to surround the thick crown of his cock, the slow squeeze as his glans compressed and reshaped itself to fit through such a tiny hole. Adam stroked himself, spreading the cool gel over his entire length, growing longer and thicker with each pass of his fingers over his shaft.

He let go of his cock and ran his fingers through the gel covering Oliver's anus. Oliver's cheeks tightened and closed against his finger. Adam pressed his middle finger against Oliver's sphincter. The muscle stretched and gave, and he slipped his finger deep inside.

Oliver groaned and his cock twitched. His muscles flexed and tightened around Adam's finger as he slowly withdrew and pushed back in. On the third thrust, he added a second finger, scissoring in and out, stretching the muscle, relaxing the opening.

Oliver's lips parted. He sighed and whimpered notes of ecstasy as Adam slowly fucked him with his fingers. After a few deep thrusts, Adam slipped his hand free and stood up. Leaning over Oliver, he wrapped his fingers around his shaft and pressed the thick head of his cock against that tiny opening. The softened ring flexed in and out. Adam pressed forward, slowly, steadily.

Oliver's hands tightened around his shins and he pulled his knees tighter to his chest. Just as Adam had pictured it, the tip of his cock seemed to reform and elongate as he drove forward and forced Oliver's sphincter to relax even more. Finally Adam rolled his hips forward and slipped through the tight opening into heat and pressure.

Hot, wet muscles clamped down on his shaft.

Oliver groaned.

So did Adam. No matter how often they loved this way, there was always the sense of the forbidden, the feeling that this dark pleasure brought with it a deeper intimacy than two men could ever know otherwise. The slow spasm of tight muscles rippling along his length was almost more than Adam could take. The amazing connection of bare cock to bare ass, the wet, fiery heat, the sense of life was almost too much.

Almost.

After a few moments, Adam caught his breath and slowly, steadily pushed all the way in, burying his full length deep inside Oliver. Muscles rippled and clenched around him, sending shocks of pleasure from his dick to his toes. He took long, deep breaths and struggled to hang on. It had been so long.

So damned long. Adam closed his eyes and began a slow and constant rhythm in and out, filling and retreating, going deep, pulling back in a steady cadence he could keep up for hours if he wanted.

His hands were still slick with the lube. He wrapped his right hand around Oliver's cock and slowly stroked his full, fat length, sliding his foreskin over the tip on each careful pull. He cupped Oliver's sac in his left hand, rolling those perfect nuts between his fingers.

When he raised his head, he gazed directly into Oliver's eyes and everything Oliver felt, every thought, every emotion, spilled into Adam's mind.

The depth of feeling stunned him.

Love and gratitude. His lifelong debt to Adam, the man responsible for Oliver's rebirth. His memories filled Adam's head—the first time he'd made love to a woman, to Eve Reynolds on the night of her first shift. Oliver was still a eunuch then, his cock hard only because of the link with Adam.

Yet Eve had never guessed, and Oliver had experienced

what every other man already knew, that amazing physical connection two people can share. It had blown the lid off his life, opened him up to want more. So much more.

And because of Adam, Oliver had made his first shift, carried along from man to animal through Adam's powerful link, a link that had given him more than fangs and fur—it had given him his manhood. He shared it now, his shock and surprise when he first realized he'd not only become a wolf, he'd become a complete male with a powerful body and a perfect set of testicles.

He shared his fear, how he'd felt when it was time to shift back, the overwhelming fear that all he'd have between his legs was a penis good for nothing more than pissing, followed by his utter amazement when he stood before Adam as a man—a real man—for the first time in his life.

He'd sat and cried, so overwhelmed by the hormones suddenly coursing through his system, by the knowledge his life had changed in ways he'd never dreamed could happen. Making love to Adam now was only part of that change. He'd found Mei, shared her ability to become a snow leopard even as she learned from Oliver how to become a wolf.

All because Adam had managed to think outside the box. He'd been willing to try things no one else had considered, not even Anton Cheval with all his many skills.

And you wonder why I love you so much? Don't you see, Adam? All these things you did for me, every change you made in my life was just for me. You didn't expect anything in return. You merely set out to fix what was broken. I was broken. I'm not. Not anymore, and it's all because of you.

Adam blinked back the tears filling his eyes. Damn it all, he'd cried enough tonight. He tightened his grasp on Oliver's cock, stroked the full length in time with each thrust of his hips. In, out, deeper and harder, sharing his body, reaching for Oliver's heart and soul.

They reached orgasm together, their minds linked as tightly as their bodies. Connecting deep and true. Oliver's cock jerked in Adam's hand. He covered the broad tip with his palm, felt the thick jets of seed spilling out and over, running in creamy trails through his fingers, down Oliver's dark shaft.

Lightning raced from Adam's spine to his balls, down the full length of his cock and he exploded deep inside Oliver's bowel. Muscles tightened along his full length, clasping, clenching, pulling him deep, sucking him dry until, long moments later, it was over.

Oliver lowered his legs. Adam lay down on Oliver, his feet still planted on the floor, supporting his upper body with his elbows. His cock still jerked deep inside Oliver's hot sheath, his heart pounded out a rhythm that eerily matched Oliver's.

They were both hot and sweaty, covered in ejaculate and blowing as if they'd run ten miles. Adam leaned close and touched his forehead to Oliver's. "I can't live without this," he said. He kissed Oliver, breathed in his breath, tasted his lips. "I need you, Ollie."

"That's a really cool thing," Oliver said, smiling at him. "We don't have to live without it. I need you every bit as much, and I will always love you, even if you do insist on calling me Ollie. It's Oliver, you jerk, but I'm glad you're back." He ran his fingers along Adam's stubbled jaw and softly asked, "You are back, aren't you?"

Adam nodded. Realized he was grinning like a complete idiot. "I am. For better or for worse, in sickness or in health."

"Good." Oliver wrapped his arms around Adam and pulled him down, until Adam's chest rested on Oliver's and the thick length of Oliver's cock swelled between them. "That's exactly the way it should be."

Muscles tightened around Adam's cock. He felt himself swelling, growing erect once more. With a practiced tilt of his hips, he picked up the rhythm and made love to Ollie once again.

Heart pounding, body trembling with need, Liana finished her shower in record time and slipped into a soft knit gown that fell in warm black folds to her toes. The sleeves were long, the neck broadly scooped, and with her blond hair drifting about her hips she felt almost frighteningly feminine.

And more aroused than she'd ever been in her life. She hadn't really understood the Chanku physiology, the unbelievable need for sexual release following a run, until she'd actually experienced it herself. Thank goodness she'd been welcome in the various pairings among the different packmates, but always as a second woman with one of the men.

Never as the only woman with two men, but if it was going to happen, tonight was the night. The added adrenaline rush of healing Logan had her keyed to a fever pitch. Expectation, knowing both Anton and Stefan awaited her, had her body shivering with desire and her sex already wet and swollen. She walked on trembling legs through the quiet house, down the hallway from the guest wing where her room was, to the quiet study where Anton and Stefan waited.

She stood in the doorway, watching the men for long moments before they noticed her. There was very little light in the room, but a single lamp cast a soft glow on the two of them. They stood close beside one another in front of the big window. Anton wore dark slacks and a white shirt with the sleeves rolled back along his forearms. His long hair brushed his shoulders, hanging loose instead of tied back as it normally was.

Stefan had on a pair of comfortable jeans with a soft, gray v-necked sweater. His hair hung loose as well, as dark as Anton's but shot through with glistening strands of silver. Both of them were barefoot, so alike in appearance and stance they could have been brothers. They looked completely relaxed, standing together, gazing at a herd of deer in the back meadow.

One of the deck lights illuminated a section of the grassy area, giving the deer an almost mystical appearance. The temperature had dropped and a white mist drifted about the animals' legs. It looked as if they wandered through clouds and made Liana think of her life as a goddess, of the beautiful, impossible things she had seen on the astral plane where she'd existed for so long.

She wondered what Eve saw, if she enjoyed the mysteries without answers, the amazing things that existed in that place out of time. She wished the new goddess well, and at the same time, wondered how any woman could choose the lonely life on the astral plane compared to this life, here with these amazingly sensual creatures.

Stefan noticed her first. He turned and smiled. Then he walked to the bar and plucked a crystal brandy snifter off a shelf, tipped an ornate decanter filled with golden liquid and poured about an inch into the bottom of the bowl. Liana walked across the room and he presented it to her with a flourish and a perfectly executed bow. Then he took her hand in his and pressed a kiss to her palm.

A tingling warmth spread out from the point where his lips met her hand. "Gallant, aren't we?" She dipped her head, acknowledging his gesture. Then she took a long, slow sip of the cognac. She loved the burn of it going down her throat, loved the taste and the heat as its spirit spread to all points in her body. As aroused as she felt, the single sip of liquor seemed to push her even higher.

Anton set his cognac on the sideboard and stepped between Liana and Stefan. "Gallant? Stefan? He tries." Anton winked at Stefan, wrapped an arm around Liana's shoulders, took her glass and set it beside his on the sideboard and tipped her back. He leaned over her, his lips a mere fraction of an inch from hers. She gazed up into his glittering amber eyes and felt as if she looked into the heavens, as if the knowledge of all the world resided in those dark pools.

She'd sensed Anton's power when she'd brought him to her world just a couple of months ago, when she'd swept him up with young Matt Rodgers and held both men against their will. She hadn't even been close to comprehending what Anton was capable of, what magic he wielded. This was a man who might have bested her, had he truly understood her nature.

Now, her nature had changed. She was Chanku—no more, no less—but her needs were even more powerful than when she'd been a goddess. Then, her sexuality was a tool, something she wielded to gain strength through sexual energy.

Now it was a physical need, arousal so all-consuming she felt close to orgasm from the mere suggestion of his kiss. He held her, not kissing her, his lips so close, his breath smelling sweetly of the cognac he'd been drinking.

But this passivity wasn't her. She had been a powerful goddess for much longer than she'd been Chanku, after all. Liana reached around Anton's neck with both hands, buried her fingers in his thick, black hair and brought his lips down to hers. She opened her mouth to his kiss and thrust her tongue between his lips.

He groaned and kissed her back. His long, lean body curled around hers and she heard the rush of blood in his veins, the pounding thunder of his heart against her chest. Anton wrapped his arms tighter around her and pulled her body even tighter against his. The thick length of his penis pressed into her belly and his long, strong legs encased her thighs.

Stefan stepped behind her, wrapped one arm around both of them and swept her long hair aside with the brush of his fingers. He kissed the back of her neck and the line of her jaw while Anton took her lips, took control of her kisses and made love to her mouth.

She was feeling almost numb with their kisses, as if her body floated in a world of sensation, when the two of them suddenly stopped and pulled away. She stood there a moment, uncertain, shivering with need while Stefan and Anton stood back and admired her.

Anton handed Liana her cognac. She took the glass in shaking hands, took a sip, and then a bigger swallow, and gave the glass back to him. He set it aside, reached for her gown with both hands and slowly lifted it over her head. She shivered harder, whether from the cool rush of air across her naked and needy flesh or the new level of arousal that swept across all of her nerve endings.

When she was naked, Anton led her to a low couch and had her lie down. He unbuttoned his shirt and peeled it over his shoulders. Then he slipped out of his slacks and kicked them aside. She watched him bare his absolutely perfect body, unaware that Stefan had disrobed until he moved close to Anton and stood beside him.

The sight of two such exquisitely beautiful men made her wet. There was no other way to describe it, that hot rush of moisture between her thighs, the sense of feminine tissues swelling, softening until she knew she must feel all buttery and warm, slick with her own juices, ready for one of these men to enter her.

Then she realized they both intended to take her. Both

huge men, entering her fore and aft at the same time. They'd not said a word, but the image filled her mind and she knew that Anton was showing her exactly what they would do.

And in showing her, he was giving her a choice. Did she want to try this? Was she willing to take a chance, to trust her body to men who were not her mates, who were, in fact, not only committed to, but in love with other women?

She must have broadcast her concerns. Anton knelt in front of her and took her hands in his. "Keisha and Xandi have chosen to sleep tonight. They sent both of us to you with their blessings, but Stefan and I would never ask you to do anything you're not comfortable with. It's your call."

"In all my years as a goddess, the only time I ever brought two men to my bed was the time you and Matt were with me."

He chuckled softly. "Hmmm . . . as I recall, there was no penetration that night."

She ran her fingertip along his cheek. "Much to my dismay. I have such fond memories of you as my lover the first time I brought you to my bed. I imagine both of you would have been an amazing experience."

Anton glanced toward Stefan, shared a look that might have made her more curious at another time, as if they spoke on a level beyond her ability to listen. Then Anton turned and kissed her fingertips and she concentrated once again on the sensations coursing through her body.

"That was a long time ago," he said. "You're still as young and lovely as you were then. I, on the other hand, have aged a bit."

Stefan laughed and sat down on the floor next to the low couch. He ran his fingers over her breasts and belly, stroking her gently while she lay there trembling with arousal. "A bit, you say? More than a bit, my friend."

Anton raised an eyebrow and glared at him with mock outrage. "I like to think I've improved with age."

"Anton, cognac improves with age, we don't."

Liana giggled, more relaxed than she'd been in longer than she could recall. "Gentlemen," she said, reaching for a hand from each of them. "No more talk of age. Compared to me, both of you are but infants. I was alive at the dawn of man's creation. Take that into consideration when you speak of age."

Chapter 9

Anton chuckled as he raised Liana's hand to his lips, but at the last moment he turned her palm and kissed the sensitive pressure point on her wrist.

Liana felt the touch of his lips like an arrow of sensation shooting from the inside of her wrist to a point directly between her thighs. Her level of arousal leapt. Her nervousness faded away.

Stefan suddenly grew serious. "I'd like to think we both have learned at least something with age, my friend." He leaned over to the sound of Anton's soft laughter, and kissed Liana. Then he scattered more kisses across her chest and over her breasts, where he paused to tease her sensitive nipples with his tongue. He sucked one between his lips and worried it with his teeth, shocking her with the sense of pleasure verging on pain.

Anton parted her thighs and ran just the tip of his tongue over her folds, separating the petals of her needy sex and lapping up her cream as if she tasted better than the expensive cognac he'd poured for them tonight. He continued licking and sucking, teasing her clitoris with gentle licks and pulling sucks, taking her higher and closer to her peak with every intimate touch and taste.

She whimpered and lifted herself to him, but he kissed her inner thigh and backed away before she could find her release.

Stefan seemed to know exactly how hard to suckle, how much to bite and lick and nibble to drive her totally insane. He worked one breast and then the other, slowly, methodically. Once again, Anton kissed and licked between her legs, but he, too, seemed to know exactly how far he could go without taking her over the top.

She didn't know she could be this turned on without coming, had no idea how high it was possible to fly. Desperate little whimpering sounds escaped from between her lips and unexpected shivers raced over her sensitive skin. She bit back a cry when Anton suddenly stood up and grabbed her around the waist, turned her quickly to face him as he sat down on the couch and lowered her gently over his straining erection.

She cried out as he filled her, stretched her to the point of pain, both of them moving slowly as he settled her down on his lap with her legs folded beneath her at either side of his hips. Reclining, Anton gave Liana the freedom to set their pace.

Eyes closed, lips parted for each tortured breath, she slowly raised and lowered herself on his shaft. The swollen mouth of her sex clung to his rigid length as she moved over him, drove him deep inside and then raised up to encompass nothing more than the fat crown.

She turned as if in a trance and watched as Stefan rolled a condom over his swollen penis. He smoothed it over his thick length, stroking himself for a moment. She turned away, unwilling to watch when she felt his fingers exploring the crease between her buttocks, the cool slide of some sort of gel as he forced it in and around her taut sphincter.

The intimacy of his touch was too much . . . not nearly enough. She whimpered again when he slowly inserted one finger and then two inside her bottom, sliding in and out of her in perfect synchronization with every deep thrust that Anton made.

She knew what was coming next and her body tensed. Stefan didn't say anything, but he stroked her back and hip, kissed her shoulder and reassured her with his gentle touch. She tried to relax as Stefan rested the broad tip of his penis against her anus. He pressed forward and Anton stilled, waiting patiently as Liana consciously willed her tension away while pushing against Stefan to help ease his way through her tight opening.

He was so careful and moved so slowly that the pain was minimal, the burn of entry far outweighed by the pleasure of full penetration. She felt stuffed full of him, of both of them.

Even so, when Anton moved forward, thrusting deep within her vaginal canal, Liana's body jerked. Fear flashed with the very real concern whether two such well-endowed men could not only fit, but safely move inside her.

There was no need to worry. They were both so careful, so loving and considerate of her comfort, their every move made for her pleasure, that Liana finally began to relax, to enjoy the pure carnal joy of taking two beautiful men inside her at once.

Two men who loved each other, who loved without boundaries, without any concern for anything beyond their feelings for one another, for their mates and now, for Liana.

She sensed Anton's thoughts at almost the same time she picked up Stefan's, their shared feelings about this most intimate of acts, their curiosity about her, their interest in her perception of them as men, as lovers. She sensed what they felt, experienced her vagina as a tight, wet sheath surrounding Anton's cock, the rhythmic clench and release of her powerful muscles as she clasped him tightly and drew him deep.

She sighed when she slipped into Stefan's thoughts, saw through Stefan's eyes, and actually watched the slow, steady glide of his penis slipping in and out of her snug channel. He loved watching the stretch and give of that small, pink ring of muscle, the way it rolled over the length of his penis and contracted around the softer tip when he almost withdrew.

Almost, but not quite.

She felt her body relaxing even as sensation grew, drawing her closer and closer to orgasm. So amazing, the thick slide of hard, male flesh deep in her vagina as Anton slowly and carefully loved her, touching her clitoris on every downward stroke, coupled with Stefan's gentle yet deep penetration in that darker, *oh, so sensitive* channel. She tried to concentrate on just one sensation at a time, but it was impossible to separate the amazing feeling of two large men making love to her, knowing they couldn't help but feel each other on every penetrating glide.

She realized her mental barriers were softening and quickly reinforced the blocks she kept in place at all times. She might be a mortal woman now, but she still had the mind and memories of a goddess, one who had lived with almost unlimited power for many thousands of years. Mental links with those around her were perfectly safe, as long as she guarded her deepest, oldest memories, her eons of knowledge, her lost immortality.

Anton's thoughts drifted into hers once again. He shared the most intimate details, the sense of his cock riding over Stefan's through the thin wall separating her twin channels, the clasp of her body, the pulse of her blood racing ever faster as her arousal grew.

Stefan's images took hold and she felt the taut muscle clasping his cock, the slick heat, deep inside her body, the thick length of Anton's erection gliding so close to Stefan's, just a thin layer of tissue away. In and out, hearts beating

in sync, now, racing to the tempo of the profoundly intimate images shared among the three of them.

Liana's body became even more pliable, more a vessel
to hold two men than the temple of her own thoughts, her
own being. She felt herself spiraling upward—higher, freer.
The barriers separating the three of them softened as the
images passed, one to the other, as sensations grew and
flew from Anton to Liana to Stefan and back again, a
never-ending loop of sensation, of arousal explored and
desire fulfilled, of knowledge.

Lights flashed behind Liana's eyes as she set herself free
and flew, her body shattering with the light of a million
stars, her muscles clenching, spasming and then convulsing with the sudden thrust of a powerful mind—Anton's
mind—seeking knowledge.

Breaking down the last of her goddess barriers, driving
through her protective walls into the dark, chaotic morass
of unimaginable knowledge.

Screaming in anger, wanting to weep with the utter despair of betrayal, Liana managed to shatter the link with
Stefan before her body tumbled into the abyss and her
world went dark.

The scream was mental as much as audible, a man's
tortured scream of unbearable pain, and images of black,
insurmountable walls, flashes of fire and bursting lights,
the impossible vision of time without end, and fear. Indescribable fear.

Adam leapt out of bed, heart thudding, mind a morass
of confused visuals and feelings, of darkness and exploding lights and terror. He shook his head to clear his mind,
reached out for Oliver, and realized he was alone. Oliver
must have returned to his cottage and his mate while
Adam slept.

Why then, did he sense the presence of another?

Adam flipped on the light. The room was empty, the sense of something *other* fading. Until a voice, familiar and beloved, whispered in his ear.

Eve?

Go to Anton. He needs you. Quickly, now. In his study.

Adam slipped on a pair of sweats and raced barefoot down the outside stairs and into the house. It was the middle of the night, but the kitchen was brightly lit. He heard voices coming from Anton's study. He ran through the empty kitchen and the dark dining room, into the small study beyond.

The first thing he noticed was the potent scent of sex and the overlying acrid odor of fear. The second was Keisha, kneeling beside Anton. He appeared to be unconscious, lying on the small couch with a blanket thrown over his hips and legs. Liana sat on a low stool off to one side, shivering even though she was conservatively dressed in a black, full-length knit dress. Tears streaked her face and her long, blond hair fell in snarls and tangles to the floor.

Stefan had put on a pair of worn jeans without a shirt, as if he'd thrown them on in a hurry. The button at the waist was undone and his hair uncharacteristically mussed and unbound. He sat at the end of the couch with one hand wrapped around Anton's foot, as if the connection anchored him.

Adam took in the scene without a word. Then he knelt beside Keisha and rested his hand on Anton's forehead. His skin was cool, but he was out cold. Adam used his healing abilities to slip inside for a quick look, to check for cerebral injuries or heart problems, but nothing looked or felt wrong.

After a moment Adam slipped back into himself, turned to Keisha and rubbed her shoulder. She was tense as a bow string. "Keisha, I think he'll be okay in a minute or two.

His breathing is fine, his heart rate's normal. His thoughts seem a little chaotic, but I think he's beginning to come around. What happened?"

Keisha looked to Stefan. He shot an angry glance at Liana and shook his head. "We were fucking Liana," he said, practically snarling when he said her name.

Adam jerked his attention from Anton to Stefan at the harsh sound of accusation in his voice, but he kept his thoughts to himself.

"Everything was great, we were all reaching orgasm at once when she shouted something and Anton screamed like he was in incredible pain. Then his eyes rolled back in his head and he went into convulsions that lasted almost a full minute."

Keisha nodded. "He was just coming out of them when I arrived." She glared at Liana. "What did you do to my mate?"

Liana bowed her head, but she said nothing.

"Why do you blame Liana?" Adam glanced at her and then at Keisha. "What do you think she did?"

"Something with her mind." Keisha ran her hand over Anton's forehead. "I can sense that much in him. Can you do anything?"

Adam shook his head. "He'll come around on his own. I feel his consciousness returning." He glanced once more at Liana. "Are you sure it was her?"

"Yes. I felt it too. Just not as powerfully as Anton." Stefan stood up and stalked over to the woman. He stood over her, more dark and menacing than Adam had ever seen him. "What happened? What did you do to him?"

Liana slowly stood up and pushed her long hair over her shoulders. She looked regal now, not beaten as she'd appeared a moment ago, and her voice carried an air of command Adam hadn't heard from her.

"It appears that while you were *fucking* Liana, she was making love. While she was blissfully enjoying an orgasm,

Anton was raping her mind, going where he had no right, where he had neither been invited nor been given permission to enter. Whatever happened, he did it to himself."

"You bitch." Stefan's low curse laced with an unspoken threat raised the hairs along Adam's spine.

"Stefan! Back off and leave her alone. Anton's coming to. Let's see what he has to say before we jump to conclusions."

"I will be gone by morning."

Liana looked every bit the powerful goddess, but Adam sensed something unexpected beneath her cool façade. An unspoken pain, and terror that had her teetering on the edge of hysteria.

"You'll go nowhere," he said.

Liana's eyes flashed—hurt and anger and other emotions he couldn't interpret, but she didn't lower her gaze. "I am a free woman—my own woman. I'll not stay where I'm not trusted. Where I can't trust."

Anton groaned and struggled to sit. Keisha helped him, murmuring soft, soothing words of encouragement. Adam moved quickly to support his shoulders, but Anton motioned him away and stared at Liana. "Trust works both ways, Liana."

She bowed her head, acknowledging nothing.

Silence settled over them, a silence broken only by the sound of breathing, of many hearts beating. Adam glanced behind him and realized the small study was filled now with silent packmates. Mei and Oliver, Xandi, Logan and Jazzy Blue, all of them here.

All apparently ready to pass judgment on the woman they'd welcomed so openly just a few short weeks ago.

Anton's eyes narrowed. "You have nothing to say for yourself?"

Liana shook her head and smiled, but there was no humor in her steady gaze. "Always so arrogant, Anton. So quick to set blame. I was not the one searching your mind without permission. I did not force my way through protective barriers set up for your own good. That was you, Anton. Breaking my trust. Using my body, weakening my defenses with yours and Stefan's skillful lovemaking to search, uninvited, through my thoughts. How dare you accuse me of breaking trust?"

She dipped her chin in acknowledgment of the assembled pack. "You have all welcomed me without question. You have taken me into your home, into your beds. I am most appreciative, but I cannot and will not stay where I am not trusted, where I am not accorded the same honor and integrity you ask of me."

She walked toward the door, passing close by Adam without glancing right or left. The small group parted for her and she left the room, her exit as regal, as powerful, as if she were a queen. Stefan stared after her, his face a mass of conflicting emotions.

Adam sat back on his heels and glanced from Anton to Stefan and again at their pack leader. Anton was sitting upright, unaided now, staring at the door where Liana had disappeared down the hallway in the direction of her room.

"Is she right, Anton? Did you invade her mind without permission?"

Anton glanced at Stefan. "Invade? That's rather a harsh word, don't you think?"

"Is it?" Stefan clenched his fists at his sides. "I was there. I was making love with a beautiful woman who was giving freely of her body, her sensuality. We were sharing our experiences, linking as we do when the sex is especially good. I remember a swirl of darkness and then I was suddenly forced out of the link. Was that your doing?"

"Forced out?" Anton shook his head. "No, I didn't have a chance to protect you. The moment I slipped past her barriers I got caught up in power so unimaginable, so terrifying . . ." His voice drifted off.

Adam frowned. "You're admitting to breaching barriers she'd not lowered on her own? Anton, you're the first one to condemn that kind of conduct."

He glared at Adam, immediately on the defensive. "What I do, I do for the good of the pack. She was holding secrets back, hiding a very large part of who and what she is. I needed to know she was safe to have here among us, around my packmates, our children. That she meant us no harm. I tried to see and she attacked." He sighed and rubbed the back of his neck. "I discovered something the hard way, something I didn't realize—that Liana is still a very powerful woman."

Keisha sat back and studied him for a moment. "Couldn't you have asked her, my love? Was it necessary to use subterfuge—which obviously failed?"

Anton took a deep breath, as if he prepared to argue. Then he let it out and leaned back against the couch. "You're right. I did fail, and I still don't know if she means us harm, though she's obviously powerful enough to cause it. I have no idea what she's hiding, what she intends."

Adam stood up. "She intends to leave. Where will she go?"

"What do you care?" Anton glared at him, sounding uncharacteristically defensive and angry. "You've hardly spoken to the woman since she arrived. You've avoided meals and gatherings where you knew she would be present. What is it to you if she leaves?"

"Fairness, Anton. The fact you've treated her unconscionably and yet you're trying to make it appear the fault is Liana's." He jerked his head in angry denial. "No, I don't want to be around her. I still hold her responsible for Eve's death, but that's my issue. My problem. Not yours and not Liana's. If you searched her mind without permission, you were wrong, Anton."

"She hurt him." Keisha turned away from Anton and gazed at Adam. "Even though what he did was wrong, she hurt him. Could have damaged his mind. I saw him convulsing, Adam. That's not a simple thing, for someone to come back at another through a mind link and send them into convulsions."

"Gave me a hell of a headache, too." Anton rubbed his fingers over the back of his neck, but he was smiling. Probably already wondering how Liana's mind worked, curious about the knowledge she could share with him—if she was still willing after what had happened. "I'll talk to her in the morning, explain my concerns but . . ." He gazed directly at Adam. "We've got a lot of history with her, very little of it good. She's failed us on so many occasions. Failed us as a people. When I saw how quickly she was accepted by everyone here, I started worrying she might have some other motive for insinuating herself into the pack."

"So now you're into conspiracy theories?" Adam stared at Anton, bemused. "That's not like you. You're generally the logical one here. What's going on?"

Anton stood up and glanced at the others in the room. "Let's just say I've had my confidence sadly shaken over the past year. I don't trust as easily as I once did. I'm concerned I might have given my trust to Liana too quickly. She's an unknown. She's not like the other Chanku who have come to us from normal, human lives. She's something else entirely, and I want to know exactly what that something else is."

Adam laughed, a harsh burst of sound as anger surged through him, unexplained and unexpected. "Shit, Anton. There's nothing remotely normal about a single one of us. Why the fuck are you holding her to higher standards than anyone else? You screwed up. You owe her an apology. If she attacked, it was to protect herself and nothing more."

He turned away then, disgusted with Anton as well as himself. He didn't have to like Liana to see her side, but then he'd always had a need to protect the underdog. And he had a terrible feeling Anton's apology in the morning was going to be too little, too late.

Adam left the study with the eyes of his packmates watching him, and the awareness that the thoughts of every single one in the room were tightly closed to him.

Liana sat alone in her room in the horribly uncomfortable hardback chair by the small desk. She'd chosen it because it seemed more apropos to her emotions to sit in a chair that forced her spine straight, her shoulders back. She'd need every crutch she could find in order to survive after what had happened tonight.

It was killing her, but she fought the overwhelming desire to give in to her emotions and cry. She knew she couldn't let go, because once she started, she'd never be able to stop.

How had everything gone so wrong?

You let down your defenses.

Okay, so she'd relaxed her barriers, but there'd been no hint of Anton's intentions before that sudden foray into her mind, no reason she should have suspected he would try to learn more without asking.

Wasn't he the one always spouting off about honor, about trust and doing the right thing? Hadn't he been infuriated when he found out she'd once manipulated his thoughts without permission? What gave him the right to burst through her carefully constructed barriers?

She hadn't attacked him. If he was so damned smart, why couldn't he figure out that her mind had just been too much for his, her memories too dark, her knowledge too filled with power for even his superior intellect to handle?

She shifted in her chair and realized she was still all sticky and wet, still covered in ejaculate and saliva from two men. Two men who had shown her unimaginable joy tonight. She'd never known such arousal in her life, never felt so close to anyone as she had to Stefan and Anton—which made Anton's betrayal even more painful.

Thank goodness she'd managed to sever the link with

Stefan before he got caught in the psychic backlash. As intelligent as he was, he didn't have the mental resources that Anton possessed. She probably could have done the same for Anton as well, but she was too damned angry to care if he got hurt. He'd attacked her. Attacked her mind without warning, used the thrill of her climax to sneak past her barriers—barriers she'd erected for his own damned protection.

He deserved the headache. She hoped it stayed with him and made him miserable all night long.

She stood up and stripped the filthy dress over her head. Her body was covered in love bites and bruises, her inner thighs a sticky, disgusting mess of mingled fluids from their climaxes. What had begun as a beautiful night of new experiences, of sharing and the sense she had been accepted by this amazing pack of Chanku, had ended in a complete and total disaster.

All she had were sticky thighs and a body covered in bruises, aching from one end to the other to remind her of the heights she'd reached, and the pit where she'd landed.

Maybe this was all part of the Mother's plan. Maybe she hadn't been given a second chance, but was instead condemned to suffer the punishment she rightfully deserved. So be it. If she was to suffer, she'd do it somewhere else. On her own, if need be, apart from her kind.

Except that right now she really needed a shower.

Liana wrinkled her nose. It was bad enough that both Stefan and Anton had marked her with their scent, but even worse, it took her back. Back to the way they felt, closing her in with their strong, male bodies. Back to the fullness, the sense of her body as a vessel filled to overflowing with sensation, awash in arousal, powered by desire.

Even now, angry and hurt, stinking of sex and reeking of degradation, she felt a rush of need, of desire for their touch. For both of them . . . for either of them.

For that amazing, intimate connection, even though she knew, now, it had all been a lie. A ploy to invade her personal memories, to literally rape her mind.

She'd been a fool. Had trusted when she should have studied and learned. She'd allowed her heart to lead when she should have used her mind. Never again. Liana closed her eyes and prayed for strength. Then she went into the small bathroom to wash away the reminder of her folly.

Halfway up the stairs to his room, Adam stopped midstride and cursed. He looked over his shoulder toward the house. The lights were still on in Liana's room. Was she packing? Would she gather up her few things and leave under cover of darkness? Where would she go? How would she survive? She'd never even ridden in a car, much less driven one.

Never used a telephone, never read a book. Hell, he didn't even know if she could read. There was no way an ex-goddess, cast out of her familiar yet timeless world, could ever survive in twenty-first century Montana.

Muttering, angry with himself, with Anton and even Liana, Adam spun around and headed back down the steps. He went in through the kitchen, quietly when he realized the lights in the study were off and everyone seemed to have dispersed and gone back to their rooms.

He walked quickly down the hallway of the guest wing and paused in front of Liana's room. He stood there and did his best to talk himself out of getting involved. Argument lost, he knocked quietly. There was no answer. *Damn.* He hoped she hadn't taken off. The idea of tracking her through the woods after the day he'd had really didn't appeal, but he knew that was what he'd do if he had to.

He tried the door and the knob turned, so he opened it just a crack, softly called out, "Liana? You in there?"

She didn't answer, but he heard the shower running so

he slipped quietly into her room and closed the door behind him. Then he locked it, for whatever reason.

He gazed around her room and saw nothing more than a fairly sterile guest room. Other than her black dress lying in a crumpled heap on the floor, it was totally spotless. Nothing at all to identify it as Liana's room. Nothing beyond a closet filled with borrowed clothing and a hairbrush lying on the dresser with a few long strands of blond hair caught in the bristles.

There were two comfortable chairs in front of the sliding glass door that led to the back deck, a small desk with a straight back chair sitting at an angle in front, and a large, king-sized bed, the dominant piece of furniture in the room.

Just like every other guest room, identical even to the one he and Eve had shared when they'd not stayed in Oliver and Mei's cottage.

He took one of the overstuffed chairs and sat back to wait. The curtains were open, but the outside lights were turned off, so all he saw when he looked out the big window was his own reflection.

He looked like hell, which was probably to be expected, but it had been one hell of a night. It could have been worse. Between falling apart in the shower and that intense lovemaking with Oliver, he'd passed through some sort of barrier he'd not been able to cross before. Just now he'd thought of Eve without the horrible, burning regret that had been attached to her name whenever it popped into his mind.

Tonight he was sure he'd heard her voice, but he'd taken it for what it was—a warning that Anton needed him. Only it appeared that Liana needed him more, whether he wanted to help her or not—but it was Eve's voice that had sent him.

A voice he'd listened to without breaking down.

That was a good sign, wasn't it? It meant he was moving forward, didn't it? He stared at the partially open door to the bathroom and tried to think of Liana with an open mind.

His muscles immediately tensed and he realized he'd folded his hands into tight fists. *Guess I'm not there yet.*

The sound of running water ceased. He didn't want to frighten her, but he wasn't ready to leave, either. Gently, he called out to her. "Liana? It's me. Adam. I didn't want to startle you, but I'm in your room. Can we talk?"

Had she heard him? He waited impatiently for her answer.

Finally, a soft reply. "I'll be out in a minute."

She sounded beaten, as if the night had been too much for her, and he realized he didn't have a clue what he was going to say. What he could offer her when he didn't even like her.

Liana stepped out of the bathroom, wrapped from chin to toes in a faded blue chenille bathrobe. It was big on her, and with her wet hair slicked back from her face, the sleeves hanging over the tips of her fingers and her toes barely peeking out beneath the hem, she looked about twelve years old.

He expected her to take the chair next to his, but she chose the one by the desk instead, which was farther away. He couldn't blame her. He hadn't been his most civil toward her.

She studied him out of those gray-green eyes of hers while he tapped his fingers and tried to figure out what to say.

Finally he just blurted it out. "Liana, I don't want you to leave. Anton's planning to speak to you in the morning, but I was afraid you'd be gone before he got here."

She nodded. "I plan to be." She shrugged. "Why would you, of all people, ask me to stay? I don't understand."

He shook his head. "I'm not sure. I only know that if you leave, I'll worry about you. I'll wonder if you're okay or if you're in danger. You don't know this world well enough to survive in it. It's a scary place."

"Anton believes I attacked him."

Adam shook his head. "That's his ego talking. He can't believe there's someone out there with a mind more powerful than his. His arrogance has landed him in hot water before."

Liana's eyes flashed. "His arrogance could have gotten him killed. And Stefan, too. I was able to sever the link with Stefan in time, but I didn't do it with Anton. He's lucky he only got a headache."

"What happened, actually? What did you do that sent him into convulsions, that knocked him unconscious?"

"Nothing. I did absolutely nothing, but that's something Anton refuses to admit."

She stood up and paced across the room and stared at a framed picture on the wall. It was a forest scene. Tall trees, blue skies, a creek running over rocks and ferns growing beside the water. Adam wondered if she actually saw it, or merely used it to hide from him.

After a moment, Liana turned and faced him. "I have barriers blocking my deepest, most ancient memories. I am ancient, Adam. I may look like a woman in her twenties, but I am very old. Much older than any of you realize, and I carry knowledge that even Anton can't process. Not without warning, without a slow and cautious approach. He burst through my barriers when I reached orgasm and dove headfirst into my mind. It was too much, too fast, and his brain couldn't handle it. Everything that happened to him was merely his mind's reaction to a complete overload of information. I didn't do a thing to Anton. He did it to himself. Then he had the utter gall to blame me for his trespass."

So that's how it was. Knowing their pack leader as well as he did, Liana's explanation made perfect sense. "Don't let Anton's error chase you away. At least give him a chance to apologize."

"And then what?" She sighed and sank down on the arm of the chair across from him. "If I stay, I will remain a pariah here. Anton is beloved by his entire pack, and for good reason. He puts them first. He loves without reservation, adores his wife and child, and has the intelligence and the skills to keep his people safe. As he reminded everyone tonight, I have failed all of you in more ways than any of us, me especially, care to count. I think this may be what the Mother had in mind when she cast me out of my world. Maybe I am meant to wander without a home, without friends. It would be a just punishment."

Adam shook his head. As much as he fought it, he couldn't help but admire Liana's acceptance of the horrible changes in her life, her willingness to admit fault. No excuses from her. None, even though he couldn't imagine the Mother punishing Liana with exile from her kind. That was tantamount to a sentence of death for Chanku.

They were pack animals. Their need for one another, for the support of the pack and all it stood for, was as necessary as breathing. Merely easing the overwhelming need for sexual release following a run was something neither man nor woman could do on their own. They'd all tried, at one time or another, to find relief through masturbation.

It wasn't enough. It was never enough. They needed the connection. The physical contact, the mental connection with their own kind. He raised his head and gazed into Liana's tired eyes—and he saw himself. The loneliness, the frustration, the sense of a life with so many important parts missing.

He was missing exactly what Liana was missing. Even

though he could never love her, he was getting past his unbearable hatred. She wasn't a bad person and she was trying really hard to fit into their mortal world.

All she needed was someone on her side. Someone who
wouldn't look at her and see the enemy, which was what
he'd seen for long enough. They needed each other, sexually if not in other ways. They didn't have to like each
other to fuck. That much he'd learned as Chanku. It was
all about gratification when you were with someone besides your mate or your friends.

At least he could offer her that much. It would solve a
problem both of them had as the only two unmated adults
among this group. It would give them the connection they
needed.

"Liana, we're both tired, and you need to sleep before
you think about going anywhere. Please, promise me
you'll wait until you've had a chance to talk to Anton. Can
you do that?"

She stared at him for so long he wasn't sure what to expect. Finally she nodded, a short, sharp jerk of her head.
"All right. I owe you that much, Adam Wolf. I will wait,
but I can't promise to stay after Anton and I speak."

"Agreed. Then I have one other proposition for you.
You and I both know there're going to be some hard feelings after what happened if you decide to stay. The others
can't help it. Anton is their leader. They'll rally around him
and protect him, which is as it should be. That doesn't
solve your problem or mine."

She frowned. "What problem is that?"

"We're both unmated. We're going to run and shift and
come back here ready to explode if we can't find physical
release. I'm not asking for a relationship with you. I don't
want one and I figure you're not interested in one with me,
but I would like to suggest a compromise."

He studied her face for any indication she knew what

he meant, but she watched him with that same open, guile-less look he'd learned to expect from her. With Liana, what you saw was pretty much what you got. No sub-terfuge, no secrets. She wore her emotions openly, as inno-cent, as transparent, as a child.

He knew she was more. So much more, but he was afraid to find out exactly what the woman was like who existed behind that artless façade. "I would like to suggest we come together as sexual partners. Physical gratifica-tion, minimal emotional contact. No more, no less. I'm not asking for a commitment, for any deep emotional rela-tionship. For one thing, I'm not ready for one and I doubt you are, either, but I've avoided shifting because of the arousal that follows. I miss running with the pack. Miss the hunt and the joy of spending time with my feral side. How do you feel about it?"

Her smile changed everything. Adam stood up, sud-denly feeling awkward and unsure. She stood as well and stopped him with her fingers against his forearm.

He glanced at the spot where they connected, aware of the heat, the sense of intimacy between them. Could he handle this? He raised his head and gazed into her clear gray-green eyes.

They sparkled now, filled with the light that had been missing just a short time ago. "Good, Adam. I feel good about it. I will welcome you to my bed whenever the need is there, as long as you will accept me when I have need of you."

He covered her fingers with his hand and wondered if he should kiss her to seal their bargain. She solved the problem by rising up on her toes and placing a very soft, chaste kiss on his lips. "Go, now," she said. "This has been a very long, very emotional day. We both need sleep."

He nodded and stepped away. Then he turned and left the room without looking back. His heart pounded in his chest and he had to remind himself this was a business proposition only. He needed sexual release and so did she. That was all.

"You stupid bastard." He muttered the phrase like a mantra as he took the steps to his room. That was the only way to describe an idiot who'd make a bargain like theirs.

He might as well have made a deal with the devil.

Stupid, stupid bastard.

Chapter 10

It took every bit of courage she could muster, but Liana appeared in the dining room for breakfast at her usual time. She'd chosen a sleek pair of form-fitting black jeans and a dark forest-green sweater with a wide neck that showcased her pale skin and the sharp cut of her collarbones. It fit her feminine curves like a glove, yet made her feel more powerful than womanly.

She'd never really thought of clothing as armor before her mortal life began, but she realized now she'd always chosen clothes and colors for the way they made her feel. For some reason, when she'd been a goddess she'd preferred gossamer gowns in white or pale blue, as if those styles and colors somehow added to the ethereal look she thought an immortal goddess should have.

How foolish she'd been. If she'd only realized that bright colors, dark colors, colors that caught the eye and held attention were the colors of power. Well, she'd figure all those tricks out eventually and for what it was worth, she felt powerful this morning as she poured a cup of coffee to soothe her wonderful new addiction to the drink. She added cream and sugar and then she filled a bowl with cereal and fruit.

Mei, Oliver, and Logan were here. They each greeted

her, but she sensed a wariness that hadn't existed before. It literally made her heart hurt, to think she would be so quickly shunned by people she'd thought were her friends.

Friends who'd shared her bed, or invited her into theirs. Her packmates.

Adam wasn't here, but it was early yet. Maybe he'd already come and gone—it was hard to say, but neither were Anton or Stefan or their families. She took a seat away from the big table, at one of the smaller chairs near the window, sipped her coffee and watched her cereal turn to soggy mush in the bowl.

"Good morning, Liana."

She almost jerked her hand and spilled her coffee. Almost, but she'd sensed Anton bare seconds before he spoke. She turned and smiled at him, but she was brittle inside. His shields were in place, strong barriers to his thoughts and feelings. It took every bit of her control to keep her hands from shaking.

"Good morning, Anton." She did her best to put warmth into her smile. "Are you feeling better this morning?"

He grabbed a chair, pulled it close and sat beside her. "I am. A bit of a headache, but in retrospect, I imagine it's well deserved." He shook his head and, if it were at all possible for a man with an ego like his, looked sheepish. "You didn't do a thing to me last night, did you? It was all my doing."

Liana shrugged. "I'm sorry, but yes. It was."

Again he shook his head. "No. I'm the one who's sorry." Sighing, he looked away. "What I did was wrong. Keisha and I spoke last—" He chuckled and smiled at her. "Let me rephrase that, Keisha spoke last night, and I listened. As usual, she was correct. I had no right to force my way into your thoughts. No right at all, especially since I'd not even attempted to ask you, first, for access. I should have done that. If you'd denied me, I might have taken the chance, but a sneak attack during sex, especially one I'd actually planned in advance, was a pretty cowardly thing to do. Will you forgive me?"

She hadn't expected an apology. Not really, and especially not one as gracious as this. "I will," she said. Then she focused on him, let him feel the strength that still simmered beneath her mortal soul. "But only if you promise me never to try that again. Anton, I do not want to be the instrument of your death."

He nodded, frowning. "Will you at least tell me what happened? I remember nothing beyond pain and then darkness."

She took his hand in hers and ran her thumbs across the back, tracing the veins that pulsed with life. "I am mortal now, but I carry an immortal's burden of ancient knowledge. It's not all accessible, even to me, but it's there, a part of my past, carved into my memories, I imagine, for the rest of my mortal existence. What you tried to access was more than your mind could accept. So much knowledge could have killed you, and Stefan as well, since he was part of our linked consciousness. I severed his link to protect him. I apologize for not severing yours as well, but I was angry."

"Angry enough to kill me?"

She sensed no censure in his words. No, he was curious. Forever curious. Liana shook her head and stared at her hands still holding his. "I don't think so. At first I was more frightened than angry. I thought it was a terrible accident, that I'd dropped my barriers by mistake and flooded both of you with too much. Then I realized you had consciously breached my barriers. I was furious, but had to take into consideration you were ignorant of my inherent mental strength. So no, I did not want to kill you, though I will admit I wanted you to suffer."

She took her hands away from his and raised her head.

He truly was a beautiful man, with his long, dark hair pulled back from his face and tied in a neat queue at his neck, his amber eyes glistening with intelligence and wry humor, and the deep, dark slashes that might have been dimples in a lesser man. They bracketed his mouth, adding strength and character to an already powerful appearance.

She realized, though, it wasn't the physical perfection that made him beautiful. It was his intelligence, his remarkable wit, his ability to see his mistakes and learn from them—and it was the love he gave without reservation to his mate, his daughter . . . his pack.

And she knew, in spite of everything, he still saw Liana as one of his pack.

He chuckled and his barriers faded away, leaving his every thought, every emotion, open to her. *For what it's worth,* he said, humor evident even in his silent mental speech, *I did suffer. I still do. My mate is still furious with me. Stefan now sees your side and is angry I included him in my unwelcome intrusion into your private memories. I honestly wasn't certain of your forgiveness.*

She smiled. Almost laughed. "Well, that's only fair, you know, since I wasn't certain of yours. I am sorry, Anton. I know you didn't realize what you were going to find, but you had no right to steal my thoughts." She shook her finger, as if chastising a child. "It was theft, tantamount to rape, you know. Or would have been, if not for your failure to take anything."

He at least had the decency to look sheepish. "I know. I was thinking of the pack, of our safety, but I neglected to think of you." He tilted his head and looked at her, eyes twinkling. "I also neglected to think of the consequences. I guess I have you to thank for the not so subtle reminder."

She dipped her chin in silent acknowledgment, but her heart felt lighter. It was much easier to smile when it was an honest expression of your mood.

Adam stepped into the dining room. She sensed his unease almost immediately. Without thinking, Liana stood and went to him, drawn by the concern in his eyes, the worry that seemed to surround him.

"Adam? Is something wrong?"

He squeezed her hand and nodded. Then, still holding her hand, he turned toward the long dining table, where most of the pack now sat with breakfast or coffee in front of them. "Listen up, guys. I've been on the phone with the incident commander at the forest service office in Kalispell. That fire that's been burning north of us has moved this way. It's currently just outside Glacier National Park. It's still a few miles from us, but with the north winds picking up, we could get spot fires around here from blowing embers. The combination of drought and unusually warm weather has everything dry as tinder, and with so many fires burning around the state, they're short handed on both men and equipment."

Anton refilled his coffee and leaned against the sideboard. "Do they want us to evacuate?"

Adam shook his head. "Not yet, though he did suggest we think about getting ready to leave in a hurry if we have to. I turned on the outside sprinklers to get the meadow good and wet, to stall the flames if need be, just in case."

Keisha stood in the doorway with Lily on her hip. "I hate to mention this, but there is no such thing as 'leaving in a hurry' with toddlers. Anton? How do you feel about Xandi and me getting a room in town for the next few days?"

He walked across to Keisha and took Lily from her mother's arms. "I would feel much better if you were safely away from here, if you want to know the truth."

Stefan came into the room with Alex on his shoulders. "I agree. In fact, I just booked rooms in that B&B you had your eye on, Keisha. Actually, I reserved the entire place in case we all need to hide out for the duration. Xandi's already packing and Mei and Jazzy said they're going into town, too."

His gaze settled on Liana and he smiled. "Good morning. I take it you already know Anton and I figured out we were totally in the wrong last night. I'm sorry, Liana. My lack of faith in you was unfair. I should never have blamed you. I need to learn to trust my instincts."

"Instead of mine, you mean?" Anton laughed. "Liana, do you want to go into town with the rest of the women? It would give you a chance to do some shopping, stock up on your own clothing instead of stuff borrowed from the others."

It really was her choice. No one was forcing her to do anything she didn't want to, which made it easy to shake her head. "No, but thank you. I think I'd rather stay here, in case my healing skills are needed." She gazed out at the dry forest and thought of all the creatures that couldn't just pack up and move into town. "There are so many wild things in danger when a fire burns their forest."

Anton shrugged. "Like I said, your choice."

"I'm going to worry about you." Keisha stroked Anton's arm and her dark amber eyes sparkled with unshed tears. "The wind has definitely picked up."

"Go pack." Anton leaned over and kissed her. "We'll be fine, and if the fire does come this far, even if the house burns, we always have the caves to escape the flames. There's enough food and fresh water down below to keep all of us safe and well fed for a lot longer than we would need for shelter from the fire."

"Should we stay, then?" Keisha seemed to hover, as if the decision was more than she wanted to make.

"Absolutely not. Think of it as a vacation." He gave her a wry grin. "You were ready to ship me off the planet last night, as I recall." He handed Lily back to her mother and kissed his daughter's nose. "Maybe Mommy will appreciate me more after a few days away. What do you think, sweetie?"

Lily giggled and grabbed his ears. Keisha snorted. "After the stupid stunt you pulled with Liana, you deserved what you got and then some." She turned toward Liana. "I'm sorry I was so sharp with you last night. You didn't deserve my anger." She nodded in Anton's direction. "He did."

"And I got it," he mumbled.

Just then Logan walked into the room. "Anton? If you don't mind, I'm going to jump ship and head out with the women and children."

"What is this? Every man for himself?"

"Anything but." Logan gestured with the portable phone in his hand. "I've been on the phone with the regional med center. They're short handed at the firefighters' staging camp. I volunteered to set up a first aid station there and do triage in case they have any serious injuries. Since you've got Adam and Liana here for any medical problems you might run into, I figured my skills would be better put to use there."

Liana touched his shoulder. "Do you feel strong enough?"

"I do. Between you and Adam, all my parts are working fine. No pain. That's the only reason I'm comfortable leaving these guys. They'll be in good hands with the two of you."

"Thank you. I appreciate your confidence." Liana stepped back as Mei and Jazzy cleared the dishes away and Oliver wrapped up the leftovers from breakfast. Laughing and talking, the pack split up, with everyone heading off to either pack or help load the cars. Liana remained behind with Adam. He gave her a tentative smile. "I take it you're serious about not leaving?"

She nodded her head. "You're right. I'm staying. Anton was very gracious in his apology."

"Good. Are you still interested in . . ." He took a deep breath and merely shrugged.

She thought his nervousness was kind of cute. "I am, Adam." She laughed, teasing him. "No-strings sex."

He nodded, but he didn't smile. "I promised to follow the women into town with the cribs and stuff for the babies loaded in Stefan's truck. Logan's going straight to the staging camp, so he'll be headed in the opposite direction from the B&B. Will you be all right?"

"Of course. Why wouldn't I be?"

Shaking his head, Adam laughed. "I have no idea. I think it's just my nature to worry."

It seemed deathly quiet with the women and children gone, as if the life and laughter had been sucked out of the place. Even Oliver had decided to go along at the last minute, convinced the women needed at least one man to stay in town and watch over them.

Adam and the others had teased him about wanting to be the only cock in the henhouse. He'd laughed, but he hadn't denied it, and he'd definitely been strutting when he headed to the car.

Alone in the house for the first time since she'd become mortal, Liana cleaned up the dishes in the kitchen, washing them by hand since she'd never quite figured out how the dishwasher worked. If she looked out the window over the sink, she could see the big irrigation sprinklers that usually watered the front meadow spraying water now on the trees at the north side of the house. Stefan had explained earlier how he planned to set them up to dampen the forest upwind of the house and cottage.

Now Stefan was up on the roof, setting out sprinklers to soak the slate shingles. Stone wouldn't burn, but wetting everything down made sense. He'd already set a couple on the cottage roof.

There were a couple of large generators ready in case

the power lines burned, though most of their power came from solar panels built discreetly into the roof. Even so, no one wanted to take a chance of losing power and the ability to pump water from any of the large wells supplying the house and irrigation.

Anton was working along the north side of the main house, cutting back some of the shrubs that grew too close, using the manual hedge clippers. He'd explained to Liana that it was too dry for the gas powered equipment. He'd removed his shirt in deference to the unusual heat, and wore faded jeans and heavy work boots. From what she'd observed, this was not his usual style, but she'd found any number of excuses to watch him.

Anton epitomized lean strength with his broad shoulders and long, ropey muscles rippling down his back and over his long arms. With faded jeans riding low on his hips and perspiration dotting the dark hair on his chest he looked much more approachable than she normally found him.

Even sexier like this than last night, entirely naked and aroused. Curious, she thought, what sights could stir desire.

Adam wouldn't be back for a couple of hours. Even so, Liana realized she was glancing out at the driveway at least every other minute, as if she could bring him home by force of will alone. She hadn't planned to miss him like this. Her feelings confused her, but so did a lot of things about life as a mortal.

Like her sudden interest in Anton Cheval in faded jeans.

By the time Adam made it back from town, the northern sky was a dirty brown and the fresh scent of pine and cedar had disappeared beneath the thick odor of wood smoke. He parked Stefan's beloved Ford truck in the garage so it wouldn't end up covered in soot and ash, and went directly to the main house.

Liana met him at the front door with a cold beer in her hand.

"You must have read my mind." He took it from her and almost leaned close to give her a kiss in thanks, caught himself and took a long swallow of beer instead. Then he followed her back to the media room. Stefan had the local news on with scenes of firefighters and aircraft battling the huge blaze just a few miles to the north of them.

"Hey, Adam." Stefan moved aside and made room on the couch.

Adam sat beside him. "How's it looking?"

"Hot and dirty, but the winds have died down and they've got the burn closest to us partially contained. With any luck they'll get it under control by tomorrow or the next day. You up for a run? Anton wants to check on the north border, make sure we don't have any spot fires smoldering. Liana's coming, too, but I wasn't sure if you were interested after moving all the kid paraphernalia."

"There's no such thing as traveling light with a toddler, is there? Sure. I'll go." He upended his beer and drank it down.

Stefan stood up and turned off the television. "It certainly explains why our mates chose to leave for town now instead of waiting until there's fire coming over the hill."

Liana looked up at Stefan and smiled. "I think they were looking forward to the vacation. And, the entertainment."

Stefan frowned. "Entertainment? What entertainment?"

Liana glanced at Adam and mentally shared a secret Mei had given her. Adam almost snorted the last swallows of his beer. "It appears Mei has taken a lot of her toys, and Oliver."

Chuckling, Stefan followed them out of the room. "Well, crap. Four dominant alpha bitches, a shitload of battery operated toys and restraints, and one very willing submissive. I hope they remember they've got babies along."

Liana grabbed Adam's arm and whispered loudly in his ear. "Doesn't he realize the B&B he chose offers baby-sitting?"

"No wonder Xandi jumped at the chance to stay there." Grumbling now, Stefan headed out to the back deck with Liana and Adam right behind. Adam felt almost light-headed, sharing laughter and a joke with Liana. She seemed to understand him, his humor, even his basic needs. As if they were a couple.

But they weren't. They couldn't be. So why did he have to remind himself how much he didn't want her?

They paused on a barren ridge above the tree line. It was the farthest Liana had ever run as a wolf, yet she still felt energized, as if she could keep going forever. The sun was setting in a haze of orange and burgundy behind the mountains west of Kalispell, and in spite of the smoke in the air, the lights of the city were still visible from this elevation.

Stefan said they might have been able to see Whitefish to the north if they'd climbed higher and the air was clear, but the smoke was too thick and it was time to head back.

At least they hadn't found any sign of fire along the northern boundary of the property, but as they turned to head down the mountain, a loud screech cut through the air. Liana turned immediately to Adam. *What was that?*

He raised his muzzle and sniffed the air. *Our spirit guide, Igmutaka. I think he's concerned about the fires.*

She knew of the big cougar that roamed these hills. He'd once been the spirit guide to Miguel Fuentes's Sioux grandfather. Liana wanted to meet him. He was not Chanku, but he had strong magic. He'd managed to do things she thought even the Mother hadn't expected. Finding corporeal form as a cougar was one of those things—it should have been impossible, yet now he wandered freely, hunted and roamed as a living, mortal cougar—but with the immortal soul of a spirit guide.

Look. Adam nudged Liana, directing her gaze to the tree line below. A large cougar sniffed the ground, raised its head and stared directly at the small pack of wolves on the ridge.

He made a loud chuffing noise, halfway between a growl and a cry. Then he carefully picked his way over loose scree as he climbed the rocky ground toward their group.

None of them moved, though Liana realized the three males had positioned themselves to protect her. From the cougar? She felt no threat from Igmutaka. She stepped forward as he approached and walked toward him. When she was only a couple of feet from the big cat, she dipped her head and lowered her tail, showing him she was no threat.

He sniffed her muzzle, her shoulder, the edge of her flattened ear, and returned to her face, watching her with crystal-green eyes alive with intelligence and understanding.

Liana sensed the others behind her and knew they were prepared to attack should she need help. Having three large males as her personal protectors was a new experience, one she thought she could grow used to.

If she needed their protection. With Igmutaka, she felt as if she were in the presence of a most wonderful and benevolent power.

Greetings, she said. *I have longed to meet the powerful Igmutaka, and to thank him for watching over my Chanku.*

The cat stared at her, obviously curious. *You were their goddess. Why do you walk among them as a mortal?*

Because I failed in my duties. Eve, who was this one's mate—she nodded toward Adam—*is now their goddess. I am mortal, but I owe you my thanks for your kindness when they needed you. I owe you much.*

The cat raised his head and stared first at Liana, silently acknowledging her thanks, and then at the three males, almost as if he assessed their worth. Then without another word, he turned and disappeared, silent as a ghost into the dusky shadows.

Liana felt almost buoyant on the long run back to the house. As if her feet flew and her heart soared. She'd watched Igmutaka from afar, had reveled in his power, his ancient wisdom. Now he, like she, walked the earth as a mortal.

And she had met him as an equal, had been able to thank him. She felt as if she'd knelt at the feet of a power greater than hers, and that thought made her smile as they drew close to the house. He was a cougar. A beautiful predator roaming the mountains, yet inside he was still Igmutaka.

Just as she was a wolf, another predator with the ability to hunt, to kill, to run with her pack. Yet inside, she was still Liana. Not a goddess, but a woman in her prime.

It wasn't just good. It was wonderful. More than she had ever dreamed over those long, long years in her other life. She'd accepted her role as goddess. She rejoiced in her role as a woman. Head high, ears forward and her tail like a great plume waving behind, she led the pack down from the mountain.

Stefan and Anton headed for their suite of rooms at the opposite end of the house as soon as they returned, leaving Liana and Adam alone on the deck, staring awkwardly at one another.

At least it felt awkward to Adam. Since coming to this place, since discovering his heritage as a Chanku shapeshifter, he'd never felt uncomfortable with nudity, with the powerful sense of arousal and the sexual drive that seemed to take on a life of its own after a shift.

When Eve was alive, they'd generally chosen each other for sex after a run, but sometimes he'd gone with one or more of the guys or a couple of the other women—it had never mattered. What mattered was the burning drumbeat of arousal, the lust that always simmered in his veins, pounding out a desperate cadence calling for release, for pure, unadulterated fucking that would at least take the edge off that almost painful sexual need.

Now, though, he stood in front of Liana and couldn't look at her. The need was there, the pounding arousal—but so were the questions.

She'd called it "no-strings sex."

Did she really mean that, or did she see him as a potential mate? He couldn't look at her that way. Not as a mate, not as a replacement for Eve. He still missed his mate with every breath he took, with each beat of his heart. This woman was the reason Eve was gone. There was no way in hell Liana was going to step into Eve's place in his life. He'd rather leave that spot empty for all time, than give it to her.

But he knew what her body looked like, all silken pale skin and flowing blond hair, and his body didn't care what his brain wanted. He couldn't help but be attracted. She was slight of build and so very feminine, though he admired her strength. Her amazing power was deceptive . . . so very deceptive, and at the same time, alluring.

Was it the novelty, the idea of sex with a woman who had been immortal? Or was it more?

He didn't want more. Didn't want the turmoil that came from even thinking along those lines. But right now he knew one thing for sure—he wanted Liana.

She watched him out of the corner of her eye, not ready to actually take him to her room or follow him to his, but Liana couldn't have not looked at Adam Wolf if she'd tried.

She felt guilt every time she was with him—guilt that she'd caused him so much pain, guilt that she could never fill the place of the one he'd lost because of her.

But she could ease the burn before it consumed them both, and it looked like she'd have to be the one to take the first step. She'd always seen Adam as a sexually aggressive lover, quick to instigate liaisons with other members of the pack. He was the one who left the women sighing and satisfied, the one so quick to lead other men into sexual trysts whether they were ready for a same sex pairing or not.

And, whether they were ready or not, Adam always had them coming back for more. He left them satisfied for the moment—then afterward, craving his touch, his sexual mastery, his ability to give pleasure in all ways possible.

He'd provided the goddess with sexual energy to spare.

She'd wondered before what it would be like, to be the object of his desire. Had watched from her lofty position as goddess when he'd joined with Eve, when he'd taken Oliver, when he'd made even the arrogant Anton Cheval beg for more. The first night he'd taken Logan Pierce had left her bursting with power.

She had watched and wondered, but she'd never expected it would be like this. Had never pictured herself standing beside him, her body burning, her thoughts so indecisive.

She stretched out her hand and took his. Raised her head and looked into his dark eyes. There was fire in their depths, amber fire that seemed to burn into her soul and find all her faults, all her weaknesses.

"I can't be Eve," she said, taking the coward's way and looking down at their clasped fingers. "I can't take the place of your mate. That's not what I want, not what I intend."

"Look at me," his voice commanded.

She raised her head and gazed into his eyes. What she saw gave her courage she hadn't expected.

"I hated you in the beginning. Despised you for taking the most important person in my life away from me. I don't love you, Liana. I can't imagine ever loving you, but I've learned to respect and admire who you are, what you're trying to become."

He shook his head slowly, smiling sadly. "Shit happens. Losing Eve was . . ." He shrugged, obviously at a loss for words. "I've never hesitated going after sex. Never had to look very hard for a partner, never felt uncomfortable or awkward. This is awkward because there will be strings with this no-strings sex. I can't be bound by them or by you."

"Good." She jerked her head in a short, sharp nod of agreement. "We need to get that straight and out in the open. I have no desire to take Eve's place in your life, no desire to step into her role as your mate. We both need the sexual release, and one day, hopefully before too long, you'll find a woman when you're ready for that kind of commitment again. It won't be with me."

She turned away and gazed at the dark forest. "It's not an option, anyway. I can never bond with any man."

He tugged her fingers and she looked at him once more. "Why not? What if the perfect mate comes to you? What if you fall in love?"

She shrugged. "Any man who tried to bond with me would die. I'm like the black widow who kills her mate. The mental link, as brief as it was with Anton, a man of unbelievable mental power, almost killed him. Imagine what would happen were I to consciously open my thoughts to another, share every intimate secret I have from the beginnings of time? I'm afraid that sex without strings is all I'm good for."

She tugged his hand and chose the direction to his small room over the garage. Going there left her the option of leaving when she was ready. No strings attached.

Without another word, Adam fell into step beside her and the two of them headed toward his room.

Chapter 11

Adam flipped on the one overhead light. At least he'd changed the sheets earlier and picked his dirty clothes up off the floor. His room was spotless and almost Spartan compared to hers. Adam tried to see it through Liana's eyes and failed. It was just a room. Four square walls with windows all around and a tiny bathroom in one corner.

It served his needs, but what about hers? How could he possibly guess what Liana was thinking? Most of the time he thought of her as a woman—just a woman, and nothing more. Not as the woman who had let his mate die. But her admission tonight, that she could never bond with a mate, had thrown him badly.

She'd been a goddess for time out of memory, a woman of amazing powers with memories more ancient than recorded history, and yet she was incapable of ever experiencing true love, complete love, the kind that only happened when two mates bonded.

Wasn't that the ultimate goal of every Chanku, to find that perfect mate, the one whose mind could forge a link with yours that lasted until death? One who would be a constant companion, no matter how far apart you were?

He'd not truly appreciated that link until his with Eve

was severed. It still felt as if he'd lost a limb, as if a major part of his body was forever missing.

Liana would never know that connection, that intimate union with another. All she would know was sex, pure, naked lust without true passion, without love. Sex devoid of the intimate link of a partner's thoughts, without the sharing that was as necessary to a bonded pair as breathing.

Liana turned to him. Her eyes glittered in the reflected light. She'd thrown on one of those colorful things the women all liked to wear after a run—a sarong. A bright splash of color, either wrapped around their bodies and tied over their breasts or, as Liana had done with hers, wrapped and tied over one shoulder.

She'd chosen a pale peach that did amazing things to her fair skin, and with her hair flowing loose to her hips and the fabric shimmering over her slim body, she looked so young, more like a teenager, than a woman older than recorded history.

More like an innocent kid, not the first woman he'd been with since losing Eve.

"Adam?" She stood directly in front of him and pressed her palm to his cheek. "Are you okay?"

He blinked. "I am, Liana. I was . . ." He shook his head. He didn't want to go there. Not now. Eve was gone and his body thrummed with need. He'd been hard since they'd returned tonight. In fact, he'd almost gone with Anton and Stefan, if not for his promise to Liana. Even so, his need was so great, his desire such a powerful force thrumming in his veins he was afraid of hurting her if he were to set the beast free.

He didn't want to hurt her. No matter how angry he'd been, he'd never wanted to cause her pain, but with his lust growing by the second, he knew he needed to find some semblance of control before he exploded.

She didn't seem to appreciate the risk. Instead she slipped her fingers inside the waistband of his sweats and swept them to his knees in one, quick shove of her hands.

"What the hell?"

"You're taking too long. I want you now." She smiled when she said it, but there was no arguing with her when she slipped to her knees in front of him, still wrapped in that shimmering length of silk.

He closed his eyes and locked his knees, prepared for the practiced warmth of her mouth around his swollen cock, but instead he felt the soft tickle of her breath, the tentative stroke of her fingertips. Innocent touches, as if she'd never explored a man before, though he knew much better. She'd been with so many men. Thousands of men.

He opened his eyes and looked down at her, at the top of her head as she bent to study his penis, perusing that familiar part of him as if she'd never seen a naked man before in her life. Her hair had fallen into a natural part down the center, and the long strands brushed the floor when she tilted her head. He was reaching for her hair, preparing to run his fingers through the shining strands when, without any hint of what she intended, she ran her tongue along the side of his shaft.

His entire body jerked with the shock of contact, the amazing sensation. Such a simple touch with the tip of her tongue, yet she left a line of fire from his glans to his groin, adding fuel to the flames when she cupped his sac in her hand.

The innocent simplicity of her touch, the coolness of her smooth, dry palm cradling the conflagration building between his legs almost had him shooting his load.

He groaned and backed away, laughing, turning his unexpected reaction into a joke. "Shit. I'm in worse shape than I thought. You're going to take me over the top before I have a chance to show you what a great lover I am. It'll ruin my reputation."

She smiled up at him. "And you have a problem with that? Your reputation is safe with me. I'm thinking, maybe I should ease some of the desire you feel. Then you can last longer the next time."

He swallowed. "That works." Cleared his throat. "So. What are you planning? How do you intend to ease all that desire?"

"Like this." Her eyes twinkled and she wrapped her lips around the tip of his cock, teasing the slit with her tongue, stroking his balls with her small hands. Then, once again she surprised him—she swallowed him, the whole damned fat length of him, all the way to the root. Her throat muscles worked over his shaft, the tip of her tongue teased the underside. Then she ran her fingernails over his wrinkled sac and both hands cupped his balls and squeezed.

He didn't even have time to think about how good it felt. One minute he was struggling for control, the next he was fighting to remain upright as his hips jerked and his seed boiled up out of his balls to his cock, and shot down her throat. No finesse. Not a bit. He didn't mean to thrust against her mouth but instinct and nature took over and he held her head in his palms and shoved harder than he should have, forcing himself even deeper.

She merely hummed around his length and swallowed every drop of his seed. He felt the spasming convulsions of her throat while she milked him and practically whimpered when she slowly slipped him free of her mouth and throat, over her teeth and lips, licking and sucking the entire way.

He'd never experienced anything like it in his life. His knees felt like rubber and he barely managed the few steps to the bed before he fell back on it with his pants hanging around his ankles. He was totally flaccid, a rarity for him, especially after a run, but what she did . . .

"I take it you like that, eh?" Liana stood up and walked

over to the bed, knelt again and pulled his sweats off over his feet. She was still chastely wrapped in the peach sarong, as untouched and pure looking as a young virgin.

Only he knew better. So did his body. She leaned forward and once again wrapped her lips around his shaft. Within seconds she'd brought him back to life with tongue and teeth and inquisitive fingers. Then she stood up and slowly untied the knot at her shoulder. "My turn," she said.

The silk whispered over her hips and fell to the floor, and Adam's cock rose up hard and proud, ready for whatever Liana wanted.

Liana crawled up over his body, intending to impale herself on that perfectly beautiful cock, but Adam had other ideas. He caught her arms and pulled her forward until she straddled his face, blushing from head to toe.

She'd not expected this, an act as intimate as oral sex. Not from a man who disliked so much about her. She tried to rise up, away from his mouth, but he held her in place, with a gentle but firm grip on both her arms.

She wasn't going anywhere. He blew a hot little puff of air against her nether lips and all her muscles down there contracted. She was already wet, but knowing his mouth was so close had her growing wetter by the second. He released her arms and grabbed her thighs, held his fingers spread along the crease between thigh and groin. She felt the callused pads of his thumbs parting her damp lips, sliding the tiny hood back from her clitoris. He touched her so gently, yet each brush of his thumbs against that bundle of nerves made her legs jerk and her muscles clench.

His breath grew hotter. She knew his mouth was close, so close, and yet he wasn't touching her. All her internal muscles rippled in greedy anticipation. Then she felt it. The tiniest flick of his tongue over her bud. She would have jerked away, but he held her firmly in place and his fingers dug into her thighs.

He did it again, barely touching her with the tip of his tongue, and again, and then again, the gentlest of licks, like a tiny kiss upon her bud. He brought her down lower, closer to his mouth, and licked the length of her sex with the flat of his tongue, sweeping up her cream like a cat at his bowl. He suckled one of her labia into his mouth, ran his tongue along the sensitive edge and then did the same to the other side.

She whimpered and tried to press closer, but he held her in place, teasing and licking, sucking and even nibbling her swollen lips with the sharp edges of his teeth. She couldn't control the way her hips seemed to move of their own accord, but he held her in his big hands and gently pushed the prepuce back from her clitoris again. Using his tongue and lips, he nursed her hard little bud. At the same time, he slipped both his thumbs deep inside her vagina.

Orgasm slammed into her. No warning, no gentle build-up to pleasure. Flashes of lightning shocked her into a scream, Adam's thumbs filled her vagina, his lips drew on her clit, suckling like a babe at the breast.

Whimpering, sobbing with the strength of her release, she curled over him, knees clamped against his face, body shaking while he gently licked and stroked her quivering sex.

She was still trembling with the aftershocks of orgasm when he lifted her away from him and stood up beside the bed. He draped her body over the edge with her feet hanging almost to the floor, stood between her legs and entered her from behind.

He was big and thick and her vagina was still all rippling, clenching muscle. She bucked her hips, instinctively fighting him off, but he held her, filled her, stretching and burning his way deep inside her channel.

Reason intruded, awareness of his size, his strength, his care with her even as he thrust against her cervix. She felt the broad head of his cock, the thick length of his shaft filling her. His sac tickled her clit, the heavy weight of his testicles pressing against her folds as he paused long enough for her to adjust to his size.

She opened her thoughts and searched for him, careful to keep the barriers to her deeper memories intact, but he was blocked to her. She had no idea how he felt, what he thought, what he wanted.

Nothing beyond the physical sensations of two bodies fucking, his sex melded to hers, his big hands grasping her waist, the curl of pubic hair brushing her ass, the heat of their bodies—and the friction.

Friction that morphed from pain to pleasure as her body slowly relaxed and adjusted to his, as her tight channel stretched and accommodated his size.

Instead of withdrawing, he pressed even deeper, taking her beyond pleasure into pain for the briefest of moments, then he rolled his hips and withdrew before thrusting hard and deep once more. He lifted her, holding her hips until her toes dangled above the floor and she reached blindly for the bedding, tangling her fingers in the bedspread to anchor herself. Holding on, she pressed her breasts into the mattress and her face against the spread. She felt helpless with only her upper body resting on the bed while he drove in and out of her tight sheath. Helpless and dominated—and more turned-on than she'd ever been in her long life.

Sound filled Liana's senses—the wet slap of flesh on flesh, the harsh burst of his breathing and hers, the thunder of two hearts beating and the more mundane squeak and creak of the bed frame.

Liana whimpered, awash in the myriad sensations—in the heat of his body, the thrust of his hard cock, the thick flood of her cream easing his way. His fingers dug into her hips and waist, and she knew she'd have bruises. Dark badges of his taking, marks that would remind her what they'd shared.

Sex without strings. Sex without ties of any kind.

Amazing sex, but empty, emotionless sex. There was no connection beyond the link of their bodies. No sense of Adam, of his goodness, his nature, his thoughts. Nothing to take this beyond an amazing exercise in mutual masturbation. His body fucked hers. Her body responded. Her heart beat to pump blood, to keep her alive, but not to connect. Her mind searched but came up empty. The link, the amazing mental joining of one to another wasn't part of the deal.

She could do this. She had to. She could share her body, but she wanted to share her soul. Needed that much from him, that connection that said she mattered, that she was more than a receptacle for his seed, more than a tight, dark, wet hole for his thrusting cock.

He knew all the right moves, all the perfect places to touch, to taste, to stroke and rub. He knew exactly how to raise her arousal to a perfect pitch, to build desire. He was a master at fucking, yet even when she'd been with Anton and Stefan, two men who wanted her only for pleasure and then, for Anton at least, for what he could take from her mind, she'd made love.

Emotional, fulfilling, and deeply satisfying love, if only for that brief time. They'd connected, the three of them. Not merely their bodies but their minds.

There was no connection with Adam. No passion. It was all about easing a need, and he did it very well. She'd tried to watch his face, to see what emotions flitted across his weathered features, but he'd managed to hide himself from her. He'd buried his face between her legs. Now he took her from behind. Only when she'd swallowed him, when she'd surprised him with her mouth on his beautiful erection, had she seen emotion in his expression.

Now, whatever emotions he felt were hidden. Trapped behind the mental walls he'd built to keep her out.

When Liana's climax slammed into her, when her body once more flew over the edge, replete and sexually undone, she collapsed forward onto the rumpled bedding. Adam shouted and thrust forward, short, sharp strokes as he emptied himself inside her. She felt the burst of his seed, the pressure of his release and then the heavy weight of his chest as he slumped over her back.

Still connected, yet miles apart. Her sex contracted around his fat length, holding him close, milking his seed until the hot semen ran down her thighs in thick streams. Full. She was totally filled by him.

And she'd never felt emptier in her life.

It took him a few minutes to catch his breath, a minute longer to realize he was probably crushing Liana, lying over her back the way he was without supporting his weight. His body felt totally drained, but he managed to roll off of her without too much difficulty and stretched out across the bed.

His lungs burned as if he'd run a mile and his muscles trembled, but he felt . . . good. He felt more at peace than he had in a while, yet at the same time there was a sense that something was missing . . . something important.

Liana lay half on the bed with her face turned away from him. For all he knew she was sleeping. She'd climaxed hard and often. He'd made certain she was satisfied, her body sated, but he wished he knew how she felt, what she'd thought of the sex.

That's what was wrong. The link. They hadn't linked at all, hadn't shared any thoughts or sensations. Afraid, at first, he'd had his mental barriers in place. When he finally realized she wouldn't hurt him, would never let him in where he shouldn't go, he'd been so caught up in sensation he'd forgotten to lower the damn things—there'd been no mental connection at all.

Sex without strings. That's what they'd promised one another, wasn't it? Why did it make him feel so guilty, then? Because he did, as if he'd cheated her out of something important.

Maybe he'd just cheated himself. Maybe Liana didn't want or need anything else. For all he knew, she hadn't even tried. Maybe she was afraid to link after what happened with Anton. He needed to think about that, maybe talk about it with her. They could do a simple link, not anything like a bond. Maybe that would make all the moves more pleasurable.

Adam closed his eyes and willed his heart rate to slow. His respiration slowed as well. He dozed a little, lying beside Liana only half awake, unfocused and dreamy.

After a while he figured he'd better get a shower before he fell asleep. He wondered if Liana was awake yet, if she planned to leave or wanted to stay the night. He hoped she didn't want to stay. That was a complication he wasn't ready for—waking up with Liana in his bed.

Adam rolled over to see what she intended.

She'd already gone. The bed beside him was cool to his touch, her silky, peach colored sarong no longer lay on the floor. Blinking owlishly, he sat up and looked around. Checked the clock beside the bed and realized not that much time had passed, but he must have slept, because somehow she'd managed to slip out without him hearing a thing.

He'd wanted her to leave, hadn't he? So why did it bother him that she'd gone so quietly, that she'd left his bed without a word? Shaking his head, Adam stretched out and got up. He stood beside the bed for a moment.

Shaking his head, uncomfortable with the direction his thoughts led him, he headed into the shower, remembering.

There'd only been one other woman who'd left him like that. One woman who'd made love to him and rocked his world, and then she'd disappeared. He'd ended up pursuing her across the country. Catching her, finally, bringing her home, making her his mate.

Eve.

And now she was gone and Liana had taken Eve's place in his bed. And just like Eve, she'd loved him, and then she'd left him all alone.

Anton ran his fingers along Stefan's spine, tracing the familiar bumps until he reached the perfect expanse of smooth flank. He thrust his hips forward, burying his full length deep inside Stef's tight ass. Damn, after doing this for so many years, the wonder of sex with this man should have lessened by now, shouldn't it?

Instead, he felt closer each time, more deeply connected on so many levels. Their hearts beat in perfect synchronization, their level of arousal matched so beautifully that each knew where the other was on that sharp-edged climb to orgasm. Stefan teetered on the precipice, as did Anton, his muscles tense, his lips parted to draw in each short, sharp breath.

Stefan's muscles clenched around his cock and Anton picked up the pace, driving deeper, faster. He reached for Stefan's cock with his left hand and stroked the hard length, finding the same rhythm, sliding his hand back to Stefan's groin as he thrust his cock deep into his bowel, stroking to the very tip as he withdrew, before plunging deep again.

He felt the first stirrings of an orgasm he wouldn't be able to stop, the current of power roiling from spine to balls and along his shaft. His strokes sped up, short and fast now as if his body were no longer under his control, as if desire alone ruled the jackhammer thrust of his hips, the tight grasp of his fingers sliding along Stefan's thick length.

He narrowed his mental focus, blocking out all but the man who consumed his attention right now. The one man who truly knew all there was to know about Anton Cheval— and loved him anyway.

Images flooded his mind as Stefan opened his thoughts, shared the sensation of Anton's thick cock filling his ass, hard balls slapping his sensitive perineum, the brush of hair as Anton's thighs rubbed over the back of his.

Anton felt as if he floated with the connections that bound them, connections as intimate as one man's penis buried deep inside the other's ass, as simple as the touch of fingers along another's flank or the way his thumb rolled over the smooth tip of Stefan's glans on each powerful stroke. Connections and a love more powerful than either of them had ever expected—powerful and as deep and emotional as the love each of them felt for his mate, for his child.

Anton gave into sensation and set his body free. He experienced their shared orgasm as two become one, what Stefan felt, what he felt. Semen flooded Stefan inside and out—Anton's ejaculate filling his rectum, Stefan's own pulsing into the palm of Anton's hand. Wet and thick, spilling over his fingers, as warm as blood, the essence of life.

Anton used the slick semen to continue stroking Stefan, rubbing his fingers over his veined shaft, cupping Stef's sac and rolling the hard orbs inside between his thumb and fingers, slipping and squeezing over his flesh with hands coated in thick cream, all the while continuing his slow but steady rock and sway, thrust and retreat.

Stefan grew hard once again even as Anton's erection regained strength. They'd been fucking now for well over an hour. The connection hadn't dimmed. If anything, it was stronger now that Anton had blocked his mind to all but his immediate surroundings, and the pleasure was far from over.

Anton loved the earthiness of the two of them fucking until they could barely stand, muscles screaming for a break, their bodies covered in sweat, and semen, stinking of sex.

He almost laughed with the image they made. Keisha and Xandi would be running them off to shower by now, disgusted with their thorough enjoyment of the ripe smells, the sweat, and sticky ejaculate. He shared that thought with Stefan, knowing he, at least, would appreciate it.

Stefan laughed out loud. Then he groaned and glanced over his shoulder at Anton. "They really don't understand, do they?"

Anton thrust deep and held the position. "No," he said, slowly withdrawing. "They're much too civilized."

Stefan lowered his head on his folded arms and pushed back against Anton's cock. "Probably a good thing or we'd be stinky and sticky all the time."

"True." Anton continued stroking Stefan's fat length, as if the grasp of his fingers around his lover's cock were merely an afterthought. "However, I know I'll never leave your bed wishing for more . . . not that I ever leave Keisha needing more."

Stefan's laugh was muffled by the tumbled bedding. "When it's just the two of us, you generally don't leave my bed, period. The last time we were together you fell asleep with my cock in your mouth."

Anton snorted. "I didn't hear you complaining."

Stefan turned his head, glanced over his shoulder and raised one eyelid. "I couldn't. My mouth was filled with yours."

It wasn't easy to laugh out loud while climaxing. In fact, Anton decided the grunt he made was more apropos, but this one took him down, left his body limp and his muscles weak and trembling. He rolled to his side and took Stefan with him, the two of them still connected, Anton still buried deep inside.

Finally, when his breathing had returned to its near-normal rate, he slowly withdrew and Stefan rolled out of bed. Anton's damp penis lay against his thigh, totally spent. It took him a few minutes to regroup, and he lay there listening to the sound of the shower. A minute later, he got up and headed to the bathroom and stepped under the spray beside Stefan.

Another time he might have continued with more sex, but tonight, with his body momentarily sated, he merely bathed, dried off, and followed Stef back to bed. There was no need to find his own room, no need to sleep alone.

Not when he had Stefan.

Anton lay down beside him, soothed by the deep, even breathing as Stef settled into sleep. He lay quietly and let his thoughts wander over the events of the past few days. He wondered if Adam and Liana had ended up together tonight after their run. He hoped so. Hoped the two of them could learn to take comfort in one another.

Both of them, in their own way, were such wounded souls. Wounded and in need of the connection that could only come between two who shared every intimacy. He understood better than most. He'd lived alone for so long, had gone without that connection for the better part of his life.

No longer. Anton reached for Stefan, found his lover's hand resting on top of the blankets and wrapped his fingers around it. Connecting once again.

Holding lightly to Stefan's hand, Anton drifted into sleep.

Liana caught the cry for help as if the voice echoed out of her dream. Blinking, she sat up and listened with all her senses. She heard it again.

Igmutaka.

But the big cat's powerful mental voice was weak, muffled by pain. He was hurt, somewhere up near the ridge where they'd met earlier.

Hurry! Before it's too late.

Liana called to the big cat, but there was no answer. She sent out a plea for help, but Adam's mind was blocked to her. Then she tried to call Anton, but there was nothing where his mental signature should be.

Unable to ignore Igmutaka's cry for help, Liana quietly slipped out through the sliding glass door and ran to the back deck. The sprinklers still pulsed a steady beat out on the meadow and near the forest. The powerful, rhythmic rush of water was the only sound Liana heard. She shifted the moment her bare feet touched wood. A gray wolf leapt over the railing, raced across the wet meadow and hit the dark forest at a full run.

Anton awakened in darkness, aware of a subtle change, of something that brought his senses to full alert before his mind was awake enough to interpret what he perceived.

He blinked. His eyes and nose burned.

Smoke!

He struggled upright, unable to focus in the absolute darkness. Leapt out of bed and almost ripped the cord out of the wall when he jerked it to raise the window blinds. The sky just to the north of the house glowed a brilliant orange. He couldn't see actual flames, but the fire was much too close for comfort.

Close, and moving closer. Treetops bent before the wind, and it was blowing this way.

"Stefan! Wake up. The fire's coming. We need to warn the others. I'll get Adam. Check Liana's room!" Anton pulled on his jeans and grabbed his heavy work boots from beneath Stefan's bed. He laced them quickly and raced out of the bedroom toward Adam's room over the garage. The only access was across the front yard, through the sprinklers. Smoke swirled about him. Burning cinders sizzled as they hit the wet grass.

Thank the goddess they'd left sprinklers running, or the meadow might be aflame by now. He ran up the stairs and pounded on Adam's door.

Within seconds, Adam opened the door, still naked, obviously coming out of a sound sleep.

"Is Liana here?"

Adam shook his head. "No. She left hours ago." He glanced up and his eyes went wide. An orange glow reflected in their amber depths. "Holy shit. How far away is it?"

Anton looked over his shoulder. "A hell of a lot closer than it was when I first noticed it about thirty seconds ago."

A gust of cinders swirled past the open doorway. Adam stepped back into the room. "Let me grab some clothes."

Stefan raced across the lawn. "Is Liana there? She's not in her room. The slider's open to the back."

Adam snapped his jeans and began pulling on a thick pair of socks. "She wouldn't have gone for a run without telling anyone, would she?"

Anton shook his head. "I don't know. I had my barriers up tight, so I wouldn't have heard her if she'd tried to reach me. Shit. Everything was blocked." But he was searching now, scanning for any sense of her.

Nothing. Nothing at all.

"Crap." Adam shoved his tangled hair back from his face. "I've had her blocked, too. After what happened with you, at first I was afraid to link with her during sex. Then I forgot to open up."

Flames licked over the top of the forest just a few hundred yards from the house. Anton stared at the fire, then started down the stairs. The yard lights went out and everything took on the orange glow from the firelight. The sound of the sprinklers died away. "Power lines must have gone. I'm going to start the generators. We can't let the water shut down now."

"What about Liana?" Adam grabbed Anton's upper arm, stopping him on the second step.

"What about her? There's nothing we can do. We don't know where she is, where she's gone."

"Have you searched?" Adam's fingers tightened around his biceps. "Have you dropped your barriers and called her?"

Anton let out a deep breath. "Of course I have. Since the moment you told me she wasn't here. There's no answer from her. No sense of her." He glanced at Adam's hand. "Let go, Adam. I need to get that generator going if there's any hope of saving the house."

Adam released him. Stefan followed Anton down the steps and they raced toward the outbuilding that housed the auxiliary generators. Anton glanced over his shoulder as he and Stefan reached the door. Adam was no longer on the top step.

He had no idea where his packmate had gone.

Chapter 12

Liana had only come this way a couple of times before, and always with the pack, but her sense of Igmutaka was growing stronger the farther she ran along the trail. So was her awareness of his pain—extreme pain coupled with desperation and fear. She knew she was getting close to him, but she had to fight her own panic, her very real terror that he might lose consciousness and she'd never find him.

She had no idea what had happened to him, what kinds of injuries she'd have to deal with, why he was hurt.

She knew though, without a doubt, there was no one else to save him. She couldn't understand why Anton's mind had been blocked to her. Adam she understood. He wanted no part of a link with the woman who'd killed his mate, though he'd obviously enjoyed the sex. It had been his idea, after all.

Sex without a relationship. Sex for the physical release it could bring, the chance to ease the arousal that followed shifting, running, and hunting. It had seemed like a good idea at the time.

But then, after the way she'd felt when they finished, she wasn't really sure she could do that again. Sex without strings sounded great in theory, but in reality it was the most empty feeling she'd ever experienced in her life.

Even the men she'd brought to her against their will when she was still the goddess had shared enough of themselves to connect on some level when they had sex. They'd shared their sexual energy with her, their desire, their sense of arousal. How she made them feel, what they wanted her to feel.

She'd prefer to resort to her own hand or one of Mei's battery operated toys rather than experience the loneliness of sex without intimacy, the kind of mechanical sex she'd had with Adam. He was a wonderful lover, his technique was amazing and she'd had more than her share of climaxes, but that wasn't enough. Definitely not enough. Not when it left her feeling hollow inside.

The air grew thick with smoke that burned her eyes and bit into her lungs. The wind had picked up and it carried the sound of the fire, the steady yet still distant roar of flames, like a huge, deadly machine racing toward her. She couldn't help but think how stupid this was, running toward a raging forest fire. She should be headed in the opposite direction, but Igmutaka's mental link drew her onward. She had to save him. He was an ancient like her— one with a fresh chance at a mortal life.

If the panther died, would the spirit guide live on? Would he have the strength to manifest again in corporeal form? She had no idea, though she knew that if she allowed the cat to die, part of her would die with him. She'd felt it when they met, that link, that sense of parallels, as if he understood things about her no one else ever could.

For that alone, she must do everything she could.

She burst through the line of tinder-dry trees and scrambled out onto the ridge just above the forest. Wind howled at this elevation, biting and cold, yet filled with the thick stink of smoke. From this vantage point she looked down and across a valley into what could be the very depths of hell—the conflagration boiled up through the tall forest. Huge whirlwinds of flame rose above the trees, exploding across Anton's land with the speed of a racing locomotive.

Mesmerized by the sight below her, of fire spinning and dancing over the treetops, of huge trees exploding into flames from the intense heat hundreds of yards in advance of the fire's march, Liana stared for untold moments, trapped there on the ridge top by the horrible beauty of total devastation.

She thought of the animals, the bears and deer, mountain goats and elk, foxes and wolves and other creatures of the wild. How many could she save? How could anything possibly survive such a horrible fire?

Igmutaka's weak cry ripped her back to reality. There was no moonlight to guide her—nothing but the glare from the fire raging barely half a mile away. Igmutaka was somewhere below her in the forest beneath the ridge, closer to the flames. She slipped away from her vantage point and headed down, winding through dry brush and tall trees—directly into the mouth of the fire. Senses wide open to any contact, she followed his mental voice. With her heightened Chanku senses she finally found him.

Found him and realized she needed help, and needed it fast.

The big cat was trapped beneath a limb that had broken off a huge cedar tree. She couldn't tell how serious his injuries were, but she knew she couldn't move him by herself. He was big, well over a hundred and fifty pounds. The branch was even bigger. How in the hell was she going to lift it on her own?

Liana shifted and knelt beside him. He raised his head and looked at her through eyes glazed with pain, but she saw recognition and, surprisingly, no sign of fear. Was he resigned to his death, or did he trust her to save him?

"Let me look, my friend."

The cat blinked and lay his head down on the rocky ground. She ran her hand over his shoulder, let herself flow into him, into his muscles and bones, his heart and lungs, along his spine. What she found wasn't promising. The branch lay across his hips. She thought there might be some damage to his spine and rear legs, internal bleeding, possible paralysis.

The fire was coming closer. The wind howled around them, blowing the flames before it. Down here, deep in the forest, she had no idea how far away the fire burned, but already embers were falling around them and the smoke was getting thicker.

Panic lent strength to her cry for help. *Adam? Adam, where are you? Please don't be blocking me!*

Liana? Where the fuck are you?!

Praise to the goddess! *Adam! Just below the ridge where we saw Igmutaka. He's hurt, trapped by a big branch. I can't move it. I can't get him free.*

You need to leave. Now. The fire will overrun that area before I can get to you.

I can't leave him, Adam. I won't. She glanced to the north. The glow in the sky was brighter, the sound of the fire gaining power. Adam was right. It could be here in seconds. The wind swirled around her, lifted her hair, blew soot into her eyes.

She ran her fingers through Igmutaka's tawny fur and thought of the life the big cat had lived. Like her, he'd existed for eons. In the beginning he'd been a wild puma, a creature of the forest, somehow tapped by the Mother to become a spirit guide for generations of Lakota Sioux.

When Mik Fuentes, a Chanku shapeshifter, had called on his grandfather's spirit guide to help Mei, Igmutaka had answered the call. He'd helped Mei, whose true nature was a snow leopard instead of a wolf, bond with the man she loved, a Chanku wolf.

Igmutaka had helped Oliver and Mei, and they in turn

had hosted his spirit until he'd found enough strength to manifest, once again, as a free and wild puma, a beautiful mountain lion who'd chosen to stay close, to guard the shapeshifters he had come to know and respect.

As goddess, Liana had watched it all unfold. Had watched and marveled at the mysteries of this amazing creature. She felt as if she knew him. She couldn't let him die—not like this, trapped and helpless with a raging forest fire burning everything in its path.

She'd not heard another word from Adam. She hoped he'd turned back. She didn't want him to die because of her, but she couldn't leave Igmutaka.

And she wasn't about to give up. Facing death without a fight was a coward's way out.

"If I can lift the branch, even a little, can you drag yourself forward?"

Igmutaka buried his front claws in the ground and tensed his shoulders. Liana wrapped her arms around the thick branch and tried to lift it.

Smoke swirled and clogged her eyes and nose. She strained beneath the tremendous weight of the branch, but she wasn't strong enough. Groaning, she put everything she had into her effort. Cords stood out on her neck and the muscles in her back, her arms and legs screamed in protest.

She'd never worried about her mortal strength before. Now she cursed her small stature, her human limits. The branch shifted a fraction of an inch. Igmutaka planted his claws in the hard dirt and pulled, but it wasn't enough. Not nearly enough.

Suddenly Adam was beside her, panting from his race through the forest, shifting and lifting, putting his massive strength beside Liana's until, between the two of them, they managed to lift and tilt the huge branch away from the injured cougar.

Adam knelt beside Igmutaka. "My friend, this will hurt,

but the fire's almost here." He glanced briefly at Liana, as if to reassure himself she was okay. Then, grunting with the effort, he lifted the huge animal in his arms. Igmutaka snarled. His body stiffened in pain, his eyes closed and he fell unconscious. Adam adjusted the big cat over his shoulders in a modified fireman's carry.

"Follow me," he said, striking off into the darkness. "There's a cave not far from here. If we can get inside, we should be safe."

Liana nodded and shifted. It was easier to walk through the dark forest with her wolven senses alert. Smoke and flaming embers blew around them as Adam headed down the hill, directly toward the raging fire.

She didn't question him. She refused to allow her fear to take control, but when they crossed through a small meadow and fire erupted on both sides, she had to fight feral instincts that had her twisting and turning to run in fear.

Heat and smoke roiled around them. Small fires burst to life in the dry grass, lighting their way, and the trees blazed beside them, raising the temperature until it felt as if they raced through a blast furnace.

"It's not much farther. Hurry!" Blowing hard, Adam grunted beneath the weight of the huge cougar. Burning embers landed on his back and shoulders. He shook his head to dislodge one from his hair. Thick smoke made it almost impossible to breathe.

They made it across the meadow just ahead of the flames. Adam carefully climbed up a rocky incline with fire burning small tufts of brush all around him. Igmutaka's legs dangled uselessly down his back. He still appeared to be unconscious.

Liana prayed he was alive.

"Here. Liana, see if you can tear the brush away from the opening." Bowed beneath the heavy weight of the big cat, Adam stood next to a rocky outcropping gasping for each breath. Liana shifted and ripped at the twisted shrubs growing against the wall. Within seconds she'd dislodged enough to uncover a man-sized fissure in the rock.

"Hurry. You go first." Adam moved aside. She didn't waste time arguing, and slipped through the cleft in the rock wall into a dark space beyond. Adam followed her into the inky depths of the cavern.

The air in here was fresher, though it still reeked of smoke. Liana sensed a subtle draft, as if air from another source was escaping through the fissure, drawn like smoke through a chimney.

She hoped that meant the cave stretched farther back inside the mountain, but there was no light. No way to see where they were going. Liana shifted to her wolven form, but the darkness was just as complete to feral eyes as human. She shifted back. "Have you been in here before? Do you know the cave? I'm wondering if we should stay here, or try to go deeper, away from the opening."

Adam's voice materialized out of the utter darkness. "I'm trying to find a passage I remember, but I can't see a damned thing. There's not much outside to burn along the face of the cliff, so I think we'd be okay here, but somewhere along this back wall there's a fairly wide passage into a larger cavern that has a small spring. I'd like to try to find it so we can work on Igmutaka where there's water and more room. Can you tell where the cool air's coming from? That'll be the passage."

He grunted. She heard the sound of him adjusting Igmutaka's heavy weight. "Maybe if I shift again?" She did, and this time used her senses to search for the source of fresh air. *Here. Link with me and I'll share what I sense.*

Is it safe?

He never would have asked that question before. Now, the fact he didn't trust her felt like a slap to her face.

Of course. I have my barriers in place.

She didn't wait for his reply. Instead, she opened her

thoughts to him and at the same time followed her senses, walking carefully in the dark. The floor of the cavern was littered with twigs and other crackly stuff, but she didn't mind walking through it nearly as much in her four-legged form.

She thought of Adam, barefoot, carrying the massive weight of an unconscious mountain lion, and her sympathies went out to him. Then a cool breeze tickled her nostrils and she inched forward. The sound of fire crackling and roaring outside the cavern grew closer, like a freight train barreling down on them. She sighed in relief when she stepped into what had to be the passage Adam wanted. It seemed to lead in a gentle downward slope into the mountain.

I've found it. Follow me.

Adam's shuffling steps closed in behind her as she moved carefully along the pitch-black passage. Within just a few moments the sound of the fire subsided and she heard the trickling song of water over stone.

She stepped from the hard, rocky floor of the passage to a surface that was sandy and cool. The air smelled damp. Unsure of the height of the cavern they'd entered, she stayed low when she shifted to her human form. Slowly she stood up, blinking. There was an eerie incandescence illuminating patches along the walls and ceiling. Not enough to cast light, but to at least tell her that they'd entered a sizeable cavern.

"Help me lay him down."

She spun around, startled when Adam spoke from directly behind her. Reaching out in the dark, she found Adam's arm first, and then the furry cougar. She helped support Igmutaka's body as Adam slowly lowered him to the sandy ground. Igmutaka's body shuddered with each harsh and labored breath as he struggled to draw air into his lungs. Liana knelt beside him. She ran her hands along his sides, down over his spine and along his back legs.

Adam took a moment to catch his breath before following Liana's lead. Their hands met over the cat's back legs. "He's got some kind of back injury. His pelvis is cracked or broken. Do you sense anything else?"

Liana nodded. Then she realized he couldn't see her gesture. "Some internal bleeding, but not as bad as I'd thought. He may have a punctured lung. I can't tell for sure, but I don't think his back is actually broken. I thought I sensed paralysis before but now . . ."

"I think it's the fracture in his pelvis that's keeping his legs from moving. Where do you want to start?"

"I'll check his lung first, his ribs, and the bleeding. You work on the bones. The pelvis is filled with blood and might be a source for some of it, but . . ."

Adam's hand covered hers. "I'll start there. I'll keep my mind open. You'll know where I'm working, what I'm doing. Don't hesitate to communicate while you're healing. Logan and I have learned that we can sometimes boost one another's abilities."

"I will. And Adam . . . don't worry about linking with me. I have barriers to keep you from places you shouldn't go."

He didn't answer—he'd already begun his healing work. Liana placed her hands on Igmutaka's side and belly. She lost herself in the darkness, in the sense of Adam working close beside her, in the warmth of the unconscious cougar struggling for breath beneath her palms.

Awareness of the fire raging outside the cave faded until she knew only darkness and the sound of three hearts beating, Igmutaka's labored breathing, Adam's sense of complete concentration, and the amazingly intimate and open mental link between the two of them.

As she slipped into Igmutaka's injured body, Liana couldn't avoid the thought that, in healing at least, they found a connection, an intimacy they'd been unwilling or unable to share during sex.

Then she was much too busy to think of anything else beyond saving Igmutaka, and taking away his pain.

Anton used his shovel to throw dirt on another burning ember, and then another. Stefan worked nearby as they did what they could to protect the house, though it seemed like a hopeless job at this point.

He sent out his call again to Adam and Liana, but there was no reply, no sense of either of his packmates anywhere. He couldn't allow worry to take hold, couldn't give in to grief, not while the fire raged along the northern edge of the meadow and the wind still pushed the flames and embers toward the big house and Oliver's cottage.

At least shoveling dirt over burning embers gave him something positive to do beyond worrying. He'd been in contact with Keisha, but he'd not told her of Adam and Liana's disappearance. He couldn't bring himself to say anything. Not until he had an idea what had happened.

He forced himself to take a deep breath and think—an image of Eve popped into his head, so he sent a prayer to the goddess. He felt silly and sort of awkward, praying to Eve. It wasn't easy, learning to have faith in, to pray to, a woman he knew as intimately as he'd known Eve Reynolds. They'd had sex on numerous occasions, hunted together, shared meals and laughter, even a few tears. She'd sat at his kitchen table and teased Keisha, babysat Lily. She would be, forever, just Eve to him. Not their goddess.

But she *was* their goddess, and he did it anyway, with her beautiful image in his mind and her laughter in his heart. *Eve, if you can hear me, watch over Adam and Liana. And if it's in your power, sweetheart, send us rain. A whole shitload of rain.*

Then he went back to work, shoveling dirt over burning embers, checking the sprinklers that continued to pump water over the big meadow and against the trees at the forest's edge.

"Did you feel that?"

Stefan's comment caught him by surprise. Anton turned toward his voice. They'd been working so hard, been so worried about Liana and Adam, neither of them had spoken for the past hour. "Feel what?"

"That! Raindrops. I think it's raining!"

"You sure it's not spray blowing from the sprinklers?"

"Yeah."

Stefan grabbed his flashlight and pointed it toward the heavens. Raindrops, falling in silver streaks toward the light, poured from the sky.

Anton took a deep breath and leaned on his shovel. "I don't believe it. I asked Eve for rain. Do you think she had a hand in this?"

Stefan laughed. "I asked her, too. It's hard to think of her as our goddess, but damn, if she can come through like this, she's got my vote."

"I just hope it's enough." Anton stared at the flames exploding over the treetops. The rain came down harder.

Stefan nodded. Black streaks of soot ran down his face, dripped from his chin. "And not too late." He didn't need to explain what he referred to. "Anything at all? Any sense of either of them?"

Rain poured out of the sky, sizzling on the hot spots, falling so hard now the flames were beginning to lose height and energy and the brilliant orange glow was fading. Anton shook his head. He was so damned tired. Tired and frustrated. "Not a word. Not a sound or any sense of them." He glanced at Stefan. "Maybe if we link, try it together?"

Stefan nodded and leaned the shovel against the side of the house. Then he walked over to Anton and threw his arms around him, holding him tight.

It really wasn't necessary, hugging one another to tighten the link, but damn, it felt good. So very good to hold Stefan's strong body in his arms. Anton pressed his forehead against Stefan's, held him close, and once again he sent out a search for Liana and Adam.

Liana blinked, brought out of a sound sleep of total exhaustion by . . . something. Whatever it was had slipped away. She lay on her back on the cool sand with Igmutaka's coarse fur warming her side. She knew Adam slept somewhere close by in the darkness, but she couldn't see him, didn't know what form he'd taken, if he was wolf or man.

Igmutaka's injuries had been repaired and she felt empty inside. There was no longer any need for her to connect with Adam. No need to share thoughts and healing in what had been, for her, an almost religious experience.

She'd first experienced that sharing with him when they'd repaired Logan's injuries, but Igmutaka's had been much more severe, their time working together longer, more intense. Adam's power to heal amazed her. They each approached injuries differently, repairing what was broken in their own way, though their results were the same.

Once he rested, Igmutaka should be as good as new.

There. Something interrupting her thoughts. She sensed it again, whatever it was that had awakened her, and opened her senses to the night.

Liana? Are you out there? Are you all right?

Anton! She sat up and mentally reached out. *I'm okay. Adam's with me. We're in a cave not far from the ridge where we saw Igmutaka. He was injured. We brought him inside the cave to heal him. The fire was too close.*

Thank the goddess!

She waited and wondered if he passed on her message to Stefan.

We're coming. What do you need?

She almost laughed out loud with relief. *The stretcher we used for Logan. We need to keep an eye on Igmutaka for a couple of days, so I want to bring him back to the house. It's still there, isn't it? Please tell me the fire hasn't damaged it! And flashlights. It's dark in here! But what of the fire?*

It's out. The house is fine, and it's raining cats and dogs. Give us a couple of hours. We'll need to come as men to carry all this stuff. Tell me about the cave you're in. I think it links to the one under the house.

Liana described it as best she could. Anton seemed to know exactly where she was. When he broke off the connection to gather what they'd need, she looked into the darkness, searching for Adam's mind. There was no sense of him, so she listened with her ears instead of her tired brain.

She heard it then, his deep, even breathing. Moving carefully so she wouldn't bump into Igmutaka, she found Adam sleeping on the other side of the big cat.

"Adam?" Lightly she stroked his shoulder. "Wake up."

Adam jerked awake. He sat up and grabbed her arm, connecting with her in the dark. "Is he okay?"

"Yes. Igmutaka's fine. He's sleeping soundly. Anton's contacted me. He and Stefan are on their way. Wonderful news, though. It's raining outside. The fire's almost out. They're bringing a stretcher and some flashlights, and planning to come through the caves. He thought it might be faster that way, but I wanted you to know."

She heard his soft sigh in the darkness. Sensed his complete exhaustion. Damn. She should have let him sleep.

"Good. That's good. How's Igmutaka?"

"Sleeping." She rubbed her fingers through the cat's coarse coat. "Thank goodness he's just sleeping." She reached for Adam and her fingers bumped his naked chest. Instead of withdrawing, she spread her palm over his heart. "Thank you."

"For what?" He covered her hand with his.

"For coming when I called for help. I tried to tell you

when I left, but you were blocked. Anton was blocked. I didn't even try Stefan. I just left because I knew Igmutaka was hurt."

"I wonder if that's why he called you, because your thoughts were open."

She didn't know how to answer that. Could she tell him the truth? That she and Igmutaka were very much alike. They understood each other. They'd lived lives much longer than mere humans and they grasped one another on a level far beyond human comprehension. Unwelcome realization came to her, that if anyone among these people she'd come to love could be her soul mate, it would be the spirit guide.

"You would have to live as a cougar, should you mate with him. Can you do that?"

"What? But how . . . ?"

Adam's fingers curled over hers. "I've been listening to your thoughts. You're so open right now. Unguarded. I can feel the barriers to your older memories, but everything else is . . ."

She sensed his helpless shrug.

"Anyway, I'm not sorry I'm snooping. You really do have a fascinating mind." He chuckled. "Ah, Liana. I wish I'd met you under other circumstances. Wish I could have known you without all the baggage between us."

His heart beat steadily beneath her palm. Liana sighed. "Eve's not baggage, Adam. Never that. She's the woman who loved you. The one you chose as your mate. Because of me, she's lost to you. That will always be between us. Facts are facts."

Adam squeezed her fingers. "I know. The thing is, I believe Eve is happier now, in the role she's taken on as goddess, than she ever was as my mate." He took her hand from his chest, wrapped his fingers around hers and rested their linked hands on his thigh. "I loved her, but part of that love was built on my need to fix anything that's broken. Eve was broken when we met. Abused and broken. I needed to make her whole."

"She needed you as well."

"Not that much. She left me in the beginning because she had to prove she could stand on her own feet. I resented her like you wouldn't believe when she left, though I didn't let anyone know how I felt. When she called me to come and get her, I knew she hated the fact she'd missed me. She didn't want to need me, much less love me. Eventually, even though she loved me with all her heart, there was part of her that still craved that independence. She wanted to prove she could make it on her own. She's got that now. What she really wanted all along."

"How do you feel about that?" Liana stroked her thumb over the back of his hands. Felt a couple of scabs, an old scar. His hands were always a mess, always healing from some injury or another. She imagined he was probably covered with burns from their trek through the forest, too. He was like that. Always putting others first.

Fixing things.

"How I feel about Eve isn't really what's important. It's how Eve feels about herself that counts. I believe she's truly happy now. Happier than she was with me, even though what we had was wonderful. At least from my point of view."

He paused. In the silence that followed, the quiet drip of running water and the soft sound of their steady breathing filled the cavern. Adam cleared his throat and his voice had a deep catch when he spoke. "From Eve's point of view, I'm thinking maybe it wasn't so wonderful. Looking back, she spent her time trying to be what I wanted. Always anticipating my needs, deferring to what I wanted over her own desires. Even in sex she was never demanding. She was my shadow and I didn't even see that she was subjugating her own needs to mine. I loved her, but I can see where being a goddess with control of her life would be pretty appealing. She might not have known that if not for you."

Liana felt tears gathering in her eyes. "I'm sorry, Adam. I . . ."

"No. Aren't you listening to me? Liana, Eve's got what she wants. She's happier now. My feelings aren't important. It's Eve's turn and you've apologized enough. It's time for all of us to move forward, and that includes you."

He let out a huge gust of air. "I hated you, that morning when you and Eve kept me from killing myself. That's when Eve told me her death shouldn't have happened, that it was your fault because you made a mistake. I've had a lot of time to think about it, though, and I've wondered if that's true. Was it a mistake? Or was the Mother taking a hand in this? Anton and Stefan are always arguing over fate versus coincidence. Anton thinks all things happen because they're fated to happen. Maybe Eve's death, your disgrace . . . maybe that was fated. Maybe it was Eve's turn to finally have control of her life. Maybe it was your turn finally to experience life."

Liana thought of that. She wished she could believe it was so, wished she could peel away the burden of guilt that covered her like a shroud, but Eve's death wasn't her only mistake. There were so many others.

She locked her thoughts away. Hid them from Adam and the sleeping cougar, just in case, while she allowed herself the luxury of contemplating her biggest mistake of all.

She'd fallen in love with Adam Wolf. She hadn't expected it, wasn't sure how to deal with it. Love hadn't come to her all at once. It still wasn't something she was absolutely certain of, but tonight, healing Igmutaka, sharing their skills as they repaired broken bones and torn muscles and saved the cougar's life, she'd linked with Adam on a deeper level than before.

Linked with him and discovered more of the man he

kept hidden beneath the surface. Honorable, intelligent, a man of quiet dignity, one capable of great love. There was nothing about him not to love. He had so much to give, yet no matter how much Liana wanted it, no matter if Adam could get past his convoluted feelings toward her, she could never accept or seek that deepest part of his soul.

She could never risk a mating bond with him, that perfect subjugation of self, a sharing of everything she was, of all that made him unique. She'd asked Eve about it once, before she realized the impossibility of ever doing it herself.

After Eve had explained the depth of the bond, Liana knew she wanted it more than anything. Wanted the connection, the pure intimacy of a mating bond with someone who could truly love her. She'd never felt such yearning to be mortal, never wanted anything so badly as love and that amazing bond that was literally a melding of two souls.

She tried to imagine what it would be like, to share that kind of bond with someone like Adam, a man she admired and respected so very much.

Admired, respected, and loved. But it wasn't going to happen. Not With Adam Wolf. Not with any man. Not if she expected him to survive.

Survival was a big part of a relationship, right? She had to bite back a nervous laugh. As if it mattered. As if Adam could ever truly love her in return. No matter what he said, Eve would always be there between the two of them.

Yet thinking of a future without someone to love, without hope of love, was admitting that she had no future at all. Not with a mortal. Yet she was mortal, or as mortal as Chanku could be. They still didn't know of their amazing lifespan, how each shift renewed cells and gave them more time.

She'd have to explain all that one day. So much knowledge she had to share, but then, wasn't that the reason

Anton had tried to invade those ancient memories? How much could she tell them without creating even more questions? Poor Anton. He was never happy unless he was searching for answers.

Thank goodness he'd found Keisha, the one mate in all the world who could put up with his never-ending quest to know, to understand. That was her worry, though. Liana couldn't help but wonder as she ran her free hand through Igmutaka's coat, felt the steady beat of his heart, the warmth of his body, if she could ever love another.

Igmutaka was the only one she knew of who could withstand a bond with her. Except she didn't love him. Even if she could become a cougar, she couldn't see herself ever loving him. Not the way she loved Adam. She glanced into the darkness toward Adam with the horrible feeling that, for better or worse, love had chosen her, not the other way around.

Chapter 13

The stale smell of smoke in her bedroom was almost suffocating, but morning sun was shining brightly through the big sliding glass doors and the outside air was clear with that "after the rain" brilliance. Liana stretched and sat up. Her muscles ached and she'd pulled something in her neck.

Probably from moving that huge limb off of Igmutaka, but thank the goddess, he was safe and alive. Most of the night was a blur to her this morning, but Anton and Stefan had brought all of them safely through the twists and turns of tunnels and caves and they'd slept in their own beds last night.

Liana did recall Adam asking her to stay with him. Instead, she'd chosen her own room, closer to the one where they'd put Igmutaka in case the injured cougar needed her during the night.

At least that was the excuse she'd given to Adam. She had too many questions to stay with him right now. She wished she had answers, but there were none. At least not this morning.

So she got out of bed, showered, and headed for the kitchen.

Liana heard the squeals of children and Xandi's voice

as she walked down the hallway. They'd all come home. The aroma of fresh coffee and soft laughter drew her into the bright kitchen.

Xandi sat at the table feeding Alex. Stefan stood by the sink with his coffee. Anton was at the small kitchen table next to Xandi. A strange man sat across from him. Strange yet sexually compelling, with an androgynous beauty that trapped and held Liana's attention.

Dark bronze skin, coal-black hair, brilliant green eyes. Tall and lean like the other men she'd come to know, he was dressed in nothing but worn Levis with holes in the knees and ragged cuffs. His feet were bare.

He wore no shirt and his smooth chest glistened, sleek and rippling with muscle. His thick black hair was pulled tightly back from his face, accentuating his high cheek-bones. His single braid hung over the back of the kitchen chair. He watched her with a most unsettling intensity.

Almost as if he knew her. Liana stumbled. Stefan moved forward and grabbed her arm. Laughing.

"Sort of a shock, right?" He grinned as if she should know what the joke was. Who the man was. "Don't you recognize him?"

She did. She did recognize him. "Igmutaka? Is that you?"

He smiled. The expression transformed his entire face. "It is," he said. "Thank you for saving my life."

She sat. Thank goodness Stefan had shoved a chair under her butt. Anton stood up and poured a cup of coffee for her. Added cream and sugar the way she liked it, and stuck the cup in her hand. He leaned over and whispered loudly, "That was sort of my reaction, too, when he wandered out and joined us for breakfast a bit ago."

Holding her cup in both hands, Liana glanced at Anton and took a huge gulp of her coffee. Blinking slowly, she looked back at Igmutaka and shook her head. "I thought you couldn't shift."

He shrugged. The smooth ripple of muscles made her

think of the cougar. "I never said I couldn't, merely that I had no reason to shift. I didn't. Then."

"Oh." What else could she say? She wanted to ask what his reason for shifting now was, but she wasn't certain she wanted to hear the answer.

Her mortal life was complicated enough already.

Adam slipped on a pair of faded blue sweatpants and shoved his wet hair back from his face. He thought of combing it, but it always ended up looking the same whether he did or not, so he left it, pulled on a green sweatshirt that definitely didn't match the pants, and headed out the door.

Smoke hung low over the burned forest, but in the light of day he could see green patches where trees had survived. Some that were burned still had green on them as well, which meant that, though damaged, they might make a comeback.

He hoped so. The forest in these mountains had been beyond beautiful. He hated to think of acre after acre of blackened ground, of damage that would take a lifetime to grow back.

As he walked toward the house, Adam sensed the minds and laughter of the missing pack members at the same time he noticed familiar cars in the driveway. It appeared everyone was back, including Logan.

That was good. He wanted to go out today with Logan and Liana and check for injured animals. Hopefully there'd be some they could save. He'd need to check on the cougar, too.

And Liana. Damn. What was he going to do about his feelings for Liana? He'd never expected to do a one-eighty like he had last night, when he realized how his feelings for her had changed so dramatically.

And it hadn't happened with the sex, either, though he'd discovered that sex without the connection was more like a hand job than making love. Goddess, his head was spinning with all the crap he needed to sort out. At least he was certain of two things—Eve was gone and probably happier without him, which meant he really had to let her go, and the feelings he had for the ex-goddess were too powerful, too intense, to ignore.

But where did they go from here? They couldn't bond. She'd made that perfectly clear. He didn't even know how she felt about him. In fact, he'd caught her looking wistfully at Igmutaka.

Grinning broadly, Adam stepped into the kitchen. At least that wasn't an issue. He couldn't see Liana spending the rest of her mortal life with a cougar.

"Good morning, Adam."

Damn but Liana looked beautiful this morning. Just hearing her voice sent a shiver along his spine. "Good morning." He smiled at her and almost lost himself in her gray-green eyes.

"Good morning, Adam."

The greeting jerked his attention away from Liana. He didn't recognize the voice or the face, yet he knew this man. Knew him intimately—like, from the inside out. "Igmutaka?"

Shit. He'd never once considered the cat could shift.

The man nodded. "Yes. Thank you for saving my life. I am most grateful. I would not be here this morning without you and Liana."

He probably shouldn't be thinking what he was thinking right now. Instead, he said, "I'm glad we could help."

Igmutaka tilted his head and smiled. "Are you, Adam Wolf? Truly?" He laughed. Then he pushed his chair back from the table and stood. "Anton? I would like that tour you promised me."

Anton stood as well. He turned to Adam and winked. "Sounds good, my friend. Come with me." The two men left. Adam realized the kitchen had emptied out. Only he and Liana remained.

She glanced up at him and then took a sip of her coffee. When she grimaced, he knew it must have grown cold. Without asking, he reached for her cup. She handed it over.

"Rough morning?" He filled a fresh cup for himself, dumped Liana's cold coffee and refilled her cup, along with the cream and sugar he knew she liked.

She took the cup and stared into its milky depths. "You don't know the half of it."

"You were looking at him with interest last night. Maybe he picked up your thoughts." Adam sat across from her and sipped at his coffee.

She snorted. "It wasn't interest like that. It was interest only in the fact I could bond with someone like Igmutaka because he was an ancient, same as me. My memories probably wouldn't fry his brain."

"Ouch. Not a pretty picture." Adam smiled at her. She looked awfully upset. "So, you were thinking about bonding. Anyone in particular, if not Igmutaka?"

She shook her head and looked miserable. He took pity on her, reached across the table and raised her chin with his fingertip. "Look at me, Liana. Please?"

She raised her head. Tears spilled from her eyes.

He hadn't expected tears. Anger, maybe, or frustration. Not tears. "Liana? What's the matter?"

She shook her head. He took a quick look at her thoughts and just about bounced off the walls she had up, they were so high and tight. No help there.

"Nothing," she said. She stood up and began gathering the cups and dishes Anton and Igmutaka had left on the table. She carried them to the sink, which was overflowing with dirty dishes, and began to methodically rinse and stack everything.

She'd turned her back to him. It was obvious she preferred to be by herself right now. He grabbed a cold Danish off a tray on the counter and went in search of Logan. He'd invite Liana along later, when she wasn't trying so hard to shut him out.

Adam left the room and Liana wanted to scream her frustration to the heavens. Instead she carefully rinsed the plates and utensils, filled the sink with hot, soapy water, and began the huge task of washing dishes for such a big crowd.

She knew the dishwasher was big enough to handle everything but she still hadn't gotten the hang of loading it, and there was something soothing about washing plates in warm water, rinsing the soap away and stacking them neatly in the rack.

Not a job she'd learned as a goddess, but it was a skill she was proud of in her mortal form. A job any person could do.

It was infinitely more relaxing than strangling Adam, which was what she'd like to do about now. How could he just leave her? Ask her what was wrong and then leave. The jerk.

Didn't he know that when she said there was nothing wrong, that was his opening to pry a little? To persist in spite of her denial? If she'd had any idea she'd end up wondering about him like this, she would have asked Eve a little bit more about handling men. They'd had a few chats, but nothing specific.

Obviously, there was a lot she didn't know.

"What are you doing?"

Igmutaka's deep voice startled her. She turned around and smiled at him. It was just weird, seeing him as a man when she'd not realized he could shift.

Of course, he wasn't Chanku. He was a Sioux spirit guide, or had been. A totally different kind of shapeshifter.

"I'm washing the breakfast dishes." She shrugged and rinsed the pan she'd been scrubbing. "Do you want to help?"

He frowned. "Of course not. Stop that. You are a goddess, not a common servant."

She laughed. If only he could see himself, and Anton, for that matter, who was reaching for a dish towel even now. "I *was* a goddess. Past tense, and a big difference. Now I'm merely a resident of this house and a member of Anton's pack. We all have chores. It's how things get done. Grab a towel, Ig," she added, feeling positively flippant.

He stared, wide-eyed. "I think not. I'll be outside if you need me for something besides menial labor." He continued on through the kitchen and slammed the door on his way out.

Liana glanced at Anton out of the corner of her eye. He was trying, unsuccessfully, to bite back a grin.

"Ig?" he asked.

Liana chuckled. "Sort of fits, don't you think? Igmutaka's a mouthful, especially if he plans to hang around."

Anton carefully dried a plate and stuck it in the cupboard over his head. "I don't think he's going to stay."

"Really? Why not?" Liana concentrated on the silverware she was rinsing.

"There's no reason for him to remain. He prefers life as a cougar and doesn't really understand the intricacies of modern life." Anton finished drying another plate, stacked it on top of the one he'd just done. Grabbed the next.

"I guess that could be difficult, if you're not willing to change."

Anton nodded. "Change isn't always easy. Sometimes it requires great sacrifices."

She wasn't sure what he meant by that. Wasn't even certain she wanted to know. She changed the subject instead. No sacrifice there.

*　　*　　*

The dishes were done, Anton had returned to his office and Liana was wiping down the counter when Adam and Igmutaka walked into the kitchen. She felt sweaty and sticky and not at all in the mood for men, but Adam's smile had a way of stopping whatever she intended to say.

All she could do was smile back at him.

"Logan's exhausted and wants to catch some sleep, but Igmutaka said he'd come. I want to see if there are any wounded animals that need care. That fire had to be devastating to wildlife. Will you join us?"

Liana folded the damp towel over the edge of the sink. "Give me five minutes. I'll meet you on the back deck." She turned to go back to her room when Adam stopped her with a gentle hand to her wrist.

"Thank you. I wasn't sure if you'd want to go."

She frowned and wished she understood him better. "Of course I do. Why wouldn't I?"

He shook his head. "I don't know." He leaned close and kissed her quickly on the lips. "Back deck. Five minutes."

Confused, she backed away and nodded. Caught Igmutaka watching her over Adam's shoulder, dark eyes narrowed and mouth pressed in a firm line. He was bigger than Adam. Bigger, broader, more intimidating. She'd not realized quite how big a man he was, not with his androgynous beauty, his finely cut features and that smooth, leanly muscled chest.

He was most definitely a cat. Even as a big man he still had the lean, sinewy body of the puma. Fascinating. A little bit scary, but definitely fascinating. She quickly left the kitchen and headed back to her room.

Adam really hadn't expected her to show up, but Liana was there in four minutes, not five. She'd changed out of her jeans and sweater and was wearing that old, ratty blue robe she seemed to like, but she shucked it immediately when she saw that he and Igmutaka had already shifted.

The big cougar sat off to one side and licked his paw, just like an oversized housecat. Liana glanced his way, but she was more focused on Adam. He liked that. Liked knowing she wasn't indifferent to him, at least.

She dropped the robe and shifted before he had a chance to admire her perfect body, though she was every bit as perfect in her wolven form. He studied her long, lean lines and wondered if she could shift and become a cougar. He'd never thought to ask.

That could make things more difficult for him, as if they weren't difficult enough already. Every moment he spent with her, now, every single thing she said or did reminded him how hopeless this was. How impossible.

They couldn't bond. Ever. Couldn't mate. He fully appreciated Oliver and Mei's quandary for the first time, but they'd managed to work things out perfectly. He didn't see that happening for Liana and him.

Of course, he hadn't asked her for any input, either. Hadn't let her know how he felt, but what was the point?

The three of them cut across the meadow and headed into the forest. There were a surprising number of untouched trees and shrubs along the trail. The fire must have crowned when it blew through so fast last night, burning the tops of trees but missing the living things at ground level. Thank goodness the rains had prevented more serious damage.

Or should he thank Eve? If what Stefan and Anton said was true, that they'd each begged the goddess for rain that had suddenly started falling in huge amounts when it wasn't even in the forecast, then they all owed the woman who'd been his mate a huge debt of gratitude.

It made him feel good, to think of Eve up there, wherever *there* was, sending down enough rain to put out the fire in time to save the house and most of the forestlands on Anton's huge estate. He tried to imagine her watching over all of them. It was surprisingly easy to see her in that role. Easier now than it had been just a few days ago.

They headed into the forest, away from the ridge where they'd found Igmutaka the night before. It wasn't long before Liana gave a mental shout and headed off to the left. The sow grizzly they found was unharmed, but her cub, about nine months old and at least thirty or more pounds, lay in the burnt grass whimpering. His feet were badly burned and there was a long, bloody slash along his shoulder.

How are we going to treat him with Mama standing guard? Liana stopped just a dozen feet from the pair.

Leave the sow to me.

Igmutaka snarled and moved closer to the bear. She growled, and rose up on her hind legs, slashing at the air. The puma didn't act at all intimidated. He took another couple of steps toward her. Then he sat and stared at the bear. A moment later, she dropped to all fours and backed off, growling low, never taking her eyes from her cub.

Looks like he speaks bear. Adam went straight to the cub's side, but he kept his attention focused on the mother. Liana didn't hesitate either. Ignoring the mother, she shifted and knelt beside the little guy and placed her hands over his injured shoulder. Before Adam even thought to shift, the wound had closed and pink, healing flesh covered the gash.

She ran her hands over the cub's paws and they healed just as quickly. The little guy stopped whimpering, rolled over and dashed to its mother's side.

Ungrateful little beast, Adam said. *Let's hope he re-members how you fixed his boo-boos when he's all grown up and decides he doesn't like wolves.*

Liana flashed a quick smile at him and shifted. Igmutaka trotted alongside and nodded to Liana, as if he acknowledged her skill, but Adam didn't pick up any communication from him. He wondered if they spoke privately, and if so, what they said.

Then he felt petty and small for his jealousy. Who was he to stop Liana from getting to know Igmutaka better? At least the spirit guide was someone who could offer her what Adam never could—the total intimacy of a mating bond.

If they could figure out the different species part of the equation. *What a mess.* Seething with silent frustration, he followed them back to the main trail.

It was dark by the time they returned to the house. Adam was exhausted, but exhilarated as well. They'd saved so many wounded animals today. A few had been too badly hurt, and those had been given a quick and painless end. There was only so much he and Liana could do. It was definitely a kindness to end suffering, especially when all Liana had to do was touch a creature and give its spirit permission to move on.

She'd treated each death not as a failure, but as a chance to ease pain. In doing so, she'd given Adam a new perspective on life and death. On life after death. All creatures survived, she said. Each of them moving on across the veil, living on as energy, as part of the universe, self-aware, their choice to return in some other form an option always open.

Some chose life again. Others preferred the simplicity of existing on the astral plane, the perfection. He'd have to ask her more about that. More about that place where she'd existed for time out of memory. That place where Eve was, even now.

They'd eaten earlier in the evening, feeding on an elk that had died in the fire. So many animals dead, but even more had survived. Fascinating, he thought, how the creatures of the forest could manage to escape such a raging fire.

Igmutaka had been a steady and welcome presence beside them. He had the ability to communicate with all the creatures of the forest, no matter their species. His voice had eased the animals' fears and made the job of healing them not only easier, but safer for all involved.

Adam didn't want to like the guy. In fact, he really wanted to hate Igmutaka, especially in this drop-dead gorgeous human form he'd taken. Wanted to challenge him for the right to pursue Liana, but he couldn't. Not when Igmutaka's pursuit of the beautiful gray wolf appeared as hopeless as his own.

The house was quiet when they trotted up the steps to the deck. Igmutaka shifted first and straightened up, tall and lean and absolutely breathtaking. His body was so perfect it made Adam's mouth go dry. Desire raged through his veins, but he had no idea how the spirit guide was wired. Would the man be insulted if Adam were to suggest they get together?

Liana shifted and stretched her arms over her head lifting her firm breasts high. Her nipples pointed up and out, dark rose against her fair skin. An even more powerful need boiled up in Adam, a fierce, driving need that went beyond even his usual state of arousal after a run. Then he saw how Igmutaka watched her, saw the man's huge erection rise up against his belly in a vivid display of sexual excitement.

Adam shifted, already hard as a post. He wondered if Mei and Oliver were still awake, if they'd welcome him in their bed tonight, because this was a hard-on he knew he couldn't handle on his own. Liana smiled at Adam, but she turned to Igmutaka and wrapped her fingers around his hand. Adam's heart sank.

She reached for him as well. "I feel absolutely high right

now. I want you both," she said. "I don't want this day to
end. Will you come to my room? Stay with me tonight?
Both of you?"

Igmutaka looked at Adam and raised one expressive
eyebrow. "Yes," he said. "I would like to share your bed."
He paused a moment, as if considering, and then added,
"And your man."

Adam thought his heart might pound right out of his
chest. He hadn't allowed the thought he might be Liana's
man even enter his mind. Igmutaka said it—she didn't
deny it. And he wasn't going to deny the fact he'd suddenly developed a serious case of lust for the sexy spirit
guide.

He couldn't speak. His cock stood so high and hard he
ached, and he couldn't have formed words if his life depended on it. Instead, he nodded his head, a short, sharp
affirmative jerk of the chin.

Liana's smile grew even wider. "Good," she said. And
then, still holding their hands, she led both aroused men
into her room through the open sliding glass door. And,
like two very bemused little boys, they followed the alpha
bitch.

It was, after all, her choice.

She stopped beside the bed. "I'm going to shower. It's
not that big, but you're welcome to join me."

She turned away without waiting for an answer. Adam
wanted to laugh out loud at the sudden attitude she'd developed. Liana was in charge and she wasn't leaving any
doubt she was the boss.

He glanced at Igmutaka and choked back a laugh at the
confused expression on the big guy's face. He wasn't
Chanku, wasn't used to women taking control, especially
during sex. Hell, he wasn't even used to a human form.

Adam almost felt sorry for him.

Almost. He followed Liana into the bathroom, well
aware that Igmutaka was right on his heels.

The shower wasn't as big as some of them in the house, but it wasn't bad. They actually bathed, and after a day dealing with burns and other injuries and breathing in way too much soot and smoke it felt wonderful to stand beneath the cleansing spray. Not that they were all that dirty—shifting took care of just about everything—but the water beating against sensitive skin seemed to make all his senses sharper.

Adam stepped out of the shower first and dried himself. When Liana stepped out, he grabbed a fresh towel and dried her as well. Igmutaka watched as if he wasn't certain how to proceed, but then, this was probably his first shower, much less his first time making love with a woman. Adam wasn't really sure what Liana wanted from the two of them, either.

He knelt and swept the soft towel over her legs, and she was too close, her scent too intoxicating to ignore. He nuzzled the blond curls between her legs and loved the sound of her quiet whimper when he gently licked her clitoris. She was already wet. When he slipped his tongue between her folds, the sweet taste of her cream dragged a groan out of him and another whimper out of her.

He heard a low moan and glanced to his left. Igmutaka had his fist wrapped around his huge shaft and a look of pain on his face, as if the sight of Adam licking at Liana's sex was almost too much for him to handle.

But Adam had no intention of making love to Liana in the bathroom. Not when there was a king-sized bed just a few steps away. He stood up and tugged her hand. She followed, but she grabbed Igmutaka on the way out. Wrapped her fingers around his big hand and dragged him along behind as she followed Adam.

Adam paused beside the bed, so turned-on that his legs were shaking and his cock banged against his belly. Igmutaka was in no better shape, and the sight of that huge cock, larger even than Adam's, standing straight up against his flat stomach was almost too much.

Adam grabbed Liana's face in both his hands and kissed her, hard. "What do you want, sweetheart? How can we please you?"

She bit his lower lip, tugging it none too gently. He realized she was as turned-on as he was. Maybe more, the way she panted the words. She turned loose of his lip and her eyes glittered with green fire. "I want Igmutaka inside me. And I want you inside him. The three of us together." She touched the side of his face. "And link with me, Adam. Don't shut me out. I'll keep you from the things you shouldn't see. Will you do that? Will you please share what you can with me?"

"You know I will." He kissed her again, harder this time. Then he glanced at Igmutaka, who looked stunned by Liana's request.

"I've never . . ." He shot a frantic glance at Adam.

Liana grinned at him. "Well, Ig," she said, laughing, "it's about time you did." She dropped to her knees in front of the spirit guide and wrapped her hand around that huge cock of his. Adam licked his lips and linked with Liana. Her arousal was like a living, breathing entity, a force more powerful than anything he'd felt before. As she sucked Igmutaka's erection between her lips, Adam experienced the flavor of the man, the texture of his cock. He felt the tautly stretched foreskin caught behind the bulbous head and tasted the small drops of ejaculate that leaked from the narrow slit at the tip.

Igmutaka groaned and thrust his hips forward. Instead of choking on him, Liana somehow swallowed him down her throat, taking all of him. Adam stepped around behind the man he couldn't wait to fuck and pressed against his back. Forcing his cock down until it rode in the tight crease between Igmutaka's buttocks, he groaned each time the sensitive tip connected with the firm cushion of a taut scrotal sac on every downward thrust.

Adam felt the spirit guide's struggle not to climax and took pity on him—for the moment. He backed away, circled around to the front and tugged Liana to her feet. She had a glazed look on her face, as if she could have suckled that huge cock forever, but he helped her onto the bed, set the pillows behind her and put a couple beneath her hips.

Igmutaka eagerly crawled up on the bed between Liana's legs. Curious, Adam wondered what it would be like for the man, taking a woman in human form for the first time. He tried to observe dispassionately, but it was impossible. He searched for Igmutaka's impressions and slipped into his thoughts, into the visuals and sensations filling his mind and body.

Igmutaka was fascinated by the moisture glistening on her folds, but too aroused to do more than follow instinct, grab his shaft in one huge fist and slip the broad head of his penis between her labia. She arched to him and spread her legs wide as he cautiously worked his huge cock inside, moving slowly, carefully, obviously realizing how big he was, how small Liana was—and how much of him needed to fit inside of her. Finally, his pubic hair mingled with her blond thatch.

Adam almost climaxed with the vivid impressions racing through Igmutaka's mind. The damp heat surrounding his human cock, the ripple of Liana's muscles as her body adjusted to his huge size. The way her full breasts with their dark nipples drew his eyes and made him salivate with an almost painful desire to suckle and lick.

Liana sighed and wriggled her hips, seating him even deeper. Adam sensed how Igmutaka's attention was drawn immediately to the way her sex had stretched to surround and clasp the length of his cock. Then Liana glanced at Adam and grinned. "Your turn," she said, rubbing her hands over Igmutaka's shoulders, down his sides, over his smooth flanks.

The mental link between them snapped. The spirit guide's head jerked up and he glared at Adam. Obviously he wasn't all that sure if he was going to like what was coming next.

Adam's hands shook so badly he could barely open the drawer in the bedside table. Lust roared through his body, fueled by frustration. Igmutaka was sliding in and out of Liana's tight sheath and Adam was still fumbling with the fucking condom. He tried to tear open the packet, gave up and ripped it with his teeth. When he grabbed his cock to roll on the condom, just the touch of his own hands almost made him come. He gritted his teeth and treated himself to a few good strokes of his shaft.

And he made certain Igmutaka watched.

Igmutaka's eyes glittered as Adam stroked himself. Then, with an arrogant look of lordly dismissal, he returned his attention to Liana and slowly began to move. His powerful hips rolled with each thrust, his balls swung between his muscular thighs and he buried himself fully inside her. Liana's head was thrown back, her eyes closed, lips parted. Adam watched the thrust and withdrawal, fascinated by the rhythmic swing of Igmutaka's testicles between his legs.

So much arrogance in the spirit guide. There was a swagger to his style, a sense of hubris that begged to be quelled. Adam grinned, feeling like a predator kneeling behind the man with a tube of lubricant in his hand. He knew this was a first for him.

If Adam pulled it off, he knew it wouldn't be a last.

He rubbed Igmutaka's flanks with his palms, getting him used to the touch of another man. At first he jerked away, but Adam kept up his slow, sensual massage until he felt Igmutaka's rhythm change, knew he was anticipating each smooth sweep of Adam's hands. Adam slipped his fingers between the tight crevice separating the man's muscular cheeks. He cupped that fascinating sac, fingered his testicles.

Igmutaka's body jerked in surprise. Adam kept it up, rolling the hard balls between his fingers, stroking the sensitive skin over his perineum.

Once again, the spirit guide acquiesced.

Adam added a thick dollop of gel to his fingers and rubbed it along Igmutaka's sweaty crease, stopping at the tightly puckered band of muscle guarding his ass. Rubbing soft, insistent circles over that sensitive ring, he almost laughed when he felt Igmutaka pressing back, silently asking for more.

Seduction had become his goal. Adam didn't want to take the man's anal virginity so much as he wanted it offered. He continued rubbing and retreating, rubbing harder, pressing a bit deeper, until the muscle relaxed and his middle finger slipped all the way inside.

Igmutaka went entirely still. His body quivered, pulled taut as a bow string. Adam slowly thrust his finger in and out, feeling the moisture, the heat, the tremendous strength of internal muscles as they contracted around his finger. He stayed clear of Igmutaka's prostate. The last thing he needed to do to this proud warrior was force an ejaculation on him that he wasn't expecting.

After a few moments of slow and steady thrusts, Igmutaka once again took up his rhythm with Liana. Remembering his promise, Adam opened his thoughts, sharing with Liana and with Igmutaka what he was doing.

In return. he was almost overwhelmed by the combined lust of the two of them. A wave of sensation and need rolled over him, roaring past his control with the speed and power of a tsunami.

Controlling his basic urge to just go for it and forget technique, Adam added another finger, and then a third as he softened Igmutaka's tight sphincter. He caught a silent litany of what sounded almost like poetry but had to be curses. Sioux? He wasn't sure of the language, but the meaning was obvious. Ig was doing his best to hang on.

Adam figured the spirit guide had to be ready for full penetration by now. He knew he was. His penis throbbed with the pressure of too much blood and not enough action, swollen much bigger and thicker than usual. He sent a silent apology to Igmutaka, lubed himself with an extra layer of gel, and slowly forced his way through Igmutaka's virgin opening.

Breathe easy. Push back against me with deep breaths. Tell me if I hurt you. I don't want this to hurt.

Are you certain of that, wolfman?

Igmutaka's harsh burst of laughter seemed more a dare than an admission of pain. He was obviously on the edge of orgasm.

So be it, cat. Adam rolled his hips forward. He felt the tip of his penis compress and slide through the tight muscle. Once that breach was made, he easily buried himself fully inside Igmutaka. Adam's balls rested against the man's perineum and the press of his groin separated muscular cheeks. He held perfectly still, giving Igmutaka time to adjust to the fullness, the strange new sensation of his ass being stretched and filled entirely by a man's cock.

Adam tried to recall the first time he'd been screwed by a man. There'd been a certain amount of fear, the sense that it could hurt really bad, the pressure and the burning pain at first entry.

Then, after just a few moments, arousal had risen up and slammed him across the balls. He thought of that now and shared it with Igmutaka and Liana, the way he wanted it to feel, the way it should be.

Igmutaka opened his mind. Out of him spilled the almost frightening level of lust that had him trembling over Liana, afraid if either he or Adam moved, he'd spill his seed before he wanted. He'd never known anything like this, never imagined the way fucking as a man would feel, much less the sensation of being fucked by a man.

Images poured out of him, sensations shared with Liana and Adam. That thick cock stretching his tight anal ring, the seductive fullness deep inside, the purely sensual connection of his own huge cock buried inside Liana's warm, wet sheath while Adam was buried in him. All so new, so unexpected, doing things in human form what he'd only known as a cougar—of doing other things he'd never known at all.

Liana smiled and touched Igmutaka's cheek with her fingers. "I wanted you to experience this. To share this connection. You're so alone all the time. I wanted you to understand what can come to you here, as a man, should you want it."

"What if I want you?"

Adam stilled. He started to raise his barriers and give them privacy, to block out their thoughts and his, but Liana's answer brought his carefully constructed walls tumbling down.

"You can have me—like this. When your body needs release, when you just want to fuck until the tension goes away. But that's all of me you get. I'm sorry." She looked over his shoulder, directly at Adam. "I'm afraid another has my heart. I don't even know if I'll ever have his, but once mine was given, I could never take it back."

"I thought as much." Igmutaka seemed to take it in good humor. He leaned over and kissed Liana. Then he began to thrust, his hips driving his cock in deep and hard in a pounding rhythm that pulled Adam along with him.

The three of them found perfect synchronicity, a perfect sense of unity, and finally, a perfect orgasm that shot them up and over the peak together. Igmutaka shouted and buried himself deep. Liana arched her back and raised her hips upward into his final hard thrust and screamed.

Adam felt the thick rush of his ejaculate pouring into the condom as his cock jerked and spasmed deep inside the spirit guide—a climax that seemed to go on forever as the three of them, linked physically and mentally, shared each sensation, one with the other. The orgasmic loop grew and expanded until, like a dying sun, it finally collapsed in upon itself.

Bodies sated and replete, minds stunned into quiescence, Liana, Igmutaka, and Adam collapsed right along with it.

Chapter 14

Liana lay in the darkness while undeniable arousal simmered awake. She had no intention of acting upon it, but she enjoyed each, individual sensation—the slow but steady clench of muscles between her legs, the yearning, burning need that tightened her nipples into nubby peaks. The way Adam's soft snore tickled her left ear and Igmutaka's furry body warmed her right side. Her body simmered and burned—so alive with desire. So much more alive than she'd ever been as goddess.

Igmutaka's coarse fur teased her sensitive skin. He'd shifted to his cougar form after their final orgasm, stretched out on the bed and had immediately fallen asleep.

Or pretended to sleep. She wished she knew him better. Had sex with Adam bothered him? He'd been so surprised when she suggested it—had she been wrong? He wasn't, after all, Chanku. His libido wasn't the primary force the rest of them understood—a libido that welcomed all sexual partners. Igmutaka was definitely heterosexual. Had she somehow insulted him?

Men could be such confusing creatures.

Too late to worry about that now, especially when she had more pressing matters. Ignoring her body's insistent clamor for sex, moving slowly so as not to awaken either male, she crawled out of bed and found her old blue robe. She had no idea who it had belonged to before she claimed it, but something about the soft chenille always seemed to comfort her when she put it on.

She needed comfort right now. Badly.

Liana slipped out of the bedroom without waking the guys, unsure exactly where she was headed. She was desperate for some time alone, a quiet place where she could think without the sensual distraction of warm, male bodies close to hers. She tiptoed down the hall until she reached Anton's study. Perfect. She peeked through the open door. It was empty.

Well of course, silly. It's three in the morning.

A nightlight burned against one wall, vaguely illuminating Anton's big old leather recliner. The room carried the subtle aroma she associated with the pack's über-alpha—a combination of aftershave and cognac, warm leather and his personal, musky scent she found so attractive. She took a deep breath and let the peace of the room settle over her, ran her hand across the worn leather on the arm of his chair and then curled up in its comfortable depths.

The shades on the window looking out over the back meadow were open. One of the outside lights burned brightly, sending its stark glare across the grassy expanse.

Was that rain? No. Snow was falling. Tiny ice crystals shimmering in the beam of light, coming down thicker and faster even as she watched. Finally, the first snowfall of the season, weeks behind schedule.

It must have just started, but snow was already sticking to the deck and the railings. She sat and stared as it fell, as the deck disappeared beneath powdery drifts and the wind picked up, swirling the flakes this way and that in a silent dance against one beam of light slicing through the darkness.

As hypnotic as the view was, it couldn't pull her away from her problem. What in the hell was she going to do about Adam? She loved him, but she couldn't have him, and that was absolutely unacceptable.

Leaning her head back against the chair, she closed her eyes and asked the impossible. "Eve, what can I do? I need your help, but I want your man. After what I did to you, can you ever forgive me enough to help me figure this out?"

Obviously, there would be no answer. A goddess, after all, wouldn't respond to such a selfish request. Liana sighed and settled into the soft leather chair. She set her worries free until her thoughts were lost in the swirling snow, until she drifted, like the shimmering flakes, into sleep—or had she?

Liana opened her eyes to a familiar scene. Somehow, she must have slipped through that mysterious veil separating the astral planes. She certainly wasn't in Montana.

She lay on freshly cut grass beside her favorite pool, the one so far away, in another time and space. She raised her head and gazed about her. The water bubbled and frothed, a soft breeze whispered and the air felt tropically humid and warm. She'd always loved it here, though now it seemed rather dull and insipid, compared to Montana. She sat up and stretched, pushed the sleeves of her ratty old robe back so they didn't cover her hands, and looked into the eyes of the goddess.

Eve sat on the grass just a few feet away. She held a bouquet of bright blue larkspur that glistened against her long, white gown. Her eyes swirled with that mysterious combination of green to gold to gray, just the way Liana's used to.

"How are you, Eve? Are you okay?"

Eve laughed. It was such an unexpected, joyful response, Liana returned her smile. "I guess that answers my question. Was that you? Did you bring the rain?"

Eve nodded. "I did," she said, and her soft southern

drawl sounded just the same as it always had. "My first true act of power. It was amazing. I called on the Mother for rain and watched the clouds boil and seethe and voila! It rained and the fire went out. But Liana, are you okay? You seem troubled."

"What am I going to do?"

"Ah. You've come about Adam. I expected you to show up eventually. You've gotten yourself in a pretty good fix, haven't you?" She ran her fingers over the brilliant blue flowers in her lap. When she raised her head and looked at Liana again, her expression was serious. "Remember what Anton said about change requiring great sacrifice?"

Liana nodded, certain her heart would break. "I have to give up Adam. That's the sacrifice, isn't it?"

Eve frowned. "No. What makes you think that?" She stood up and walked across the neatly mowed grass and handed one of the bright stems of larkspur to Liana. "I love the fact I can have my favorite flowers here, no matter the time of year."

Liana stared at the flower in her hand and thought of all the things she'd loved about this life. Loved, but didn't really miss. Flowers out of season were one of them. She glanced up and took the hand Eve held out to her.

Eve pulled her to her feet. "What holds you apart from Adam—from the entire pack, for that matter—is what you have in your memories, the overabundance of knowledge stored in that brain of yours. It's too much. It's what keeps you from being entirely mortal. It almost killed Anton."

Liana stared at the larkspur in her hand. "I know. I had barriers up, but I had no idea . . ."

Eve sighed. "The Mother didn't tell you, but she left your memories and your knowledge intact so that you'd still have a choice. You can choose to take back your role as goddess once again, should you want it, or you can keep your mortality."

Shocked, Liana laughed this time. "Why would I want it back? I was a horrible goddess! Eve, you're so much better at this than I ever was. It's your role to play, not mine."

Eve squeezed Liana's hand in both of hers. "Are you saying you freely renounce your claim to the power, even though you could take it back, should you wish?"

Liana shrugged. "I already thought I'd given it up, when the Mother cast me out."

"I think she only meant to punish you, to teach you a lesson."

Liana glanced from the impossible stem of larkspur in one hand to Eve's fingers wrapped around her other. She let go of Eve's hand and brushed the goddess's cheek with her fingertips. "I must have learned the wrong lesson, then, my friend. I love my new life. I was frightened at first. Afraid of the change from the only life I'd ever known to one that was totally unfamiliar, but I've come to view the Mother's action as a wonderful gift, not punishment. I don't want to come back here."

Eve brushed the petals of the flowers she held against her lips and blushed. "To be perfectly honest, Liana, I don't want you back here, either." She laughed. "Just now, when I saw you, I was so afraid you were coming to reclaim your job."

"Never." She blew out a big breath of air. "Thank goodness we've got that cleared up! What I need to know is, if there's some way to clear that knowledge from my mind, at least enough to make me entirely mortal? Enough so I can bond with Adam, should he ever love me?"

Eve's eyes closed and she stood very still. Conversing with the Mother? It had never been that easy for Liana. When Eve finally opened her eyes, she sighed. "The knowledge you have can never be lost. You hold the mystery of our kind, the history of the Chanku. History I, if I'm to be an effective goddess, will need."

Liana frowned. "Then how? Is there some way to

transfer those memories, move them from my mind to yours?"

Eve nodded. "There is, but that's where the sacrifice comes in. It's a horrible risk, Liana. You could lose everything you know, everything that makes you who you are. Your memories of your childhood, your ability to heal, your knowledge of our history. Are you willing to take that chance?"

Shivers raced along her spine. What if she forgot Adam? Forgot that she loved him? What if she forgot how to shift? Would she even recognize her packmates?

Did it really matter, if she could never bond with the one man she fell more in love with every day?

"I have to." Liana twirled the larkspur in her palms. The flowers spun, faster and faster, until she clasped her hands together and stopped the spinning. She held the single stem tightly between her palms and stared at the brilliant blue, at flowers that shouldn't be blooming this time of year at all. "I failed as their goddess," she said. "You haven't. The Chanku—I—need you. You're already better at this job than I, with all my eons of training, could ever hope to be. If the knowledge I have makes you even better, able to help the Chanku more, it should be yours. I offer it freely."

Eve nodded. "Go back now. What we'll need to do is similar to a mating bond, except I will take and you will give. I promise to be careful, not to take more than I need. Tell Anton what you want to do. Ask him if he can help us. Then gather everyone together and call me. Your combined strength will bring me through the veil. Once I'm there, we can proceed, and with any luck, it might actually work."

"And if we fail? Are you at any risk?"

Eve shook her head and stroked Liana's cheek with the backs of her fingers. "No, my friend. The risk is entirely yours."

Liana blinked back tears. If they failed, she could end up an empty shell. "Promise me, Eve. If anything goes wrong, please promise you'll bring me back here with you. I wouldn't want Adam left with a mindless wraith instead of a woman."

Eve leaned close and kissed her. "Go, now. Call Anton and ask for his help. I'll be waiting."

Liana blinked, caught in the swirling colors of Eve's eyes, in the brilliant blue larkspur blending with green and gold and gray. Then she was waking up in Anton's recliner, watching snowflakes swirl and dance outside the window in the half-light of early dawn. Over a foot of the white stuff blanketed the deck. Had she dreamed her meeting with Eve?

She glanced at her hands folded in her lap, at her fingers wrapped around a single stem of bright blue larkspur. Then she sent out a mental shout to the one man who would know what to do next.

Anton!

Adam awoke alone in Liana's bed, fuzzy headed and blinking in the pale gray light before sunrise. Liana was gone. The warm spot on the bed next to him carried the pungent odor of mountain lion. He sat up, noted the fresh snow on the deck outside the window and the partially filled-in prints of the big cat.

He stretched to the pop and crackle of his back and shoulders, which reminded him of some of the acrobatics the three of them had managed the night before. His mouth tasted like something had died inside, so he got out of bed and headed into the bathroom.

Still no sign of Liana, but she'd probably gone in search of coffee. For someone who'd just discovered the brew, she'd become an addict awfully fast.

After he splashed cold water on his face and brushed

his teeth with Liana's toothbrush, Adam went looking for his pants. That's when he noticed Igmutaka out in the middle of the meadow, sitting by himself in the snow, staring toward the forest.

Curious, Adam forgot the pants, stepped out through the glass slider and quietly shut it behind him. Bitter cold raised goose bumps over his skin, but thick fur warmed him as soon as he shifted. He trotted through the snow to see what was up with the cat.

Igmutaka turned his head toward Adam as he picked his way through the soft, powdery snow. The temperature had definitely fallen during the night and his breath left soft puffs of steam, but after wondering for so long if winter was ever going to show up, the snow and cold were more than welcome.

Ice crystals shimmered on Igmutaka's fur. He must have been out here for a while, sitting in the snow and staring at the dark woods. The cat watched Adam come closer. Then he turned his attention back to the trees. Adam sat beside him and studied the dark forest, thinking how odd it would look, were anyone to see a cougar and a wolf sitting side by side on a snowy morning.

He waited, but the silence stretched out between them. Not uncomfortable, but not entirely relaxed, either. Finally Adam turned to the cat. *Something bothering you, cat?*

Igmutaka let out a long, slow breath. *I have never been with a man before.*

Ah. I wondered if that was it. I'm sorry if we pushed you into something that felt wrong. That was never our intent.

The cougar snorted and turned to stare at Adam out of glittering green eyes. *Far from it. I think that's what bothers me. I liked it too much. I felt . . . complete. Connected in a way I've never been before with a sexual partner in my animal form. Even when I was with Mei and Oliver, sharing their desire, their sex with one another, it wasn't this good.*

And there's a problem with good? Adam didn't want to laugh, but the spirit guide seemed unaccountably serious for merely enjoying a good fuck.

Among the Lakota, one who shares the female spirit is called winkte. *They have great spiritual power and are held in high regard by the tribe. I am not* winkte, *not homosexual, yet I was your bitch last night, and it was good. Then I awakened this morning, my staff swollen with seed, wanting to make love to you, not Liana. So I must ask you, wolfman—have you somehow changed my nature?*

His deep sigh echoed in the morning silence and underscored his confusion

Adam thought about it before answering. They were such different creatures, their very natures different. Wolf and lion, Chanku shapeshifter and Lakota Sioux spirit guide. One began as a human not even four decades earlier, the other as a wild cougar long before recorded time.

So very, very different.

A powerful libido drives the Chanku, he said, speaking carefully. *The need for sexual release, especially after a run in our animal form, the need for connection. Maybe your nature as a shapeshifter is more like ours when you're a man than when you're in your animal form. The sexual desire for others, no matter their gender, is normal for us. Have you been a man before? Made love to a woman as a man?*

The cougar turned and stared at him for a long, long time. *No. I've not been human before. My natural form is the cat. I began as a wild cougar eons ago, before I became a spirit guide.*

Why did you shift now?

His ears went back, and he snarled. *For Liana. To make*

love to a beautiful female, wolfman. Not to fuck your ugly hide.

Then his dry chuckle took the sting from his words. Arousal surged, and Adam shot back, *You still haven't fucked my ugly hide, cat. I fucked yours.*

That can be remedied. Igmutaka tilted his broad head and dared Adam with his sparkling eyes.

Follow me. Without another word, Adam turned away and trotted through the snow. Not back to the house—instead he headed directly to his little room over the garage.

Igmutaka kept pace right behind him.

"You're saying that if we all gather in the meadow and call on Eve, she can materialize here, on this plane? I've done it before, when I brought Ulrich's mate, Camille, back, but she was trapped on the astral, not there by choice as an immortal goddess." Anton sat on the footstool in front of Liana with his forearms resting on his thighs, a cup of hot coffee cradled in his hands. His hair was mussed, his shirt undone and he'd not fastened the top button on his jeans.

Still warm and sexy from his bed, he'd come to Liana the moment she called. Now he questioned her, and it was more than obvious his level of interest grew with every answer she gave.

"That's what she said. She has to come here in order to transfer my knowledge. For some reason we couldn't do it there."

"What are the risks?"

She'd really hoped he wouldn't ask that question. Liana shook her head. Shrugged away her concerns. "I could lose too many memories, too much of what makes me, me."

"Then it's too dangerous."

"No, Anton." She shook her head so hard her hair whipped around her shoulders, but he had to understand.

"It's not. Not if the choice is to exist without ever bonding with someone I love."

Slowly he nodded. Smiled and shot her a glance out of the corner of his eye. "Anyone in particular?"

She blushed and stared at her toes.

"I thought so. And Eve is willing to help you?"

Liana raised her head and forced him to meet her eyes. "Like I said, she's a better goddess than I ever was."

The Chanku, by nature, were predators. Times like this, taking a man to his bed who still questioned the basic morality of sex between them, made Adam feel like a sexual predator. Had he forced Igmutaka to do something against his nature? Was he wrong to encourage even more experimentation?

The spirit guide was not Chanku, though Adam vaguely recalled someone saying that all shapeshifters had originated in the same area of Tibet, all children of the same Mother. Maybe they were related in some convoluted way—except Igmutaka had never actually been human.

If that were the case, why had he manifested as such a beautiful man? His features, while entirely masculine, could have been every bit as lovely if he were female, but there was no doubt that Igmutaka was all male—a powerful, imposing male—and he was following Adam up the stairs to his room with a purposeful stride and the obvious intent to have sex.

The kind of sex that took two strong men to their most basic, primal level. Alphas both, one choosing to submit, not bowing beneath domination. Never bowing.

Trembling more with anticipation and need than the cold, Adam opened the door. He'd shifted at the foot of the stairs and walked through snow barefoot to reach his room, yet his body felt flushed with heat.

Only his toes were cold.

Igmutaka followed on four feet. His hot breath bathed Adam's flank and the deep, chuffing sound he made sent shivers along his spine. Adam wondered if he should rethink the situation. He'd long thought of himself as a predator. Igmutaka fit the part much better than he.

Adam opened the door and stepped back.

The cougar entered. He stayed in cat form, padding softly around the room, sniffing at the corners and under the bed, peering into the bathroom and the closet, reminding Adam he was truly a beast at heart. At one point, he lifted up slowly on his back legs and rested a paw high on the wall for balance, sniffing along the edge of the window, raising little puffs of dust as he explored. Then he delicately dropped back to all four feet and gazed at Adam.

When he finally shifted and stood on two feet in the center of the room, Igmutaka filled the space, not only with his size but his presence. Adam stepped close to him and pressed his palm flat against Igmutaka's chest. "Okay, cat. Whatever you want," he said. "However you like it. Feel free to experiment." He ran his fingers across the jutting collarbone, over his shoulder, across his chest. Slowly, gently, he rubbed the dark berry colored nipple over Igmutaka's heart.

Igmutaka's eyes drifted shut. Adam took the lead and rubbed both nipples, pinching and squeezing, bringing them to taut little points. He stepped closer until the hard length of his cock brushed against the underside of Igmutaka's, tilted his head and worried first one nipple and then the other with his teeth.

A low rumble vibrated the skin beneath his mouth, the growl of a needy beast. Adam laved the nipple with his tongue. The growl grew louder, more insistent.

"Well, Ig . . . either you really like that or you're about ready to shift and take my head off."

"I like it too much, wolfman. Now give that same attention to my cock." He glared at Adam. "And do not call Igmutaka 'Ig.'"

Adam lifted one eyebrow. "Getting bossy now, aren't you? Had no idea you were a dom." But he smiled when he said it, went to his knees and cupped the man's sac in his palm. The heat and weight spiked his arousal another notch. He couldn't blame this on the shift. It was all the man, the circumstances, the scent of his body, the velvety weight of his balls—and most of all, the visual of Igmutaka's heavily engorged penis rising high and hard against his belly.

The color fascinated Adam and reminded him of Mik. Not really brown, not red, but a beautiful dark bronze shade with a darker map of thick veins running just beneath the surface. The single drop of milky pre-cum glistening on the curve of his dark, silky glans was all the invitation Adam needed.

He wrapped his fingers around the thick base and brought the crown to his lips, ran his tongue over the sensitive tip. He dipped beneath the foreskin that had rolled back behind the thick flare and lightly stretched it with his tongue, sighing with the unimaginable pleasure of taste and texture.

He tightened his fingers around Igmutaka's huge ball sac, fascinated by its weight and size, the warmth of those two firm orbs within their pouch, the perfect fit, nestled in his palm.

There was no way he could swallow this cock, and he didn't intend to try. That was Liana's trick, not his, but he could still tease with lips and tongue and teeth, still fit the thick knob inside his mouth and suck hard enough to hollow his cheeks.

Igmutaka's hands came down hard on top of his head and held him perfectly still. His breath rasped out in harsh staccato bursts as Adam continued teasing and tasting. He squeezed his fingers around Igmutaka's balls, ran his middle finger up the crease between his cheeks and spun little circles over the tight pucker guarding his ass.

Igmutaka trembled and images spilled into Adam's mind. The way his lips looked, circling the smooth glans, his tangled, dark blond hair tickling Igmutaka's belly and the thick length of Adam's forearm disappearing between his thick, muscular thighs.

It was too much—not nearly enough. With a rumbled curse, Igmutaka backed away from Adam's grasp, away from his mouth. He leaned over and braced his hands on his thighs, just above his knees, and the air whooshed in and out of his lungs. "I want you there, wolfman," he said, pointing to the side of the bed. "Lean over it. Where's that slick stuff you used, that stuff to help you get inside me? I want it now."

Adam stood up and laughed. "Pushy bastard, aren't you? Whatever you want, big guy. No need for a condom if it's just the two of us. The call's all yours."

Igmutaka grunted, but he watched everything Adam did with dark, glittering eyes. Adam found a tube of KY next to the bed. He put it in Igmutaka's hand, showed him how the lid flipped open. Then he turned around and assumed the position, leaning over the side of the bed. The mattress was tall enough that he knew his ass was at the perfect height for penetration.

A wave of total vulnerability washed over him. He wasn't all that certain how much he was going to enjoy this. Igmutaka was hung like a bull moose, but he didn't seem to appreciate the subtleties of good foreplay. Of course, if no one ever thought to teach him . . .

Adam imagined Igmutaka going down on his knees behind Adam, using his tongue and lips on Adam's balls and cock, licking in and around his ass. He shared the visual, the way it turned him on. He felt Igmutaka's surprise, sensed when it segued into interest and blatant curiosity that quickly turned to arousal.

Igmutaka dropped to his knees behind Adam and spread his thighs and butt cheeks apart. Then he sucked Adam's entire sack inside the hot cavern of his mouth.

"Holy shit, man. You don't kid around, do you?" Adam gasped as Igmutaka sucked and tongued his balls. His cock rose hard and full against the mattress, trapped between soft bedding and his belly. The intimacy of Igmutaka's oral foreplay, the hot sweep of his tongue, the pressure of those big hands holding him open and vulnerable, took Adam to an unimaginable, unexpected level.

He wasn't sure how long he could hang on, not with Igmutaka's unpracticed yet wildly erotic exploration of so many erogenous places. He hooked a ride on the spirit guide's mental and physical journey, absorbing his own taste through Igmutaka's touch, the scent and texture of his buttocks and balls.

Swept up in the mind play, he felt Igmutaka's fascination with this intimate foray into a human male's body. His tongue found Adam's sphincter and he poked and probed that sensitive ring. Then, recalling what Adam had done to ease his way the night before, he opened the tube of KY and dribbled a glob of the cool gel down the crease in his ass.

One thick finger slipped in, and then a second. He sawed in and out a few times until the pleasure was almost unbearable before adding a third. Adam moaned, a tortured sound of pleasure, not pain. When Igmutaka slipped his fingers free, Adam felt bereft, unaccountably empty.

Then the sleek, broad tip of what had to be the largest cock to ever come in contact with his ass pressed softly against his taut ring.

He immediately tensed. Igmutaka didn't seem to notice. He increased pressure slowly and steadily, forcing that huge glans against Adams comparatively tiny, puckered ass. He had to fight his instincts, the voice screaming in his head to get up and get the hell away from this guy before getting split wide open.

Those instincts weren't easy to overrule, but he pushed back against the pressure and ordered himself to relax. Igmutaka grunted and leaned against Adam, forcing the thick crown hard against, and finally through, his tight sphincter.

The pain was indescribable—delicious and agonizing, seductive and dark and, he feared, something he could easily become addicted to. Breathing in short, sharp pants through parted lips, Adam willed his tense muscles to relax in spite of the sharp burn of entry—a sharp burn that grew worse, not better, as Igmutaka slowly forced his massive cock deep inside.

Adam swore under his breath. Then he swore out loud and fisted his hands in the rumpled bedding. He felt every single millimeter of that huge cock pushing its way into his bowel. His body fought the intrusion, tensing against the pain, making it worse.

Contrary jackass that he was, the more it hurt, the more turned-on he got. The deeper Igmutaka went, the more Adam wanted. Finally, when the rough hair at Igmutaka's groin brushed Adam's buttocks, both men paused, blowing as if they'd just run a mile. Igmutaka held perfectly still, giving Adam time to adjust—as if adjusting to that monster was even possible.

Adam wasn't about to move at all. Not with all of that rammed inside him, and he wondered when it would finally start feeling good. Except the pain, the fullness, the living blanket of this man's big body covering his so gently with that massive boner jammed up his butt was the most erotic thing he'd ever experienced in his life.

Igmutaka had never done this before and his mind was awash with the new sensations, spilling them in graphic, vivid detail into Adam's head until the two of them were flooded with images and feelings, a continual loop of Adam to Igmutaka and back again.

Then Igmutaka groaned and rolled his hips forward, thrusting even deeper. Adam grunted and shivers covered every inch of his skin, a rippling of sensation that ran from his toes to his scalp. Igmutaka withdrew, slowly pulling out until only the thick crown remained, trapped by Adam's taut sphincter.

He thrust forward, a little bit faster, withdrew slowly, then faster the next time, and deep. So terribly deep. In and out, his body ruled by a primal rhythm only he could hear.

Pain and pleasure wrapped Adam in a seductive coil. His cock rode against the bedding, his balls jerked with each slap from Igmutaka's full sac until his body gave in to the darkness, gave in to pain and turned it fully to pleasure, embraced the pounding penetration, the burning and tearing that never quite ended, yet seemed to change as time passed.

Changed and expanded. It wasn't just his ass getting fucked, it was all of him, his very existence caught in the throbbing rhythm, Igmutaka's rhythm, a drumbeat pounding in his blood, ruling the cadence of his heart. He was the spirit guide and Igmutaka was Adam Wolf, yet Adam remained aware of the barriers in the man's mind—barriers guarding ancient secrets and knowledge he could not share.

Even so, this time he knew what was coming, anticipated the tug and separation as his mind and body loosed the tethers holding them, rejoined, becoming one with the man who continued to drive deep inside with every powerful thrust of his hips.

He sensed Igmutaka's curiosity, but there was no fear when the two of them connected overhead, as if they floated near the ceiling of the small bedroom. Looking down as if through a fish-eye lens, Adam watched the sensual buck and sway of Igmutaka's powerful body, watched as he rose up, pushed back to meet the man on every thrust.

What is this, wolfman? Not a usual part of fucking, is it?

Not at all, but it happens sometimes when the sex is really good.

Igmutaka's spirit self merely grunted. Then, very quietly, he said, *That's good. I was afraid I might have hurt you.*

Only in a good way, my friend. A very good way. Come . . .

And with that simple command, Adam was back and his orgasm blossomed in both body and mind, coiling tight and charging through his system, bursting free in a flash of power and sensation that exploded out of him.

Igmutaka jerked against his buttocks and he cried out. His words were a jumble of languages old and new, his jubilant shout of conquest as old as time. He fell forward, slumping over Adam with all the tension gone from his massive body.

They lay there together, intimately connected, muscles still clenching and rippling with the shock of their climax. Adam felt Igmutaka's chest rumble against his back.

"What's so funny, cat?"

"I am thinking if this is my nature, it's going to kill me."

Adam laughed. "Yeah. Me, too."

"Do you want me to move? Can you breathe?"

"No and yes. Don't move. I like you inside me when you're not the size of a Louisville Slugger."

"A what?"

"Never mind." Adam's muscles felt like jelly. His belly

was sticky from his ejaculate and he felt Igmutaka's running down the insides of his thighs. Definitely time for a shower. Soon. Sometime soon.

Damn. Looks like I'm too late.

"Anton?" Adam nudged Igmutaka. "Did you hear Anton Cheval just now?"

You both heard me. I wanted to ask you to practice abstinence this morning. We need to harness your sexual energy tonight.

You're right. It's too late.

Igmutaka's voice intruded. *I'll make sure he's built up more by then.* He pumped his hips against Adam's butt.

Anton's laughter rippled over Adam's thoughts, but Igmutaka's teasing thrusts already had him growing hard. *Why do you need the energy boost?*

There was a long moment of silence. Liana's voice cut in. *We want to call Eve and bring her through the veil. She needs the knowledge stored in my memories if she's to do her job as goddess. We can only make the transfer here, with Anton's help.*

Eve? Alive once again, if only for a short time? Once more a living, breathing woman? Adam's head fell forward on the bed. Igmutaka pulled slowly out of his ass and his body sagged against the sticky bedding. He hadn't seen Eve since that fateful day just weeks ago when he'd tried to kill himself. Could he see her again without reawakening all the old pain?

He wasn't sure. Wasn't certain he wanted any part of Liana's plans, whatever they were. His life was so fucked right now, he didn't know if he could take the pain of seeing Eve . . . and then losing her once again.

Chapter 15

It was almost midnight when they gathered in the meadow behind the house, eight wolves, a snow leopard, and one large mountain lion forming a silent circle beneath the pale light of a waning moon. Snow had fallen on and off all day long. The soft powder reflected the light that threw ghostly shadows across the shimmering surface.

Adam sat apart, watching, unsure still whether or not he could participate. He'd watched quietly as Keisha set a small, white monitor on a convenient tree stump before joining the circle, and would have laughed if he'd been in his human form. He might have lost his courage but at least his sense of humor was intact.

Somehow, bringing a baby monitor to a mystical gathering of shapeshifters come together to summon the dead seemed just a bit out of place, but Anton insisted everyone needed to be here.

Keisha and Xandi weren't about to leave their babies unguarded, even though both children slept soundly right now.

Maybe he should offer to watch them himself. He had no business being here. None at all. If guilt could screw up a ceremony, it would be his. Guilt over not being enough for Eve, guilt over loving Liana, guilt over his cruel treatment of the ex-goddess, over his selfish ways when he'd been with Eve . . . was there any place in his life where he hadn't screwed up?

He turned and caught Igmutaka watching him. Hell, he even felt guilty about the damned cat. He'd created a monster, showing him what sex between two guys could be like. He'd lost count of the times they'd fucked today, at least until the cat had disappeared with Liana.

He had no idea where they'd gone, what they'd done, and he'd been too damned stubborn to ask. Shit. One of these days, he really needed to grow up. Movement caught his eye and he glanced again toward the circle. He'd have time to deal with all his failures later, but now Anton had moved to the center, a huge black wolf against the pristine surface of white snow, and all attention was on the pack leader.

Mei shifted. The leopard became a wolf, probably so she could understand whatever Anton said. The cougar, of course, remained a cat, but Igmutaka was able to understand their mindtalking when they were wolves, unlike Mei, whose leopard wasn't as multilingual.

Adam. You need to join the circle.

I'm not really sure about this, he said, finally admitting it to everyone here. *I'm afraid my presence might affect your chances of calling Eve.*

Only if you're not with us. Join us now, Adam.

The quiet command behind Anton's words left no room for argument. It was all it took to bring him into the circle, sliding into place between Logan and Igmutaka. Liana sat directly across from him. She watched him out of her beautiful gray-green eyes with her ears pointed forward and her thick brush of a tail wrapped daintily about her front toes.

In the center, Anton raised his head and howled. He'd already explained that since their power was stronger in their wolven form, and since Eve was expecting to be called, this would be more effective.

It certainly felt powerful. Adam raised his head and joined the chorus. His human mind processed the power, the sense of the pack and the perfect unity of their voices raised together in wild song.

His feral side rejoiced in the strength of the pack, but his mind wasn't on the logic behind calling their goddess to them in her corporeal form. No, it was on the bitch sitting across the circle from him, the beautiful gray wolf with the mystical eyes and the scent of her coming heat.

He wanted her. Needed her on a level he'd never admit to himself in his human shape. The human side still grieved for what was lost, what could never be replaced because, in many ways, it was perception, not reality that was forever gone.

His wolf admitted the truth—Liana filled all those empty places in his heart. She was the perfect match to his imperfect, needy self—a better match than Eve had ever been. Eve, so willing to accommodate his desires, so quick to do what she thought he wanted, be the woman he thought he needed. In truth, she'd been an enabler, giving him everything he wanted, but not necessarily what was good for either of them.

It had taken him so long to figure it out—why she'd leapt at the chance to exist as a goddess on another astral plane, choosing a thankless job, in his mind, over being his mate, but he understood now.

She'd given up herself when she mated him. She hadn't known how to remain true to herself, to be her own woman. After a lifetime with abusive men, she'd automatically fallen into the role of the woman she thought he wanted. She'd lost herself in loving him, and he, like a fool, hadn't realized just how much she'd given up.

No wonder she ran from him in the beginning. She'd

seen it coming even then—the loss of her newfound freedom as the helpmate to yet another demanding male.

Liana wasn't like that. Not at all. She had her own sense of power, an innate knowledge of who and what she was. She was a healer, if not more powerful than he was, at least of equal skills. She had a mind that could kill him, should either of them grow careless, held knowledge that even the great Anton Cheval lusted after.

There was no risk of Liana subjugating herself to any man, much less to Adam. She was the perfect mate for him, except it was impossible. Without the mating bond, they could be lovers, friends—but never soul mates.

So be it. If it meant the rest of his life without a life mate, without that amazing mental and emotional bond he'd once shared with Eve, they'd still make it work. Somehow.

Their song ended. Igmutaka's scream cut through the bitter night, a fitting, final note. It was time. Adam opened his mind to Anton, allowed his energy to flow into the huge black wolf at the center of their circle. Somehow, Anton absorbed it all, the shared energy from every creature here, until he seemed to glow with their accumulated power. His fur stood on end. Sparks flashed over his head and shoulders.

The air above Anton shimmered. Adam felt a slight *pop*, as if the pressure had suddenly changed. He blinked, and Eve stood beside Anton with one hand resting on his broad skull.

His amazing Eve, perfect and beautiful as always, yet no longer the woman he'd loved. No longer human. Not Chanku. She was their goddess, an immortal power gowned in white with shimmering eyes swirling in that hypnotic gray to green to gold that caught and held him motionless.

She smiled his way, acknowledged him with the tilt of her chin. Then she turned to Liana and reached out her hand. Liana shifted, but as she rose to two legs in human form, she turned and looked at Adam. Her soft *I love you* echoed in his mind.

He was still reeling with her unexpected declaration when Liana glanced away and, barefoot and naked in the snow, walked to Eve. Eve drew her hand through the air. A clear bubble of energy encased them all, snow disappeared and the wolves sat in lush green grass, their fur warmed by a breeze as soft as summer.

Still rattled, his mind spinning, Adam tried to concentrate as Eve swept her hand over the front of her gown and the silky fabric shimmered to the ground and puddled around her feet. She gazed steadily at Liana. "Of your own free will, among witnesses, do you choose to give up all knowledge pertaining to the role of goddess?"

Liana's eyes never wavered and her voice was clear and strong. "Of my own free will, among witnesses, I give unto the Goddess Eve that which I know."

"So be it." Eve dipped her head in solemn acknowledgment of Liana's pledge. Then she wrapped her arms around Liana and drew her into a tight embrace. Eve was taller, stronger than Liana. She held her close with one hand placed just above the round curve of Liana's lush behind and the other hidden in her blond hair, supporting the back of her head. Then Eve kissed Liana.

Their mouths came together, open, searching, fusing both women, one to the other, in a kiss that lasted an eternity. Liana wrapped her arms around Eve and strained up on her toes so that their full breasts met and pillowed together, and their pubes meshed, blond curls to blond curls.

Thighs straining, bodies touching from top to bottom, they writhed together in a sensual dance that was all the more powerful, bathed as they were in the shared energy of the pack.

With Liana's *I love you* echoing in his head, Adam felt his cock expand beyond his wolven sheath. When he managed to tear his gaze away from the women, he saw that every other male in the circle was just as aroused. Even the big cat was erect, his unsheathed penis a red brand against his belly, while the female wolves squirmed against the soft grass as if they couldn't bear to remain still.

Finally, long minutes later, Eve straightened up, ending the kiss. Liana remained perfectly still, obviously supported in Eve's embrace. Her eyes were closed. Adam remained in place, but he began to worry at Liana's silence, her stillness.

Eve brushed her hand over Liana's long hair and sighed. "I think it worked. I have the knowledge Liana promised me, the memories so ancient they threatened those of you who might link too deeply with her."

Eve knelt and lay Liana down in the thick grass. She still hadn't moved. Adam glanced at Anton, but the leader's mind was blocked to him. He asked, anyway. *What the fuck is going on?*

Eve brushed Liana's long blond hair back from her face and stared directly at Adam. "Liana asked me for a promise, one I refused to give her, that should anything go wrong, I take her back with me. I don't know if she will be all right or not, but I'm not taking her. Liana was cast out of her world because of her failure to guard those she was charged with protecting, but she grew to love her mortal life. Offered a chance to return as goddess, she chose mortality of her own free will. I am only here because she asked me to take what knowledge I needed, better to do my job as your goddess."

Eve raised her head, but she still looked directly at Adam. Pleading with him? "I warned her, Adam. I told her she might never be the same, that the process could leave her nothing more than an empty shell, but she insisted. She said that if she couldn't bond with you, she didn't care to live. Foolish woman."

Adam's blood ran cold. He stared at Liana, lying so still and silent in the grass. Then he looked closely at Eve. Her concern was honest, but at the same time he felt her satisfaction—she'd gotten exactly what she wanted, what she needed.

Knowledge. Power. More power than she'd ever known in her life, and if it meant the destruction of one woman's mind, it was worth it, a justifiable sacrifice to the new and rightful goddess in the overall scheme of things.

Had Eve always been like this?

"No, Adam." She shook her head and stood up beside Liana. "You can't blame me for this. Liana asked me to do this. She knew the risks. She was willing to take them."

His shift was fueled by anger, by the pure frustration of not knowing what to do, how to fix what was obviously so badly broken. "Why, damn it?" Tears blinded him. He stood upright as a man, went to Liana and knelt beside her. Touched his fingers to her throat, but he had to search to find her weak pulse. "If this was all to give you some damned information, why couldn't she just tell you? Why all the mumbo jumbo? Why would she do such a stupid, reckless thing?"

Eve touched her fingers to his shoulder. They felt ice cold against his skin. Inhuman. He glared at her, aware of a side to Eve, a selfish side he'd never seen before. Maybe he'd just never wanted to see it.

"She did it for you, Adam. It was all for you."

Eve didn't merely fade away—she disappeared with a rush of icy wind and a change in pressure powerful enough to make his ears pop. Without hesitation, Adam scooped Liana's limp body up in his arms and stalked back to the house through the snow. "Logan, open the clinic. Now."

Logan raced past him on all four feet, shifted at the deck and ran inside. Adam never broke stride as he walked through the open door and carried Liana up the steps to the pack's small infirmary. The others followed him, but he noticed Anton stayed to the back of the pack.

Anton knew this could happen. Damn it all, but he had to know there were risks. How the hell could he ever allow . . . No. Not allow, he'd made it happen. He'd done the fucking spell that brought Eve back. Practically snarling in frustrated rage, Adam carried Liana through the door to the clinic and carefully stretched her out on the bed.

She looked so peaceful—perfectly relaxed, as if she were merely taking a nap. He picked up her hand and wrapped her limp fingers in his. No response. No sense of Liana at all. Adam turned and glared at Anton, who'd finally stepped into the clinic. "Why, Anton? Tell me why."

Hours later, Anton leaned against Logan's desk in the small office beside the room where Liana slept, and sipped at the cognac in his glass. He wondered, once again, how he could have prevented this terrible tragedy from happening. Adam stared out the window. Like Anton, he'd slipped on a pair of worn jeans but his bare back and naked feet gave him an oddly vulnerable look. A man of immense power, of even stronger passions, he reminded Anton now of a lost kid.

Like so many of them, Adam's childhood had been one of betrayal and loss. Anton hated being the cause of yet another horrible chapter in his life, but partly because of his actions, Liana lay on the bed in the next room like a broken flower, her sweetness extinguished, the woman they'd come to know and love, for all intents and purposes, quite possibly gone forever.

"You're saying that she knew, going into this, that she could end up wiped clean of everything? No memories, no personality, nothing at all that made her who she was? She knew?" Adam spun around. He held his clenched fists at his sides, but his eyes were dark, empty pools, devoid of any light.

Anton nodded. "She went to Eve of her own free will. Told her she'd almost killed Stefan and me and wanted to get rid of her ancient knowledge, her memories of so many thousands of years. She wanted a mortal's mind with a mortal's knowledge. Eve needed that knowledge to fulfill her role as goddess, something she told Liana. It was Liana's choice to attempt a transfer. She told me that herself. Not Eve's."

"But Eve, knowing the danger, accepted her offer? Bitch. That damned bitch."

"She was your mate, Adam. The woman you loved, and yet you can stand here and curse her?" Anton shook his head. "Think of what you're saying."

Adam glared at him. "I am. Eve knew the risk to Liana but she was willing to do it anyway to get what she wanted. Liana took the risk because she was thinking of all of us, not of herself."

Anton shook his head. "Actually, Eve was thinking of her role to all Chanku, not just you. Liana? She was thinking of you, Adam. Only you. She loves you, but she knew there could never be anything between you until she did something about all her centuries of memories, all that marvelous knowledge that just about reformatted my brain."

Adam bowed his head. "She said she loved me. Just before she joined with Eve. Totally blew me away, because we'd never said the words, had barely accepted the fact we could be friends." He laughed, but the sound was fueled by a terrible anger. "It's like whatever I touch is screwed. Manda stayed locked in her cell for twenty-five fucking years, Eve died, Liana . . . shit. What's wrong with her? Will she ever wake up?"

Anton studied him over his glass. "Have you thought of going into her mind?"

Adam sighed. "Yeah. Of course I have, but I'm afraid of what I'll find. What if I get in there and there's nothing? What if Eve stripped her of everything?"

"You'll never know until you try. Remember, you saved

Eve's life doing something you really didn't want to do."
The day Adam had literally traveled inside Eve's damaged
skull and repaired a deadly blood clot had changed more
than Eve's life. It was the first time Adam realized he had
the power to heal.

"Yeah. I did, didn't I? Wonder if she thought of that
when she raped Liana's mind?"

Before Anton could think up a suitable reply, the door
opened and Igmutaka walked into the room with Logan
behind him.

"What are you going to do for her, wolfman? Her spirit
needs you."

Anton glanced at Logan, who merely shrugged as if he
didn't have a clue. "Why do you say that, Igmutaka? Can
you hear her?"

Frowning, the spirit guide looked from Adam to Anton.
Back at Adam. "Of course I can. Don't you hear her crying?"

Adam straightened up. "No." He shook his head. "I
don't hear anything when I go to her. Nothing at all. Is she
saying anything?"

Igmutaka shook his head. "She weeps and waits. I feel
her spirit. It's all alone in a very dark place, waiting. I
think it waits for you."

Adam pushed by him and went straight for Liana.
Logan and Igmutaka followed, while Anton brought up
the rear. He stood in the doorway while Adam knelt beside
Liana's bed. He touched her temples with the tips of his
fingers and closed his eyes. A moment later, he raised his
head. "Nothing. I can't find her."

Igmutaka stood beside him, staring down at Liana.
Then he knelt beside Adam. "Hold my hand, wolfman. I'll
take you to her."

Adam wrapped his fingers around Igmutaka's hand.
The spirit guide placed his left palm on Liana's chest over
her heart, and closed his eyes. After a moment, he tilted his

head back and began to chant. The words meant nothing to Anton. He guessed they were in the Lakota language, but he wasn't sure.

There was power in their rhythm, though. Power that surged through his veins and beat a perfect cadence with his heart, ancient power that called to the elements, to the life force in each of them in this room.

Without turning Igmutaka's hand free, Adam crawled up on the bed and lay beside Liana with his head on the pillow next to hers. His and the cat's linked hands rested on her flat stomach.

Igmutaka's chant rose and fell, like the flow of the tide washing inexorably to shore. His broad palm covered Liana's heart, his voice continued to draw power, to focus it on the woman lying so still upon the bed. Anton felt his thoughts floating, as if his mind had been freed from the tethers of his body. His life's essence swirled in the room, dancing with the others, singing with the spirit guide as he called Liana home.

It was dark, but darkness wasn't the worst of it. No, the worst part was how lonely she felt. She knew her name was Liana, knew she was Chanku, but she couldn't find her pack. Couldn't find the one who loved her. She wandered, entirely alone in the darkness, searching for the way home.

She wasn't even certain how she'd come here. One moment she'd been with so many who loved her, the next she'd felt a terrible pain in her head and there'd been a loud, loud noise, as if all the sounds of all the world had suddenly gathered in her skull.

And then it was silent, and so dark. So very dark where she wandered. She'd wept, but crying accomplished nothing. She'd called out, but she couldn't remember who to call for. There was a name, a man, one who wanted her.

At least she hoped he wanted her. She knew she'd made

a great sacrifice for him, if only she could remember what it was. Wandering certainly wasn't getting her anywhere. She folded her tired legs and sat. The ground was hard and smooth and flat, and she decided to concentrate on her surroundings. There must be someone looking for her. There had to be.

There were no birds, no sounds of insects, but she sensed a rhythm in the air, a pounding rhythm that seemed to ebb and flow with the beat of her heart, the rush of blood through her veins. The rhythm grew stronger, louder, and she recognized a man's voice chanting in one of the old tongues.

She used to understand the words. Not now. Now they were merely sounds, beautiful sounds calling to her. She listened more closely. Maybe she could recognize the words. No, they were foreign to her . . . but the voice was familiar. She remembered! Igmutaka? Was he the one chanting?

Where was Adam? How could she have forgotten Adam! She was almost certain he would come looking for her, if ever she were lost. Maybe she needed to ask him. That was it. She only had to ask.

Adam? Adam! Where are you?

Liana! I'm here. Liana, I can't find you. I hear your voice, but I can't see you.

Adam. She sighed, unbearably relieved. *I knew you'd come.*

There was a pale glimmer of light, almost swallowed up by the darkness, but she slowly rose to her feet and began walking. If she took her steps in time with the chant, she actually seemed to cover ground faster, so she paced herself, walking toward the light.

She saw a man, barely visible in the darkness and distance, but so achingly familiar she almost started crying again. Instead, she lifted up her feet and ran like the wind, running for the man, the light, the song she recognized now as the voice of Igmutaka chanting.

Adam held out his arms and she threw herself into his embrace. His body shuddered and she knew he wept, but it was okay now, and the chanting grew louder and the strength of the man's arms around her lifted her up. Lifted her up and carried her home.

She blinked, almost blinded by the overhead lights after the tomblike darkness where she'd been lost, but things were still blurry because the tears wouldn't stop flowing from her eyes. She was lying on a hard, flat bed and Adam's face was buried against her breasts. His shoulders were shaking and the front of her was wet, so she knew he cried as well.

She ran her fingers through his tangled hair and he lifted his chin and gazed at her, looking at her as if she'd been raised from the dead.

Well, maybe she had. Slowly, Liana turned to her right and smiled at Igmutaka. He knelt beside the bed, her proud warrior with glistening eyes and suspicious damp trails over his bronzed cheekbones. She reached for him, hooked her fingers around the back of his neck, and pulled him close.

"Thank you, both of you. I was lost and you found me."

Adam grabbed her fingers and kissed them. "It was the damned cat. I couldn't reach you, but he sensed your spirit. He knew how to call your spirit back, or we might have lost you."

"What happened?" She remembered kissing Eve, and then nothing. Nothing until she awakened in the darkness without any idea how to get back.

"When Eve transferred your memories, she either took too much or it was a shock to your mind. For whatever reason, you collapsed. Do you remember any of what happened?"

Liana nodded. "Help me sit up, please?"

Igmutaka arranged her pillows while Adam helped her

sit. Logan and Anton were in the room as well, both of them watching her with huge grins on their faces. She felt her energy returning, and with it a stronger sense of who and what she was, why she'd been lost, why she'd taken such a terrible risk.

It was all about Adam . . . and maybe, just a little, about the beautiful native American standing beside her bed. She patted the spot beside her. "You look ready to fall over. Sit beside me, please?"

Igmutaka nodded and sat carefully on the bed next to her. Adam had taken the other side and the two of them made her feel safe and protected.

"Why the hell did you do it, Liana?"

Her sense of well-being vanished. "Do what?"

"You know what, damn it! Eve could have killed you, stripping all that out of your mind."

"I knew the risks, Adam. I was willing to take them."

"Well I wasn't. You had no right to—"

Liana burst out laughing. She glanced at Anton. "You were right, you know. He does think it's all about him. The two of you are much more alike than I realized."

Adam grumbled. "What are you talking about?"

"This was about me, Adam. Not you. Me. I wanted to be mortal, and the only way I could swing it was to get rid of a lot of immortal baggage. Eve wants the role of goddess and that includes immortality, but she didn't have the knowledge to handle it, so a trade seemed like the perfect solution. Now she's got the information I've been storing since before recorded history."

"What did you get out of it then? Anything?"

She touched his face, ran the backs of her fingers along his jaw. "I got the best thing of all, Adam. A blank slate. A chance to write new memories. A mind that's not something I have to guard for fear of harming those I love." She looked up at Anton. "You can wander through my brain all you want now, Anton. I'm sorry you won't find much of interest in there anymore."

"Are you absolutely sure of that?" Anton stepped close to the bed and grabbed her hand. "Do you remember your childhood?"

She thought about it a moment, recalled a little girl with pigtails and a big brother who teased her, younger brothers who followed her around and made her crazy. "Yes. Anton, I do. More than before, in fact. I remember! I was afraid those memories were lost forever."

"Then I imagine there are still treasures to uncover. Will you still be a healer?"

Liana thought about that a moment, searched inside herself and felt the power spring to life. Smiling, she nodded at Anton. "I will. I am." She laughed, feeling such an amazing sense of joy, of contentment. "I was afraid I might lose that part of myself."

Anton leaned over and placed a very courtly kiss on the back of her hand. "I'm glad. It appears all those parts that make you special, that are the heart and the strength of you, remain. Sleep well, Liana. It's been a very long day and a longer night. We'll see you in the morning."

Anton and Logan left the clinic. Liana sat in the narrow bed with Igmutaka and Adam on either side, like bookends holding her close. She was absolutely wide awake, and sleep was the furthest thing from her mind. "What time is it?"

Adam glanced at a clock on the wall behind her. "Almost four. We couldn't find you for over three hours." He leaned close and kissed her lips, a chaste kiss that still made her toes tingle.

"I'm sorry. I couldn't tell you what I planned. I didn't have the energy to argue with you, and it really wasn't about you, Adam. It was a decision that affected me, affected the rest of my life—a life which, if everything worked, would be changing from never ending to one with a finite number of years—and it was a decision I had to make alone."

He nodded. "I understand. I don't have to like it, but I do understand." He glanced at Igmutaka and shook his head. "If we hadn't had the cat here to help, though, you'd still be wandering in the dark."

"You would have found her eventually, wolfman." Igmutaka slid off the bed and stood up. "Her spirit and yours are connected. I felt it when I searched for her. That's how I found her. I followed the life threads from your spirit to hers."

Adam grabbed Igmutaka's hand and held on. "Where are you going, cat? I was thinking of taking Liana up to my room so she can sleep in a comfortable bed instead of this thing." He smiled at her. "That is if you want to come to my room. It's up to you." Then he laughed. "See? I'm learning."

She smiled at him and nodded. "I'd like that. Igmutaka? It's a very big bed."

The spirit guide shook his head. "I've been inside these walls far too long. It's time for me to go back to the forest. I need to see how much of my home is left."

"You're leaving? Just for tonight, right?" Adam swung his legs off the bed and stood up. "I thought maybe you were going to hang on to this new shape for a while."

Igmutaka rested his hand on Adam's shoulder. "I won't go far, wolfman. Whenever you call me, I will come, but my life is in the forest, not here."

Adam took a deep breath. "I've grown used to your ugly mug. I'll miss you."

"I think you'll miss my . . . what did you call it? Louisville Slugger?"

Adam laughed. "Yeah. I'll definitely miss that."

"So will I." Liana reached for Igmutaka's hand and wrapped her fingers in his. Then she pulled him close and kissed him. "Thank you. You are always welcome in my life and in my bed. I will keep you in my heart forever. Remember that, even when you're far from your human self."

He stood straight and nodded. Then he reached for Adam and pulled him into his arms. Two powerful men who'd formed an amazing bond over the past few days. Liana wondered if she'd ever see him in this beautiful human form again.

The two separated. Igmutaka slipped out of his jeans and shifted much too quickly. Where once a perfect human male had stood, a large mountain lion waited for someone to open the door.

"I'll be back in a minute. I need to get the door downstairs for him, too." Adam and the big cat left the room.

Liana slowly climbed off the bed and waited for Adam to return. When he finally came back to her, she wrapped her hand, her very mortal hand, in his, and followed him back to his room over the garage.

Epilogue

Igmutaka perched on a rocky promontory on a ridge at the top of the world and gazed out over the snow-covered forest. Rows of blackened treetops stood like dark soldiers across the burned hillside, but the promise of new life showed in scattered patches of living trees, somehow left unscathed by the fire.

The forest would return. Not soon, but it was the way of all things, this cycle of birth and death, devastation and renewal. For one who was immortal, a forest fire was but a small thing, a normal event in the circle of life.

But these woods were special, this time in his existence filled with new experiences. Everything had changed from the moment Miguel, the one they called Mik, had called him from the spirit world. To manifest as a living cougar after untold eons as spirit had been a wondrous thing. To take corporeal form to another level altogether, to experience life as a human male for the first time in his existence, had proved to be a truly fascinating experience.

One he hoped to continue.

He'd grown to respect these Chanku. They understood the spirit world much as the old tribes had done. They respected the link between the living and the dead, yet they did not fear that which they didn't truly understand. No, they accepted.

Accepted and loved. He thought of the woman and the man, two souls so different, yet so tightly linked that their life forces were already forming a single strand. Liana, once a goddess, had chosen mortality over her immortal life, while the wolfman was still learning the powers with which he'd been gifted. They loved one another, yet they welcomed Igmutaka into their lives and their bed.

Welcomed him with their bodies and their hearts. It was enough to give an old spirit guide hope for the future. Enough to make him leave his forest once again, and make that trek back down the mountain. He'd been a fool to think he could walk away from them—he'd discovered he liked their friendship, their intimacy, too much.

Plus, they'd told him that Miguel would be returning to these mountains, bringing his mates, both male and female. He owed his very existence in this world to Miguel Fuentes, and Igmutaka always paid his debts. Mik's female carried two babies, each fathered by one of her men. He should be there for their births, especially for the one who was Miguel's. He'd guarded the man's grandfather for many years. Watched over Mik as a child. Maybe Mik's child would have need of Igmutaka's guidance.

One never knew, but one could hope.

He'd discovered that even an ancient one such as Igmutaka relished that feeling of being needed. It had been a rather humbling discovery, but he could handle it. He was a powerful spirit guide, an immortal—it was his choice to spend time with these mortals.

With a flick of his long tail, Igmutaka leapt from his rocky perch and made his way through the snow, back to the ones who welcomed him in whatever form he chose.

Adam lay beside Liana in his big bed in the room atop the garage and watched the snow pile higher against the window. After a couple of weeks of heavy storms, they'd almost caught up to the average for this time of the season, which meant they'd be rolling into December with the usual blanket of white on the ground. Hopefully, the melt in the spring would be enough to begin the long, slow restoration of the burned-out forest.

He rubbed his chin over the top of Liana's head and inhaled the sweet scent of her shampoo. Vanilla this time. He liked it. She sighed and rolled closer to him, and he couldn't help but think what a perfect fit she was in spite of her small size. Tough and determined, strong willed and more than his match in any argument, she kept him on his toes, and always kept him coming back for more.

She kept that damned cat coming back too. He thought of Igmutaka out there now in the storm, and hoped he was okay. He hadn't been around for a couple of days and, as much as Adam hated to admit it, he missed him.

Of course, there was really no reason to worry. The spirit guide was immortal, a true creature of mystery when it came down to details, though he'd become more human each time he shifted, each time he showed up at their door, or in their bed.

As Liana said, he was always welcome. Adam couldn't agree more, though he'd feel a bit better about sharing his woman with another male once he and Liana mated as wolves.

They'd decided to hold off, for now. Get to know each other as man and woman without the baggage of grief or immortality between them. One man, one woman, going through the give-and-take of falling in love, learning more about each other, one day at a time.

So far, he was thoroughly enjoying the courtship.

Liana shifted in her sleep and mumbled something under her breath. Her soft hand trailed along his side and settled on the hard root of his cock, stroking that sensitive juncture between penis and groin.

He groaned and arched his back into her touch, swelling beneath her fingers as his body roused. Her soft fingers stroked and stoked his fires, until a blast of cold air caught his attention. Adam glanced toward the open door. Igmutaka stood in the doorway, tall and lean and gloriously naked. His long black hair hung free. Ice crystals sparkled in the dark strands.

He had a broad smile on his perfect lips, and a boner the size of a damned baseball bat between his legs. Chuckling, Adam lifted the blankets beside him. "Get in here, cat, and shut the damned door. You're letting the heat out."

"Good morning to you, too, wolfman," he said. Then he closed the door, swaggered across the room like the cocky bastard he was, crawled beneath the blankets and pulled the soft down comforter up over the three of them.

Adam cursed when icy feet hit his warm legs. Then Liana stretched along his other side and her fingers tightened around his shaft. He bit back a grin. Not in his wildest dreams could he ever have imagined a morning like this—waking up to an immortal spirit guide warming icy toes against his legs on one side, and a naked ex-goddess on the other, with her slender fingers wrapped lovingly around his cock.

Life just didn't get any better.

Then he thought of the mating bond, how it was going to be when he and Liana finally came together as wolves, when their hearts and minds literally became one.

It was definitely going to get better. A lot better.

Something to think about in the cold, gray light of dawn. Something to dream of, surrounded by those he loved, those who loved him in return. Liana's lips brushed his shoulder. Igmutaka's hand settled atop his thigh. Smiling, Adam drifted back to sleep.

If you enjoy Kate Douglas's super-erotic WOLF TALES
novels and her "Chanku" novellas in the SEXY BEAST
anthologies, you're in for a different but equally
delicious treat as she moves into paranormal
romance!

DEMONFIRE

Don't miss it!

A Zebra mass-market paperback on sale now.
Turn the page for a special preview . . .

Chapter 1

He struggled out of the darkness, confused, disoriented . . . recalling fire and pain and the soothing voices of men he couldn't see. Voices promising everlasting life, a chance to move beyond hell, beyond all he'd ever known. He remembered his final, fateful decision to take a chance, to search for something else.

For life beyond the hell that was Abyss.

A search that brought him full circle, back to a world of pain—to this world, wherever it might be. He frowned and tried to focus. This body was unfamiliar, the skin unprotected by scales or bone. He'd never been so helpless, so vulnerable.

His chest burned. The demon's fireshot, while not immediately fatal, would have deadly consequences. Hot blood flowed sluggishly from wounds across his ribs and spread over the filthy stone floor beneath his naked hip. The burn on his chest felt as if it were filled with acid. Struggling for each breath, he raised his head and stared into the glaring yellow eyes of an impossible creature holding him at bay.

Four sharp spears affixed to a long pole were aimed directly at his chest. The thing had already stabbed him once, and the bleeding holes in his side hurt like the blazes.

With a heartfelt groan, Dax tried to rise, but he had no strength left.

He fell back against the cold stones and his world faded once more to black.

"You're effing kidding me! I leave for one frickin' weekend and all hell breaks loose. You're positive? Old Mrs. Abernathy really thinks it ate her cat?" Eddy Marks took another sip of her iced caffé mocha whip and stared at Ginny. "Lord, I hope my father hasn't heard about it. He'll blame it on the Lemurians."

Ginny laughed so hard she almost snorted her latte. "Your dad's not still hung up on that silly legend, is he? Like there's really an advanced society of humanoids living inside Mount Shasta? I don't think so."

"Don't try to tell Dad they don't exist. He's convinced he actually saw one of their golden castles in the moonlight. Of course, it was gone by morning." Eddy frowned at Ginny and changed the subject. She was admittedly touchy about her dad's gullible nature. "Mrs. Abernathy's not serious, is she?"

"I dunno." Ginny shook her head. "She was really upset. Enough that she called nine-one-one. I was on dispatch at Shascom that shift and took the call. They sent an officer out because she was hysterical, not because they actually believed Mr. Pollard's ceramic garden gnome ate Twinkles." Ginny ran her finger around the inside of her cup, chasing the last drops of her iced latte. "I heard there was an awful lot of blood on her back deck, along with tufts of suspiciously Twinkles-colored hair."

"Probably a coyote or a fox." Eddy finished the last of her drink and wished she'd had a shot of brandy to add to it. It would have been the perfect finish to the first brief vacation she'd had in months—two glorious days hiking and camping on Mount Shasta with only her dog for company . . . and not a single killer garden gnome in sight.

She grinned at Ginny. "Killer garden gnomes aren't usually a major threat around here."

Ginny laughed. "Generally, no. Lemurians either, in spite of what your dad and half the tourists think, but for once Eddy, don't be such a stick in the mud. Let your imagination go a little."

"What? And start spouting off about Lemurians? I don't think so. Someone has to be the grown-up! So what else happened while I was out communing with nature?"

"Well . . . it might have been the full moon, but there was a report that the one remaining stone gargoyle launched itself off the northwest corner of the old library building, circled the downtown area and flew away into the night. And . . ." Ginny paused dramatically, "another that the bronze statue of General Humphreys and his horse trotted out of the park. The statue is gone. I didn't check on the gargoyle, but I went down to see the statue. It's not there. Looks like it walked right off the pedestal. That thing weighs over two tons." She set her empty cup down, folded her arms and, with one dark eyebrow raised, stared at Eddy.

"A big bronze statue like that would bring in a pretty penny at the recyclers. Somebody probably hauled it off with a truck, but it's a great visual, isn't it?" Eddy leaned back in her chair. "I can just see that big horse with the general, sword held high and covered in pigeon poop, trotting along Front Street. Maybe a little detour through the cemetery."

"Is it worth a story by ace reporter Edwina Marks?"

Eddy glanced at her. "Do not call me Edwina." She ran her finger through the condensation on the scarred wooden tabletop before looking up at Ginny and grinning. "Maybe a column about weird rumors and how they get started. I'll cite you as Ground Zero, but I doubt it's cutting edge enough for the front page of the *Record*."

Ginny grabbed her purse and pulled out a lipstick. "Yeah, like that rag's going to cover real news?"

"Hey, we do our best and we stay away from the tabloid stuff . . . you know, the garbage you like to read?" Laughing, Eddy stood up. "Well, I'm always complaining that nothing exciting ever happens around here. I guess flying gargoyles, runaway statues, and killer gnomes are better than nothing." She tossed some change on the table for a tip and waved at the girl working behind the counter. "Gotta go, Gin. I need to get home. Have to let Bumper out."

"Bumper? Who's that? Don't tell me you brought home another homeless mutt from the shelter."

"And if I did?"

Ginny waved the lipstick at her like a pointer. "Eddy, the last time you had to give up a fostered pup, you bawled for a week. Why do you do this to yourself?"

She'd be lucky if she only bawled for a week when it was time for Bumper to leave. They'd bonded almost immediately, but she really didn't want a dog. Not for keeps. "They were gonna put her down if no one took her," she mumbled.

Ginny shook her head. "Don't say I didn't warn you. One of these days you're going to take in a stray that'll really break your heart."

Eddy heard Bumper when she was still half a block from home. She'd only left the dog inside the house while she went to town for coffee, but it appeared the walls weren't thick enough to mute her deep-throated growling and barking.

Thank goodness it wasn't nine yet. Any later and she'd probably have one of the neighbors filing a complaint. Eddy picked up her pace and ran the last hundred yards home, digging for her house keys as she raced up the front walk. "Bumper, you idiot. I only left you for an hour. I hope you haven't been going on like this the whole time I've been gone."

She got the key in the lock and swung the front door

open. Bumper didn't even pause to greet her. Instead, she practically knocked Eddy on her butt as she raced out the front door, skidded through the open gate to the side yard and disappeared around the back of the house.

"Shit. Stupid dog." Eddy threw her keys in her bag, slung her purse over her shoulder and took off after the dog. It was almost completely dark away from the street light and Eddy stumbled on one of the uneven paving stones by the gate. Bumper's deep bark turned absolutely frantic, accompanied by the added racket from her clawing and scratching at the wooden door to Eddy's potting shed.

"If you've got a skunk cornered in there, you stupid dog, I swear I'm taking you back to the shelter."

Bumper stopped barking, now that she knew she had Eddy's attention. She whined and sniffed at the door, still scratching at the rough wood. Eddy fumbled in her bag for her keychain and the miniature flashlight hanging from the ring. The beam was next to worthless, but better than nothing.

She scooted Bumper out of the way with her leg and un-latched the door just enough to peer in through a crack. Bumper whapped her nose against Eddy's leg. Shoving fran-tically with her broad head, she tried to force her way inside.

"Get back." Eddy glared at the dog. Bumper flattened her ears against her curly fur and immediately backed off, looking as pathetic as she had last week at the shelter when Eddy'd realized she couldn't leave a blond pit bull crossed with a standard poodle to the whims of fate.

She aimed her tiny flashlight through the narrow open-ing. Blinked. Told herself she was really glad she'd been drinking coffee and not that brandy she'd wanted tonight, because otherwise she wouldn't believe what she saw.

Maybe Mrs. Abernathy wasn't nuts after all. Eddy grabbed a shovel leaning against the outside wall of the shed and threw the door open wide.

The garden gnome that should have been stationed in

the rose garden out in front held a pitchfork in its stubby little hands like a weapon, ready to stab what appeared to be a person lying in the shadows. When the door creaked open, the gnome turned its head, glared at Eddy through yellow eyes, bared unbelievably sharp teeth, and screamed at her like an avenging banshee.

Bumper's claws scrabbled against the stone pathway. Eddy swung the shovel. The crunch of metal connecting with ceramic seemed unnaturally loud. The scream stopped as the garden gnome shattered into a thousand pieces. The pitchfork clattered to the ground and a dark, evil smelling mist gathered in the air above the pile of dust. It swirled a moment and then suddenly whooshed over Eddy's shoulder and out the open door.

A tiny blue light pulsed and flickered, followed the mist as far as the doorway, and then returned to hover over the figure in the shadows. Bumper paused long enough to sniff the remnants of the garden gnome and growl, before turning her attention to whatever lay on the stone floor. Eddy stared at the shovel in her hands and took one deep breath after another. This was not happening. She *had not seen* a garden gnome in attack mode.

One with glowing yellow eyes and razor-sharp teeth. *Impossible.*

Heart pounding, arms and legs shaking, she slowly pivoted in place and focused on whoever it was that Bumper seemed so pleased to see.

The mutt whined, but her curly tail was wagging a million miles a minute. She'd been right about the gnome. Eddy figured she'd have to trust the dog's instincts about who or whatever had found such dubious sanctuary in her potting shed.

Eddy squinted and tried to focus on the flickering light that flitted in the air over Bumper's head, but it was jerking around so quickly she couldn't tell what it was. She still had her key ring clutched in her fingers. She wasn't quite ready to put the shovel down, but she managed to shine the narrow beam of light toward the lump on the floor.

Green light reflected back from Bumper's eyes. Eddy swung wider with the flashlight. She saw a muscular arm, a thick shoulder, and the broad expanse of a masculine chest. Blood trickled from four perfectly spaced pitchfork-sized holes across the man's ribs and pooled beneath his body. There appeared to be a deep wound on his chest, though it wasn't bleeding.

In fact, it looked almost as if it had been cauterized. A burn? Eddy swept the light over his full length. Her eyes grew wider with each inch of skin she exposed. He was marked with a colorful tattoo that ran from his thigh, across his groin to his chest, but other than the art, he was naked. Very naked, all the way from his long, narrow feet, up those perfectly formed, hairy legs to . . . Eddy quickly jerked the light back toward his head.

When she reached his face, the narrow beam glinted off dark eyes looking directly into hers. Beautiful, soul-searching dark brown eyes shrouded in thick, black lashes. He was gorgeous. Even with a smear of dirt across one cheek and several days' growth of dark beard, he looked as if he should be on the cover of *People* as the sexiest man alive.

Breathing hard, her body still shaking from the adrenaline coursing through her system, Eddy dragged herself back to the situation at hand. Whatever it was. He hadn't said a word. She'd thought he was unconscious. He wasn't. He was injured . . . not necessarily helpless. She squatted down beside him, and reassured by Bumper's acceptance and the fact the man didn't look strong enough to sit up, much less harm her, Eddy set the shovel aside.

She touched his shoulder and grimaced at the deep wound on his chest, the bloody stab wounds in his side. Made a point not to look below his waist. "What happened? Are you okay? Well, obviously not with all those injuries." Rattled, she took a deep breath. "Who are you?"

He blinked and turned his head. She quickly tilted the light away from his eyes. "I'm sorry. I . . ."

He shook his head. His voice was deep and sort of raspy. "No. It's all right." He glanced up at the flickering light dancing overhead, frowned and then nodded.

She could tell he was in pain, but he took a deep breath and turned his focus back to Eddy.

"I am Dax. Thank you."

"I'm Eddy. Eddy Marks." Why she'd felt compelled to give her full name made no sense. None of this did. She couldn't place his accent and he wasn't from around here. She would have recognized any of the locals. She started to rise. "I'll call nine-one-one. You're injured."

His arm snaked out and he grabbed her forearm, trapping her with surprising strength. "No. No one. Don't call anyone."

Eddy looked down at the broad hand, the powerful fingers wrapped entirely around her arm, just below her elbow. She should have been terrified. Should have been screaming in fear, but something in those eyes, in the expression on his face . . .

Immediately, he loosened his grasp. "I'm sorry. Please forgive me, but no one must know I'm here. If you can't help me, please let me leave. I have so little time . . ." He tried to prop himself up on one arm, but his body trembled with the effort.

Eddy rubbed her arm. It tingled where he'd touched her. "What's going on? How'd you get here? Where are your clothes?"

The flickering light came closer, hovered just in front of his chest, pulsed with a brilliant blue glow that spread out in a pale arc until it touched him, appeared to soak into his flesh, and then dimmed. Before Eddy could figure out what she was seeing, Dax took a deep breath. He seemed to gather strength—from the blue light?

He shoved himself upright, glanced at the light and nodded. "Thank you, Willow."

Then he stood up, as if his injuries didn't affect him at all. Obviously, neither did the fact he wasn't wearing a stitch of clothes. Towering over Eddy, he held out his hand to help her to her feet. "I will go now. I'm sorry to have . . ."

Eddy swallowed. She looked up at him as he fumbled for words, realized she was almost eye level with his . . . *oh crap!* She jerked her head to one side and stared at his hand for a moment. Shifted her eyes and blinked at the blue light, now hovering in the air not six inches from her face. What in the hell was going on?

Slowly, she looked back at Dax, placed her hand in his and, with a slight tug from him, rose to her feet. The light followed her. "What is that thing?" Tilting her head, she focused on the bit of fluff glowing in the air between them, and let out a whoosh of breath.

"Holy Moses." It was a woman. A tiny, flickering fairy-like woman with gossamer wings and long blond hair. "It's frickin' Tinkerbell!" Eddy turned and stared at Dax. "That's impossible."

He shrugged. "So are garden gnomes armed with pitch-forks. At least in your world. So am I, for that matter."

Eddy snapped her gaze away from the flickering fairy and stared at Dax. "What do you mean, you're impossible? Why? Who are you? What are you?"

Again, he shrugged. "I'm a mercenary, now. A hired soldier, if you will. However, before the Edenites found me, before they gave me this body, I was a demon. Cast out of Abyss, but a demon nonetheless."

He knew she was bursting with questions, but she'd taken him inside her home, given him a pair of soft gray pants with a drawstring at the waist and brewed some sort of hot, dark liquid that smelled much better than it tasted.

She handed him a cup, then as she left the room, she told him to sit.

He sat, despite the sense of urgency and the pain. The snake tattoo seemed to ripple against his skin, crawling across his thigh, over his groin and belly to the spot where the head rested above his human heart. He felt the heat from the demon's fireshot beside the serpent's head burning deeper with each breath he took. Exhaustion warred with the need to move, to begin the hunt. In spite of Willow's gift of healing energy, he felt as if could sleep for at least a month. Instead, he waited for the woman, for Eddy Marks. He sipped from the steaming cup while she opened and closed drawers in an adjoining room and mumbled unintelligible words to herself.

The four-legged creature stayed with him. Eddy called it "damned dog," but she'd also said its name was Bumper and that it was a female. The animal appeared to be intelligent, though Dax hadn't figured out how to communicate with her yet. She was certainly odd looking with her bullet-shaped head, powerful jaws and curly blond coat.

"Sorry to take so long. I had to hunt for the first aid kit."

The woman carried a box filled with rolls of bandages and jars and tubes of what must be medicine. He wished his mind were clearer, but he was still growing used to this body, to the way the brain worked. It was so unlike his own. This mind had memories of things like bandages and dogs and the names for the various pieces of furniture he saw, but too much in his head felt foggy. Too much was still trapped in the thinking process of demonkind, of kill or be killed. Eat or be eaten.

All that was absolutely clear was the mission, and he was woefully behind on that.

Of course, he hadn't expected to encounter a demon-powered gargoyle armed with fire just seconds after his arrival through the vortex. Nor had he expected the power of the demons already here. Eddy had no idea she had truly saved more than his life.

So much more was at stake. So many lives.

Her soft voice was laced with steel when it burst into his meandering thoughts. "First things first," she said. "And don't lie to me. I'm trusting you for some weird reason when I know damned well I should call the authorities. So tell me, who are you, really? Who did this to you? How'd you get this burn?"

Blinking, he raised his head. She knelt in front of him. Her short dark hair was tousled and her chocolaty brown eyes stared at him with concern and some other emotion he couldn't quite identify. Thank goodness there was no sign of fear. He didn't want her to fear him, though she'd be better off if she did.

He shook his head. He still couldn't believe that blasted demon had gotten the drop on him. "I really am demonkind. From Abyss. The wound on my chest? It was the gargoyle. He surprised me. I wasn't expecting him, especially armed with the fire."

She blinked and gave him a long, narrow-eyed stare. "Hookay. If you say so." She took a damp cloth and wiped around the burn on his chest. The cool water felt good.

Her soft hands felt even better. Her touch seemed to spark what could only be genetic, instinctive memories to this body he inhabited. He felt as if his mind was clearing. Maybe this world would finally start to make sense.

She tilted her head and studied the burned and bloody wound. "That's the second reference to a gargoyle I've heard tonight," she said, looking at his chest, not his face. "They're not generally part of the typical conversation around here."

Shocked, he grabbed her wrist. She jerked her head around and stared at his fingers. He let go. "I'm sorry. I didn't mean to startle you. Have you seen it? The gargoyle? Do you know where it is?"

She stared at him a moment, and then sprayed something on the wound that took away the pain. She covered it with a soft, flesh-colored bandage before she answered him. "No," she said, shaking her head, concentrating on the bandage. "Not recently."

Her short dark hair floated against the sharp line of her jaw. He fought a surprisingly powerful need to touch the shimmering strands. He'd never once run his fingers through a woman's hair. Of course, he couldn't remember having fingers. He'd never had any form beyond his demon self of mist and scales, sharp claws, and sharper fangs.

She flattened all four corners of the bandage and looked up at him. He wished he were better at reading human expressions. Hers was a mystery to him.

"Last time I saw it," she said, "it was perched on the corner of the library building where it belonged, but I heard it flew away. It's made of stone and most definitely not alive, which means it shouldn't be flying anywhere. What's going on? And what are you, really? You can't be serious about..." She glanced away, shook her head again and then touched the left side of his chest, just above the first puncture wound. "Turn around so I can take care of these cuts over your ribs."

He turned and stared at the fireplace across the room. After a moment he focused on a beautiful carved stone owl, sitting on the brick hearth. The owl's eyes seemed to watch him, but he sensed no life in the creature. It was better to concentrate on the bird than the woman.

Her gentle touch was almost worse than the pain from the injuries. It reminded him of things he wanted, things he'd never have.

He was, after all, still a demon. A fallen demon, but nonetheless, not even close to human. Not at all the man he appeared to be. This form was his for one short week.

His avatar.

Seven days he'd been given. Seven days to save the town

of Evergreen and all its inhabitants. If he failed, if demon-kind succeeded in this, their first major foray into Earth's dimension, other towns could fall. Other worlds. All of Earth, all of Eden.

Seven days.

Impossible . . . and he'd already wasted one of them.

He would have laughed if he didn't feel like turning around and heading back to Abyss—except Abyss was closed to him. With only the most preposterous luck, he might end up in Eden, though he doubted that would happen no matter how he did on his mission. The promises had been vague, after all.

So why, he wondered, had he agreed to this stupid plan?

"I asked you, what's going on? I'm assuming you know how my cheesy little Wal-Mart garden gnome suddenly grew teeth and turned killer. Try the truth this time. With details that make sense."

He jerked his head around and stared at her, understanding more of his new reality as each moment passed, as the memories and life of this body's prior owner integrated with his demon soul.

Eddy sat back on her heels and her dark eyes flashed with as much frustrated anger as curiosity.

He glanced down at his side. There were clean, white bandages over each of the wounds from the demon's weapon. The big burn on his chest was cleaned and covered. The entire length of his tattoo pulsed with evil energy, but if he ignored that, he really did feel better.

Stronger.

He sensed Willow's presence and finally spotted her sitting amongst a collection of glass figurines on a small bookcase. Could demons enter glass? He wasn't sure, but at least Willow would warn him in time. He caught the woman's unwavering stare with his own. She waited more patiently than he deserved for his answer. "I always tell the truth," he said. "The problem is, will you believe me?"

She nodded and stood up. "I'll try." She stalked out of the room. He heard water running. A moment later she returned, grabbed his cup and her own and left again. This time, when she handed him the warm mug of coffee, he knew what to expect.

He savored the aroma while she settled herself on the end of the couch, as far from him as she could get, yet still have room to sit.

She was close enough for him to pick up the perfume from the soap she'd used to wash her hands, the warm essence of her skin, the scent that was all hers.

He shrugged off the unusual sensations her nearness gave him. Then he took a sip of his coffee, replacing Eddy's scent with the rich aroma of the drink. He couldn't seem to do anything about his powerful awareness of her. Of this body's reaction to her presence, her scent, to every move she made.

He could try to ignore her, but he didn't want to. No, not at all. It probably wouldn't work, anyway.

She curled her bare feet under herself and leaned against the back of the couch, facing him. He turned and sat much the same way, facing her.

Bumper looked from one of them to the other, barked once and jumped up on the couch, filling the gap between them. She turned around a couple of times and lay down with a loud, contented sigh. Her fuzzy butt rested on Dax's bare foot, her chin was on the woman's ankle.

"Bumper likes you." She stroked the silly looking beast's head with her long, slim fingers. "If she didn't approve, you wouldn't be sitting here."

Dax smiled, vaguely aware that it was an entirely new facial expression for him. Of course, everything he did now, everything he felt and said, was new. "Then I guess I'm very glad Bumper approves. Thank you for battling the demon, for taking care of my injuries. You saved my life."

She stared at him for a long, steady moment, as if digesting his statement. There was still no fear in her.

She would be safer if she was afraid.

"You're welcome," she said. "Now please explain. Tell me about the garden gnome. What was it, really?"

He steepled his fingers in front of his face and rested his chin on the forefingers. Had the one who first owned this body found comfort in such a position? No matter. It was his body now, for however long he could keep it alive, and resting his chin this way pleased him. "The small statue was inhabited by a demon from the world of Abyss. They've broken through into Earth's dimension, but the only form they have here is spirit—that dark, stinking mist you saw after you shattered the creature was the demon's essence. They need an avatar, something made of the earth . . . ceramic, stone, metal. Nothing alive. The avatar gives form and shape, the demon provides the life."

She nodded her head, slowly, as if digesting his words. "If I hadn't seen it . . . good Lord . . . I still can't believe I saw what I saw out there." She glanced around the room. "Where's that little fairy? The one you called Willow?"

"She's actually a will o' the wisp, not a fairy. She's a protector of sorts. She gathers energy out of the air and shares it with me. Helps me understand this unfamiliar world, this body. Right now, she's sitting on your bookcase. I think she likes being surrounded by all the little figurines on the top shelf." He looked over his shoulder at Willow. Her light pulsed bright blue for a second. Then, once again, she disappeared among the tiny glass statuettes.

Eddy shook her head. She laughed, but it sounded forced, like she was strangling. Mostly, her voice was low, sort of soft and mellow. It fit her.

"I'm generally pretty pragmatic, unlike my father who believes every wild story he hears. I can tell it's going to be really hard for me to deal with all this. Just point to Willow as a reminder that the impossible is sometimes possible . . . you know, when I look at you like I think you're lying."

"I promise to do that." He smiled over the edge of his cup and took a sip of the dark brew. She'd said it would perk him up, whatever that meant. He did feel more alert. He hoped it wasn't because danger was lurking nearby. He still didn't understand all this body's instincts.

"You said you were a demon, but you look perfectly human. What exactly do you mean?"

"Exactly that. I'm a demon from the world of Abyss. It exists in a dimension apart from yours, but I was sent here by people from another world, one called Eden that's in yet another dimension. The two worlds never touch, never interact. They exist, complete yet apart, entirely dependent on the balance that holds them apart as much as it connects them."

"So what does that make Earth?"

He stared at his cup of coffee a moment, picturing the three worlds as he imagined them. "Earth is the fulcrum," he said, raising his eyes to study her reaction. "Eden on the one side is a world of light filled with people who are inherently good. Abyss, on the other, is a world of darkness, a land of fire and ice populated by creatures who personify evil. Earth is in the center, holding them apart, keeping them in perpetual balance . . . or, at least, that's the way it's supposed to work. The way it's always worked in the past."

Her brows knotted over her dark eyes and she looked confused, but at least she was still listening. Dax ran his fingers through Bumper's curly coat. The dog was a hard-muscled, frilly contradiction—she had a powerful body with strong jaws, yet she was covered in a curly blond coat that made her look utterly ridiculous. Dax couldn't imagine anyone creating an animal like Bumper on purpose, yet somehow the combination worked.

Sort of like Earth. "Your world is mostly populated by

a mixture of different kinds of humans—some who will always try to do the right thing as well as those who are set on doing something evil. The best of you and the worst of you are balanced by the vast majority who are sort of like this dog of yours, a blend of both good and bad, beautiful and ugly." He laughed. "Smart and stupid. Somehow, it all works and, on the whole, humans get along and live their lives."

She snorted. He grinned at her. "Well, most of the time, anyway."

Shaking her head, she set her cup down. "I beg to differ with you, but people don't get along that well. There are wars going on all over the world, people are starving and dying, we have to worry about terrorists blowing things up, and . . ."

"I know. That's why I'm here. Evil has grown too powerful on your world. It's giving demonkind a foothold. Balance has reached a tipping point. It's slipping over to the side of darkness. The people of Eden recognized the danger, but they're incapable of fighting. Their nature doesn't allow it. They can, however, hire fallen demons to fight their battles."

She ignored his reference to himself and instead asked the one question Dax didn't want to answer.

"What happens if the balance slips too far?"

He didn't want to think about that. Couldn't allow himself to consider failure. Bumper raised her head, stared beyond Dax, and growled. Dax looked down at the dog, but he spoke to Eddy. "Then the demons of Abyss take over. If Evergreen falls to the demons, they gain a powerful foothold in your world. If this town falls, others may follow. The fear is that all of Earth will fall to darkness and demons will rule. There's a risk that eventually, even Eden will be overrun."

"Dax? I think you need to turn around."

He snapped his head up at the quaver in her voice and

Eddy's terrified gaze. He spun around on the couch and his feet hit the floor just as the stone owl by the fireplace stretched its gray wings and clicked its sharp beak, as if testing to make sure things worked.

Willow shot up from the bookcase so fast she left a trail of blue sparkles in the air behind her. Dax leapt to his feet, pulled in the energy Willow sent him and pointed both hands at the owl, fingertips spread wide.

Fire burst from his fingers in long, twin spikes of pure power. He caught the owl as it prepared to take flight, trapped the creature in a blazing sphere of heat and light and blew it right through the wire screen and into the fireplace.

Eddy screamed. The creature screamed louder, sounding eerily like the garden gnome Eddy had flattened. The cry cut off the moment the flaming owl hit the back of the firebox and shattered. A dark wisp, stinking of sulfur, coalesced in front of the broken pieces, but before it could race up the flue to freedom, Dax called on Willow's power once again.

This time a blast of icy air caught the amorphous mass of darkness, freezing it before it could make its escape. It hovered a moment, quivering in midair, then fell to the hearth and shattered into a thousand tiny pieces of black ice.

Dax hit the ice with a burst of flame. The pieces sizzled and disappeared in puffs of steam.

He took a deep breath and turned away from the mess. Eddy sat on the end of the couch, with Bumper caught in her shaking arms. Both of them gaped, wide-eyed, at the fireplace. Before Dax could assure Eddy that everything was all right, at least for now, she raised her head and stared at him.

"Okay." Her voice cracked and she took a deep breath. "I take back what I said. You won't need to point to Willow for proof. I promise to believe anything you tell me. Explain, please, what the hell just happened?"